THE PERFECT GENTLEMAN

JULIE COOPER

Quills & Quartos
PUBLISHING

Edited by Kristi Rawlings and Jennifer Altman

Cover by London Montgomery Designs

ISBN
978-1-951033-11-8 (ebook)
978-1-951033-12-5 (paperback)

To Dennis, the perfect gentleman for me, and to Mom and Dad, for first showing me what love looks like

To our dearest, loveliest
Allyson ~ with much
love, to the perfect baker!

Julie Cox

TABLE OF CONTENTS

THE PERFECT GENTLEMAN: VOLUME I

THE PERFECT GENTLEMAN: VOLUME II

A Not-so-Merry Chase

The Perfect Gentleman
Volume 1

Longbourn, Hertfordshire

Margaret Bennet Bingley exchanged the cloth upon her brother's forehead for a newly wetted one, sighing. The act would do little to combat the fever, and in a few short minutes it would be as heated as its predecessor. Nevertheless, she would continue her pitiful efforts to save her brother's life, futile though they were. Thomas Bennet might be a curmudgeonly, stubborn bachelor, but he was all the family she had left.

"Margaret." Thomas's voice was hoarse and barely discernible

"I am here," she said. In the low light from the hearth, his eyes appeared glazed and bleary, but at her touch he turned towards her.

"Margaret…"

"Do not speak," she said, seeing what the effort cost him. "Try and drink." Lifting the glass of barley water from his bedside table, she held it to his lips. After the briefest sip, however, he collapsed upon his pillows, exhausted.

She brushed his hair off his face, noticing the cloth had fallen from his forehead. But as she moved to get a new one, he clutched her wrist, stilling her.

"Must tell you," he began. His voice faded, then strengthened, and she could see the enormous effort he put forth. She curbed her instinct to quiet him, lest the distress of being unable to communicate did more harm.

Moving closer so she could hear every word, she bent nearer his lips.

"Must tell…I am…married," he said.

Her eyes widened in shock and astonishment, certain she misheard. "Wha–what? I do not…Thomas? M–married?"

He waved weakly at his dressing cabinet, until she understood he wanted something from within.

Uncertainly, she went to it, placing her hand on the top drawer, looking at him for confirmation. At his nod, she opened it. There, underneath the cravats, peeked a leather portfolio. Carefully she removed it from its hiding place and deposited it into his trembling hands, afterwards lighting a candle so they might better view its contents.

Thomas fumblingly removed the papers within, resisting any efforts at assistance. After shakily sorting through the few pages inside —an official-looking sheath of papers along with a few letters in rounded, childish handwriting—he handed over the official ones.

"Young…a boy, a foolish boy," Thomas muttered, and Margaret realised he spoke of himself.

She peered at the papers. It appeared to be marriage documents between Thomas and one Fanny Gardiner, dated some twenty-one years past. Thomas would have been barely nineteen at the time.

She had so many questions, but the first was obvious. "Did Papa know?"

"No," he answered. "He…was already ill. Knew I would have to leave school, come home to Longbourn. When I went to…seaside to…"

He fluttered his hand—a gesture for "final orgy of excess" she supposed. She remembered that dark time, when their father's illness brought all their youthful plans to an end. She never had the London season promised, and Thomas gave up the scholarly pursuits he loved. Father wasted away slowly, taking years to die. Vaguely she recalled Thomas making a trip to the coast for a few months, remembering her envy of his departure while she nursed their ailing parent. Perhaps she noticed the downturn in Thomas's nature after his holiday, perhaps she even imagined some youthful failed romance leading to his bitter feelings towards marriage, but she never dreamed this!

"Marriage, Thomas? But…why is—*where* is she?"

"Ramsgate," Thomas said. "I...she was a...strumpet."

"*What?*" Margaret cried.

Thomas grasped her wrist with a grip grown surprisingly strong. "She lied!" he gasped. "Thought...a widow. Already had...a young daughter. Fooled me, utterly. Told me she...with child. *My* child."

"But she–she was not?"

"Oh, she was," he replied bitterly. "But who is to say...mine? She... mistress to a baron. First child...some peer's by-blow. Told me after... we wed."

Margaret's first thought was that *he* certainly played a part in the dreadful affair, since he believed in the possibility the child was his. But this was not the time for recriminations; she needed more information before Thomas's strength faded.

"The other child, Brother? The baby? Are you sure it was not yours?"

He was silent, and a sick feeling arose within her breast.

"So, you do not know for certain," she said. "And it might now be—"

"Gave her a house!" he cried out, startling her. "Adequate payment for a few nights on her back. Told her she could keep...as long as she stayed away, kept her mouth...shut."

He must have read the disapproval in her eyes, because he added sullenly, "Had you... to think of. Could hardly bring a...a harlot to Longbourn as its mistress and 'spect you to make a decent match."

Margaret nearly rolled her eyes at this fine bit of self-justification. He had not helped her find *any* kind of match, being perfectly content to have *her* act as Longbourn's mistress while refusing to go to town for any reason. If she had not spent a month with an acquaintance in London and met Robert, she would never have had even her few years of wedded bliss. But she could not waste his strength with reproach.

"Was any provision made for the child?"

"After some years," he began gruffly, "...and I had time to...calm, I...inquired. I thought...if it were a boy, I might...take him. But...'twas a girl," he revealed sulkily.

"Brother," she said, struggling for equanimity, "we must—"

"I know," he said, his voice faded now and irresolute. He made a trembling attempt to pick up the papers still on his lap, but his weakness overcame him. Margaret carefully extracted one of them from his weak grip.

It was a letter, the childish writing carefully spaced with a minimum of blots.

Dear Papa,

Mama said it is permisable that I shoud write you a few words. I have a cat named Snow Queen. She ackshully lives in Mr Hawes stables but I pretend she is mine. Mr Hawes calls her Kitty. He is Not good at naming cats. He has a Horse that is mean and tries to bite me when I visit Snow Queen but I do not let him get to close. His name is Gallant that is another silly name for he lacks manners. I can run real fast but Jane says running is not for ladys but I am not a lady yet so for now I win races. I dont think ladys have much fun. Jane has a new Governess. Her name is Miss Persons. She says I am not a Modil Pupil.

Do you have any animals? I hope you have a Dog. I think Dogs are the friendest animals. But I do not tell that to Snow Queen it woud hurt her feelings. What is your dogs name?

Sincerely Your Daughter,
Lizzy

AFTER READING IT, MARGARET GLANCED AT HER BROTHER. HIS EYES WERE closed, the shared confidences obviously having taken their toll. She read the next letter, dated a month later, and then the next, a month after that. She formed a picture of a girl with boundless energy, sweet and smart and loving. A girl who desperately wished her papa to acknowledge her as his.

She picked up the last one. It was much briefer than the others and dated a good three months after its predecessor.

Dear Papa,

Mama says you Dont want me to write to you and I shoud Stop. I think you are a Very Bisy Man with heaps of Important Bisness. So I shall make it very Easy. If you are too Bisy to write to me but woud enjoy receiving letters from your Daughter circle the Yes. If you Dont want to read them circle No.

YES   NO

Sincerely Your Daughter,
Lizzy

MARGARET BIT HER LIP AND BLINKED SEVERAL TIMES TO STOP THE STINGING pressure behind her lids. She was certain her brother had not extended the little girl the courtesy of replying to her simple request. No, he dealt with her in the way he usually dealt with difficult or painful problems in his life—disregarding, while hoping they would disappear.

Well, he had his wish. There were no more letters.

Margaret had hoped for children, very much. Sadly, it had not been thus ordained. Yes, she could understand her brother's pride was sadly trampled and this Fanny person's deception might have doomed their brief affair. Heavens, at Thomas's age *she* likely would have been scandalised and disgusted. It was only with maturity and loss that she learned how important love and family ought to be, and how precious and finite such things were. Fanny Gardiner ought not to have revealed her secret regarding the parentage of the elder daughter to her young, proud husband. But Lizzy was not to blame for any of it, and the thought of that little girl eagerly looking for the post, for a letter that would never arrive, smote her. How long before the child put that hope away for good? Three months? Six?

Rage nearly overwhelmed her. *Fool! You discarded her without even an attempt to learn if she was yours! And she could have been yours, whether by blood or simply a shared lifetime of care. She could have been here, at your bedside now. Instead, I am the only one in this world who cares for you, and I am terrified to leave your side for fear you will die alone.*

She sank back into her chair, slowly regaining control of her emotions. What was done could not be undone. Perhaps Lizzy was married with a brood of her own, perhaps she followed in her mother's footsteps, or perhaps she died of some childhood illness long ago. But she knew this: her brother's conscience was not a clean one and some part of him deeply regretted not answering those letters. Why else had he not destroyed them? Why show them to her now?

A long sigh escaped her lips, and she released her anger with it. Obviously, Thomas felt he was not long for this earth. He revealed this, knowing she would do right by the girl. Thomas had nothing to do with his money except grow it along with his crops. There were investments from their mother's portion of which she was aware, and for which she was his heir. Her husband left her comfortably situated. She had no need of her brother's money, and if he died now, she would ensure the family he shamefully neglected would receive it instead. If he lived, she would see that somehow, some way, he made up to the girl for his abandonment, if such a thing were possible.

THE DAYS AT LONGBOURN WERE AS BLEAK AS THE WEATHER. CHARLES Bingley found himself in his Uncle Bennet's bookroom on a flatly damp Monday afternoon, uncharacteristically troubled. Of course, he was anxious on his step-uncle's behalf, though he did not know the man well. Uncle Bennet only recently began imparting his knowledge on estate management, and Charles found him a practical and intelligent man, if too given to cynicism.

His step-mother refused all of his efforts to assist her with Mr Bennet's care and Charles resolved that another nurse must be hired before his step-mama ran herself into the grave as well.

Charles—unlike his sisters—was kind to his step-mother since the moment his father introduced her as his soon-to-be bride. As a little-known gentleman's daughter, their match was judged by Louisa Hurst and Caroline Bingley as too plebeian for their wealthy father, though Robert himself was always in awe of her gentility. Robert unreservedly supported Margaret's idea of moving from London to Hertfordshire, leasing Netherfield, and giving his son an opportunity to learn the business of estate management from her brother. He knew Margaret blamed herself for her husband's death, for moving them into the plague-ridden county, but Charles had a more philosophic view of these things.

Charles was in London visiting his friend Mr Darcy when illness struck the area, and so swift was its trajectory, he barely returned in time to say his farewells before Robert was lost to them.

The door opened as he stared at the bookshelves, and the house-keeper appeared bearing a tray, setting it beside him with a grunt.

"Thank you, Mrs Hill," Charles said, accepting a cup of tea from the grumpy female. "You are a treasure."

"Hmph," the woman replied, departing unceremoniously. Hill was immune to male charm of any sort, even Charles Bingley's.

Finally, Margaret appeared. Charles waited until she poured her own tea before speaking, though he took in his step-mother's pale complexion and anxious eyes.

"Has Uncle Bennet taken a turn for the worse?"

"No worse," she said. "And no better. He is delirious half of the time and insensible the other half. In truth, he seems worse than your father before he passed. Every time I lie down to rest a few hours, I fear the nurse will wake me with bad news. And yet, he lives."

"He is younger than Papa, and stronger. We must remain hopeful."

"I am, I am," she agreed distractedly.

"What else is it?" he asked gently.

As if she had come to a difficult decision, she met his eyes directly. "I do have something else on my mind."

The situation called for discretion, naturally, so Margaret attempted to explain it as delicately as possible: her brother's secret marriage, the betrayal, the child he never saw, the unanswered letters from a young girl, her fears for Lizzy's fate.

Charles was slightly appalled, of course, that Bennet would be so careless with matrimony. Whatever opinions he might harbour regarding by-blows and uncertain parentage, his first concern was his step-mother's anxiety.

"Where is Mr Bennet's family now?" he asked gravely.

"Ramsgate."

"What an amazing coincidence!" he cried. "Darcy told me he was going to look in on his young sister soon, this month, perhaps, and Ramsgate is where she set up housekeeping! The very place! I will send him an express today, asking him to look in on them while there. Will it do?"

Margaret's heart lifted at the thought of something, *anything*, being done to at least provide more information. But *Mr Darcy*? Everyone knew he was a paragon, a shining example of one who stayed on the straight and narrow path, never deviating an inch. In all likelihood, being asked to concern himself with such a morally dubious affair would offend the gentleman's sensibilities to an unheard-of degree.

"It would, of course, relieve my mind greatly if we could arrange for matters to be investigated, and the sooner the better. But Mr Darcy? It is likely this business would be an affront to–to his honour."

"I know he sees things in rather more black and white than the average man," he said. "But he is discreet and trustworthy and would do anything he could to assist a friend in need."

Truth to tell, with the notable exception of her step-son, she was not sure Mr Darcy—master of the great estate Pemberley, possessor of a family tree littered with aristocracy, rumoured to have rejected an offer of a peerage from the king, and high stickler for propriety and virtu-osity—*had* any friends besides Charles and a cousin or two. He was too *much* a paragon. Mothers and fathers alike held him aloft as an example for their progeny to follow, and regularly offered up their eligible daughters as likely candidates for mistress of his home and properties. But this, of course, was not the same thing as popularity or amiability.

"The Bennets could hardly be considered Mr Darcy's friends," she murmured.

"Perhaps not, but he *is* mine. I am sure he will want to help," Charles insisted.

Margaret was not completely certain, but in her exhaustion, was willing to accept Charles's reassurances. He pledged to send out the express this very afternoon, that Darcy might have it in hand by even-tide. He thus took his leave, bent upon persuading Fitzwilliam Darcy to undertake a mission of mercy.

However—perhaps due to Margaret's natural discretion when explaining the matter, or perhaps to some inarticulacy caused by her fatigue and general distress—she inadvertently omitted an important bit of information. Charles departed Longbourn believing Thomas Bennet's alleged daughter was a child...an eight-year-old child.

Darcy House, London

Fitzwilliam Darcy stared at the blotted muddle before him, attempting to decipher Bingley's message, tilting the parchment this way and that, hoping an altered perspective would make a difference. What he read—or at least, what he interpreted from what he read—was disagreeable indeed.

Darcy felt some guilt for his part in Bingley letting Netherfield, even knowing he could not be blamed for the fever that took Bingley's father. At the time, it seemed ideal. Margaret Bennet Bingley was highly respected in her home circles, despite marrying beneath herself socially. Robert Bingley, and hence his son, would fare much better in the country than in London, where society turned up its nose at those without the proper pedigrees. Close proximity to Mr Thomas Bennet, Mrs Bingley's brother, made the Netherfield property even more attractive. Mr Bennet managed his Hertfordshire estate very well, and Darcy agreed he would be a sound tutor for the Bingleys in estate management. The respectable society there might be small, but knowing Bingley, he would find ample opportunity to make friends and enjoy himself.

From the contents of this letter, however, it appeared Mr Bennet's honour was compromised on several levels. Astounding that the unspeakable marriage had not come out before this; even more astounding that fusty, confirmed bachelor Thomas Bennet had somehow become embroiled in such a disastrous affair. And now there was a child to consider, who must be deemed legitimate issue regardless of the truth. What an ugly, ugly muddle. If Darcy's father were still alive, he would instruct him to send an agent to look into the situation and never be associated with any part of it. But then, George Darcy had ample reason to keep clear of anything remotely smacking of moral decay.

As do I, Darcy reminded himself. Though he had not heard so much as a whisper of scandal linked to the Darcy name for several years, he knew it would not take much of a spark for the old stories to ignite. Profligacy was, as ever, much more interesting than virtue.

Certain of his years at Eton were marked by such whispers, followed by fisticuffs, much to his father's dismay. But those days were long over, and the ire—no, the *fury* possessing him then—had dissipated as well. Just as he had mastered the scorn of schoolchildren, he had mastered his disposition, his passions, his life. By the time his father passed away, Darcy had earned his approval in society.

Of course, his father had wanted to see him safely wed to a bride of equivalent virtue and rectitude, with his nursery begun, and was disappointed in Darcy's unwillingness to oblige him. At the onset of his father's long illness, Darcy was too young to consider marriage. He had thrown himself into learning the management of their holdings and estates. His sister, too, had needed his care and consideration.

But beyond the excuse of general busyness, he had wished for... more. More than a merger of two people with similar upbringing and more than another dignified notch in his family's distinguished pedigree. Obviously, *his* parents' marriage had not been a happy one; perhaps begun with the best of intentions, uniting an earldom and a gentleman's fortune, the consequences were a disaster from which his father had never fully recovered. Darcy was not a romantic. He did not know if he believed in love, but he believed in harmony, and such was only possible if partners were genuinely interested in each other.

He had not found any such "more" as yet, and even wondered if the notion was mistaken. He wanted a wife; or, rather, his body, base creature that it was, wanted to attend to the business of procreation with what he considered extremely inconvenient enthusiasm. Other men might take mistresses, treating the matter of feminine companionship lightly, but no rakehell life for Fitzwilliam Darcy! Thus, he had attended an unusual number of parties this season, and with much keener interest than years past, attempting to acquaint himself with the latest crop of young society misses without starting gossip—a hideously difficult task, since he had never troubled to bestir himself before—and he was no closer to convivial matrimony than to the moon.

Despite the potential for scandal, a trip to Ramsgate at least gave him an excuse to avoid a fortnight's worth of salons, assemblies, and balls. His cousin the colonel, who had undertaken to accompany him to these festivities, would be disappointed, but would undoubtedly contrive to enjoy the season without him. Darcy could only feel relief at the idea of ducking out. Besides, he had not liked the brevity of Georgiana's last letter, and had been meaning to visit her. This could be a perfect opportunity to ensure the fresh sea air and her new, more maternal companion were helping her to get past the unhappiness she experienced since their father's death.

It was decided then; he would pay a quick visit to Ramsgate, discovering what he could about the situation of Mr Bennet's young daughter, under the very real cover of satisfying himself as to his sister's wellbeing. No one need know he might be required to visit fallen women and their natural daughters.

JANE SPOKE LIZZY'S NAME LOUDLY. LOUDLY, AT LEAST, FOR JANE.

Lizzy startled. She could tell, from the faint note of annoyance in Jane's voice, it wasn't the first time her sister had called her.

"I am sorry," Lizzy replied, wiping her hands upon a stained towel kept near for the purpose. "I was minding the pincers and didn't hear you."

Jane looked at the lifelike sculpture of a lobster Lizzy was modelling and gave a delicate shudder. "It looks very...real," she said. "Are you sure Mr Dobbs would not like more of those sweet little seals instead?"

"He probably would. But I should have to poke my eye out with your darning needles if I had to make another. What did you need?"

"Mama wonders if you have taken her silver hair comb. Again."

Lizzy dug around in her assortment of "tools" until she found the clay-encrusted item. She scrubbed at it with her towel before handing it over to her sister. "I needed it for the mermaids' hair. The comb teeth are perfectly spaced and sturdy enough to make grooves in the clay."

"Oh, Lizzy. Not mermaids again."

"*Nothing* sells as satisfactorily as the mermaids, and well you know it. Mama needs a new wardrobe before her next round of parties if she's going to replace her 'dear Percy,' and good brandy doesn't come cheap."

Of course, once I have a worthier agent than Mr Dobbs, I shall be able to earn more.

She tamped down her exasperation with Jane's scruples by silently repeating her goals. *See Jane happily wed and earn enough to take care of Mama without relying upon the men. Oh, and never again sculpt anything in the least bit nautical.*

Jane's eyes briefly closed, her usual smile disappearing. "I will ask Father," she said.

"You cannot do that, Jane," Lizzy replied. Jane hated reminders of their main source of income, preferring to pretend Fanny Bennet's gentlemen callers were there to take tea and discuss the weather. "It will remind him that he hasn't approved of your betrothed and the madness will begin all over again."

"He only wishes to see me settled," Jane offered.

There was a smattering of truth in this. Even though Jane was his natural daughter, Sir Walter's fondness for her exceeded his brief interest in their mother. Though he was a vain and capricious man, Jane was haphazardly provided for; sometimes with money, but more often nice clothing, governesses, and a completely impractical education. Lately, he provided several candidates for her hand in marriage, none of whom Jane had the slightest interest in encouraging. Jane's heart belonged to Captain Worth, currently earning his fortune privateering, fighting both the French and the English smugglers. Sir Walter was mightily displeased with her choice. Any requests for money would recall Jane to his attention, along with the dramatic fits for which Sir Walter was known.

Lizzy preferred to avoid dramatics whenever possible, although living with Fanny meant they were sometimes unavoidable, bless her.

"Mermaids are much easier to cope with than your father," Lizzy said. "Have you had any letters from the Captain lately?"

This was an obvious diversionary tactic, but Jane fell for it. Jane was so good that nothing dark or devious could touch her. They ought to make a scientific study of her and attempt to discover what implacable substance her character possessed that would not allow sin to stick.

Or maybe, Lizzy thought ruefully, *I hold a special allurement for it, and draw it all away from her.*

FANNY CLASPED HER HANDS TOGETHER NERVOUSLY. "OH, LIZZY, I'M NOT certain of the peach. Do you think it too girlish?"

"Not at all," Lizzy said. It was very important to be firm with Fanny's indecisiveness, or she would fret the day away. "It does wonders for your appearance. Besides, you are not so very old."

Fanny's expression turned hopeful. "I know I could pass for ten years my junior." Then she frowned. "But even that is no longer young. Perhaps I should accept Mr Goulding's offer, after all."

Lizzy set her hands to her hips and stared her mother down. This was much easier to do now that she was half a head taller.

"Mr Goulding is an atrocious pig. Do you not remember what he did to Hattie? She will wear that scar on her face forever."

"I know. I know you're right," Fanny agreed, wincing at the thought of her friend's injury. "'Tis so vexing. At Lucretia's salon last week, Lydia wondered if I might be taking ill. I am so pallid, she says. What is to become of us if I cannot replace dear Percy?"

"You are not to be concerned. You are still beautiful, and have forgotten more about men than Lydia Younge ever knew. She is simply jealous. Isn't she now a companion for some spoiled heiress since her London girls' school failed? Besides, I do not care for that red dress, as flattering as the cut might be. If you were pale, it was the fault of the cloth. We shall sell that one, so we might add the cream satin for a new negligee."

Fanny still looked anxious, but gossip and the thought of a new negligee soothed her. "Lydia is ever so fortunate she had any students at all," Fanny opined. "The very idea of putting her in charge of training up young ladies! I'll wager she barely escaped London before the whispers began. One can only wonder what *this* heiress's guardians are thinking, giving her charge of an innocent. Lyddie always boasts of her blue blood and her marriage to a gentleman, but everyone knows she carried on with Lord Fitzwilliam well before her widowhood, and who knows how many before and after him. The luck of her! The cream satin, you think?"

Lizzy spared a moment of sympathy for the unknown heiress. Promptly, however, she called a halt to this line of thinking. *For all you know, the heiress is a nasty piece, while Lydia is unlikely to give cause to be sent packing from that fine Albion House property. You have problems enough of your own without borrowing from strangers.*

If only she could see her mother's household set comfortably for a few years, she could leave and make her own way! She even had a plan for how to begin: by seeking out the kindly man who'd taught her those first lessons in her art, the man who showed her how to unleash life inside of clay, freeing her imagination into visible permanence.

The fact that Lizzy had not laid eyes on this man since she was nine years old might, perhaps, create a challenge.

Paying only half-hearted attention to her mother's chatter, she recalled that long ago time. Despite having been warned to stay upstairs and out of sight while her mother entertained, Lizzy was rash, impetuous, and unsupervised. Due to her highly irregular family, she was not welcomed everywhere in the neighbourhood and Jane was often kept busy with governesses and lessons from which Lizzy was usually excluded.

Still, at her young age, she fretted over her mother and the gentlemen who buzzed like bees around her, half-hoping one of them would become her Papa, half-terrified of the same. And so, she spied. Hidden in stairwells, behind furniture or even inside it, she eavesdropped, she listened, and she kept watch during her mother's salons and entertainments.

One gentleman in particular captured her attention. He performed little courtesies for Mama, his manners beautiful, his smile gentle. She sought an opportunity to make his acquaintance, and because he had become a regular visitor, it was not long before she found one. At dawn's first light, as he was quietly departing, she popped up from the sofa where she waited.

"Oh!" he exclaimed, raising his walking stick before realising his assailant was a little girl.

Lizzy held out a hand. "My name is Lizzy. I've wanted to meet you this age. Just so's you know, not only is Mama beautiful but she is kind, and would make a fine wife, if you were wanting one. She has two daughters, but we've room for lots more children here. The baron insists Jane have her own room, but *I* am happy to share. Jane has loads of manners, too—she's ex-emp-lary," Lizzy enunciated carefully. "Which is a great thing in an elder sister, don't you think?"

"Hmm…why, yes, I suppose so," the gentleman replied, his cheeks stained red, though he had shaken her hand politely. "Ought you not to be tucked into your bed?"

"Oh, yes," Lizzy nodded, "but no one knows if I am or amn't, so it don't truly matter if I keep an eye out for Mama instead. And I been watching you and see you're a real fine gentleman, and since Mama is forgetting to ask about important things, I thought I might do it for her. I help her with lots of affairs," she confided importantly.

"You do?" he asked, at a loss.

"Oh, yes. I'm a wonder with the pawnshops and bargaining with the butcher."

He shook his head, finally smiling, and then sighing. "Now, listen to me, Little Miss Lizzy, you can't be listening at doors and such, and most of all, you can't be presenting yourself to your Mama's guests."

Lizzy's regard turned mulish. "How'm I supposed to help things along if I don't?"

"You have to trust me on this, Little Miss. Tell you what—you promise to stay well away from your Mama's company, always and forever, and next time I visit of an afternoon, I will bring you an important gift. How's that?"

"I suppose," Lizzy said, a little sullenly.

But he shook her hand firmly, tapped her nose, and bid her farewell as politely as if she were a fine lady, and Lizzy awaited his next visit with overwhelming eagerness.

When the great day came, Lizzy was ushered into the parlour at the gentleman's summons, her mother smiling uneasily at the irregular request that he be presented to her daughter. At first puzzled by the lumpy substance he held, Lizzy was fascinated when he transformed the lump into a kitten, then, a lump once again, and then a puppy. He could make an endless variety!

He left the clay with her and was agreeably impressed with her attempts at reproducing the kitten, proudly displayed to him by Fanny on his next visit. He brought more clay, books on modelling and the arts, and what was more, shared tales of his boyhood, with his Italian, artistic mother and English father who was a land steward like himself, in a place called Derbyshire near a village named Lambton.

He dabbled in painting and sculpture for his mother's sake, he said, and learnt some of what she taught, but he hadn't her "gift;" he could reproduce technical perfection in a subject, but was unable to capture its true essence.

Lizzy hadn't a notion of what he meant by such words. She only knew he spoke to her as though she *could* understand. With every visit, she loved him more, investing every minute in improving her modelling until she produced figurines that delighted and amused him —and he rewarded her with praise and more instruction. One grand morning he even brought a labourer, who built a working kiln in a corner of the garden, and spent days showing her how to fire and glaze her pieces. One afternoon, as they experimented with the size of the flame in the firebox and the timing, Lizzy felt such a surge of worshipful love for the older man, she could not contain it.

"Oh, sir," she said, "if I have the 'gift,' like your Mama, won't you please, please marry us and live with us always?"

In the sudden silence, she knew immediately she had made a mistake. His cheeks reddened, and he smiled sadly. "No, Little Miss," he said. "It cannot be."

He did not come the next day, or the next. When she pestered her mama for his whereabouts, Fanny could only shrug and tell her not to be a nuisance. One evening, he did come—but not to see Lizzy, and since she'd left off spying, she hadn't learned of it until long after his departure. Mama told her later—he'd given her something called a congé, which meant he would not be back—leaving a tiny bundle and letter for Lizzy.

She sat with the unopened letter for some hours, not knowing how she could bear to read his good-bye. But of course, she finally did.

Dear Little Miss,

Thank you for your offer of friendship and family. You do me a great honour, if undeserved. My Mama went to live in heaven not long ago, and I was so sad, I left my home and family to take a holiday. But it is time I return to them, and thus I must take my leave of you. Please believe me when I promise you do *have Mama's gift and astounding talent. Someday you will be a distinguished artist. All of England will pay you homage, and I will tell any who will listen I helped plant your feet on the path to greatness.*

I enclose a ring given me by my Mama. It was her father's, and is precious to me. Whenever you see it, please remember the promise you made.

Your friend always,
Mr H. Wickham

LIZZY SHOOK OFF THE MEMORIES. *I WAS SUCH A SILLY CHIT.* HER MORE mature self was very grateful to him for more than just the clay, for undoubtedly that promise had kept her safer than she might otherwise have been. After she had grown older, she took control of the lackadaisical household; she plagued and scolded her mother into being more selective of her beaus and staying away from the more "exciting" candidates for her attentions. This sensible advice led to much longer-lasting liaisons, which in turn helped preserve much of her mother's beauty. Fanny would always desire a lively circle and her parties and assemblies were well known, but she kept her most intimate associations to very unadventurous, stolid, elderly sorts, such as dear departed Percy.

Since Mr Wickham's parting, Lizzy had laboured tirelessly on developing her own talents, until she felt she was ready to take on the world. Or at least a corner of it, enough to secure some safety and peace for herself and for her mother—and Jane as well, if her captain did not come back from the war. As little respect as Lizzy had for Mr Dobbs, at least he paid her for something that did not involve sexual favours. What she had already sold, she knew, was the least part of what she was capable of creating. Her dream was to find Mr Wickham in Derbyshire, remind him who she was by showing him the ring and letter, perhaps with a few pieces of her recent work. He had spoken of art dealers and auction house owners as though they were his dear friends; perhaps one of them could help her sell her pieces under a man's name. In her wildest fancies, she dreamed he sent her to his mother's family in Italy, where she would finally try her hand at stonework and Carrara marble...but, even if the kindly Mr Wickham could only give her a letter of introduction to someone useful, she would be grateful.

She fingered the ring that hung, always, on a chain about her neck. One more protector for Fanny. Once more, and then never again. *I will extract us from this life, and I will prove my gift.*

Fanny's words interrupted Lizzy's mental ramblings.

"I should perhaps mention…Mr Goulding is sending his man over with an offer," she said tentatively.

"Mother! Why would you encourage him?"

"Oh, Lizzy, what is to become of us? I'm not as young as I once was, and 'tis all so…oh, how I miss dear Percy. Whatever shall we do?"

Lizzy sighed. Her mother's feelings for Percy were real, if somewhat shallow. Men were shallow creatures, requiring almost nothing of a woman's true nature. Fuss over them as if doing so was life's greatest pleasure and treat every word they uttered as insightful wisdom. Luckily for the state of their pantry, she had never had to do it, and for that, she was grateful to her mother.

"You do not have to stoop to such as Goulding," Lizzy said sternly. "That is why we invested in the fabrics for a beautiful new wardrobe. You will shine at your salon Friday evening, and the gentlemen will fall at your feet."

"Are you certain, Lizzy?" Fanny asked anxiously, her hand sliding over the sensuous, silken nap of a daring hat à la Hussar the milliner recommended.

"Completely."

Attic Above Fanny Bennet's Drawing Room

"Lizzy," Jane whispered. "Do you *have* to do this?"

Lizzy glanced up, giving Jane a "*You know the answer*" look, and refitted her eye into the eyepiece. The device, her own invention, gave her a good view of the drawing room on the floor below. Mirrors in one of the drawing room's chandeliers, when slowly rotated, allowed her to see nearly everything and everyone. It required her to lie flat on her stomach in the middle of the attic floor to man the eyepiece, and she could hear only murmurs wafting upwards like warm air from a hearth. Still, she could keep an eye, literally, on who was paying attention to Mama, and, if the crowd grew unruly, summon Jacob—their "bully"—to quietly remove offenders. She took note of admirers, judged who was most acceptable and made it her business to discover everything she could about them. In this way, she learnt enough to assist her mother's undependable judgment.

The assembly progressed nicely. Fanny, resplendent in peach silk, was beautiful and the centre of attention. Other female invitees had been carefully chosen—all of them less voluptuous, older, and harder-edged so Fanny could shine. The men came from a variety of spheres, for Fanny's little affairs had a small but certain reputation amongst Ramsgate society for good food, excellent liquor, and general gaiety. While most guests were hardly good *ton*, there were a few members of the neighbouring gentry and a peer or two, all hoping for more excitement than the coastal town usually offered.

"Lizzy," Jane whispered again, more urgently. "We have a problem!"

Lizzy lifted her head. "What? What problem?"

"Jacob says there is a–a gentleman here who insists upon speaking to Mama *immediately*. Jacob believes him too important to send away."

Lizzy sighed. Jacob *looked* intimidating, with his pugilist body and lofty height, but the right authority could intimidate him. No doubt, Mr Goulding's man—or heaven forbid, Mr Goulding himself—had chosen *this* evening to appear with his unwelcome offer.

"I will see to it. Go on to bed."

"Are you sure, Lizzy? I can accompany you."

"Not necessary. I will get rid of him."

Jane said, unmistakable relief in her tone, "I told Jacob to put him in the small blue parlour. Oh, here." She handed her sister a card.

Mr Fitzwilliam Darcy was the name printed on expensive vellum. But then, Mr Goulding was a wealthy man; he would pay his solicitor well.

Lizzy stood and brushed at her dark skirt in case her sojourn on the carpet had left dusty evidence. "I will send him on his way."

Before entering the parlour where Mr Darcy waited, she squared her shoulders, firmed her chin, and prepared to make her point quickly and succinctly. This was not the daunting Mr Goulding, she reminded herself, only his hireling. Jacob was nearby in the kitchen and would come quickly if called. She had dealt with pawnbrokers, spongers, drunks, and harlots; she could certainly deal with a solicitor. She opened the door, prepared to speak, but instead stood with her mouth open, caught mid-syllable. "Mr Dar—"

He was the handsomest man she had ever seen. Tall, with broad shoulders, a dimpled chin, and a patrician nose the envy of any aristocrat—a nose worthy of much finer forebears than a mere solicitor ought to possess. He was dressed all in black except for a hint of silver thread on his waistcoat, making his shirt and cravat appear ruthlessly white. Even the stone in his stickpin was black—onyx, perhaps. There was a day's growth of dark whiskers on his chin, giving him a rougher appearance, as though he had added the extra touch of *noir* purposely to suit his attire.

DARCY WHIRLED AT THE SOUND OF THE WOMAN'S VOICE, IMPATIENT TO finish this ugly errand. Evidently, he had timed his visit with some sort of soirée, forcing him to insist upon an audience using the infamous Darcy stare. Now he found himself staring once again, but for an entirely different reason.

By all that's holy. No wonder Bennet lost his head.

The harlot was beautiful. He was no expert on female clothing, especially *this* sort of female, but her frock clung to her light, pleasing figure in an extremely promising fashion. Her hair was piled untidily upon her head, with curls escaping at her nape. She should have looked frowsy and unkempt, but instead she brought to mind pale skin in sultry moonlight and the last thousand nights he spent alone. Her eyes were wide, thick-lashed, dark, and appraising. She appeared much younger than she ought—part of her arts and allurements, he supposed—and he wondered how she maintained such a fresh, inno-cent aspect. Perhaps *innocent* was the wrong word, what with those eyes. No female with such eyes could be an innocent. Eyes so deep a man could drown in them, never remembering to come up for air.

Before he went down, he fiercely reined himself in. Doing so made his words emerge more sharply than he meant.

"I have come about the girl."

"You have no business here," the woman replied.

"I believe I do," he said. "I was informed she was agreeable to the connexion. Before any meeting, I mean to assess her general health."

"Do you mean to inspect her teeth and hooves? Go back to where you came from, sir, and tell your patron that Mrs Bennet wants nothing to do with you."

Darcy drew himself up, all thoughts of her beauty gone. "Your sarcasm is unappreciated and highly suspect. I mean to see how well cared-for she is, and I warn you not to trifle with me. You do not know the trouble you bring upon this ramshackle household if I am not satis-fied with the results of my inquiry."

"Do not threaten me or my house. I swear you will live to regret it!"

"What are you hiding?" He scowled. "If you do not bring me the child this minute, I will have you arrested. If I find you have abused her in any way, I will see you in Newgate!"

"Child? What child?"

He answered in his coldest tone. "Do not play me for a fool, madam."

"I think there has been a mistake. You have the wrong household. There are no children here."

Darcy was beyond irritated at her prevarications. "Shall I call a constable? The magistrate? Do you deny the presence in your home of Elizabeth Bennet?"

The woman blinked. "No-o," she answered.

Darcy found it difficult to speak through his clenched jaw. "Then bring her to me."

"Elizabeth Bennet?" she queried slowly.

"Yes!"

"*I* am Elizabeth Bennet."

It was Darcy's turn to blink. "You are not a child," he said.

"Plainly," she replied. "Why would you think I was?"

"I did not. I thought you were the harlot," he said.

"Do you represent Mr Goulding?"

"Never heard of him," Darcy replied. "Are you certain you are the only Elizabeth Bennet here?"

She rolled her eyes. "What is your business with this house? Who *are* you?"

After a day in the saddle, Darcy had anticipated nothing more than a reunion with his sister and a long, hot bath. But his over-active conscience had begun fretting over the supposedly neglected "child" of Bennet's. There had been no trouble finding the place; Mrs Bennet was hardly unknown. And now he was facing, *not* a defenceless child, but a dark-eyed, tempting Prime Article.

What a happy twist of fate! his body cried.

Do not even consider it, his brain ordered.

"I am a friend of the Bennet family. As my young sister is currently living in Ramsgate with her companion, I was asked by a family emissary to judge your situation upon my next visit," he cautiously replied. "Obviously, there is some misperception at work."

"Bennet family?" she repeated. Her open gaze became guarded. "Do you mean Mr Thomas Bennet?"

Darcy felt an instinctive abhorrence of the shadows crossing her expressive visage. "This upsets you," he said, making it a statement, not a question.

"Of course not," Miss Bennet replied. "'Tis nothing to me what Mr Bennet does or does not do."

"He is very ill," Darcy began.

"So sorry to hear it."

"I suppose you find this difficult," he tried again, feeling fully out of his depth.

"Let me make this plain," she interrupted. "Obviously, you were under the mistaken impression that I am a child. You may now assure all that I survived my infancy, without the kind nurture of my absent parent. You may also reassure them I have no intention of embarrassing the family by making myself kno—" She stopped mid-word, a thoughtful expression replacing her frown.

"Do you believe they would pay for it?" she asked conversationally.

"Pay for what?"

"Pay. Money. So I stay away or keep quiet about myself. I wonder how much silence would be worth? Of course, if he has a new wife, then the marriage is illegal and—"

"I hate to disillusion you, but Thomas Bennet has no illicit second wife to abet your blackmail scheme," he answered drily. He knew he should be disgusted and angry, but it was oddly attractive to see her brighten, a dreamy gaze replacing her former cynicism.

She frowned. "Oh. I suppose it *could* be considered a blackmail, put like that."

"How else would you put it?" he asked, interested to know the workings of her criminal mind.

"I am his daughter, and yet he has never provided so much as a meal, much less a dress or a ribbon. I consider I am owed something for that."

"I understood he provided this home," he said, gesturing around him.

"If you had a child, and you gave her mother shelter but no food to put on the table and no coal for the stove, or heavens, no table or stove, would you say you'd done your duty by her?" she asked in a tone of mild curiosity.

He thought of Georgiana, for whom a settlement of thirty thousand seemed but a small fraction of her worth. Of course, Georgiana was the granddaughter of an earl, not the daughter of a harlot.

"It seems ample payment for services rendered," he answered, irritated at himself for comparing his dear sister to someone so far beneath her.

Elizabeth shrugged. "That is what I thought you would say. If you will excuse me, please." She turned and left the room abruptly, leaving Darcy standing in the dim parlour before he could think of a protest.

And why should I care if I insulted her? he thought. *There is no child in need here, but a scheming female, and whatever happened in the past cannot be undone. Bingley misunderstood the situation.*

Or had he? Bingley's letter had been deuced difficult to decipher. Perhaps Darcy had been the one to misunderstand. But what, then, had Bingley expected his friend to do?

Stupidly, he had left the letter in London. He did not know what his next steps ought to be.

Your next steps ought to be out the door and to Albion House and your sister, as quickly as may be. Thank the fates you need have nothing more to do with this house of sin and a female who considers extortion as indifferently as you might consider a selection of waistcoats.

But those eyes! They had weighed and measured his character and found him wanting. Wanting! Fitzwilliam Darcy, of Pemberley! As if such as *she* could be any judge!

He strode out of the dim parlour, pausing to look in both directions. To his left was the passage towards exit and escape; to his right, a closed door. Without allowing himself to consider his decision—he could hear muffled laughter and music, and who knew what one might find?—he opened the door, only to find himself in a tidy kitchen. The bully was there, flirting with a maid. Such a lax household!

"I need writing materials, at once," he said, using the note of command he had learned at his father's knee. The bully quickly made himself scarce and the maid scurried about, returning momentarily with the requested objects.

He dashed off a note to Miss Elizabeth Bennet, giving her his direction, informing her he would be writing to her father's family regarding the situation, as he would be several days in the neighbourhood for his aforementioned visit with his sister. In the meantime, if she wished him to convey any message to Mr Bennet, he would be happy to do so, closing the missive with gracious thanks.

There, he thought with satisfaction, after giving the maid instructions for its delivery to Miss Elizabeth. Despite her discourtesy, despite the fact that she was completely undeserving of his superior attentions, he had delivered a polite farewell. *I am now at liberty to enjoy visiting Georgiana.*

But how much of his satisfaction came from having had the last word, he would not admit to anyone, least of all himself.

LIZZY STARED INTO THE EYEPIECE, VIEWING THE PARTY BELOW, BUT TAKING in nothing. The question of whether the elderly Lord Cumberbatch might be interested enough in Fanny to make her an offer, or whether to encourage Mr Tippets, a successful draper, was the furthest thing from her mind.

It is not as though your father wrote to you. The fastidious Mr Darcy, so overly addicted to scrupulousness, was very careful to leave Mr Bennet's name out of it. But who wanted to know me? Or know of me?

Fanny had always maintained Thomas Bennet to be Lizzy's father and she, his legal wife. Though Fanny's grasp of honesty was somewhat flexible, the whole subject of her marriage was sore enough that Lizzy believed her. Fanny had loved him, and they nearly starved before she had finally taken a protector.

Lizzy viscerally understood his abandonment. Fanny liked to call him unforgiving and heartless, but most men would not easily accept that the bride they thought a widow was actually a baron's former mistress. Fanny was also fond of blaming Sir Walter, whose unwillingness to part forever with Jane meant Fanny could not maintain the lie of her "widowhood." As a child she saw the torch Fanny carried for him was not completely extinguished; Mama had encouraged Lizzy's letters to her absent father.

As an adult, Lizzy could also recognise why he had not answered her. Fanny deceived and humiliated him; Lizzy was a reminder. His dreams of the future were ripped apart by a baron's leavings and her mother's lie; it was doubtful he believed Lizzy to be his daughter. Lizzy had faced these truths long ago, and no longer dwelt upon what could never be. She had her own dreams, of a small cottage with a spacious studio, away from the false glamour of Fanny's life, happily producing the creations her limitless imagination supplied. If Fanny had a generous allowance, perhaps she would stop relying upon men for attention and security. Or perhaps not.

"Excuse me, Miss," Clara, their maid, said softly.

"Yes, Clara," she replied, getting up from the carpet. She wasn't doing her mother's interests a bit of good tonight, regardless.

"The toff said as I ought ta give you 'is note. At once, 'e said." She handed over the piece of foolscap.

"Thank you," Lizzy said, dismissing the maid with instructions to make sure the cold meats and cheeses for supper were ready to serve. It was unsurprising that Clara obeyed Darcy's orders rather than her employer's. The Bennet family obviously lived in a sphere far above her own, sending such a one as him; he had an air of command exuded only by those born to wealth and great fortune.

She was equally unsurprised that Mr Darcy's handwriting was bold and elegant. It matched what she noted of his clothing and general appearance. With a mixture of curiosity and annoyance, she read what he had written.

Hah! I, send a message for Thomas Bennet? I would wager Fanny's next dressmaker's bill that he would not deliver any letter I would write!

She glanced at his note again, almost instinctively, and this time, her eye caught on the words "Albion House." Was that not where her mother's least favourite crony-adversary now resided? Lydia Younge, the governess of an unknown heiress?

Lizzy had supposed the heiress's guardians were careless and neglectful, to have accepted any references produced by Lydia Younge. Plainly, however, Mr Darcy was the conscientious sort, if perhaps a bit naïve. After all, he was willing to make a fuss over the wellbeing of a child he did not even know, simply because he had promised to look in on her. Someone ought to inform him that his sister was not in good hands. Perhaps many of the *beau monde* thought little of profligacy, but some of Lydia's predilections went beyond the usual infidelities. *Far, far beyond,* Lizzy thought with a shudder.

But why should *she* be that someone? And would he even believe her if she did tell him?

Who cares if he believes me or not? she reasoned. *I am not responsible for any of it. But I do not like Lydia, and I am not so hard-hearted as to withhold the information from Mr Darcy because he is a fastidious, arrogant, condescending male with an unfortunate connexion to my absent parent.*

Briefly, she considered writing him a note. But if meddlesome Lydia saw any note with Lizzy's name on it, she would immediately be suspicious; if Lizzy sent it without identifying herself, she could not be sure if it would be disregarded or given to some secretary to decide if it should be acted upon. Only by confronting him herself could she be certain he would have an opportunity to accept the truth.

She decided she would go on the morrow to Albion House, early enough that Lydia would still be abed. With a sigh, she gave up tonight's party as a loss. She needed to plan her clothing and words to convey sincerity about his sister's companion. It would require she borrow one of Fanny's more subdued fine dresses simply to get past the butler or housekeeper, taking Clara along for an appearance of respectability.

If he understands how poor a choice he made in Lydia, I will have done my duty by my conscience.

But how much of that satisfaction came from knowing she would be taking the mighty Mr Darcy down a peg or two, she would not admit to anyone, least of all herself.

Albion House, East Cliff, Ramsgate

Darcy was displeased. His displeasure did *not* stem from the fact that he had driven all the way to Ramsgate, mostly in order to visit Georgiana, only to discover Georgiana was nowhere to be found. What he could not understand was *why*.

Arriving last night, feeling somewhat unsettled after his meeting with Elizabeth Bennet as well as fatigued from his journey, he expected a warm if surprised welcome from his sister. Instead, the housekeeper, Mrs Douglas, informed him that Georgiana and her companion were away on a visit to Lady Catherine at Rosings Park.

That Georgiana would willingly stop with their estimable aunt defied imagination. Georgiana was a dutiful niece, but their aunt was a difficult woman, over-critical and temperamental. To say their annual sojourn, so recently endured, was anything but a necessary evil was to whitewash the truth. Lady Catherine *must* have summoned her, but Mrs Douglas was certain no letter from the great lady had been delivered. Also, Georgiana had taken her carriage and her companion, but no footman, and what is more, they left *his* coachman behind in favour of another, hired by Mrs Younge. The trip to Rosings Park was only a day's journey on good roads, but Georgiana *had* to understand that if she arrived there with any less than a contingent of attendants, she would never hear the end of it.

Last night he was too exhausted from his journey to consider all the oddities. If Lady Catherine bid her come, at the very least he would have expected an express from his sister delivered to Darcy House in London, begging him to accompany her. What *could* Georgiana be thinking? Was she so lonely here that even Cousin Anne's spiritless company would be an improvement?

Darcy was lifting his pen to begin his own express to his lady aunt, when a quiet scratch sounded on the library door.

Mrs Douglas entered, disapproval stamped upon her features. "Please excuse me, sir, but a young lady insists upon an audience. I told her you were not receiving, but she says she will not leave without speaking with you."

Darcy lifted one brow and plucked the card from Mrs Douglas's outstretched hand.

Miss Elizabeth Bennet

"She is alone?" he asked, forcing a note of censure into his voice. It would not do for the servant to detect any eagerness on his part to meet with forward young females.

"Her maid accompanied her," Mrs Douglas sniffed.

He pretended to think about it. "It will be easier to hear what she wants," he finally said in an appropriately disinterested tone. "Show her in."

Mrs Douglas was too well-trained to argue. Shortly thereafter, Miss Bennet was ushered into the library

Darcy fought to keep his expression composed, but it was difficult. He had been expecting the somewhat dishevelled, unfashionably garbed beauty from last evening. The female before him now bore little resemblance, except in her dark, flashing eyes and the slightly cynical curve of her mouth.

She wore a modish fur-trimmed walking dress, with a short pelisse of deep lilac shot with white, on each hip a Spanish button accentuating her extremely agreeable figure. Her bonnet, of the same purple as the pelisse, was adorned with white ostrich feathers, quivering in the air around her head like a trembling halo. From her boots of unexpectedly bold plum-coloured leather, to the lime green gloves encasing her hands, she gave the impression of a brightly coloured ice treat he had once been served in Gunter's Tea Shop on Berkeley Square. Oh, for a taste!

"Mr Darcy," she began. "It is good of you to see me. I trust I have not upended your sensibilities by appearing uninvited on your doorstep."

She closed the library door and his heart thundered in his chest. Nevertheless, he maintained his air of ennui as he stood to greet her with a small bow.

"My sensibilities are intact, thank you, Miss Bennet." He motioned carelessly at the settee, and hid a smile as she made herself comfortable, as if she were cosying up for a nice chat.

"For now," she agreed. "No doubt before I am finished, you will be outraged, aghast, and annoyed. Perhaps *fainting* with fury. You seem like the sort. All that remains to be seen is whether you will be offended enough to have me tossed from the house—an outcome, I might add, to be heartily endorsed by your housekeeper."

"Indeed?" Darcy asked, stifling his shock. No one who knew him would even dream of such a response. "You have a very ill notion of my fortitude. I assure you I have never fainted in my life, furious or otherwise."

"Never thrown things when you're in a fit of the sulks?"

"Gentlemen do not lose control, especially in the presence of the fairer sex," he reassured, with equal parts annoyance and amusement. "Even when faced with such extreme provocation."

Miss Bennet laughed. "Do gentlemen come in different species, like roses? I have witnessed tantrums from your sort that put spoiled tots to shame. But perhaps you are *homo generosus tranquillitas*…or would it be *homo generosus moron*?"

He was briefly distracted from his protest by her use of Latin, even if her application only ran to personal insults. He shook his head to clear it, and to prevent himself from bantering with her in ancient languages.

"Very witty, Miss Bennet. Perhaps you ought to come to the point of this potential provocation, instead of attempting to goad me into anger beforehand…which, if you consider, does not seem a particularly rational plan."

"You are correct, Mr Darcy. I shall make this brief. I understand Lydia Younge is in your employ. My mother has known Lydia for a number of years, and I certainly know *of* her. What I know is not flattering and, in fact, she is the last person who ought to have charge of a delicate young girl."

She paused to take a breath.

"Whatever you wish to think about my mother, her life is positively dull compared to Mrs Younge's," she continued. "A fact Lydia never fails to mention in their conversations, by the way. Lydia lived in Ramsgate for years before moving to London to start a school, for which she had minimal qualifications, and we have known her for most of that time. She is not...right. Not for your sister."

"Revealing this is very...altruistic of you," Darcy said coldly. "Astoundingly so."

"I do not give a fig if you believe me or not. Go right ahead and have the harlot's daughter thrown out of your superior presence. I have informed you of the truth, as I set out to do, and now you cannot claim ignorance. At least, on *this* matter."

She expected it, Darcy realised. Even through his shock and suspicion at her words, he could see she was waiting for him to heap abuse upon her. She was convinced of it. It was not in his nature to defend himself, but he *would* demonstrate how an honourable man ought to behave, no matter his own expanding consternation and confusion.

"Mrs Younge gave excellent references," he said instead. "Her 'Academy for Younge Ladies' was well regarded, with students from other good families."

Miss Bennet gave a sharp, negative shake of her head. "Her birth is well enough, her husband was a gentleman, her lovers discreet—and some very highly placed—but one cannot always keep such things completely quiet. She complained to Mama about the high sticklers pulling their daughters and refusing to pay her over silly rumours. She said she hated rusticating in Ramsgate, especially with a spoiled heiress in tow, but at least she was not so far from town that she could not *entertain*."

Darcy fought his desire to growl in frustration and anger. It was a temptation to begin pacing—and perhaps tearing his hair—but his self-control was absolute. *A gentleman does not display his emotions for an audience.* Still, he said more than he might have, had he been in greater possession of his wits.

"When I arrived last night, I was told my sister and her companion departed on a journey to my aunt's estate, Rosings Park. There are a number of reasons why I find this information...surprising," he said. "It is very irregular. Very irregular indeed."

"Perhaps she truly did go to your aunt's," she said suddenly, reversing her previous belligerent tactic. "If Lydia wished to travel to someplace near there, she could easily have urged your sister into a visit."

"*Not* easily," he muttered. "My aunt is not a person who Georgiana would willingly…"

He suddenly seemed to recollect the presence of his visitor. He straightened. "I thank you for bringing me this information," he said formally. "I shall have you driven back to Harbour Street."

"Wait! What do you plan to do?" Miss Bennet asked, moving in front of him and laying one hand upon his arm.

"Find my sister, of course," he answered stiffly. "I shall write to my aunt immediately to determine if she went to her. I was in the process of doing so when you were announced. I shall also make inquiries on the main roads."

She removed her hand, but continued to block his path. "No."

"No?" he questioned, his voice registering an octave lower in dangerous warning.

"If you make inquiries, it will be noticed. Too many people here know Lydia, and her reputation. Your sister's…she could be harmed."

Though Darcy wanted nothing more than to shove her aside and run out the door—hauling strangers off the street shaking information from them—a portion of his common sense could acknowledge the truth of her words. He paused to listen to her instead of beginning the shoving and shaking.

She proceeded to pace back and forth, the silly feathers on her hat fluttering wildly in her wake. He fought the impulse to snatch it off her head, to still her; ladies never paced, but of course, she was no lady. He did not even know why he so quickly believed her. But though he might not be of a social temperament, his social experience was vast. Every instinct told him she spoke the truth. *Devil take it!*

"According to you," he pointed out resentfully, "it is too late to rescue Georgiana's reputation. I have apparently had her installed with the devil for the last month." He made a sudden sound, like a groan or a roar. It made Miss Bennet jolt in alarm, but she quickly stiffened her spine against it.

"Which is *not* the case," she stated emphatically. "Lydia has not trumpeted the name of her heiress, and she would not. The very last thing she wants is gossip to reach the wrong ears. Consider—if anyone connects her with a Darcy, the likelihood becomes greater someone might tell *you* of her unsavoury reputation, as I just did. Miss Darcy is her cow, so to speak, and she will protect her for as long as there is milk. The only reason I put it together was that you left your direction on that note, and I knew Lydia lived here as a companion. I never heard your sister's name until you mentioned it a moment ago. They have been living very quietly. We have time to calculate the best method of rescue, *if* rescue is even needed. Is your aunt discreet?"

"Wha-what? Aunt?" His head ached, trying to follow her thought processes.

"The aunt to whom Georgiana has supposedly travelled."

"Yes, but—"

"Is your aunt to be trusted?"

"Lady Catherine? Giving her secret information would not be my first choice," he said. "Even if she does not gossip, she would bludgeon Georgiana with reminders for the rest of her life."

Miss Bennet nodded. "Then we shouldn't inform her unless we have to. I will need a description of your sister and of her carriage and coachman. Did she take a maid as well?"

He shook his head in the negative, one sharp movement.

"How old is your sister, Mr Darcy?"

"Fifteen," he replied shortly.

Miss Bennet nodded. "The servants here—did they infer any suspicion about the journey? Perhaps not outright, but was there anything in their manner, anything at all, conveying a hint of misgiving or hesitancy, no matter how slight?"

He ran a hand through his hair, a betraying nervous action, trying to think upon nuances of behaviour and speech. It was difficult in his current state of primitive outrage mixed with anxiety, but he managed.

"No," he said at last. "All seemed unexceptional. Mrs Douglas was distressed I had missed her by a day, but that is all."

"Has Mrs Douglas been in your employ for long?"

"No. She was hired by my usual London agency when we established this household." His gaze narrowed. "Why? Do you know anything of her?"

"Nothing," she assured. "She seems rather a dragon, which would not be to Lydia's liking. It could be Lydia wished to escape her eagle eye. Does your aunt run a lax household? If Lydia believed she could have more free—"

"No," Darcy interrupted firmly. "Just the opposite, in fact. Rosings Park is the last place one would go for...diversion."

"Then I believe it would be the last place Lydia would wish to go. She could easily learn the nature of the place from your sister. However, I could possibly imagine a scheme to leave Georgiana there for a visit whilst she went elsewhere, perhaps in search of said diversion."

"No, my sister is very timid, and Lady Catherine's nature is not a placid one. We returned not long ago from our Easter visit. Believe me when I say Georgiana would not look forward to another. She is reserved, but also stubborn. No one would be able to compel her into taking such a journey willingly."

"You mean, no mere companion would be able to compel her."

Darcy glanced at her, expecting to see the smirk returned, but she appeared serious, thoughtful and...concerned.

Why? Why should she possibly care about a stranger? He did not realise he had asked the question aloud until she looked up sharply.

"You do understand, Mr Darcy, that I do not live in your world?"

He stopped himself, barely, from rolling his eyes. "Of course," he replied.

"Of course," she agreed. "Do you understand Georgiana does not live in your world, either?"

His brow furrowed.

"I know what you think. You believe Miss Darcy and I have nothing in common. But you, sir, are wrong. We are both females surrounded by peril. The difference, however, is that I have understood this from the time I was very young, whereas she has been insulated and kept ignorant of it. Her blood and birth were supposed to protect her—*you* were supposed to protect her. She has never been expected to care for herself. She is a lamb let loose in the wilderness. Believe whatever you wish about me, I have a great deal of compassion for lambs, whether they are prize specimens of the nobility or the shabbiest of the flock."

She looked him straight in the eye with a clear, direct gaze he found oddly irresistible. "I will find your sister."

"If there is any chance my sister is in danger, I must begin the search immediately," he pronounced, shaking off the spell of her. "I thank you for your concern, but this problem is mine."

He watched her sigh heavily. "I do not say she is in danger, *per se*, no more than any female. In fact, I believe Lydia Younge would not do anything apurpose to harm her, and would in fact protect her. Why should she betray the hand that feeds her? I simply do not understand this situation, and I do not *trust* Lydia. The likely risk facing Miss Darcy is a minor scandal for being associated with her. The worst *possible* thing you could do is hire curious searchers and Bow Street Runners and gossipy henchmen. Leave this to me. I will find her."

Darcy made a contemptuous noise. "How? Will *you* hire the curious searchers and gossipy henchmen? What can you do that I cannot?"

Miss Bennet closed her eyes. "One, two, three, four, five, six, seven, eight, nine, ten," she counted aloud.

"What are you *doing*?" he asked incredulously.

"Practicing patience with obtusity," she replied. "I may have to count to one hundred."

His feelings were divided between abject frustration and an inappropriate, inexplicable desire to smile. "Obtusity? I do not believe there is any such word."

"If there is not, there should be. You are the picture of obtusification. *Listen to me.* I have kept my family safe all these years through the judicious acquisition of information. I learn who is safe and who to shun. I have cultivated acquaintances for miles around. I know who to talk to, and even more importantly in this case, who to avoid. I know people who know people who can discover anything, and better still, everyone hereabouts is accustomed to me doing the asking. While you draw unwarranted attention wherever you go, my questions will not cause the slightest bit of curiosity. At least allow me to *try* before you go haring off half-cocked and make a muck of things."

Darcy stared; it was all he could do. Those expressive eyes of hers were flashing, her posture warrior-like and ready to charge. Dressed as she was in her silly purple frock, she looked like some sort of avenging butterfly. He wanted to argue with her and point out that it was his *duty* to keep his sister shielded from the darker side of life. Her comment about protection stung, as it was no doubt meant to do. At the same time, he acknowledged she had made several reasonable points. And taken him down a notch or two.

It was a novelty. An astonishingly refreshing, odd novelty. She attempted to push him down far enough that she might help him up. No one ever stood up to him or stood up *for* him. In charge. A world of responsibility on his shoulders, always.

A gentleman never contradicts a lady, he thought. Even a not-quite lady. If she lied, he would find her out and she would regret it. If she told the truth, it was a reasonable offer of assistance, and Georgiana's best hope. For his sister's sake, he would accept it. *Only* for Georgiana's sake.

5

Darcy received the first note within six hours of Elizabeth Bennet's departure. A dozen times, he decided it was utter foolishness to trust the woman in *anything* having to do with Georgiana; the heart-wrenching thought of scandal affecting his dear sister always stopped him from assuming the search himself. But the note brought with it a deep feeling of relief and he calmed for the first time since Miss Bennet had taken her leave.

> *They were seen at St. Lawrence crossroads. It appears you shall have the best possible outcome—they are almost certainly bound for Rosings Park.*

He would go to Lady Catherine's, he decided, and speak with Georgiana himself. She must have heartily wished to leave Ramsgate, and it upset him that he had not seen her loneliness. He buried himself in estate duties—and lately, the duty of acquiring a bride—while allowing his responsibilities to consume him. He should have abandoned London weeks ago and spent the time with her. The season had been an utter waste, regardless. He was no closer to finding the mother of his future children than if he stayed nearer his sister.

Unbidden, an image of Elizabeth Bennet, her belly rounded with his child, rose up in his vision. A wave of primeval yearning accompanied the picture. *Devil take it!* He never had such a foolish fancy in all his life. Annoyed with himself, he sat down at his desk and began composing a letter to his sister, a process sure to divest him of any improper feelings.

Several hours later, another note was placed into his hands. He read it and swore. Miss Bennet had a rather disagreeable flair for drama, turning a simple inquiry into some sort of gothic novel scene!

Sent agent to ensure they reached Preston. (Do not be alarmed. He is discreet!) He could find <u>no one</u> who has seen your carriage. Am investigating another <u>clue</u>.

Clues! Pah! Most likely, her 'agent' was an idiot who could not find a lit candle in a dark room. He was certain Georgiana's party simply had not left any impression on the people of the Preston coaching inn.

When the final note came some hours later, he suffered an intense temptation to give way to fury and outrage. Dread collected in his gut like an infection. In her capital letters and underlined words, she scolded him like an overdramatic fishwife, demonstrating a complete lack of awe for his station. It was devilishly irritating—and strangely alluring.

Not, I repeat, <u>NOT</u> on the way to Rosings Park. They have gone <u>else-where</u>. I have <u>clues</u>. Do <u>NOT</u> choose now to forget you are a Gentle-man. Do <u>NOT</u> indulge in some ill-considered tantrum and spoil everything!! <u>WAIT</u> for me. I shall attend you <u>IMMEDIATELY</u> as soon as I have verified <u>important</u> information.

And then, a little further down the page:

<u>Restrain</u> yourself! Do not act in haste!

That last line drew him up short, pausing him in the act of throwing the note aside and calling for his horse, his servants, and every ill-begotten constable in this ill-begotten town.

For an instant, he saw red. How dare she order him to stay motion-less when he needed movement, action! Why had he agreed to trust such a woman in the first place? Perhaps she was in league with Mrs Younge, sent to distract him because he had unexpectedly appeared at

Albion House. His fists clenched, his heart beat hard in his chest, urging engagement.

It was a familiar feeling, though he had not experienced it in years. It meant he was about to free his rage, allow it to make decisions for him. His moods, his passions, were red-eyed maddened beasts he kept chained with iron self-control. Each stake in the fence of that control was forged in conflict and despair, by a youth determined to make more of himself than the world's opinion foresaw. Not his mother's son, but his father's.

He made himself breathe slowly. In and out. In and out. He had once had to do this daily, or several times per day, over every provocation. Send each emotion separately into a deep and frozen space within. He had practiced, until the forced calm became habit, and his tempestuous blood ran cold. Or cool, at least. Manageable. It had been years since he had to remind himself to breathe.

With the return of a modicum of calm came the return of common sense. If Miss Bennet had not come, he would have had the truth from his aunt at the same time—or even later—than he had learnt it from her. Except, of course, he would then have had Lady Catherine to deal with as well, the potential for indiscretion magnified. Miss Bennet was correct in that Mrs Younge had no reason to hurt Georgiana and every reason to protect her. The most likely explanation was that she was making this journey for reasons of her own, and Georgiana was along for the…the adventure. He had been young, once upon a time. Richard's elder brother had proposed several escapades in which he had longed to participate. Of course, he refused…but he had certainly been tempted.

He had, possibly, shielded Georgiana overmuch from their family stains. In protecting her from the shame he suffered, had he failed to teach her how narrow the path and how steep the fall if she succumbed to dishonour?

There is still time, he assured himself, though he cringed at the thought of the three days of distance now separating them. How much longer while he waited for "clues" to be discovered by his amateur detective? Nevertheless, he easily reached the conclusion that Elizabeth (as she was indecorously becoming known in his thoughts) was his current most likely resource for a happy outcome.

He searched Mrs Younge's room himself, and found nothing until, opening a thin book he discovered a series of lewd drawings. Sickened, he sent off an express to Darcy House in London, instructing his servants to treat as urgent and immediately forward all personal correspondence to him. However—instead of the letter from Georgiana he longed for—the messenger returned with a single note from Richard asking how Georgiana fared. He could not bring himself to answer.

Despite the near-desperation lurking just beneath his surface calm, when a frowning Mrs Douglas entered to announce Miss Bennet, his spirits lightened a degree.

"Show her in," he said, before Mrs Douglas even finished speaking.

"In here?" she asked, a new layer of dismay added to her inflection.

Darcy glanced around at the fine front parlour usually reserved for the most distinguished visitors. He did not stop to consider why he had awaited her here. "Yes," Darcy answered. "Without further delay, if you please."

The servant noted the gentle reprimand and made haste to fetch the visitor.

Although Darcy was frantic for news, he could not fail to see the difference in its bearer. Not only was she back to wearing one of her dark, nondescript dresses, but her beautiful eyes were shadowed with fatigue. Had she slept at all since she left him?

"And bring a tea tray, Mrs Douglas," he added, noting the paleness of Elizabeth's fair skin.

Shortly thereafter, the housekeeper returned with tea and an array of delicacies worthy of the parlour, if not the company. Pleased when he saw Elizabeth's eyes brighten at the selection of cakes, he reined in his impatience long enough to encourage her to eat. Soon Elizabeth was serving him tea from silver that had been in his family for a hundred years. She poured like a great lady, observing little formalities he did not know how she could have learnt, and he momentarily forgot his anxieties. But only for a moment; they were too close to the surface to allow him calm.

Still, he could see she had obviously foregone personal comforts in order to see to this business with his sister. What kind of person did such a thing for a total stranger?

"As I wrote, I have ruled out Rosings Park as their destination," Elizabeth said, once her immediate hunger was sated.

"How?" Darcy questioned, hoping against hope he would find her reasoning flimsy.

"There was no sign of them at the coaching inns in Preston. I was prepared for this, and instructed my agent to follow the trail all the way to Rosings looking for any sign of our travellers. He returned very early this morning. He found no sign of them."

Darcy set his cup aside. "They went west, as you first noted, as if they were indeed bound for Rosing Park. Why?"

"That is more than I know. However, I did not limit my search for them to the roads towards Rosings," she added. "I have ruled out the south coast, Brighton, and Devon as well. Just after the tollgate at Margate, instead of continuing westward, they veered north. They were seen at The George in Margate, because one of their horses went lame. A stableboy there overheard the 'red-haired female' talking to her coachman about the next stopping point. The good news is, we know the general direction they took. North. I have the name of the coaching inn where they meant to stay the night."

"They must have gone to Darcy House in London," Darcy said. "It is the only explanation that makes sense."

"If they were going to your home, why did they take such great care to leave the impression of journeying elsewhere? Why not simply inform the household they were visiting you?"

Darcy held himself still, with great effort.

"Because, plainly, they did not want any word of this journey reaching me," he said through stiff lips.

"Quite so," she agreed, as if he were a dutiful student correctly answering his teacher's query. "Lydia is up to some mischief. However, I still believe Miss Darcy remains safe. I cannot see a gently bred girl willingly accompanying her on some dangerous adventure, or Lydia relinquishing the safety and income of her position in exchange for brief entertainment, not to mention losing all future possibility of respectable employment."

He observed the play of expressions upon her face as she spoke, and he had his answer regarding what kind of woman would put her entire life on hold, foregoing creature comforts, for a school girl's indiscretion. It was the kind of managing female whose current life offered not nearly enough challenge for the sly, intricate workings of her mind. She ought to have been born a man, able to lead governments or better still, military campaigns.

Face the truth, Darcy. You are devilish glad she was not born a man. With effort, he returned his wayward mind to the current conversation. "I hope you are not suggesting I sit about and wait for their return."

She sighed, as if this was precisely the answer she expected from him. Exaggerated patience was obvious in her response. "Of course not. But neither must you create an uproar."

"I was young once, and whatever you believe, I am no ancient now, Eliz—er, Miss Bennet."

Her delicate mouth curved upward in the barest hint of a smile, an action that caught his eye immediately. Plainly, she had noticed his near slip.

"I did not mean to imply you were old-fashioned and staid, or that you would insist upon making a hash of everything by noisily flinging about your vast and prestigious influence," she said.

Minx. That was exactly what she implied. But a sparkle had returned to her fine eyes. Evidently the nourishment rejuvenated her lively nature.

"Since you reject my vast and prestigious influence, what do you propose we do instead?"

She appeared startled at the use of "we." *He* certainly was, but it was too late to retract it without a loss of dignity. Besides, he was certain she had several schemes floating about in that devious brainbox of hers, and he was wildly curious to hear its workings aloud.

"I will go after her, of course," Elizabeth said."You should return to your London home, where I will send word of any developments. I have rented a carriage and can be on the road within the hour."

"So I am to be relegated to London now?" he asked. "Useless fumbler that I am, I shall play no part in my sister's rescue?"

Her lovely mouth firmed in disapproval as sharp as his housekeeper's. "Of course you have a part to play. I hope you do not expect me to pay for rented carriages, not to mention rewards for information, from my own purse?"

His displeasure rose; ruthlessly, he suppressed it. "I am sure I already owe you a great deal, and money is the least of it. But I hope you do not believe I will be sending a lone female across England, searching for *my* relation?"

"You will not. I will take Clara and Jacob. Neither has a great deal in the upper story, but they'll do for appearances and safety, and I trust their discretion."

"You cannot believe I shall sit with my boots propped in London, awaiting news?" From the look on her face, it was exactly what she expected. Almost overcome by the desire to quash that expression with further sarcasm, he rose from the settee to face away from her, trying to moderate his anger.

"As I have already explained—"

He interrupted her, his words flat. "Pray do not do so again. I am too well known, I shall attract attention, et cetera, et cetera. You cannot make it any clearer you have placed me in the same empty-headed category as your Clara and Jacob."

"Of *course* you are not as ignorant as my servants. I would never dream of such an implication. But *surely* an important man such as yourself has better things to do than chase about the countryside, whereas I—"

He whirled, his eyes blazing. "Miss Bennet, please do me the very great favour of pretending—at least while in my presence—that you do not believe all men to be fools and idiots."

She opened her mouth to deny it, then obviously reconsidered. He could almost see her dilemma—agree with him and insult, or disagree and lie? The mild humour he found in her quandary lessened his annoyance somewhat.

"I only want what is best for Miss Darcy," she settled on at last, sounding sulky.

"On this, at least, we agree. Finish your tea while I think, if you please."

Her exhaustion rendered her obedient to him although he could see her reluctance. Such was her fatigue that motionlessness became almost immediately a doze. He watched her for longer than he ought, then gently shook her shoulder. "Miss Bennet! You must wake."

She blinked stupidly. "How long did I sleep?" she asked, stifling a yawn.

"A few minutes, no longer. I would have let you continue, but the servants would find it passing strange, and I am sure your own family will have something to say about your prolonged absence, as well."

"Not really," she muttered, yawning, still half-awake. "They are not much in the habit of looking after me. 'Tis more the other way 'round." She shook her head, attempting to clear it. "But time is wasting. I must be on my way."

"You shall not," Darcy said firmly, stating aloud the conclusions he had drawn—especially after seeing her all but collapsed with fatigue upon his sofa. "You are exhausted, and this is not your problem. I appreciate your assistance for the information you have obtained, and I shall repay you for your time and any expenditures you have made on my behalf. You are owed my deepest gratitude. But I shall take the reins from here."

She opened her mouth to protest, but he quickly held up one hand in a halting gesture. "I assure you I am capable of discretion. I shall take the carriage you hired, as planned, and call myself Mr, hmm, Jones. I will avoid inns the Darcys usually frequent, and no one shall know the difference."

"And what will you say—that won't arouse suspicion—to explain why you are chasing across the countryside after a young girl?" she asked tartly, fully awake now.

"I will say I am searching for…my, ah, niece," he said, annoyed he felt obliged to defend his position.

"It will not do," she said, shaking her head.

"Why not? What would you say that would be so much better?"

She adopted that condescending tone he hated, the one that said she humoured a buffoon.

"I would not have one story, but several, which I would amend according to whom I questioned. Furthermore, 'tis not so much your story, but your manner. There is no mistaking you are a gentleman who is accustomed to having his own way. A hired carriage would not disguise it. Even if you could manage to invest your accents with some token humility, you are a male. You would be taken for some libertine, prowling across the country after a young lady. Most would be deeply suspicious, and you'd attract all the more attention because of it."

Darcy despised the fact that she had a point. Nevertheless, his opinion remained unchanged. He would do whatever had to be done, none of which included sitting at home doing naught.

"Be that as it may, I refuse to return to London and leave my sister's fate in the hands of another. I can*not* do it, and I will not."

"Very well," she said with a pained sigh. "You may come along. I don't suppose anyone would believe you are my manservant. You will have to be my brother."

Darcy could not help it. Despite the strain, the frustration, the anxiety, he almost smiled. It was *so* ridiculous.

"You are labouring under one or two misunderstandings, Miss

Bennet. The first one being that *you* will decide *anything* about this journey, including the extent of my participation."

Her brows knit together in consternation, but she recovered quickly. He had to give her that.

"I merely assumed you are as devoted to finding Miss Darcy as quickly and as *discreetly* as I am," she said with a sniff.

"Oh, I am," he said. "But even if *I* decide to *allow* you to come along, there is a flaw in your suggested ruse."

She put her hands on her hips and glared at him. Salacious thoughts flooded his brain. He stuffed them back into the armoured chest where he kept such feelings, but even so, he could feel the pressure of them, much too near the surface.

"What is that?" she asked, with all the hauteur she regularly accused him of exhibiting.

He leaned in close, letting her feel how much larger and stronger he was. It was imperative she understand precisely why the idea that she accompany him, under *any* pretence, was out of the question. "Do not be a green girl. No one who sees how I look at you would *ever* believe you my sister," he whispered.

6

Lizzy did something she hadn't done in years; she blushed.

In truth, she felt stupid. After all, she had been avoiding the traps which men presented since she was a child. She stayed clear of what went on in her mother's world, but she was *not* a "green girl." Nevertheless, she had behaved as though she was, ignoring the fact that he was male and a stranger. That must end at once.

"You are speaking of sexual attraction, of course," she said bluntly. "Are you the sort who would take advantage of an unwilling female?"

He stepped back, appalled and horrified—as she had suspected he would be. She could spot a lecher at fifty paces. Mr Darcy did not qualify.

"Of course not!" he cried.

"Then I fail to see a problem. I am *not* willing. You are *not* a despoiler of females. If you do not believe you can play the part of brother, then you can play the part of husband. I shall be Mrs Jones. If or when we must stop for the night at inns, you may procure us separate rooms, as is often done."

He shook his head, obviously scandalised by her speech. "Miss Bennet, such a journey would be *most* improper. If it was to be discovered you and I had travelled together, it would be a scandal of the worst sort!"

"Why?"

He gaped at her. "*Why?*"

His astonishment almost made her smile. "Mr Darcy, as you have so helpfully pointed out on more than one occasion, I am a harlot's daughter. I have no reputation to lose or to protect. If any part of our little adventure is discovered—and the whole point of my going is so no word of this ever *does* leak, be so good as to recall—it would simply be assumed you had a brief *rendezvous* with a *lady of the town*. Such a scandal, no matter how distasteful or embarrassing you might personally find it, would serve to further obscure your sister's disappearance. And it would only be scandalous until the next *on dit* arrives to amuse the gossips."

Because she had been so blunt, he was as well. "I do not keep mistresses or visit brothels. I would not care to be known as a *man of the town*. My reputation is very important to me."

She cocked her head. "Is it more important to you than your sister's?" she asked.

"Has anyone ever told you how annoying you are?" he demanded.

Lizzy broke into a chuckle. "Often. 'Tis a sad habit of mine," she agreed. "I will leave you now to gather up a selection of your most sober waistcoats so you can become a more believable Mr Jones. If you come to Harbour Street in an hour, I shall be ready to depart."

LIZZY HAD BELIEVED THE HIRED HACK COMFORTABLY SPACIOUS, BUT SHE hadn't adjusted for the amount of room a Darcy and his glacial stare must occupy. Neither had she missed his disdainful sniff at the musty smell, or the deprecating sneer levelled on the torn and shabby squabs. Did he think rented carriages were plush and comfortable? This one was better than many! He ought to try riding atop a mail coach! This was *luxurious* in comparison!

He smelled delicious, sandalwood with some exotic hint of spice, and clean, solid male. Even in his dark, plain clothing, he would not fool many. Arrogance was bred into his bones, the hard and authoritative manner as natural to him as forming figures in clay was for her. It was astounding he had allowed her to defy him at all, much less accompany him. Undoubtedly, accepting her assistance required lowering himself a good deal, and then only for his sister's sake. It was likely a personal flaw that she admired him for it.

"We have many miles to pass, Mr Darcy. Shall we do so in silent scorn?"

His eyes returned to her face with some surprise, as if he had forgotten her presence. "Please forgive me, Miss Bennet. I am impatient, but I did not mean to be uncivil."

"We should at least have our stories straight, so we do not tell different ones if it becomes necessary."

"Let us simply agree to say as little as possible. Increasing deceit only increases the odds we shall be caught in a lie."

She chuckled. "Oh, you do need me, Mr Darcy. If we wish for people to actually tell us things, we need to chat, gossip if you will. To do *that*, we must have something to say. We require a story that explains why a grumpy, brooding Mr Jones along with his amiable, charming wife are searching for a young girl and her companion, casting neither suspicion upon us nor aspersions upon your sister. In general, merely glaring at people does not loosen tongues."

"We should have rented a nicer carriage," he said. "Others may find it suspicious that we chase after our betters."

"You lack imagination," Lizzy replied, shrugging. "If you are an employee, you might be chasing after your betters for many good reasons, at the whim of your employer."

"If you have so much imagination to spare, devise a story that embraces driving in a more comfortable vehicle," he grumbled.

"How many do you own?" she asked curiously.

It was Darcy's turn to shrug. "I miss my phaeton at the moment. 'Tis very fast." His hand smoothed over the cracked leather seat. "And better furnished."

"Exchange this for a better one if you must," Lizzy said, just managing to subdue an eye roll. "But the more superior the vehicle, the more attention it draws. Now, from whence come Mr and Mrs Jones?"

"London, I suppose," he answered disinterestedly.

"Hmm, very well. Do you think I could pass for a town wife?"

To her surprise, he stared at her intensely, making her glad for the shadowed carriage. How uncomfortable to have him searching for flaws!

"Perhaps not," Darcy said at last. "You are too exciti—, um, exuberant to be from town. The weather and pollution of London keep most confined to indoor pursuits."

"Is that a gentlemanly way of pointing out I get far too much sun?" she asked. "You will be happy to learn that you and my mother are in perfect accord. The trouble is that I am addicted to walking along the sea's edge. Oh, and of course, my kiln is out-of-doors, in the garden."

"Your kin?" he asked, confused.

"My kiln—a sort of forge for my clay. I sculpt."

"You sculpt? What do you sculpt?"

"Oh, whatever the tourists will buy," she answered nonchalantly, having no intention of revealing her deepest dreams to a critic. "Fish, lobsters, even seashells and the like, for the most part."

Deciding discretion was the better part of valour, she didn't mention the mermaids. "Something to commemorate a holiday spent at Ramsgate."

"Ah. Trinkets."

She raised a brow. "My kiln is fairly small, and thus I am limited in size to what pieces I can fire." *And by Dobbs as to what I can offer.* "That the price makes them affordable to many does not mean they are of inferior quality."

He held up a hand as if to halt her words. "I do not doubt it. I meant no insult."

She shrugged to show it didn't matter what he thought of her or her art. Seeking to change the subject, she said, "I doubt anyone will take notice of my complexion. We will say we are from London. You can be a solicitor who is searching for a young lady about an inheritance."

"Of course! That would explain my search beautifully. And it is a reason for which I do not require a wife."

She returned his gaze innocently. "Do not blame me for your slothful imagination. Besides, I wager I will *still* acquire more information than you, Mr Jones."

"Is there anything else about us that I ought to know?"

"We have been married for only a few months, and you could not bear to be apart from me while you searched for the Missing Heiress."

"Perhaps *you* could not bear to be apart from *me*," he said.

"Because you are so charming," Lizzy shot back. "I very much doubt Lydia would disclose Miss Darcy's identity, so there is no need to use her name in the search," she continued. "We'll refer to our Missing Heiress as Miss…Danforth. She is the only living relation of a rich uncle in America, who has recently died in a carriage accident.

You were charged with informing her of this unexpected bounty, only to discover she's left on a journey and as you must speak to her immediately, we have followed."

Darcy nodded.

Lizzy went on, "I wish you would tell me more about your sister, beyond her description. I feel if I understood her better, I might be able to understand this situation...what and why Lydia has taken her away."

She peered carefully at him as she spoke. While his face expressed anger and annoyance easily enough, anything else was stifled behind his mask of bland impassivity. But now, after a few hours in his company, she was beginning to see signs there might be more than arrogance and grumpiness to his character—though of course, grumpy arrogance was obviously quite a habit with him. Still, a slight quirk of the lips might be full-blown laughter in other men. A twist of the brow was a thoughtful question; a blink, an expression of astonishment. How remarkably self-contained this gentleman was! Coaxing him to express emotions—even negative ones—was beginning to seem an irresistible challenge. She had always been too competitive for her own good.

Darcy scratched his chin contemplatively. "Georgiana is...delicate," he said at last.

"She does not enjoy good health?" Lizzy asked.

"No, she is healthy enough. She is tall for a girl, and slender, so perhaps that is part of it—one feels as though she is breakable. Quiet, and perhaps restrained. She fosters a protective instinct, naturally."

"Oh, naturally."

He frowned. "Sarcasm, Miss Bennet?"

"Not at all. But you'd think I had asked you to describe your finest china, not your sister."

His mask was back in place, but his offence was plain.

"Fifteen years is a difficult age for a young lady," she said, rather more gently. "Too young to be taken seriously by most adults, and too old to be distracted by more childish pastimes. By the same token, persons of the opposite sex become incredibly...interesting."

He sat up straighter in his seat, his posture so stiff, she knew his affront had swelled to anger.

"My sister is not the same kind of female with whom you are accustomed," he said tautly.

Lizzy laughed. "Ah. You are one of *those* sorts of men," she said frankly.

"What sort?"

"The kind who thinks there are only two sorts of females—good ones and bad ones. The good ones sit like your fine china on a shelf. You dust them off for parties and their duty is to impress, and then retire quietly to the shelf once more, at least until they produce a place setting or two. They aren't allowed feelings like love and passion. You expect them to barely tolerate marital intimacies, and then only when *you* say 'tis time to set the table.'"

"You *are* bold," he said, scandalised.

"Bold. Another word for 'bad.'" She nodded.

Darcy was obviously taken aback by that statement. "You misunderstand me," he said quietly.

Lizzy waved this off. "Nevertheless. My point is this—your sister is a person, a lady. It is natural she should struggle with a number of new feelings at this age. Feelings that *all* females possess, to one degree or another." She stared straight at him. "Harlots and heiresses, both."

DARCY TOOK REFUGE IN THE PRETENCE OF SLEEP, NOW AND AGAIN emitting a soft snore. The poorly built coach made the ruse difficult, yet their conversations were like picking one's way across a partially frozen river; he could hear the cracks in the ice with every step. Sleep might be cowardice, but infinitely less treacherous. Through his lashes, he stole frequent glances at his travelling companion. She stared out the window, watching the passing scenery burnished by late afternoon sun and road dust.

Her posture was easy, as if the jouncing carriage troubled her not at all. An unusual woman, Elizabeth Bennet. She spoke as if he thought *her* a strumpet; he did not. Her beauty could have been a powerful weapon, had she chosen to use it. Instead, it was all unconscious, as if she neither knew of nor cared for its existence. She practiced no arts or allurements; he watched for it, and even—if he were being honest— hoped for it. She was no pious, delicate miss; yet, she would have him think she and *Georgiana* had much in common.

Perhaps, in her circle of friends and acquaintances, she had never met anyone quite so innocent as his sister. For all that Elizabeth—as he dared call her in his thoughts—was no doxy, neither was she an innocent. Those lovely dark eyes of hers had seen too much. Likely no admission—no matter how scandalous—about human nature would surprise or shock her. He could even tell her, if he chose, all about the Darcy heritage of shame, and she would probably shrug it off with a *c'est la vie*.

It was a tremendously freeing thought, though of course he would never so choose.

It took him a moment to realise the carriage was slowing. It was too soon to have reached The Five Bells, their first planned stop, and hopefully where Georgiana and Mrs Younge had changed horses. Immediately he was on his mettle; while this was a good, well-travelled road, dangers were everywhere. He sat up, and as the carriage heaved to a stop, saw Elizabeth's hand already reaching for the door. He grasped it, halting her movement.

"No. Wait here," he commanded. He stared down her instinctive protest until she released her grip on the handle. Before departing, he had replaced her hired hand with his own coachman, who could be counted upon for both discretion and pistols upon his person. Frost would deal with the situation, whatever it was, but Darcy took no chances. He reached underneath the seat for his own stashed pistols, noting the first signs of alarm in Elizabeth. Still, she remained remarkably composed, simply giving him an eloquent look.

He had no trouble interpreting her expression. *Don't bungle this*, it said. He almost smiled as he stepped from the coach, vigilant, ready for anything.

But there was only Frost, standing next to the team, arms akimbo, staring at a disabled landaulet a good distance ahead. From their vantage point they could see but not be seen. A man paced in front of the incapacitated carriage, alternately pulling at his hair and pausing as if speaking to an unseen someone in the interior of the vehicle.

"What think you, Frost?" Darcy questioned. They both were well aware of a common ruse involving thieves lying in wait by a seemingly disabled vehicle.

"Likely, all's as it should be," the thickset man answered. "A bad place for hidin' and too exposed for surprises."

Darcy agreed with his coachman. Still, he murmured a few words of explanation to Elizabeth before climbing up on the box and riding beside Frost. No sense taking any risks.

They had no choice but to slow to a stop once near the landaulet—it was either that, or flatten the man who ran into the road on their approach, gesticulating wildly. Both Darcy and Frost had their hands upon their pistols as they drew up.

"My wife, my wife!" the man cried.

Darcy and Frost glanced at each other with varying degrees of alarm. Darcy swung himself down to face the stranger before Frost had the team quite halted.

"Calm yourself, man," Darcy ordered. "Tell me what you are about."

The man was not immune to Darcy's commanding presence. He ceased shouting, giving his name as Darrow. His explanations thereafter were erratic, but definitely contained the words "wife," "baby," and "coming *now*." He pointed to the landaulet listing drunkenly on its broken axle. Faint moans could now be heard emerging from its depths.

Darcy's gaze met the wide-eyed Frost. "We will fetch help," Darcy offered.

"Sent my coachman on ahead two hours ago or more. He ought to have found someone by now!" Darrow wailed.

Darcy sighed. The coachman had taken one of the horses; he should have happened upon the nearest village within an hour and must have run into difficulties. At that moment, Elizabeth climbed out of the carriage. Her gaze flickered over the three men, but she disregarded them to stride towards the landaulet. Darcy ran after her, catching her sleeve.

"What are you doing, Miss Bennet?" he hissed. "There is a female possibly about to...to—" he hesitated, unable to articulate his dismay.

"So I heard," she said, not pausing. "I will look in on her."

"Are you some sort of–of midwife?" he asked, a note of disbelief in his lowered voice. More muffled cries emanated from the interior of the vehicle.

"Not at all," she replied.

"You cannot! It is beyond unseemly!" he whispered vehemently.

"Obviously, you've forgotten much about your wife, Mr Jones," she bit out.

He tightened his grip on her arm. "Very amusing. Now listen to me —we do not have time for this. We will make certain assistance arrives. Please return to the carriage!"

She turned an appalled regard upon him. "Are you deaf? Can't you hear the fear in her cries? We cannot leave her like this. We simply cannot!" She shook off his hand and marched in the direction of the keening wails.

LIZZY WASN'T AT ALL AS CONFIDENT AS SHE STROVE TO APPEAR. IN FACT, she felt queasy. She had never witnessed a birth, though she had heard Fanny and her friends discussing it in what Darcy would no doubt consider shocking detail. It sounded anatomically impossible, but it had been occurring since the beginning of time and hopefully would progress as per usual regardless of the inexperience of any attendants.

She opened the door and looked into the face of a woman perhaps a few years older than herself, sprawled across the carriage cushions. Her hair was damp with perspiration, and she panted and moaned. The broken axle meant the benches listed strongly to one side. Lizzy wedged herself in and took hold of her hand.

"What is your name?" Lizzy asked, stroking hair off the woman's sweaty forehead.

"Katherine," she gasped.

"Is this your first child, Katherine?"

"N–no. A boy, died of fever before three-month."

Lizzy nodded sympathetically. "Your body knows what to do, my dear. All will be well."

"'Tis too soon," Katherine sobbed. "I thought we had time enough to reach my ma's house. But I was thrown off the seat and—"

"Hush, hush," Lizzy soothed. "Try to calm yourself. Deep, slow breaths will help," she suggested, though she had no idea if it were as true in childbirth as in other stressful situations.

Time had no meaning while Lizzy reassured her patient; minutes or hours passed, possibly years. Her hand ached under the pressure of Katherine's hold whenever the pains came. Beyond fanning her with her hat brim, giving her infrequent sips of water obtained from Mr Darrow, and breathing along with her whenever hysteria threatened, Lizzy was completely at sea. Just when it appeared the labour came to some kind of crisis of agony, noises beyond the carriage indicated the arrival of others. An older woman flung the door open, allowing a breeze inside the airless interior. Lizzy moved as if to leave, but Katherine clung more tightly to her sore hand.

"Her name is Katherine," Lizzy said, offering what little information she had. "She says the babe comes early."

"Aye, well, babes will come when babes will come," the older woman said. "I am Aggie, and if anyone can deliver your wee one, 'tis I." After a cursory examination, she competently rearranged Katherine so Lizzy supported her from behind, half-sitting up. Aggie gave them a heartening smile. "Let's bring this babe now, eh?"

DARCY WATCHED AS ELIZABETH FINALLY EMERGED FROM THE CARRIAGE. She did not look so coolly confident as she had when entering. Her hat lay limply at her back, held in place by ribbons around her neck, stray curls framing her very pale face. In fact, he would call her pallor a definite shade of green. He was striding towards her before he was even aware of it, sliding his hand underneath her elbow as she stumbled. She leaned into him, accepting his help, which he found ridiculously satisfying; he must remind himself of his vexation with her for forcing this delay upon them. The sound of a new-born baby crying had alleviated much of his annoyance, however.

"I am sorry," she murmured. "I was too long in a cramped position, and I've lost feeling in my limbs."

He did not know if she apologised for delaying them, or for having to accept his assistance. *Undoubtedly the latter.* Slowly he guided her to where their carriage waited. He noticed she took deep breaths, breathing through her nose. He wondered if she might be ill. He paused beside the door of the hack—if she were going to cast up her accounts, he would rather she did it here.

"Are you well?" he asked, eyeing her carefully.

Her words overflowed in a sudden stream, as if she could no longer contain them. She gripped his wrist as if she needed a support for her excess emotions.

"*That* was the single most terrifying experience ever! I had *no* idea what to do. I thought Katherine would die while I stupidly did naught but hold her hand. Bloody devil!" She choked out the vulgarity, but he could summon no indignation. The situation sounded horrifying indeed. She looked up at him, her eyes full of remembered fear. "The midwife arrived in the nick of time."

His voice was gentle, if wry. "Since you were determined to dawdle, I rode ahead on one of the horses to see if I could not hurry along some assistance. I discovered their coachman at a pub, waiting comfortably for a message to be carried to the midwife. I persuaded all in the vicinity of the necessity of producing a midwife *at once*. You would be rather gratified by my gentlemanly tantrum."

She smiled up at him, her distress fading. "Indeed, I *knew* you were capable." She clutched his hand, and her smile grew mischievous. "Thank you, Mr Jones. So very much."

At least her colour was restored. "You are very welcome, Mrs Jones," he answered drily, prodding her into the carriage. Once they were on their way, he looked at Elizabeth curiously. "Why did you do it? Knowing you were helpless to assist Mrs Darrow in any useful capacity, why put yourself in that situation?"

She shrugged, leaning back against the squabs. She had not replaced her hat, having tossed it beside her on the seat, and he knew a moment's temptation to brush escaping curls away from her delicate cheekbones. Her eyes closed, and he thought she would not answer him at all.

"There was no one else," she said quietly. "And the only thing worse than suffering is suffering alone. I could spare her that, at least. Anyone would have done the same."

Darcy shook his head, unconvinced of the truth of *that* statement, and unsure as to whether he was mightily impressed, or appalled beyond belief.

7

The Five Bells was a busy coaching inn patronised mainly by the working class. Mrs Younge had mentioned it as the next stop on her journey; it was certainly not a usual stop for the Darcys. No one here knew him, which was good. Annoyingly, however, no one instinctively understood he was to be given a private parlour and the inn's finest rooms, requiring he speak more than was usual for him.

As he followed the servant leading him to his room, he glanced back to see Elizabeth still chatting merrily with the innkeeper's wife, her left ring finger sporting a gold band produced from her reticule. More than one man had taken notice of her, obliging him to aim a liberal number of menacing stares at the impudent oafs. At least the Darcy glare was still effective, with or without a retinue. Was it wise to leave her alone? She seemed entirely unconscious of the male attention following her wherever she went. Not that she would pay any mind to *his* opinion on the matter.

After washing off the road dust, he entered the private parlour where a maid laid out a meal of soup and hasty mutton. It smelled appetising, but after waiting several minutes he began to be uneasy. Even allowing time for her to pry information loose from the inn's denizens before performing her own ablutions, Elizabeth ought to be here by now.

Darcy, about to set out in search of her, startled when the door was pulled out of his grip by her entrance.

"Where have you been?" he grumbled.

"Were you waiting for me to begin eating? You should not have." Walking to the table, she lifted the cover on the mutton, inspecting the dish.

"Never mind the meal. What kept you so long?" he thundered.

"I apologise for the delay, but it took me some time to work our little matter into the conversation. Mrs Jennings was full of information, but sadly difficult to keep to the point," she explained.

"Were they here? Did she remember seeing my sister?"

"Yes, she did. They took the inn's best room for the night. She described them in nearly every particular."

"Did Georgiana seem well?"

"Very well. She said the young girl was very quiet, but obviously in good health. And," Elizabeth announced with unrestrained triumph, "Lydia questioned Mr Jennings about their proposed route. Inducing Mrs Jennings to stop chattering long enough to question her husband was what took me so long. I have not only the name of their next coaching inn stop, but the one after that!"

Delight suffused her features, entrancing him as he gazed into her sparkling eyes. "Oh, well done, Elizabeth," he said, his voice full of quiet joy, and, quite forgetting himself, pulled her into his arms for a hearty embrace. Truly, it was merely an instinctive response, borne of his great relief, and she returned it in the same spirit. At least at first.

He did not mean for it to happen. He had not been this near a female who was not a relation in years, and the feel of her body, slim and yet curvaceous and strong—so very *un*-relation-like—jolted his system. The delicate skin at her neck was inches away. Without any of the consideration marking all his actions, he gave in to impulse, pressing an open-mouthed kiss to the pale skin below her ear.

She stiffened immediately, and gave him a not-gentle shove.

"Mr Darcy!"

"Devil take it!" he muttered, stalking to the opposite end of the room.

For several moments, the only sounds were the muffled voices of the tavern's patrons on the floor below, the clink and clatter of plates and mugs and trays.

"I beg your forgiveness, Miss Bennet. It was wrong of me," Darcy said quietly, absolutely mortified.

"I know what people believe," she replied in the same subdued manner, after several more moments of awkward silence. "Like mother, like daughter. It was perhaps too much to expect you not to think it as well, especially considering my offer to pose as your wife. But what you're thinking…it isn't me. I assure you, I have kept myself safe for years by avoiding situations where my interest might be misconstrued. I should not have—"

"You will *not* take the blame for this," he interrupted. "I thought nothing of the kind. I did not misunderstand, I misbehaved."

"In the interests of total honesty, while my concern for your sister is genuine, my motives for helping you are not entirely pure. I am hoping you will express your gratitude—*when* I find her—with some sort of monetary compensation. I am trying, with all my energy, to carve a much different life for myself. Your sister's reputation, is important, of course…but I also see this as an opportunity to help achieve my goals, and possibly this expectation increases my enthusiasm for the duty."

"Blackmail again, Miss Bennet?"

"No!" she protested. "Not at all! Merely a reliance upon your natural generosity of spirit, in return for my total dedication to finding your sister."

"Does this mean if I inform you that the natural generosity you anticipate is out of the question and you shall not receive a shilling for this venture, you will accept my decision meekly?"

She peered at him carefully. "Meekness is not in my nature," she admitted.

"How shocking," he said drily. "Luckily, you have accurately calculated my capacity for generosity and need have few concerns on that account. Our dinner grows cold. Shall we eat?"

Grateful that threats of ravishment and accusations of blackmail seemed to be over and done, she allowed him to seat her and ate heartily of the repast provided.

"We are not stopping for the night, are we?" she asked. "If we can travel at a much brisker pace than they, we might catch up to them, even if they are so far ahead of us."

"It was my intention to travel on, if you were willing," he

confessed. "My sister is not a great traveller. I am counting on them not being able to go so far, for so long, as we can."

"Oh, of course *I* am. But what of Mr Frost? Is he?"

His right brow rose again. "He is willing if I say he is willing," he said mildly.

Elizabeth snorted.

"What is that oh-so-delicate response supposed to mean?" he asked.

"You don't really want to know," she answered, turning back to her meal.

"I insist," he persevered. "Truly."

She set down her spoon. "You can command a person's actions, but you cannot command a person's *willingness*," she replied. "It is the one thing you cannot order and yet you seem to expect it, no matter how unlikely."

"Why is it so unlikely?" he asked, genuinely curious.

"Because of your manner. I doubt you asked his opinion, or shared what we hope to gain by hurrying. No one likes to be commanded or compelled to perform a task not at all their own idea or to their liking."

"Of course I did not ask. But what makes you believe I have to resort to bullying or threats in order to persuade Mr Frost to do my bidding? Would not he have an indisputable interest in pleasing *me*? How very cunning you must have to be, Miss Bennet, if in order to get anything accomplished, you must convince the other person that *your* judgment is their own."

She picked up her spoon again. "Whatever you say, *Mr Jones*."

There was a pause, as he considered he had no intention of bringing Elizabeth along on this journey in the first place. And yet, here she was. "Touché, Mrs Jones," he replied, and applied himself to his dinner.

THEY FINISHED THE MEAL IN SILENCE. *IT WASN'T TOO UNCOMFORTABLE.* HE had apologised for that...that kiss, or whatever it was. Misbehaviour, he called it. Really, one could not even call it a kiss. Something less *consequential* than a kiss. Mr Darcy looked preoccupied, but he was no jaw-me-dead at the best of times, and she didn't believe he was angry or disappointed.

Still, she must learn to keep her tongue between her teeth, and practice being an agreeable but extremely *respectable* companion, so he did not buy her a ticket on the mail coach back to Ramsgate or attempt improprieties again. Her one goal was to find Miss Darcy. No victorious embraces turning into not-kisses. No arguing with him again, even if he wore that supercilious expression that drove her mad. At any rate, her outspokenness never seemed to upset him. He was very unusual and dissimilar from most men in his class, at least in this respect.

She followed him to the carriage, where Mr Frost waited with the new team. Mr Darcy handed her inside and suddenly paused, turning back to his coachman.

"Frost—are you sure you are willing to continue on tonight?"

Lizzy's mouth opened in surprise. He glanced at her with a smirk.

"Excuse me, sir?"

"I was inquiring as to whether you wish to keep on," Darcy repeated. "It is very late for travel."

Through the open door, Lizzy could see the coachman scratching his chin in consternation.

"Din't you ask me to have the team ready to go now, sir?"

"I did. I want your opinion though. Perhaps you are fatigued?" Mr Darcy asked, politely if stiffly.

"Fatigued, sir? Me? Haven't I run your teams for you whenever you've needed, for as long as you've wanted? Have I ever fallen asleep at the reins? When have I ever been any trouble?" Mr Frost asked, in tones of deep affront.

"Never, Mr Frost. You have always been extremely capable," Darcy reassured quickly.

"A man might be in his fortieth year and still outwork two men of twenty," Frost said.

"Indeed, he might," Darcy agreed quickly.

"If Harris has been hinting that he c'n do better, why, I says he's telling whiskers," Frost continued. "He hasn't the experience. Why, I've forgotten more than Harris ever knew. I'm accounted very clean with the pistols, too, which is what you want at night. Have you seen Harris shoot, sir?"

"I have not, Mr Frost," Darcy agreed again. He glanced at Lizzy again, this time with definite irritation.

Lizzy shrugged helplessly.

"A regular gollumpus with a pistol is Harris. Cain't hit the broad side of a barn at noonday, much less at night. Why, I'm an old hand with 'em. Age and experience, that be the way, sir."

"I certainly concur," Darcy agreed, almost desperately.

"That Harris, why, he has tongue enough for two sets of teeth. If you need a man who can keep his jaw shut, I'm the one, sir." He eyed "Mrs Jones" pointedly.

"I say you are the perfect man for the job, Mr Frost," Lizzy interjected virtuously.

Frost's gaze returned to his employer triumphantly. "Much obliged, madam," he replied.

"Yes, indeed, Mr Frost. Very good. Carry on," Darcy spoke quickly, heaving himself inside the carriage before the conversation could spiral any further out of control.

"*Fa*-tigued. Hmph," Frost was heard to mutter indignantly as Darcy pulled the door closed.

Darcy glared at Elizabeth with equivalent indignation.

She held up her hands in a gesture of surrender. "How was I to know he is every bit as proud as you?" she asked.

Darcy narrowed his eyes. "*You* are trouble, Miss Bennet," he said.

"Tell me something I don't know," she replied agreeably, as the carriage jolted into motion.

THE HOURS PASSED SLOWLY. IT WAS A CLEAR NIGHT WITH A FULL MOON, and the road was a good one. Darcy expected to reach The Swan with Two Necks by mid-morning, thereby officially gaining a day on Mrs Younge's party, stopping there for a few hours' rest.

The inn was in London, but situated nowhere close to Darcy House in Mayfair. Though he wished a stop were unnecessary, Frost needed rest, and Elizabeth required an opportunity to question the inn's maidservants, if possible, ensuring they were still on the scent. He would have Frost inquire amongst the stablemen.

"Have you visited London before?" Darcy asked politely, interrupting her wayward thoughts.

"Twice, to visit warehouses for fabrics with Mama. Jane has been several times, though, with her father and governess, and she told me all about it."

"Jane?" he asked, curious.

"My elder sister," Elizabeth explained. At his inquiring look, she continued, "Half-sister, I suppose I should say. Her father is Sir Walter Eden, a baronet. He is very good to her."

"Do you have any other relations?" he asked.

"Only Jane," Elizabeth replied. "Sir Walter is very attached to her. He often provided a governess, whenever his finances permitted, and most of those allowed me to sit in on her lessons. We went through many governesses, because it is difficult to get good help within my family's…situation. Believe me, one does not want persons with gin-soaked breath teaching French conjugations. Or sometimes if Sir Walter was pockets-to-let, the teacher would be let go."

His brow furrowed. "Dash it all. Bennet should have made sure *you* had a governess. A good one."

"Well, yes, that would have been ideal, especially during the times when Sir Walter was down on his luck. Or if the governess didn't want me sitting in. Though I could often stay in the next room and listen, as long as she could not see me."

"Why the deuce would she care?" he asked. "Were you a mischief-maker?"

"Oh, no," Elizabeth laughed. "I very much wanted those lessons, especially as I grew older. To learn to read and write—not to mention all the other social graces—greatly elevates one's opportunities. Mama is hardly literate, so I know first-hand how difficult life can be without learning. But Sir Walter doesn't much care for anyone except Jane, and he didn't wish his precious coin wasted upon me. Luckily, most governesses found it easier to teach Jane if I participated, and he wasn't there to see, was he?"

Darcy shook his head. "I am sorry Bennet did not do better by you, Elizabeth."

"'Tis all in the past," she replied. "I have no complaints. I am very fortunate in my education, and in my sister, who is a treasure."

DEVIL TAKE IT, he thought. LOOK AT THAT MISCHIEVOUS LITTLE SMILE. What was she thinking? About *him*? He experienced such an attraction as he had hitherto only dreamed of, a state of perpetual astonishment growing with every passing minute. The pallid, twittering ninnies presented to him as the crème de la crème of Almack's, wreathed in roses and shod in satin, could not approach the magnificence of Elizabeth Bennet in her plain grey gown. The thought of any of those "diamonds of the first water" aiding a stranger giving birth was laughable. Her staunch devotion to her natural elder sister was another sign of her goodness. No envy or resentment—only strength, determination, courage, and beauty. He had never met her equal.

If only she were the *slightest* bit respectable, if only Bennet had done as he ought and reared her as the gentleman's daughter she was born to be, Darcy might even offer for her. As matters stood now, the only offers he could make were unseemly ones. He would not do that to her, or himself, no matter how tempting.

His thoughts shifted to his sister. Where could she possibly be travelling? She had been well-insulated from the harsher consequences of their family's disgrace, being only a two-year-old at the time. She knew the necessary details and that her prospects for marriage might be more limited than they ought, as well as the possibility of unkind whispers. Lady Catherine's assurances of her ability to gain Georgiana vouchers for Almack's, the success of his investments and resultant increase in her portion, as well as ensuring his own reputation remained exemplary, convinced him she would launch successfully. Until *this* little misadventure, of course. Unless she had been kidnapped by Mrs Younge, she had no one to blame but herself.

Not comforting.

Of course, there was every possibility Mrs Younge had only mentioned the names of this inn and the next, the Bull and Mouth, as a similar ruse to the one she had used leaving Ramsgate, when claiming they were off to Rosings Park.

Still, most amusements would be found in the London metropolis. Georgiana had begged him to take her to some of the shows her friends had been allowed to attend—a naval melodrama at Sadler's Wells (too violent), a pantomime in Covent Garden (too vulgar). His mind listed several such entertainments he had refused her. He had been trying to protect her more fragile reputation, but had he also been treating her as if she were still in the nursery? Perhaps so. There could be little doubt: her companion indulged her young charge—and likely herself—in London. Mayhap he should abandon the rest of the journey, inform Richard of Georgiana's escape, and set up a search right in town.

If he were wrong, they would be even further behind. And if he were right, it was doubtful viewing a few plays would corrupt Georgiana. Doubtlessly he would discover them on their return trip to Ramsgate without involving anyone else.

He realised by the increasing sounds around him and the lightening rays of dawn, they must be nearing London. *So close to Darcy House, and yet so far*. He thought of the journey ahead; it was uncomfortable using the unknown and less competent help offered at inns. Though he trusted his servants' discretion, it was imperative he maintain utter anonymity. Besides, 'twas doubtful they would go further than the Bull and Mouth; likely they remained at The Swan with Two Necks.

Darcy glanced across at the sleeping female sharing this journey with him, her head jouncing uncomfortably against the carriage wall. Not to mention the awkward angle of her neck...though it did give him an entrancing view of her throat. He knew he ought to feel guilty for staring, but it was not like there was aught else to do. Perhaps he, too, should try to doze.

At that moment, the coach hit a particularly savage bump in the road, pitching her forward off her seat. Darcy flung himself over and caught her, easing onto the cushions beside her. She did not even waken. Blast it—she must be exhausted. She turned into his shoulder, and instinctively he shifted to make her more comfortable. In her sleep, she had no inhibitions, burrowing into the warmth of his body, nestling against him. She let out a soft snore, and he smiled.

Whatever it said about his character, this was the most fun he had had in years. Possibly ever.

Lizzy gradually returned to wakefulness, feeling the light of the morning sun against her lids. For some reason, her pillow was very hard, but otherwise she was warm and cosy and did not wish to rouse. Thoughts and memories buzzed disjointedly around her brain. Disguises. London. Her hip was sore, her bed too narrow. Lydia Younge. Mr Darcy. *Mr Darcy?*

She snapped fully awake. Dear heavens, this was no hard pillow beneath her cheek! Pulling herself upright, she jarred him in the process.

"Mr Darcy!" she gasped.

He straightened, stretching his long arms out in front of him, rubbing his eyes. Lizzy saw a rather largish damp spot on his waistcoat, where she had obviously drooled. *Wonderful.*

"Good morning, Miss Bennet," he said, making no move to shift to his proper seat. Instead, he dug into his coat pocket, removing a watch and opening the cover. "We are making good time," he added, lifting the shade and peering out. "I surmise we shall arrive at The Swan within the hour."

Lizzy now noted the noise and could not resist peeking out the window herself. They were in London proper, slogging behind lines of other vehicles. The shouts of coachmen and the din of sellers hawking goods, the relentless evidence of the million bodies surrounding them in fetid smells and polluted air, diverted her dismay at waking to find herself sprawled across her travelling companion.

"So many people," she murmured, gaping at the view. "I will never get used to the idea of so many crammed together in such a relatively small area." Of course, her remark reminded her that she was likewise crowded against *him*, their bodies pressing closely within the confines of the seat. Mr Darcy was such a large man, his shoulders wide, his legs long. Being pressed against his side was making her feel…winded.

Stop it, you stupid girl! Why doesn't he remember he is a gentleman and move back to his seat? Why do I remain here if he will not?

Rather than heed her sluggish conscience, however, she gazed surreptitiously at her seat-mate. Mr Darcy, plainly, had no difficulties with their closeness. Truthfully, he appeared to be paying no mind to her whatsoever, all his attention taken up with staring at the city passing by the window. Perhaps he regularly rode with females in coaches; he said he didn't keep a mistress and was careful of his reputation, but that did not mean he hadn't flirtations. At least he was gentlemanly enough not to mock her for using him for a pillow.

"Be careful at this inn," Darcy warned, startling her from her reverie, and she shifted herself to put a bare quarter-inch between them on the seat. A seat that seemed to shrink in size…or was he growing larger?

"This is not Ramsgate," he continued, apparently unconscious to the fact she was *well*-aware of the un-Ramsgate-like surroundings, "and a part of London I would not usually frequent. Stay away from the yard and the public rooms."

"I can take care of myself."

"Possibly, and 'tis distressing that you have been required to do so. Nevertheless, for the here and now, you are under my protection, and I would appreciate your allowing me to provide it."

Lizzy turned an exasperated glare upon him, trying not to heed the sudden feeling of warmth his solicitousness inspired. "Mr *Jones*, need I remind you of my purpose for being here? Granted, I cannot wander about the yard stalking stablemen, but I am no fragile flower who must dine in a private room."

"No one is more aware of *our* purpose than I am, *Mrs* Jones. Have you forgotten your vow to honour and obey so quickly?"

Lizzy's eyes jerked back to his face. She could swear she saw amusement lurking in his. Was the very corner of his mouth tipped up? And was that a dimple appearing? Surely not.

"Did you make a jest, Mr Jones?"

"A very small one," he said, laying his hand atop hers. "Please. I ask you in all sincerity to heed me on this point. When we arrive, speak with the maids, order a bath, ask for every assistance. In all likelihood, these would be the same servants who may have waited upon my sister, if indeed she actually sojourned here. I find it very difficult to believe she would agree to stay at such a place. I would not be at all surprised if she and Mrs Younge are in a much quieter part of town, and only gave out the name of The Swan as a ruse. It is well enough known for catering to tradesmen and the Mail."

"You think they are staying in London," she said, pulling her hand away, changing the subject and thus avoiding a promise she might not be able to keep. "Not travelling further north."

"Upon reflection I have come to the conclusion that, perhaps, I have kept too tight a rein upon my sister's activities. I ought to have allowed her some extra amusements in London where she had friends. I thought it safer but she has chafed under the restrictions. I fear it has led to her seeking out such entertainment in a more secretive fashion."

Lizzy could not help feeling sympathetic. She glanced at his hands, clenched into fists upon his knees. Instinctively, she laid her hand upon one of his. "You are a very kind brother. I think most men would be furious with her for lacking judgment and betraying your trust. She was simply out of her depth with Lydia."

"Whom *I* hired," he said bitterly.

"Lydia has connexions amongst the *ton. S*he likely presented very good references."

"I thought I was getting the best. Lord Cumberbatch is such a high stickler, and he sent his daughter to her school. And my own uncle vouched for her character. He was once a close friend to her deceased husband."

As he spoke, he unclenched his fists and absently took her hand, rubbing the scar slashing across her index finger, and one bisecting the base of her thumb. She knew she should pull it away from him immediately, but his posture eased; he wasn't conscious of what he was doing. And she had questions.

"Your uncle?" she asked.

He let go of her hand, distractedly lifting Mr Wickham's ring that hung from a chain round her neck. It had an odd design, a red garnet cross on a field of black and white, with diamond insets, but he appeared to take no real notice. "The Earl of Matlock."

"That explains much."

His attention caught on her tone, and he let the ring drop. "What does it explain?"

Lizzy's eyes widened. "Oh, nothing. I meant nothing at all."

He only stared, the force of his gaze making her cringe inwardly. Nevertheless, she tried to brazen it out.

"Forgive me," she said, her eyes sliding away from his look. "I don't know what I was saying."

Suddenly her hand was seized in an almost crushing grip. "What does it explain? Do not lie to me."

She yanked her hand from his. "You're hurting me."

"I beg pardon. Please, tell me. If it concerns my sister, I should be told."

"I don't know that it does. My knowledge is based upon Lydia's boasts to my mother. Lydia's husband *was* a friend of...of your uncle's. But she claimed she and Lord Matlock...were more. For several years. According to Lydia, her husband knew and approved, as Matlock in turn gave them entrée to more exclusive society in exchange for, ah, intimate favours."

"Devil take it," he shuddered, clutching at his forehead in obvious distress. "How could he? And to recommend her for Georgiana! Impossible! I cannot believe it!"

Lizzy was sorry to have caused him such pain. He had tried so hard to protect and shield his sister, yet his own uncle delivered her into the lion's mouth. Feeling an inexplicable impulse to soothe, she carefully reclaimed his hand.

"If your uncle cares as much about his reputation as you do, possibly Lydia required the reference of him as a price for her silence." She did not understand why a wealthy and powerful earl would think Lydia's insults could have any ill effect upon him when they could only destroy her own character, but she had to say *something*.

"He would care," Darcy replied shortly. But he did not pull his hand away.

The shock of betrayal sent Darcy into silence.

After the family scandal, his Fitzwilliam relations—at least the elder ones—cut the Darcys with brutal efficiency, in the name of *correctness*. Lady Catherine had not spoken to them for several years after. Eventually his father made peace with her by hinting that Fitzwilliam would never be able to marry her daughter and thus combine their fortunes *unless* she threw the weight of her reputation into extricating them from social disgrace. His aunt *still* hoped for the wedding, though he told her he was not willing.

His uncle was the family patriarch, a man of few words and inflexible honour. Catherine had worked on him for some years after she accepted the Darcys back into her circle, before he acknowledged them again. He had not relented until George Darcy was on his deathbed. Lord Matlock took care of his reputation more scrupulously than most men tended their estates, and he was practically treated as King Solomon amongst his cronies in the House of Lords. Matlock would *die* before allowing a blot upon the high lustre of his character.

Or so Darcy always thought. If what Elizabeth said were true…but it could not be. He stared at his hand, which had somehow become entangled with hers again—just as his every thought was growing ensnared in the very inappropriate Elizabeth Bennet. Here he was, on this strange journey with a woman who had no difficulty upending his world.

"I do not believe you," he said. "'Tis not true."

"Perhaps not," she agreed. "Lydia's word is hardly trustworthy."

For some reason, her easy agreement enraged him. "Do not patronise me. You believe my uncle indulged in a sordid alliance, coolly betraying his family while refusing to speak to *me* for *years* because—"

"Why does it matter what I believe? What is the opinion of a harlot's daughter?"

"Stop it!" he hissed. "Quit referring to yourself as such."

"It is only the truth, as you have, yourself, noted."

"I will not hear you degrade yourself with demeaning epithets. Your opinion matters to me because it is Elizabeth Bennet's opinion. And I…I respect Miss Elizabeth Bennet."

She bit her lower lip. "Why…why would your uncle refuse to speak to you for years?" she asked.

"Never mind it," he said sharply.

She lapsed into silence. The paved streets were so noisy one could hardly hear oneself think, the rattling of the carriage jarring their spines over each bump, the sounds of Frost roundly cursing a brewer's dray mixing with a hundred or a thousand other voices.

Darcy repressed arguments defending his uncle's sterling character, nearly all of which would reveal things he most certainly did *not* want to share. *I will not bother arguing with Elizabeth as to the truth of Mrs Younge's liaison with the earl.* That information came from the least dependable source possible and was not worth considering. The unscrupulous widow hoodwinked his uncle, and that was all. Elizabeth ought to know better than to repeat a thing Lydia Younge said. As for revealing his family's shameful past, it was not going to happen. Not ever. Elizabeth was his…a friend of sorts. But she would be exiting his life soon, and he must remember it.

Darcy kept tight hold of her hand. Lizzy didn't let his go. Side by side, they travelled silently through the busy streets of London.

They pulled into the bustling yard at The Swan with Two Necks, by far the busiest, largest inn Lizzy had ever seen. Since she disregarded her silent travelling companion, she stared out into the gallery-like area, breathing the acrid smell of livestock.

Horses were everywhere, men leading them about—unhitching, hitching, grooming, feeding. Stable boys called to each other, grooms and ostlers barked at the boys, livestock grunted and chewed in a noisy cacophony. Idly, she wondered what it would be like to sculpt a life-sized horse, then shuddered. Ever since being bitten as a child by a horse while trying to feed a stable cat, she preferred to stay well away from them. Watching as a black one took a nip at an inattentive stable lad's shoulder, she decided if she ever procured the materials and skill to reproduce something so large, she would select a lion or bear!

She spied the prostitutes at once—hard, skinny women eking out an existence by tupping coach passengers in dirty rooms or dark alleys. Lizzy felt nothing but pity for them; nevertheless, she did not appreciate the brazenly inviting looks cast at Mr Darcy. Of course, he did not notice *them* at all.

The innkeeper's wife, treating them with indifference, invited them inside. After some insistence on the part of 'Mr Jones,' they were given a private dining room and a plain if respectable meal of mutton, peas, and apple tart. The room was cosy, the fire burning away the early morning chill. By the time the maid arrived to inform Lizzy that her bath was ready, Lizzy was nearly falling asleep in her peas.

Darcy had obviously provided a large gratuity, because the maids attended to her with great good cheer; Lizzy had to remind herself it was not a personal gift, only an opportunity to pry for information. Still, it was nice to be treated so politely, and to have someone else wash the thick masses of her hair and brush it dry in front of the fire.

The younger of the two maids, Maggie, was by far the most voluble, so Lizzy dismissed the elder one and managed to bring the conversation around to ladies she had waited upon recently. Fortune smiled. She remembered Miss Darcy!

"We doesn't get many of the Quality 'ere, so course I remembers. Quiet like a mouse, 'er was. No trouble a'tall, I was that happy to do fer 'er. 'Er lady companion weren't so tame, let me tells you." Lowering her voice confidentially, she added, "Oh, she was on 'er 'igh 'orse. Demandin' the best and snubbin' it all as not ups to 'er taste. Then at night after the young miss be put to bed, down she comes, guzzling 'til she's drunk as David's sow. Notcher proper companion if you asks me. Braggin' 'bout how she be off t' make 'er fortune."

Lizzy perked up. "That's what she said? 'Off to make her fortune'?"

"'Er very words," the maid said earnestly. "Wondered about it, I did. Thought fer certain she meant t' abandon the young miss. I was that worried, 'cos the girl tweren't the sort as ought to be left without no one, mind you."

"To be sure," Lizzy said. "But she didn't leave her?"

"Oh, no, Mistress. They was off together the next day."

"Do you remember anything else, Maggie?" Lizzy placed her hand upon her reticule, a universal signal of remuneration offered for information.

Maggie brightened. "Well, young miss wish ta know 'bout the inns comin' up. It was plain as day she were used to finer lodgings 'n these, an' I think she 'oped fer better."

"Did she mention where they were planning to stop next?" Lizzy asked excitedly.

"Well...not jest. She asked 'bout the Bull and Mouth in Baldock, an' 'bout the Angel Inn in Stilton. I tells her that the Bull twern't much better than the Swan, if it twern't much worse. The Angel Inn is passing fair. The Talbot in Stamford be better, an' more fittin' fer such as 'er."

Lizzy nodded. It seemed confirmation enough that Miss Darcy was planning to journey at least as far as Stilton. "Is there anything else? Anything at all, no matter how small."

The girl shrugged. "She were...sad, I s'pose. Or maybe i'twere nerves. She twern't near so 'appy as that companion of 'ers, I tells you."

After Maggie left—very pleased with the sum in her apron pocket —Lizzy pulled on her clothing, eager to share this news with Mr Darcy. She crept across the hall, tapping softly on the door of his room.

No answer; perhaps he slept soundly. She knocked a bit louder. Nothing. Finally, she rapped loudly on the door, to no avail. *Blast*, she thought. He must be downstairs, perhaps even with Mr Frost. Too impatient and fatigued to wait, she made for the common room.

Despite the fact that it was late morning, the room was dim and smoky. Several shabby men sat about looking as though they were permanent fixtures, adding to a general air of dilapidation; she did her best not to meet anyone's eye. Mr Darcy was correct—this was no place for a female alone. By the time she determined he was not there, she had already attracted some attention—leers and outright ogling. Time to make a hasty exit.

She was nearly to the stairs when she felt a beefy hand upon her shoulder. The man's fermented breath soured the air.

"Where you goin' in such an 'urry-like? Come an' join me fer a nip." He stepped in front of her.

"No, thank you." She jerked away from his encroaching hold, relieved when his hand only tightened briefly before sliding away. Nevertheless, he remained immobile, blocking her retreat. "Stand aside, sir. My husband expects me."

"Pretty little bob tail like you, 'e oughtn't 'ave left you alone if 'e din't wanna share."

Lizzy overlooked the insult, wondering if it was too soon to knee him in the nutmegs. "No."

"Sweeting," he guffawed, treating her to a display of rotted teeth. "Gimme a li'l kick up. Shows you a good time, I will." He lunged forward.

It happened so quickly. Lizzy raised her knee, ready to give Mr Smiles a "kick up" he would not soon forget, when suddenly he was... gone. Blinking at the disappearance, she heard the sound of cracking wood as a large body crashed into spindly chairs.

Darcy appeared before her, his expression nothing like his usual impassiveness. Were she the dramatic sort, she'd say the flames of Hades lit his eyes.

"Upstairs!" he roared. At that moment, the drunken oaf reappeared, having regained his footing. Like a bellowing bull, he put his head down, charging straight for Darcy.

Although his attacker must outweigh Mr Darcy by two stone, Darcy ducked his ponderous fist, head-butting the bruiser right in his nose. Blood spurted.

"Upstairs!" Darcy roared again. The drunk uttered a very uncomplimentary remark about Lizzy's favoured nocturnal activities, and Darcy charged him with a silent viciousness, throwing him several feet into a table that did not survive the collision. Unfortunately, it likewise made no impression upon the brute's eagerness to continue cuffing. Scrambling up, he locked one massive arm around Darcy's throat, pummelling him with ferocious punches to the ribs.

Unhesitating, Lizzy grabbed a sturdy hardwood table leg off the floor; raising it high, she brought it down with all her might on the thick-skulled lout's head.

It only temporarily stunned him, but long enough for Darcy to stagger away. Unfortunately, Mr Smiles turned on her.

"Witch!" he bellowed.

Lizzy dashed up the stairs and into her room, throwing the bolt. Her relief was short-lived, however, as her assailant threw his colossal weight against the thin door. Scrambling across the room, she glanced out the window, searching for any means of escape. Sadly, nothing presented itself but a long, straight drop to the ground.

The door took another punishing blow, jarring it from its frame—a child could take it the rest of the way. Grabbing the stoneware pitcher from its perch upon the washstand, she braced herself for battle.

But the expected strike didn't come. Instead she heard loud thumps —fisticuffs?—in the corridor, then angry voices gradually fading to quiet murmurs. Though the pitcher grew heavy, she didn't dare poke her head out to look. When silence finally reigned, she cautiously approached her door, startling when it swung open, listing drunkenly on its hinges.

There stood Mr Darcy. Other than his extremely dishevelled appearance and a purpling bruise upon his jaw, he appeared unharmed.

"Are you hurt?" she cried. And then, without awaiting an answer, she ran into his arms.

"A re you hurt?" Elizabeth asked again, her voice muffled in the folds of Darcy's coat. The frightened tone of her voice hit him like another fist. For a very few moments, Darcy just held her, relief nearly overwhelming him. The threat to Elizabeth, not to mention her mad actions trying to fight for him, had likely taken ten years from his life.

Witnessing the ruffian nearly breaking into her room took another ten; he had aged twenty years before noonday. He had not slept in more than twenty-four hours, he was beside himself with rage and anxiety, and something inside had simply snapped.

In the frenzy that followed, Darcy tossed out every rule he had ever practiced regarding the gentlemanly art of fighting. No kick was too low, no move too underhanded. The lout was big, but he was slow, drunk, and fully dependent upon his intimidating bulk

He was even now being carted off to his hovel, the innkeeper was in possession of a large sum of Darcy's ready cash for damages, and Darcy had to somehow ensure Elizabeth never, *ever* put herself in such jeopardy again.

"I am fit. But you? Are you well?" He held her face within his hands, searching her for signs of pain or distress.

"He did not touch me," she assured.

"Never do that again." He could not continue to look her in the eye, could not bear to see his failure to protect her reflected there. Instead, he glanced at the splintered door, and steered her across the hall to his room. "You will sleep in here. Your room is no longer habitable."

He bolted the door behind him, grabbing a rude wooden chair from the hearthside and wedging it against the door for extra security. "You are safe now. Try to sleep for a few hours. As soon as I am certain Frost has had enough rest, we will be on our way."

"I need to tell you what I learned from Maggie, one of the maids."

He determinedly kept his back to her. "Probably the same thing Frost learned from others here—that Younge and Georgiana were here, and are now on their way to the Bull and Mouth in Baldock."

"Yes, but also—"

"You can tell me on the way north. You must rest."

"Where will you sleep?" she asked, after a few quiet moments.

"I will…" He waved vaguely at the hearth.

"There's not even a decent chair to sit upon," she replied. "I'm sure we could ask for a new room to be prepared."

Darcy was not sure of that at all, as the innkeeper was vexed, to put it mildly. Anxious to draw no further notice, Darcy overpaid him to let them stay, promising they needed nothing further. Besides, he wanted —*needed*—to watch over her. Just until his heart resumed its usual rhythm.

"'Tis no matter, Elizabeth. Please, take the bed."

She did not protest his familiarity or his suggestion. After a long silence, he finally heard sounds of her skirts rustling, the thunk of her shoes hitting the floor, the creak of the bed ropes as she lay down.

"It is warm enough. Will you take the blanket, so you needn't lie on the bare floor?" she asked, her voice husky with fatigue.

He glanced at the hearth, where a sooty rug lay. She was right; the room was amply heated. He hesitated, then moved backwards with his hand outstretched behind him to take the proffered blanket, tossing it on the rug.

He heard a giggle.

"I am perfectly decent, Mr Darcy. You may look where you are going."

But he would not look, lest the sight of her in a bed be too much. *It is only the aftermath of the fight*, he told himself. The fisticuffs had his blood up. He spread the blanket out on the hearth, facing it.

"This is silly," Elizabeth pronounced.

"What is?" he asked, finally giving in to the temptation to glance at her. The sight was both better and worse than he imagined, with her seated at the mattress edge, hair undone and falling nearly to her waist in a waterfall stream of long, thick, wavy locks framing her face and those vivid, expressive eyes. She smiled as she finger-combed the tresses, and he shut his eyes again, keeping the image behind his lids.

"You are exhausted, you have just taken a beating, and you desperately need rest. I can curl up at the foot of this bed and leave you the bulk of the mattress. Take off your boots and come to bed, Mr Jones."

"That is a terrible idea," he said, even as he sat down beside her on the mattress edge to remove his boots. With a grunt of effort, he managed to remove the first one and went to work on the second. He fought to think logically.

But she was already creating a nest at the foot of the bed, arranging the pillow. She curled onto her side, her feet dangling off the mattress edge, her slim ankles and bare toes peeking out from beneath her skirt hem. She smiled sweetly and sleepily at him. It was the most enticing thing he had ever seen, and his heart filled with yearning. His mouth went dry, and he swallowed.

"This is a bad idea," he rasped.

She only closed her eyes. "I won't tell if you won't."

He sat there at the cliff—ah, mattress edge—for some moments, staring at her face, lovely in its repose. She had fallen asleep instantly, trusting him. *I would die before I hurt her. I will protect her, even from myself.*

Decision made, he drew off his neckcloth and removed his coat, folding it for a pillow and throwing it upon the blanket. If it would not be a particularly restful interlude, at least he had a wonderful view of her sleeping form, her features tranquil. As he arranged himself on the hard floor, it occurred to him that he might never have this opportunity again, the simple privilege of watching her sleep. That honour would belong to some other man. Her husband.

The thought stabbed him with rapier sharpness, sliding directly into the softest, most vulnerable region of his heart with brutal efficacy. Her courage, her sweetness, her bold honesty would belong to someone else. Another man taking care of her, loving her. Another man filling her belly with his children, children that ought to be *Darcys*! But how could he marry her?

How can I let her go?

For all her sordid roots, Elizabeth was the rarest of gems. He could not fathom any of the *ton's* current crop of insipid misses beaning a huge, drunken ruffian in order to defend *him*. They would all have screamed or swooned or both, while *his* Elizabeth armed herself with a pitcher and made ready to fight. She was a fearless Athena, courageous but shrewd. From the very first, she had been helpful and resourceful in searching for his sister. Yes, she expected payment from him, but only seeking to better herself. And after the fighting finished today, she had shown how much she cared, running into his arms, asking after *his* injuries, giving no thought to her own distress. Next to Elizabeth, society's ladies were pale paste stones. Perhaps their settings were grander, but they entirely lacked her substance. As God was his witness, he wanted her.

But he had more than himself to consider. A happiness purchased at the price of Georgiana's was dishonourable. Even though he needed sleep, he could not; rather, he devoted the time to considering possibilities, discarding ideas, and planning how he might obtain what he desired so very, very much.

DARCY MUST HAVE FINALLY DOZED. HE WOKE WITH A START. SUPPORTING himself upon one elbow, he looked up.

Elizabeth was dreaming, restlessly tossing and turning. Also, he noted the fire was out; it must have been poorly banked, and the room had grown cool, despite weak afternoon sunlight peeking through a crack in the cheap draperies. She needed the blanket he used.

He was more than happy to give it to her, to see her made more comfortable; he could sit in the chair and probably be as well off as he had been on the floor. But she appeared to be growing agitated, and he could not bear to see her in any sort of distress. He looked at his watch, seeing it would likely be another two hours before Frost was ready to leave.

"Elizabeth," he whispered.

She did not respond, but gave a little, twitching moan.

His heart clenched at the thought of her in the clutches of a bad dream. He knelt at her bedside. "Elizabeth," he repeated, slightly louder.

She shrieked in response, startling him. Before he knew what was happening, she had thrown herself against him, knocking him onto his back. Her body covered his, her arms wrapped around his head. An animal-like snarl came from her lips, her legs kicking at some unseen intruder.

"Elizabeth!" he cried, trying to keep her from hurting herself against the stone floor. Her eyes opened, confused at first, gradually becoming mindful of her surroundings.

"Sweetheart," he said softly. "I have you. You are safe."

Her cheeks flushed. "I had a bad dream. Mr Smiles, coming at you with a pitchfork."

He carefully smoothed the curls off her face, using the excuse to feel the utter softness of her cheeks, her chin. "Mr Smiles?" he asked, looking up at her with a gentle expression. "That sounds like one of those dreadful puppets in a Punch and Judy show."

"That–that man you fought," she supplied with a remembered shudder. "He had that awful smile with those horrible teeth."

"I truly wish you would allow *me* to take care of defending myself and you. Waking and dreaming," he added. And then he pressed his lips to hers.

It was his first real kiss ever, though he had imagined them before. His imagination had failed him, utterly. Her lips were so much softer, the sensation far more exquisite than he could have conceived. His breathing grew laboured, his heart pounding. He never wanted it to end, and he did not want to do anything that would frighten or importune.

"I love this." He stroked her face, opening his eyes to see hers were closed, her long lashes fanning her cheeks. "Elizabeth, darling," he said, feelings of tenderness and desire almost overwhelming him. "You are so beautiful, so soft, so sweet."

He returned to her lips, revelling in the special feeling of connexion when they were mouth to mouth. He wanted to kiss her forever, to never leave this room.

"No," she whispered, turning her face from him.

"I am sorry," he gasped, moving aside to put a little distance between them.

"We are getting carried away," she said.

For several moments they stayed motionless, side by side, waiting silently for their pulses to return to an ordinary rhythm, for the cold floor beneath them to cool their heat.

"I am sorry, too," she said.

"You did nothing wrong," he protested.

"Not wrong," she said, after a moment's consideration. "At least not what most people think of as wrong. I am not sorry I had my first kiss, *kisses*, and that they were yours. I enjoyed it."

Her first kiss! She was as untried as he. *We can learn the lessons of passion together!* "As did I," he said fervently.

"I am not ashamed, either," she said, a note of defiance in her voice, as though he left some criticism unspoken but understood.

"Of course not. I would never, ever want you to feel ashamed."

She laughed a little, perhaps at him, perhaps at herself. "You must remember the lessons I learned at my mother's knee were likely the reverse of the usual maternal instructions. Mama said it is good to have passion between man and woman. Having the ability and desire to please one's husband is a gift and a joy.

"My opinion of her advice in this matter has improved, I believe. I have always thought it would be greatly to a husband's benefit to learn to please *me*. But I can see how mutual affection can be mutually favourable."

Darcy found himself wanting to smile. He was very willing to learn to please her in every way, though it did not seem politic to show amusement at her discovery. "I enthusiastically agree."

"There are rules," Elizabeth replied seriously. "Mama broke them, and she paid the price. She tried to get around them, to bend them, to make them work for her. Men may break them outright and consistently without consequence, and it wasn't fair or right that she pay for *her* errors for the rest of her life.

"Thomas Bennet pronounced her a harlot and departed, and thus that path was all that was left to her. She is not clever or wise. She had two children to feed. She did the best she could with such judgment as she possessed."

"Do you think she would have been content to be Thomas Bennet's wife? Could she have made him happy?"

"Who can know? And why should I care whether or not *he* would have been happy? She would have been faithful to him, I believe, but the past is unchangeable. My point is this—I have no intention of breaking these sorts of rules. I will not live her life. If I am blessed to have passion to give I will wait until I am certain of the man I give it to. My husband and I will have trust between us."

"We have already broken many of the rules," he pointed out.

"Not the important ones."

"Kissing is not against the rules?"

"Kissing incites feelings that make it easy to disregard the rules. I admit I have been...naïve, thinking I was immune to forgetting them, ever. I thought having the example of my mother before me, knowing all the things I want to do differently in my life would be enough. I thought having my own important goals and dreams would be enough. I thought trust in character, mine and yours, was enough. I was wrong. Even the most trustworthy can forget."

"Kissing in a bedroom, perhaps," he replied thoughtfully. "It is easy to forget the rules when we are already halfway to disregarding them entirely."

"Sexual congress can take place anywhere. There is not a safe place to forget *anything*."

"I know you are right, and yet, I want to kiss you again," he said. Before she could protest, he added, "If that is against the rules, I want to touch your hair. I want to feel it in my hands."

He matched action to words, his large hands combing through the thick tresses. "It feels like silk," he said roughly. He drew a strand up to his lips and kissed that instead, closing his eyes, just for a moment. She gazed at him with wide eyes, and he imagined he could feel her yearning reach out for his own.

DARCY LET HER GO BEFORE HE SENT RULES TO THE DEVIL, CALLING FOR A bath to be drawn for him in Elizabeth's former room, leaving only after gaining her promise to bolt the door behind him and to wait there until he came to fetch her. It was time to get ready to leave, to reach the Bull and Mouth—which destination he still thought was most likely a ruse covering his sister's continued presence in London. Why would she continue north? Unless she was travelling to Pemberley, it made no sense whatsoever.

After his bath, he dashed off a careful letter to Richard, explaining what he supposed: Mrs Younge was not a good influence and had taken Georgiana to London, to amusements that Darcy had expressly forbidden. He asked Richard to make cautious investigations, listing the entertainments Darcy had most recently prohibited...Vauxhall, two or three theatre productions, and a boxing match, of all things.

He had every confidence in Richard's discretion and resourcefulness; Richard would find Darcy's sister. Meanwhile, Darcy would continue this journey north, firstly to rule out the unlikely possibility Georgiana had actually travelled this way, and secondly, to spend more time with Elizabeth.

His beloved.

He recalled what Elizabeth said: "My husband and I shall have trust between us." He almost chuckled aloud. Elizabeth would marry him. He had devised a plan to make it possible, and now—despite his concern for Georgiana—he was almost, well, *giddy* with excitement.

But the disclosure needed the right moment, and the cooperation of Mrs Bingley and perhaps even Thomas Bennet, should that gentleman survive. Darcy had no doubt those two would eventually accommodate his ambitions and desires, but it might take some persuasion and pressure on his part.

He could hardly wait to share her good fortune with the lady herself.

Darcy inspected his timepiece once again. Where the devil was Frost? He had sent word to be ready to leave at four o'clock and it was now thirty minutes past the hour. His eyes studied the yard once more, searching the never-ending parade of teams and coaches and weary travellers being expertly herded for a quick meal. If the man were not so dependable, Darcy would be angry, but his impatience had turned to disquiet at ten minutes past.

Bad enough to be starting so late in the day. While the weather and roads were good enough, and he and Frost well-armed, it made sense for safety's sake to stay where they were until morning. However, when he suggested this to Elizabeth, she looked at him as if he were insane.

"Have you forgotten your sister is missing?"

Of course, he had not forgotten it for a moment. If he had not received assurances that his cousin was even now arranging the London search, he would not leave at all. The only way he could justify the journey north in his mind was to remember they were crossing a lead off the list of possibilities. But niggling feelings of guilt also indicated that his wish for more time alone with Elizabeth, much as anything else, might be guiding this decision to continue northward.

He imagined her now, upstairs in her room, burning with the impatience, energy, and purpose she carried with her, always. If Frost did not appear soon so he could escort her downstairs, doubtless she would defy his orders to remain where she was.

Did he want a wife who could not be controlled? One who relentlessly stirred the waters of life, rather than the calm of a reflective pool? *Yes, indeed.*

At that moment, a somewhat out-of-breath Frost appeared. "Sir," he rasped, his cheeks flushed pink with exertion and the chill of the day. "Beg pardon fer the delay. But I heard some news from the head ostler, and having time, as I thought, to spare, I did a spot of investigation. I believe you should hear this."

Lizzy startled at the sound of the brief, sharp rap at the door. She had been wool-gathering—yet again—about those kisses. About the bewildering sensation of his lips against hers. Much of what she knew regarding intimacy—which, to be sure, was a good deal more than most young ladies—left her cold. It was astonishing how different the experience was from her expectations. She could not deny anticipation to be in his arms again.

NO! Stop this! Anticipate nothing, because nothing will be happening!

But as many times as she lectured herself, the excitement would not dissipate.

She opened the door quickly, hoping to divert any wayward thoughts.

"You forgot to ask who was at the door," he entered scolding. "Always, always ask before opening."

"You are absolutely right," Lizzy agreed seriously, closing the door behind him. "I haven't quite recovered from the kissing earlier. Most distracting."

Darcy's mouth opened and then closed again, gaping at her. Immediately his gaze was drawn to her plump lower lip; his cheeks flushed.

"You allowed me far too much time for thinking. Where have you been?"

"We are not leaving," he said. "Not to go north. We stay in London."

"What?" she asked in disbelief.

"Mr Frost traced a boy by the name of Jem Abrams, a lad hired by Mrs Younge to fetch and carry for them during their stay here. He finally discovered Jem's whereabouts this afternoon. The boy says that twice Younge sent him into London proper with notes for a gentleman staying in rooms not far from here. After the first note he delivered, the 'swell' told him there was no reply, angering Mrs Younge. She sent a second note, and the boy was instructed to wait for a reply, no matter how long. Apparently, it was quite a long wait, as the man was out at gaming hells—er, beg pardon, clubs—until dawn. After much grumbling, the gentleman wrote out a reply, which Jem subsequently returned to Mrs Younge. Whatever was in the reply pleased her very much, he said, and she gave him an extra shilling for his trouble."

"So we know Lydia exchanged notes with men who frequent gaming hells. This does not surprise me in the least. However, unless he gave Frost a complete itinerary of the expected route, I fail to find this useful," Lizzy replied.

"Patience, dearest," Darcy said, giving her an affectionate tap on her nose. "Younge then announced they were to be away that very morning—the accommodations here not being up to her standards—since deciding to take in some amusements in town. She quizzed him extensively upon his knowledge of nearby inns, and he gave her the names of all those he knew. London was her sole interest. I think it obvious she remains in the city. There is no sense in pursuing a northward trail."

Lizzy was quiet for long moments, reflecting upon his words.

"Did Jem learn the name of the 'swell' corresponding with Lydia?" she finally asked.

"George Worthy. Does that sound familiar?"

She shook her head. "Not at all."

He nodded. "Canvasing the inns, as well as Mr Worthy's neighbourhood is critical. Lydia is arranging her own assignations under cover of amusing her charge. I must give London all of my attention."

It was a job requiring discretion and warranting a face-to-face meeting with Richard, or perhaps even a Bow Street runner. He would see Younge dismissed without references; a serious talk with his uncle was also in order.

"I see you must pursue this." Lizzy said at last.

"Yes. I am having Mr Frost return you to Ramsgate. I will write soon. Your gracious assistance will not be forgotten."

"Oh, but I do not return to Ramsgate," she replied.

"Why not?"

"I shall continue on to the Bull and Mouth, to carry on the search for Miss Darcy," she replied calmly.

"Did you not listen to a word I said?"

"I heard you," she said. "However, the maid who served Miss Darcy gives a different impression. From all she understood, Miss Darcy plainly believed they would continue north. If I must judge between Miss Darcy's word and Lydia's, there is no contest."

"Plainly, my sister is not commanding this expedition. I follow the tracks of the person who is."

"Did I not agree you must pursue this lead?" Lizzy asked. "Logically, however, I must pursue mine—continuing the journey north—eliminating that possibility, if nothing else."

"Miss Bennet," he said, with aggravated formality, "I understand your need to prove your worth to me. Your efforts shall be rewarded. It is completely unnecessary to go further."

"I appreciate it, but I have not yet completed what I set out to do," she answered patiently. "Miss Darcy spoke of their plan to stay at the Bull and Mouth. I go there now to discover if she actually did."

"I will send a messenger."

"And what would your messenger do if she *has* been there? Likely, learn little or nothing and return home, thus leaving an even colder trail."

"I will have him send us an express and follow her."

"And who is this discreet and trustworthy messenger, who shall trace your sister without risking scandal, hmm?" she asked. He made no reply.

"I shall send word if I hear of her whereabouts," she said. "I wish you luck with your search here."

"You cannot go alone!"

"Frost will be ample protection, but if you have a footman who can be spared…"

"Frost is not going anywhere, and neither are you!"

A loaded silence formed between them. At last, Lizzy said, "Of course, you must do with your employees as you see fit. I shall bid you good day and Godspeed."

She turned away from him, intending to depart. Darcy grabbed her arm, and for the first time, her chin went up and her eyes fired dangerously. He abruptly let go.

"Where do you think you are going?"

"I am off to see what time the post is leaving. I have shillings enough from what you've already given me. I will do as I think right and necessary."

"This is a blackmail, Elizabeth."

"I do not require your assistance. I demand nothing of you. You have my word I will be discreet."

He ran his hand through the thick waves of his hair. "As a gentleman, I cannot allow you to go off unattended into a potentially dangerous situation."

She shrugged. "Does not your set have certain rules for ladies, and others for females like me? Honour requires you to protect the innocent. Clearly, I do not fall within that class. We may separate here with your character intact. Meanwhile, I will do what *my* honour requires of me."

THEY WERE ON THE ROAD AN HOUR WITH HARDLY A WORD EXCHANGED. Darcy reminded himself frequently: *this is why I love her*.

The notion of honour in a woman, especially a woman who was not reared to be a lady—with all its implications—was rare and admirable. It was true the *bon ton* would not consider her an innocent, yet she was, in the most literal of ways. She entrusted him with her first kisses; he would not, *could* not repay her with abandonment, when she sought only to do the right thing. He could, mayhap, find her an escort, but she was so beautiful, so desirable. Who could be trusted to protect her?

It was unlikely Georgiana was in any danger, safely tucked away in London with her companion and coachman. Thus it was he was in a carriage, travelling to the Bull and Mouth, just to prove Elizabeth wrong. *Devil take it, she shall go no further. And she will have to learn obedience before she is ready to become Mrs Darcy.*

"What did your cousin say?" Elizabeth asked finally.

Darcy thought back on the conversation an hour earlier and scowled. "Richard agreed I may as well rule out the Bull and Mouth, since Georgiana told your maid it was their destination. He has a small group of handpicked men from his regiment whose honour and discretion he trusts with his life, and they shall be combing the city for Mr Worthy and Mrs Younge."

In fact, Richard felt Darcy would not be particularly useful in their

London search. He was too well-known amongst their peers for covert inquiry, with no skill for deception and guile. The conversation left him feeling devilish useless, which did nothing for his mood. Useless in London and thus on a useless journey to a useless destination. A perfect waste of time.

"He must have been scandalised at your choice of travelling companions."

A little smile accompanied her words, and his feelings of futility faded somewhat. Surprising his worldly, unflappable cousin with Elizabeth's presence was something of a coup. At least Richard was as unlike his father as was possible, passing no judgment. Darcy was not in the habit of explaining himself, but Richard was like a brother to him, and Elizabeth's character was his to protect.

"It is not what you think, Richard," he had explained. "Miss Bennet is assisting with the search. Her mother has known Mrs Younge for several years, and Miss Bennet has been invaluable in determining her schemes and in questioning female servants."

"Oh, of course," Richard concurred. "Very helpful, indeed." The slight smirk on his cousin's face, however, had quickly become annoying.

"'Tis true," Darcy insisted. "Miss Bennet is deserving of *all* of your respect, and mine."

Richard had promptly agreed but Darcy knew he would raise the subject again. Hopefully, he would support the forthcoming nuptials once he knew everything. His cousin was the *only* member of his family likely to do so, with the possible exception of Georgiana.

"He was surprised, yes," Darcy said, answering Elizabeth at last. "I do not routinely bend the rules, so to speak, in my dealings with the fairer sex."

Elizabeth's smile widened, and the sight further cheered him.

"Mr Darcy, you did not simply bend the rules, you tied them into knots, weighted them with sand, and chucked them into the Thames."

"Perhaps so," he admitted, noticing the way the fading sunlight picked out streaks of burnished chestnut in her hair. What at first appeared to be dark brown was composed of a hundred shades, from coffee and chocolate to mahogany, bronze, and burnt umber, an endlessly fascinating parade of hues. He remembered only too well the sight of those thick locks spread upon a pillow.

"Do not do that," she whispered.

His eyes shifted back to her face. Her smile had disappeared. "What did I do?"

"Do not look at me that way."

"What way?"

She folded her arms warily in front of her, turning her face away from him.

"What is the problem?"

"It is easier to remain unattracted to you while you are fuming and behaving like a sulky child than when you—" She broke off mid-sentence, astonished, as he slid off the rear-facing seat and knelt before her.

"You are attracted to me?"

"Is that the only thing you heard in that sentence?"

Darcy extracted her hands from her tightly folded arms. "Your hands are cold," he murmured, chafing them within his much larger, gloved ones. "I have noticed you seldom wear gloves. The nights grow cooler as we travel northward."

Lizzy shrugged, trying to disregard that this aristocratic gentleman knelt on the carriage floor at her feet. "I know I ought to wear them for the look of the thing. My sense of touch is important to me. I do not care to have my hands covered. 'Tis like being blindfolded."

She glanced at him, seeing if he thought her ridiculous, but he continued to look at her earnestly. He was adept at hiding his emotions, but she was growing better at discerning them; she saw no disdain, only understanding and...was it affection? She quickly quelled the temptation to tell him about her art, her sculpture. There was danger in surrendering too many pieces of her heart.

And then he did the one thing certain to further weaken her defences. He took her hand, a hand that was the furthest thing from the smooth, unblemished, soft skin of a lady's, and tenderly placed it upon his own cheek, as if he wished her acute sense of touch to connect them. She could feel the nascent roughness—his beard was thick, growing in again as soon as he shaved. Of her own volition, she traced the strong line of his jaw, the patrician nose, the dent in his chin. Memorising the shape of him. Wishing she could untie the elaborate knot of his cravat and feel the muscles of his throat work as he swallowed. Uncovering a vast curiosity within herself to understand every muscle and tendon, to recreate him in clay or even stone.

His eyes closed, allowing her this private exploration. Touching his ear made him shiver, exposing an unknown sensitivity. It was such a hidden, personal mystery, something perhaps no other in the world knew about this strong and commanding man.

Just like that, she found herself gathered up, collected into his arms, his kisses dually claiming and cherishing. He was the sort of man who was most to be feared—tall, strong, handsome, a man upon whose broad shoulders sat the lives of hundreds, who wore authority perhaps more easily than his cousin the colonel. The colonel's power required a uniform in order to display itself; Mr Darcy's required nothing more than a look, a nod, a simple gesture from one of his well-groomed hands. Even now, his kisses ordered her mind and heart to accede her independence, to hand over her love into his keeping.

One more. Just one more kiss, one more moment of enchanting closeness, my heart against his, sharing breaths and exhilaration. With the last bit of will left in her possession, she jerked her mouth away, burying her face in the folds of his coat.

She would not have been surprised had he chided her, or sulked, or worse, disregarded her attempts to halt the intimacy. After all, it was she who spoke of rules and restraint, and yet willingly yielded at the slightest provocation.

He did nothing except gather her more closely, settling her comfortably against his chest, and hold her. She ought not to have allowed it, of course, and yet it seemed of all the things she could *not* have, this one thing could be hers. Closeness. Human warmth upon a bitter cold night. Acknowledgement of this oddly fulgent friendship, so completely impossible in the light of day. Here, in the dark, they were simply a male and a female who cared for each other.

Lizzy listened to the beat of his heart, strong and steady beneath her ear, until once again she slept.

It was early in the morning when they reached the Bull and Mouth. Lizzy gazed out the window desultorily, unwilling to lose her comfortable position within the circle of Mr Darcy's arms. She felt the soft touch of his lips against her hair in the briefest of kisses, and pretended she did not notice.

"'Tis not near so busy as The Swan," she commented.

"Busy enough," he replied. "Stay close to me, Mrs Jones. I do not much care for the look of this place."

The Bull and Mouth struck Lizzy as the sort of sly place where bawds lay in wait for naïve innocents fresh from the country, promising them a glorious future after a free ride to London. Still, the investigation was uneventful. Once Lizzy was ensconced in her room, she ordered the services of a maid. The first one appeared to have no knowledge of Miss Darcy, so Lizzy found an excuse to call another. By the time she had spoken to them all, she was convinced Miss Darcy had never stayed here. One look at the none-too-clean bedding, and she did not wish to either. She sent a note to "Mr Jones," and soon he knocked upon her door.

"She has not been here," they both said at once, after she let him inside.

Darcy ran a hand through his hair, the corner of his mouth lifting in what, on another man, would be a smile. The signs of his fatigue were obvious to her, his usually impeccable clothing now wretchedly wrinkled, the scruff of his beard and reddened eyes giving him an almost piratical appearance.

"I see we have both drawn the same conclusions," he began. "I believe we should turn back to London at once. We can take a new team and we may even be able to reach town without stopping. I spoke to Frost, and he agrees."

"I must continue on. As I explained to you, it is necessary to go at least as far as Stilton. The maid from The Swan said—"

"Enough of this wild goose chase!" Darcy interrupted brusquely. "My sister is in London with her poor excuse for a companion. We are travelling further away from her."

Lizzy reminded herself again that she did not require kid glove handling, despite her disappointment in his display of anger. Patiently, she answered, "I understand your wish to return immediately. I will find passage to Stilton—a Yellow Bounder, mayhap."

"No."

"Excuse me?" she asked.

"You heard me. No. Absolutely not. You are finished with this foolishness. That is my final word. We are returning to London. At once. I shall accompany you downstairs within thirty minutes." He turned on his heel and walked out the door.

11

L izzy stared at the door, bewildered, for several moments before she collected herself.

Well.

It was a good thing, she thought, the lessons already learned from her mother's life. For one, whilst females might feel commitment and loyalty in the aftermath of intimacy, men seldom reciprocated. Also, she knew better than to surrender to the side of herself wishing to obey him now, to please and earn his favour and approval. Men were not the only ones who understood duty and sacrifice.

Then she laughed at the notion. It was only her foolish heart that thought leaving him a sacrifice; the rest of her was firmly of the opinion it was an excellent decision! She was getting too attached, her emotions already composing happily-ever-afters to fit a tale existing entirely in her mind. Lizzy knew the reality of those endings, and happiness seldom played a part.

By the quick offices of a helpful maid, she procured a ticket for the next mail coach, taking her as far as Stilton. What she would do from there she knew not, but by riding on top, she had saved a good deal—which might be important if Mr Darcy refused to fund any further explorations north, as seemed likely. If there were no signs of Miss Darcy in Stilton, in the absence of support, she must abandon the search and pray for Mr Darcy's success.

His theory regarding Lydia's desire to amuse herself in London made excellent sense. What could possibly be in Stilton, if that was indeed their destination? But comparing Lydia's noisier hints to Georgiana's quiet inquiries and apparent distress meant Lizzy could not let the matter rest, not yet. Besides, the helpful maid assured her the post ran to many towns in Derbyshire, including Lambton. If she were *very* conservative with her means, she could make inquiries there for Mr Wickham before returning to Ramsgate. Perhaps fate had led her this distance, after all.

She did not pretend to look forward to the upcoming confrontation. Mr Darcy was unaccustomed to being countermanded; he was tired, out of sorts, and beside himself with apprehension for his sister. As much as she wished he trusted her intuition, she could not see any reason why he should. With a sigh and a last brush at her skirts, she left her room to beard the lion.

She found him pacing impatiently near the carriage. For a moment, Lizzy was simply captivated by his appearance. From shoulders needing no buckram padding to the long legs leather-tipped in polished Hessians, he was a picture of wealth, masculinity, and authority. His wardrobe alone priced him beyond her reach. To have kissed him was a blunder of monumental proportions, for she could not imagine anyone else ever making a better job of it.

And yet, in an odd way, she was proud of herself. She had captured the interest, however briefly, of a formidable, aristocratic man. In this, she could understand what had driven Fanny Bennet to sacrifice herself for Sir Walter; there was a thrill in it, an imitation sort of power, for a female so often at the mercy of others.

But unlike Fanny, Lizzy had *not* succumbed. Her hopes and dreams remained intact. She would not sacrifice them for fleeting—if wonderful—sensation.

Though the odds of seeing Mr Darcy again were sadly slim, she could not be sorry she had known him. A deep-rooted fear that she was her mother's daughter was forever banished. She was Elizabeth Bennet, a sculptor, and Fitzwilliam Darcy thought her beautiful. How many could say that? She straightened her shoulders and approached him.

"I was coming to fetch you," he said gruffly, opening the door for her. "You ought to have waited."

Lizzy said gently, "I shan't be returning with you to London. I wish you good fortune, but have made my own arrangements to travel on to Stilton."

His expression turned thunderous. "I made it clear I would not countenance any further journeys north. Now stop this nonsense and *get into the carriage*."

"You may as well stop blustering, for all the good it will do you," Lizzy said. "I am not yours to command. I have explained why I must continue north. I bid you farewell."

"No!" he burst out, loudly enough that heads turned. Frost, sitting on the driver's box, carefully stared straight ahead at nothing. Darcy glanced around then took her arm and marched her to a less conspicuous corner of the large yard.

"Unhand me, sir. You do your cause no favours."

"How am I supposed to make you my wife when you defy me at every turn?" he said in a harsh whisper, not releasing his grip upon her forearm.

For once in her life, Lizzy was so completely and utterly surprised she doubted her senses. He could not have spoken those words or else she could not have heard them correctly. She opened her mouth, but no sound emerged.

Darcy did not appear to notice. "Is it not enough your entire existence reeks of degradation? You *are* the daughter of a harlot, devil take it! I have obstacles enough to overcome in whitewashing your past, never mind contending with incessant disobedience! You behave unreasonably, when I only wish to show you honour!"

Everything within Lizzy stilled. She put her hand on the larger one still gripping her arm and pried his fingers off, flinging his hand from her person as if it were week-old refuse.

"You are deranged," she said, her voice trembling slightly. "Completely mad."

"Marriage is not a mad notion. After careful thought, I know I cannot allow your past to come between us. I will bring you to your Aunt Bingley and convince her to take you under her protection. If your father yet lives, I will force him to acknowledge you as his daughter. We shall not speak of your mother. I vow no one shall mention her in your presence."

"My past? My presence?" Lizzy began, but the absurdity of his words was too much. "This is impossible. I am going away."

He chuckled. "I understand your surprise. You would have been less amiable in my eyes had there not been this little unwillingness. To be sure, I cannot make you my wife until after Georgiana is safely wed —I cannot allow her to feel the taint—but in vain have I struggled against my ardour! I will visit you in Hertfordshire often, though it may take years—Georgiana is young, if you recall."

"Years?"

"Unfortunately, yes. At least you will at last be sheltered and trained as is your right. The intervening years will give you ample opportunity to prove to any naysayers you are worthy of the Darcy name and a suitable mistress of its estates. But even if they never fully accept you, I do not much care for London. My life is spent at Pemberley, in Derbyshire, where we shall live quietly."

Lizzy's thoughts miraculously cleared. The explanation was plain: their adventure—and the kisses—violated his strict code of ethics, thus forcing a proposal. His words had been hurtful, his dismissal of her family offensive, and his conclusions simply impossible, but no man cared to be forced into a marriage, this one least of all.

"I am not insensible as to the honour of your offer," she began carefully. "Although I thank you for it, I am convinced you will be relieved to receive my refusal."

"What?"

"You have done as honour demands and made me an offer. I have refused. Honour is now satisfied. Although for future reference your proposal was more presumption than offer. It does not matter much in my case, but were you to attempt this again, you might wish to actually *ask* the lucky girl. Also, as accurately as you describe my situation, it seems somewhat ill-advised to detail every undesirable, hmm, *attribute* of your potential bride and her family. Not that your next offer will be to a harlot's daughter, I'm certain," she added kindly, patting his shoulder. "It might be best, *truly*, for you to keep to your own circles."

"What are you talking about? Why would I feel relief at your rejection? Elizabeth, I *love* you."

Lizzy made a gesture of exasperation, her patience diminishing. "Do not be irrational, please. You do not even know me, much less love me."

"I do know you. I know the sweetness of you, the wonder of your kisses, the need we share for each other." He moved closer, so near she could smell the heat and salt of him. He was plying his best weapon, a masculine fascination he possessed in abundance, to compel *her* to forget what he never, ever could: the vast differences between them.

"You do not know anything." She pushed back the sorrow clogging her throat. "One cannot build a life on kisses."

"These days with you are the sweetest *in all* my life. We can build anything we wish upon them. Forget your past and come with me."

He slayed her, flaying her weakest self with the lash of their mutual affection. He called her stubborn, but he was impossibly more so. "How could I forget, sir, when you remind me so often?"

"I will forget!" he cried, his own anger growing at her obstinacy. "I have already! I do not care!"

"You care, and always will," she insisted, using anger to stem a tide of foolish tears. "Whenever you are upset, I will become the harlot's daughter. Any time I annoy or dismay you, it will be the harlot you blame. If I disagree, you will certainly credit my inferior upbringing rather than my right to a differing opinion. A marriage of such unequals would be disastrous!"

"Do not presume to inform me *what* I shall think and *how* I shall feel. I have been kinder to you than to myself—you *are* a harlot's daughter. Nevertheless, I have accepted and acknowledged the unpleasant truth. By every measure of civility, I should never even *introduce* you to my sister, much less make you a member of her family! The least you could offer in return is obedience to my reasonable wish to go back to London and *find* her. Devil take it, is clinging to your connexion to a harlot worth dismissing out of hand the greatest of opportunities?" He ran a hand through his mussed hair, forcing his tone to gentle. "You are fatigued, we both are. Please, get into the carriage. We shall discuss this when we are in a better frame of mind."

But Lizzy had reached her limit. She had tried patience, understanding, and making allowances, but he provoked her beyond bearing. "Is it my fate to provide all the common sense in my every association? What do I want most in life, Mr Darcy? What is my most cherished dream? You cannot answer, for you do not know it—because I have never revealed it. Perhaps you assumed it was to be the wife of a great man and mistress of a great estate. Allow me to correct you, for it is not so."

She told herself to walk away, to simply end this painful confrontation. She knew he would never listen, never hear the harlot's daughter; no one ever did. Yet, even though it was futile, her anger boiled over with ear-singeing vehemence.

"Did you think I would *rejoice* in establishing an affiliation with the people who rejected me from birth? Do you suppose I have no pride at all, that I should be *grateful* for a recognition you would *force* them to impart? What a *delight*, to reside in a household where I am barely tolerated—and that only because someone who has more power than they do demands it. How would I amuse myself in this happy home? Oh, certainly, you've answered that already—while the years pass, I eagerly await the crumbs of your attention while learning to comport myself properly enough to be worthy of it. Attempt to prove myself to those who are mortified by my very existence! What a dream come true!"

She jabbed a finger at his chest. "Am I to forswear my sister and mother both? Of course I should! After all, what is filial affection compared to the privilege of hosting teas for gentlefolk who will despise me, tittering behind their hands and conveying their scorn in a hundred ways? Worst of all, sir, you do not know yourself. How easily you brand me 'daughter of a harlot' when you are in a passion. You once said my birth does not define me, but when crossed, your contempt is clear! As though I am a figure of shame, and ought to be grateful that you overlook it against your will, your reason, and even your character!"

Lizzy jabbed at him again. "Let me be understood—*I am not ashamed*. Not of myself, not of my dear sister, nor even of my mother. She has made decisions, perhaps, that I would not. But she never, not once, considered abandoning her daughters. She never dreamt of rejecting us because we interfered with her 'opportunities.' She did the best she could with what she had, and unlike my esteemed father, the *gentleman*, that *harlot* has never blamed her children for actions of her own."

She straightened her posture and lifted her chin. "I am not my mother's choices. I am not yours. I am myself, and shall become exactly who I wish to be. And *that*, fortunately for your delicate sister's sake, will *never* be *Mrs Darcy*."

Looking at his habitually impassive face—now openly showing the depth of his astonishment along with another emotion...bitterness?

disappointment?—her anger flattened. Perhaps he felt both. Perhaps neither. What did she know? Nothing at all, when it came to this man.

"I wish you well, Mr Darcy," she said tiredly. "I will find a way to send word if I should happen to discover your sister. I would appreciate it if you could have my trunk brought down. I will be taking the mail coach to Stilton."

She curtseyed to him for the first time—she did know how, after all —and left him standing alone in the yard.

DARCY WAS IN LONDON BEFORE HE BEGAN SORTING WHAT HAPPENED WITH Elizabeth. For hours, his overriding emotion was anger. She had accused him of not knowing her, but she was the one who utterly rejected him and all he offered without a thought. What hopes and dreams could she possibly have that his influence and wealth could not advance? How dare she so ignorantly disparage the benefit of the Darcy name!

Was *he* supposed to *rejoice* in the sordidness of her relations, whose condition in life was so decidedly beneath his own? Especially after he had worked so relentlessly to restore his family name, made so many personal sacrifices and difficult choices, all for Georgiana's sake. He *must* consider his sister's welfare! Five or six years, giving his sister opportunity to mature and have a season or two, time to arrange a suitable match with no blemish from his quarter to blight her chances. It was her right! Was it so much to ask?

Well, perhaps it was a great length of time, but he had been willing, nay, *eager*, to pledge his own prolonged sacrificial troth! If he, the master of Pemberley, were willing to make such a forfeit, why would not she? Was not the prize a worthy one?

'Tis for the best. She is stubborn to a fault, besides lacking in relations, fortune, and sense. Her foolish refusal saved me a world of trouble. I should feel relieved, as she said.

But relief was the only emotion he did *not* feel. Chagrin, bitterness, disappointment, anxiety, suffocating despair, a bitter flame of feelings upon which his anger simmered and boiled. By the time he reached Darcy House, the bitter brew coagulated into a hard, cold lump of regret.

He had left her there to fend for herself. He was so mortified, so horrified, and yes, he could admit to himself, so heartbroken, he had hardly known what he was about. Had not Frost marshalled him into the carriage, he might still be standing in the yard of the Bull and Mouth staring stupidly, speechless and disbelieving.

Blast and bugger, the mail coach! Alone! By neglecting to arrange an acceptable means of conveyance and companionship, he had *abandoned* her. Everyone knew the dangerous speeds at which the mails travelled; how long had she waited there until it arrived? Were her fellow travellers harmless, or thieves and ruffians? He had not even made sure she had money for travel! He had given her a goodly sum early in their journey, but knew she had freely distributed it to sundry maids and possible informants along the way, leaving a trail of grateful servants in her wake. How much remained?

He could send money north, with his fastest carriage and largest footmen. It would be indiscreet, perhaps, but that did not matter. They would be searching for Elizabeth Bennet, not Georgiana Darcy. Still, he remembered the cold dignity in her farewell curtsey, and doubted if she would ever again accept so much as a shilling from him.

Breeding tells, his father would often say. George Darcy had likely wondered how much of the blood running through his son's veins was worthy of the Darcy lineage. At this moment, he wondered too.

Despite sleeping in his own bed for the first time in days, he dozed in fits and starts, trying with little success not to think about *her* and dream about *her* and all the ways he had failed, and of all the things he would do and say differently if only he could begin the day over again.

THE JOURNEY TO STILTON WAS AS AWFUL AS LIZZY EXPECTED, BUT AT LEAST it was quick. So quick, in fact, that several times she thought the mail coach would overturn. Not that she was especially afraid. The seats up top, designed for four bodies, had eight stuffed into them; they would likely all still be entangled if it capsized, catapulting together as a giant human projectile. And frankly, she was so uncomfortable, it would probably be a relief. She thought with longing of the hired carriage, absent the sharp elbow of the woman on her left and the fishy smell of the farmer on her right. The prickly, over-large straw bonnet in front of her continuously abraded Lizzy's face, and she hated to think of the insect life teeming within the hats of the unwashed fellow travellers clinging precariously behind her.

Unfortunately, such discomforts did not prevent her from dwelling on the odd proposal—if it could even be termed such—from Mr Darcy. Could he truly have thought himself in love? How *could* he think so, when her birth was so inextricably linked to his contempt?

Most of the time, disdain did not upset Lizzy; she was nearly inured to it. From her earliest youth, everyone from the draper's son to the lowliest beggar on High Street thought himself her better. The contempt had made her stronger, since most women lived in fear of it, and their thoughts and actions were often dictated by its avoidance. Since avoiding scorn was impossible, she had fashioned her character upon her own notions of right and wrong, good and bad. Lizzy demanded respect from her associations or cut them from her life; what she lacked in friendships was more than compensated by her art.

Still, it did not mean she welcomed scorn; she yearned for the opportunity to be judged solely upon her own character and her own talents. Who would not?

Perhaps Mr Darcy's desire to improve her lot were sincere. It was naïve of him to suppose, however, that he could simply whitewash her past and force the world to disregard it. How so, when he himself could not?

Darcy was a good man, she knew that—he had never taken advantage of her, despite opportunity—but he was a man of his upbringing and birth, just as she was of hers. Why should his derision sting so much more than the rest of the world's? She lifted her chin in silent defiance of his scorn, only to have the straw bonnet retaliate against her tender cheek once again.

She was nearly dead on her feet by the time the coach arrived at the Angel Inn, which catered to tradesmen and the mails. It was an even less likely stopping place for the fragile Miss Darcy than the Bull and Mouth. With dogged persistence, however, Lizzy ordered her bath and questioned the maids. When not one of them recognised her description of Lydia accompanying a timid young girl, it was all she could do not to weep. Alone at last in her room, Lizzy collapsed upon the shabby bed, staring dismally at the ceiling.

Nothing. No one. Miss Darcy is not here, has never been here. I made a mistake. I could be with him still—abruptly, Lizzy recognised the direction of her thoughts and covered her face with her hands.

Stop! I am simply fatigued. On the morrow, I go to the Talbot, my final clue, and question the maids. If there is nothing, as now seems likely, The Adventure of the Missing Sister is concluded, my part complete.

At long last, the arms of Morpheus claimed her, but her dreams were restless. Restless and full of a grief she would never admit in the light of day.

The Talbot, less than a half-day's travel north from Stilton, catered to a much better clientele than the Angel Inn. Knowing if she appeared on the Talbot's front steps alone, she would have no luck getting a room, Lizzy spent precious coin to hire one of the maids for a bit of pretend. Sally thought it all great fun, although she repeatedly had to be reminded that Lizzy was not trying to pass herself off as a member of the peerage.

"Hush!" Lizzy remonstrated for the third time. "Do not call me 'Your Grace' or 'Duchess' or 'My Lady.' We do *not* want to draw attention to ourselves!"

Sally, who'd imagined herself the picture of an elegant lady's maid, grumbled until Lizzy reminded her of the promised extra shilling for information about Miss Darcy and Lydia. Without revealing the Darcy surname, Lizzy enlisted the assistance of the young maid, who was eager to begin her career as a spy.

Thankfully, the Talbot was busy and the innkeeper more so. He granted them a room with only a cursory inspection of appearances, and shortly thereafter Lizzy was in far nicer accommodations than she had enjoyed previously on this journey. After dismissing Sally to her sleuthing, she removed her boots and curled up in a soft chair by the hearth to wait.

Her thoughts turned to the future—namely Derbyshire. As soon as determining this inn had never seen Miss Darcy or Lydia, she must begin her search for Mr Wickham, and purge her mind of any thoughts of Darcys.

An idea had crossed her mind as she remembered her final conversation with Mr Darcy. He had mentioned Derbyshire as the location of his country estate and primary residence. Might *he,* or someone in his employ, have known of an estate manager by the name of Wickham? Would it be so dreadful an idea to write and ask? She could include the inquiry in her letter admitting that his sister had not travelled this far north. It would not be a personal inquiry. Surely asking the question was acceptable.

Satisfied she had provided herself with a justification, her mind skipped to the next problem: her need for money. Tallying what she had, she calculated she could get to Lambton but with little to spare. Would Mr Wickham make her a loan, with the ring as her pledge? She could not bear to pawn it.

Weary but not sleepy, Lizzy began to pace. She wished she could go to her clays, to lose herself in her work as she usually did whenever life became intolerable, or at least go for a long walk to dispel her pent-up energies. While the weather had been mild thus far, she wondered if her luck would continue into Derbyshire; it was colder there, she supposed, and her wardrobe was more suited to the temperate Ramsgate weather. *So cold, I feel so cold since he left. Since I left him.*

Don't be an idiot, Lizzy. You made a choice for the best, and you know it.

She *did* know it. The important thing was not to let her female emotions determine her fate. *I wish I had some clay. Even a small bit. If only I could release these provoking feelings into the clay!*

Just when she thought she would go mad, she heard a light tap. Swiftly, Lizzy opened the door, only to be almost knocked over by Sally's ebullient entrance.

"Oh, Miss, oh, Miss," she began breathlessly, hardly waiting for Lizzy to ask her what she had learned. "I was talkin' to Lottie who takes up trays to the private parlours. Cook here is a beast, she says, but if you stay outta the way o' her wooden spoon, it's not bad, she says, and it pays ever so much better than The Angel. If you were ta give me a reference, she says they need help in the worst way an' she's sure I can start now! I would give you yer coin back, Miss, if you'd write it."

Lizzy, her hopes having briefly soared thinking the maid had learned something of import, sighed deeply. "Won't they wonder why I leave you here and continue alone?" she asked.

"Doncha fret. I already says you's travelling from here ta Scotland ta be wit' yer aunt, and I've no wish ta live with foreigners." Her expression grew sheepish. "Since you had me take a box along fer looks, I brought all me best things wit' me. Just in case there were better work to be had here."

"Very well. I will be happy to write you a reference. 'Twill save me your fare back to Stilton, even if you keep your pay. Please see if you can procure writing materials."

"Oh, thank you, Miss!" Sally turned to go, but suddenly paused with her hand upon the door. "Dear me! I forgots to tell you! Lottie tells me that two females, just as you described 'em, *did* stay here not two nights past!"

Lizzy, who had given up completely, opened her mouth in shock. "Here? Two days ago?"

Sally gripped her hands together in sudden remembered excitement. "Yes, ma'am. Lottie brought the mutton in to their private parlour, just as the younger miss was cryin' and sayin' as how she din't want to be wed over the anvil, she had changed her mind and wanted her home chapel. Then the older one saw Lottie and hushed her but good."

"What?" Lizzy asked with considerable astonishment. "She's certain...'over the anvil' is what was said?"

Seeing Lizzy's sudden pallor, the maid attempted to reassure. "Sure and fer certain, Miss. But Lottie said she saw them at breakfast and the young miss weren't cryin' nor carryin' on no more. So as maybe they gave up the idea. Lottie din't know aught else."

"Good heavens," Lizzy murmured in utter dismay, "but we're under the hatches now." Then she stiffened her spine. "I need information, Sally, regarding travel north. Learn this for me and then I will write out your reference."

"Yes, ma'am!" Sally replied with enthusiasm, listening attentively as Lizzy explained what she needed to know.

THE ONLY GOOD PART ABOUT ARRIVING BACK IN LONDON ALONE WAS HIS bath and his first decent shave in days. His servants were too well-trained to comment, but he could feel their curiosity at his disreputable appearance. Donning the cravat handed to him by his silent valet, he found it difficult to face himself in the mirror. There were too many thoughts and truths he hid from, truths he could not allow himself to consider, and his own weary eyes mocked him. His secretary had many uses for his attention that long day, some of them quite urgent; but only the message that Colonel Fitzwilliam awaited him in the library brought any reprieve from his feelings of gloom.

"Cousin!" Richard cried as soon as Darcy entered the room. "Devilish good to get your note. I have news—"

"You discovered her?" Darcy asked hopefully, desperately. If his cousin found his sister, or even confirmed she was in London, then he had at least made *one* correct decision in returning.

"Unfortunately, no," Richard answered quickly. "Gads, man, you look terrible. Have a seat before we begin jawing. Can I pour you something?"

"No, thank you, Richard." Darcy wearily sank down onto the sofa opposite his cousin and stared sullenly into the flames.

"Miss Bennet?" Richard began delicately. "Did she return with you?"

Darcy straightened his posture, clenching his fists with the pain and pleasure of speaking of her aloud. "She decided to go as far as Stilton to confirm some slight information that Georgiana journeyed further north. However, Mrs Younge told others that they remain in London, so I thought it best to return."

At the mention of the name, his cousin frowned. "Lydia Younge," he said darkly. "Miss Bennet was correct in advising us not to trust her."

"Obviously. However, as much as it pains me to note, Mrs Younge's best reference came from your father."

"I am well aware. I made some discreet inquiries regarding her... and Darcy, their names are linked."

"Whose names?" Darcy asked slowly.

"My father's...and Mrs Younge's," Richard replied, not meeting Darcy's eyes.

"What? The Earl of Matlock, virtue and rectitude's greatest proponent?" he said with bitter sarcasm.

Richard made an angry sound of agreement. "Apparently my father is more a proponent of discretion and, ahem, appearances, than virtue *per se*. But who in blazes knows what he thinks? Certainly not I.

I have always considered him ruthless, but had no idea how low he would sink."

"Why the devil would he recommend her as Georgiana's *companion*?" Darcy snapped heatedly, casting off restraint to agitatedly pace the room.

"I can only assume he did not think the one thing had to do with the other. After all, who is the greatest man he knows? Himself. Younge had the good taste to fall into bed with him. In his eyes, that likely makes her *more* intelligent. Any other married man keeping a high-flyer might be blameworthy, but the incomparable Earl is justi-fied, no matter what he does.

"To think of the number of times I have been called on the carpet for *my* failings, while *he* felt entitled to do whatever he pleased...it makes me ill."

Darcy shook his head, feeling ill himself. "All those years he cut the Darcys because of—"

"I know," Richard interrupted, not anxious to hear aloud his cousin's rightful indignation. "Plainly it was the scandal, not the deed. Lady Catherine, at least, is honestly self-righteous, as difficult as she is. This whole situation is enraging, Darcy. I am sorry."

Darcy stopped before the hearth and stared into the flames. "It is not your fault, Richard. As it turns out, it was fortunate the earl cut us dead, otherwise I might share guardianship of Georgiana with him instead of you. You were always a friend to me, even when he ordered you to keep away." His thoughts turned contemplative. "Do you remember the name of that young jolter-head at school you stopped me from killing?"

"At Eton? Fletcher," Richard replied.

"Fletcher," Darcy repeated. "Right you are. The cork-brain never did know when to shut it."

"I doubt you would have killed him."

"I am not sure. I was too angry, too friendless, too big for my age, and too ungoverned in my responses. He represented every arrogant popinjay who turned up his nose at me, every gossip slyly repeating their parents' whispers. I had already been sent down twice for fray-making. That day it all came to a head. I do not even remember what he said, just the red rage obliviating all of my senses. Thank goodness you happened along."

Richard laughed. "You had become rather celebrated even amongst the older boys when you blacked Gresham's eye. You might have been big for your age, but he was in *my* class and bigger still. You were not alone in your contempt for him, though, and some of the sixth years were sympathetic, keeping me informed whenever word circulated that you were fighting again."

Darcy gave a nod of remembrance. "Do you remember what you said to me, afterwards? After you pulled me off Fletcher?"

"I have no idea."

"You asked me when I was going to stop fighting my parents' battles. You said the adults in our family had made a muck of things, and I should cease brawling with any who pointed out their mistakes."

"Good advice, if I do say so myself," Richard said. "Perhaps easier said than done."

Darcy nodded. "True enough. But I had been so fixated on trying to preserve the dashed Darcy honour, I was carrying the world's contempt upon my own shoulders. After thinking on what you said, I finally realised that we had no honour to preserve at the moment, and I was a fool to be so thin-skinned about it. I vowed I would regain honour through my personal conduct, and I made my peace with the past. That was my last fight at Eton. I give you the same advice now, Richard. Do not own your parents' mistakes."

"Devilish hard to do, Darcy. For him to inflict his appalling errors in judgment upon poor Georgiana is simply unforgivable," Richard fumed.

"I might have abandoned fisticuffs, but I do know how to fire a pistol," Darcy agreed with equal contempt. "Tell him to keep out of my sight."

"I would, except we are not speaking at the moment. I tried to get more information from him about Lydia Younge. Naturally, he would not accept any responsibility for his actions." Richard abandoned his pacing to sit down heavily on a hearthside chair.

"What possible defence could he give?" Darcy asked wonderingly.

Richard shook his head. "I will not tell you what he said so you do not feel obligated to call him out. Not that I would much care if you did murder the old dunghill cock, but I would hate to see you flee to the Continent. As he has suddenly departed for the country at the height of the Season, I would guess he avoids any requests to name his seconds."

Darcy began to pace again. "Have you had any other luck?"

"I have not, but the necessity for discretion slows us. I have more men looking into this Worthy person, as we needn't be quite so circumspect in our inquiries about him." Richard ran his hand through his hair, mussing the dark gold locks women had been known to exclaim over.

They heard a tap at the door. "Enter," Darcy called.

His butler, Pitkin, opened the door. "Excuse me, sir. A Lieutenant Summers is here to see Colonel Fitzwilliam." Darcy and Richard exchanged a glance, and Richard nodded.

"Show him in," Darcy said.

Lieutenant Summers was slim and youthful in appearance, but had a certain canniness of expression that spoke of innate intelligence. "What is it, Summers?" Richard asked, knowing the young man would not have intruded unless it were something of the greatest import. Judging from the expectant look on Darcy's face, he understood this as well.

"Sir, the watcher you stationed at Mr Worthy's place of residence observed an army officer, a lieutenant—not one of our men—approach the door to his rooms. When it was clear no one was at home, the lieutenant proceeded to force the lock to gain entry. At that point, our watcher—Sergeant Briggs—intercepted, and he took the lieutenant into custody, after some struggle."

Richard's brows rose skyward, both at what was and was not said. "Indeed. What was this chap's business with Mr Worthy?"

"That's just it, sir. The trespasser, an officer by the name of Lieutenant Denny, claims the rooms don't belong to any Mr Worthy at all, but to another officer by the name of Lieutenant George Wickham. He's gone missing from his company in Hertfordshire, and his commanding officer, a Colonel Forster, sent Denny after him. It seems Wickham owes Denny—and a number of other fellows in his company—a considerable sum in gaming debts, sir, and Denny was sent to collect on them and try to bring Wickham back to Forster. Wickham had written Denny to tell him he would soon have all the money he is owed, as he—Wickham, that is—would be coming into a fortune. Denny had the letter on his person, complete with Wickham's direction. Which led him to 'Worthy's' rooms."

Summers took in the impassive expressions upon the faces of the two other men. He paused, suddenly looking uncomfortable. "That is all. I thought you would wish to know as soon as possible, so I came here to notify you at once."

"And you were correct to do so," Richard said. "Where now is Lieutenant Denny?"

"At headquarters, sir," Summers replied, appearing relieved. "I thought you might wish to question him further yourself."

"Again, correct. I shall return to headquarters shortly. You are dismissed, Summers. Good work. Tell Briggs the same."

"Yes, sir," the officer replied, taking his leave of them.

"Devil take it," Darcy whispered, once they were alone again. "George Wickham."

"False name and gambling debts...the man sounds a right scoundrel. I thought the name seemed familiar," Richard said uneasily, "but 'tis such a common one, I cannot be certain. Do I know him?"

"Doubtful, unless you have heard me cursing the cur. He is three years my junior, the son of Pemberley's former land steward and also my father's godson. Old Mr Wickham died, thrown from his horse while inspecting some of our properties, and my father took George in, as his mother had died of illness a few months prior. Father sent young George to Eton, determined to do all he could for him, charging me to look after him."

Darcy gave a mirthless laugh. "Wickham initially made many friends and showed decent progress, but it gradually became obvious he was morally bankrupt, a charmingly dishonest little beast. I began hearing rumours and tried to counsel with him, but I was treated as his enemy. He even wrote to my father to complain of me trying to ruin his reputation in his House simply because he was a poor orphan."

"As if!" Richard said loyally. "You were always one to look after the underdog! Too smoky by half!"

Darcy shrugged. "I had repeatedly been sent down myself at that age. Thankfully, Father did not believe him and merely thought George exaggerating, having trouble adjusting to the loss of his parents. I tried to assume the same, but over time I saw his decided preference for depravity. He barely passed his courses, and likely only because he was *most* proficient in cheating. It had been decided that he should have the living at Pemberley when Mr Bradley passed, but after George impregnated a Lambton girl *and* one of our housemaids, Father changed his mind. With outraged fathers on his doorstep, my father finally saw for himself that Wickham was the last person on earth who ought to be of the Church. He told the rascal he would give him the means to study law—as long as he agreed to leave and never return."

"'Tis better treatment than he deserved," Richard retorted.

Darcy took a long pause, tension radiating from his large frame. "Not two months after Father passed away, Mr Bradley died. And who do you suppose was on my doorstep within a fortnight, claiming the living should be his?"

"Wickham?" Richard asked incredulously.

"The same. He was of course informed I had been apprised of the entire situation, that I was well aware of Father's withdrawing the offer of the living, and why. Wickham countered with spite and malice, as you might expect, but departed without another shilling from me."

Richard's forehead was creased with concern. "A rum character, certainly, and quite probably the sort who would interest Lydia Younge," he said.

"George Wickham could interest anyone in skirts when he took the trouble. He is a charming, greedy, libertine." Darcy met Richard's gaze with horror-filled eyes, as he drew a natural conclusion.

"Georgiana," he said, his face pale with dread. "The secrecy of the trip. North. They were journeying north. Wickham, writing that he is coming into a fortune. Georgiana's thirty thousand. George Wickham is eloping with my baby sister, and Lydia Younge is helping him."

13

Darcy began the journey on his Arabian, Cyclops, a beast with both stamina and strength. His cousin was similarly mounted. Grimly, they rode northward, fuelled by equal parts outrage and despair.

Why had he failed to hear Elizabeth? *She told me, and I would not listen to her. She knew. She knew about the–the connexion*—the thought curdled in his mind with wild distaste—*between Lord Matlock and Lydia Younge. I, of course, though I can barely tolerate my uncle's company, chose to defend his morals rather than believe her word.*

Despite the attentiveness the road required with only an almost-full moon to guide them, he had ample time to think. And to berate himself. Not simply for failing to continue the search with Elizabeth, but for *all* the ways he had failed her. With the keenness of recollection, he could remember every word she said to him in that stable yard, every argument he had refused to hear.

She was right, right about everything. How quickly he flung the word "harlot" at her, and after he had instructed her never to call herself thus! Would he do as she accused? Every time she disagreed with him, would he simply remind her of her roots so she would understand she was not *good* enough to argue with him? *You are not your father*, he had so easily promised his cousin, and yet he laid *her* mother's actions like a noose around her neck. If she had known his own family's chronicle, she would have called him a complete and utter hypocrite.

Why had he neglected to ask her about those dreams that were so important to her? Why fail to use the brief time they had together to truly try and *know* her? He had observed her character, learnt of her compassion and shrewdness, her steel spine, her wit and humour, her kisses…in short, all of what pleased *him*. He knew next to nothing of what pleased *her*.

Dear Lord, he had lost two days, nearly three, simply because he was a sapscull. Elizabeth *might* have discovered Georgiana's presence in Stilton. Would she have uncovered the elopement? He could not depend upon it, so she might be following much more slowly, searching inns and seeking clues. But money, he had not left her any. What would she do when she ran out? He had been a selfish, thought-less cur, and she might suffer for it.

Why, if he were not so fixated on his own family history, was he so quick to malign hers? Despite their difference in stations, she was worth ten of him. The least of what he owed her was an apology and an explanation. Whether or not she would allow anything more, he could not know.

It was early morning in Stilton when he stopped at the Angel Inn. Most everyone remembered 'Mrs Jones,' because she had hired away a maid to accompany her on her journey; they had taken the post north together. His relief was great; she had the means to hire a servant, which was something. No one remembered seeing Georgiana or Younge.

Stopping at The Talbot was pure coincidence. Richard's horse threw a shoe not far from it, and as they had been forced to stop—and as it was a quality establishment with fine horseflesh—they decided on changing their mounts. To fight fatigue, they ordered coffee at its public room while fresh horses were readied. And since they were there, he questioned the helpful early morning servants. It was not long before he was speaking to a maid by the name of Sally, who, once she realised his, er, identity, readily imparted all she knew.

"Mr Jones! Her brother! Miss Jones told me about you, sir! She wrote a letter fer you, but she din't trust it."

"She did not trust her letter?" he asked, taken aback on hearing he had been demoted to the role of brother.

"The mails, sir. She said the more important the post, the more likely it is t' be mislaid or mis-delivered. Did you get yer letter, sir?"

"Hmm, no, no I did not," Darcy replied, somewhat bemusedly.

Sally nodded, satisfied at this proof of Miss Jones's wisdom. "So she said. She were frettin' about it somethin' awful."

"Do you know the letter's contents?"

Sally glanced about furtively. "It be about the girl," she whispered. "Yer tryin' t' stop the weddin', aren't you?"

"She knows about the, ah, wedding?" Darcy asked, lowering his voice as well.

"So's you *do* know! I was the one as turned up the scheme," she said proudly. "Miss Jones hired me t' search fer clues."

"Ah," Darcy said, and because it seemed further acknowledgement was required, "Good work."

"You c'n be sure as I won't say a word," the little maid vowed. "Not one word t' no one, but you of course, as Miss Jones tol' me you'd help once you got yer letter. It's jest like somethin' out of a sensation novel, in't it? Poor young girl tryin' to save her family from the work-house by dashin' off ta Gretna Green wit' a wealthy rogue, not knowin' she's come inta the blunt. Oh, you will save her in time, won't you, Mr Jones?"

He blinked at this rapid discharge of information. Evidently Elizabeth had concocted a story that preserved Georgiana's dignity, if not her reputation.

"I shall do my best. Were you able to learn where they might be stopping next?"

Sadly, Sally had no idea of the route, only the ultimate destination. Darcy quelled his disappointment.

"When did Miss, ah, Jones leave here?" he asked.

"It were the early mail yesterday. She were lucky and there be a seat up top, an' only four others to share, not counting the babe in arms, though one of them passengers was all guts and garbage, more's the pity. I'm that sorry, sir, I tweren't keepin' on as her maid," Sally said, seeking to prolong the conversation until he remembered to give an appropriate gratuity for her helpful information.

He looked up at her, suddenly watchful. "You? You were the maid she hired from the Angel Inn?"

She glanced around, ensuring no one could overhear, and whispered, "It were her idea t' pretend, sir. They'd not have let her stay here if they'd known she was travellin' on her own. It looks *fast*, an' Mr Beedle, he be the innkeeper, he don't hold with fast females. Though of myself, I think it's Mrs Beedle who makes sure he don't. It was just t' be fer the day, sir, an' then I was t' go back t' the Angel, but they had a place here for me an' Miss Jones gave a real nice reference."

Darcy grit his teeth at this news. He had not stopped to consider *anything*. No truly decent lodging would allow Elizabeth entry alone, and she had no means to hire a companion for aught except brief pretence. But as angry as he was with himself, he had one final question for the maid; self-derision could wait.

"Miss Jones, how did she seem? She was…well?"

"Why, yes sir. Frettin' for the girl, but fit as could be. I took good care of her," she stressed.

"Thank you," he said, finally passing a coin to the expectant-looking maid. Richard waited, staring at him with unconcealed curiosity and some impatience when he finally turned to leave.

"What was that about?" Richard asked.

"Miss Bennet discovered the elopement," Darcy replied once they were out of hearing. "She left on yesterday's mail to follow and try to intercept."

"Good news," Richard said. "She is a day ahead of us and with the snail's pace Georgiana has maintained thus far, she might be able to catch her."

"Except she has little money and no clues as to where Georgiana might be stopping next. It will be sheer luck if she happens to intercept her. And she—" He broke off, unable to articulate all of his fears. Georgiana in the hands of Wickham. Elizabeth, travelling by herself on a mail coach that barely stopped for refreshments, never mind a night's sleep, with almost no money and even less protection. He shook his head in abject dismay. "We must go."

LIZZY WAS EXHAUSTED. *WITHAM COMMON. GRANTHAM. NEWARK. WESTON. East Retford.* At every stop, she let herself down and asked as many people as she could if they'd seen anyone matching Lydia's or Georgiana's descriptions. It was, perhaps, somewhat indiscreet, but her desperation was great, not to mention that, at her current speed of travel, she might even pass her prey. She had purchased a ticket to Carlisle in North Yorkshire, the nearest stop to what was commonly known as "Scotch Corner"—the point where traffic for Glasgow and the west of Scotland diverged from that of Edinburgh. It was fifteen miles yet from Gretna Green, but was as far as she had the means to travel. What she would do if she were unable to intercept them— mercy, what she would do if she *did* intercept them—was anyone's guess. Hope to get close enough to talk some sense into Miss Darcy, she supposed. Attempt to delay them until Mr Darcy received her letter—*if* he received it.

Even if he did get the letter, there was a distinct possibility he might not accept it as truth. It would be difficult for him to believe his young sister, barely out of the nursery to his way of thinking, was eloping. Lizzy, remembering her fifteenth year and a certain *tendre* for the butcher's son, had no trouble believing it. Fifteen-year-old girls did not realise it was even *possible* for a boy to pledge *his* heart on one day and break *yours* the next. Lydia was the noxious root of this exploit, the groom-to-be undoubtedly some shabby lover, willing to cut her in on a portion of Miss Darcy's wealth in exchange for coercing the unlucky little heiress.

Lizzy dozed, held upright by the bodies crammed into the small space, waking when the guard's horn sounded, notifying an inn some little ways distant of the mail coach's pending arrival. It took her fuzzy brain a moment to remember where they were.

Bawtry. We're in Bawtry. First stop in Yorkshire.

As soon as the coach halted, Lizzy stood.

"Only changing teams, Miss," the guard warned.

Lizzy nodded. The stable hands worked quickly to keep the mails running, and she had perhaps ten minutes at a maximum before they would be on their way once more. If she were not in her place when they were ready to start, they'd throw off her trunk and she would be left behind. There was opportunity to question one, perhaps two persons only, and the odds of it being anyone who had actually seen her quarry were slim indeed.

She cast about the yard with a practiced eye, searching for some-one, male or female, who looked like they might pay attention to goings and comings...and be willing to gossip. She found a likely prospect in a genial-looking elderly man lounging on a wooden bench against the brick wall of the posting house. She moved towards him, trying not to hurry, to appear as one who merely needed to stretch her limbs. As she made her way slowly past him she gave him timid acknowledgement and bit her lip, doing her best to look distressed and upset. It was unsurprisingly easy.

"Nah, then, a pretty youn' lass like thee ought nawt t' be so gloomy on a fair day," he called in his strong Yorkshire accent.

Lizzy did not have time to be anything except forthright and hope for the best.

"Oh, but it's such a tangle, sir," Lizzy cried. She was surprised when her eyes filled with real tears, but reminded herself they were a natural consequence of fatigue and *not* the nagging bleakness shadowing her since the separation from Mr Darcy in Baldock.

"Nah, nah. What's t' trouble?" he asked, sounding genuinely concerned.

Lizzy removed a handkerchief from her pocket and dabbed at her eyes. "My niece has fallen into…bad company," she said. "I have to find her, and soon. I'm following as rapidly as I can, but she has such a start on me… Oh, sir, have you seen a young girl, aged fifteen years, blonde hair and very tall, accompanied by a lady in her thirties, petite with bright red hair and a…a very forward manner?"

She needn't further describe the situation; there was only one reason for a young girl to be fleeing this far north, with her family in hot pursuit.

The old gent appeared thoughtful for a moment, staring upward with narrowed eyes. "Were they travellin' wit' a fellah, prinked up as if 'e came owt of a bandbox, nawt short nor tall but full up o' 'imself?"

Lizzy—after untangling the words from within his thick accent—answered with a heart full of genuine fear. "They may have been," she answered cautiously.

"Aye," he said. "Nawt but a day behind 'em, ye be. I thought t' young miss a propah fine laidy t' be wit' those two."

The guard's horn blew, warning that the coach would be leaving at any moment. Lizzy fumbled in her reticule to hand over a precious sixpence, but he stopped her with a gesture.

"Nah, nah. No need, Miss."

Even though a very un-ladylike sprint would be required to reach the mail coach, she paused to grasp both of the old man's hands in hers. "Thank you. Thank you so much," she said.

He beamed, then waved her on. "Go on wit' ye. Catch yer ride, Miss."

Lizzy gave him an answering smile, then dashed to the coach, feeling more heartened than circumstances warranted; after all, she did not know where Miss Darcy was at present, and an unwelcome bridegroom had joined her party. Still, she was not so far behind them as she feared, and she was making good time while they maintained their lackadaisical pace.

And there were, once in every while, kindly strangers in the world. It was a very good thing to remember.

GEORGIANA DARCY WAS IN A PICKLE. IT DID NOT HELP ONE LITTLE BIT TO know it was of her own making.

Stupid, stupid child, she lectured herself with the most stinging criticism in her vocabulary. A child. It was just how she behaved. Was it any wonder all and sundry still treated her as one?

Lydia was supposed to be different. From their first private meeting and her shocking insistence they call each other by first names, to her worldly knowledge of, well, *everything,* she had seemed to understand Georgiana's longing for love, excitement, and romance. Fitzwilliam kept her in a glass cage, and while she understood his fears and why he protected her so diligently, she yearned for freedom. Lydia had known it. So easy to recognise now, how simple she had been to deceive.

Of course, she had never intended to be caught up in an *elopement;* even with all her rebellious inclinations, she had not wished for *this.* But somehow George's poetical odes to her beauty, to her allure, to his yearning for *her*…it went to her head, as it was obviously meant to do. She would bet her fortune she was not his first dupe.

This evening, for the first time, his charm had worn thin enough for her to see the shabby workmanship beneath. From time to time on their journey, she had voiced her misgivings to Lydia but never said a word about them to George. Finally, she had determined to talk to him privately, to convince him to take her to Pemberley instead of Gretna Green. She wanted the banns read, a real wedding instead of this havey-cavey affair, and she wanted her brother to give her away. As angry as she was with him, she never meant to go so far as this. It would hurt him deeply to miss her wedding day.

George refused to even listen to her. "Best beloved, dearest heart, you know your brother would not consider letting you wed so soon. He would insist upon a wait of years, when I long to be yours now."

"But...he cares about my happiness," Georgiana had pressed. "Would it be so dreadful to wait? By my sixteenth birthday, he would be much more amenable—"

George interrupted sharply. "You know my reasons for not trusting his honour. He thinks me not good enough for you, my beloved."

Georgiana had been furious when he first told her about Fitzwilliam's treatment of him, but upon reflexion, she considered it very out of character. "I am sure there is an explanation. I cannot help but think there is some misunderstanding. Once he knows we are in love, he will *have* to make sure you are treated fairly."

But George's expression had grown mulish. "I am a man, with a man's needs. I cannot go without companionship for months or years, waiting for your brother to decide you are grown enough to *be* that companion."

Always before, when he made veiled references to the marriage bed —usually accompanied by kisses—she grew excited. This time, though, she caught a threat. *Do what I say, or I will find someone else who will.* Even though he pressed kisses now to that special place on her neck that usually made her so shivery, the warning sounded loud and clear.

Would a man in love behave thus? And so, she did not allow herself to be put off, did not let it go. She pressed, and pressed hard for what she wanted.

"I do not want to be married at Gretna Green, with a blacksmith presiding. I do not want my friends to laugh at me behind my back or– or to my face! I want a real wedding!"—and she burst into tears.

Whatever response she expected, it had not been the one she received.

He grasped her chin with bruising force, his eyes narrowing. "Stop your caterwauling, you tiresome—"

At that moment, Lydia bustled in, all noisy sympathy, separating them, gathering Georgiana up in her arms, declaring that all this trav- elling put everyone on edge, that George should understand her dear girl only needed a hot bath and her supper for all to be well.

Georgiana had allowed her to smooth everything over, but it was as if some magic spell had broken. Suddenly, she caught the looks between Lydia and George, like a wordless language.

Be quiet, idiot, or you'll ruin everything, Lydia's look said to him.

And George's looks to Lydia? What *those* looks spoke brought heat to her cheeks. He had never, ever looked at her that way. And…she was not sure she wanted him to. There was nothing of romance in those looks.

Somehow, a part of herself had always known if she refused to elope, the whole shining daydream would disintegrate into the sham it had always been. Perhaps that was why she had pressed at last. Perhaps she *wanted* to stop deluding herself. Perhaps she could now admit this was the *real* reason she had slowed their pace at every turn, insisting she would be ill if they failed to stop frequently.

It hurt to know that the man she thought she loved betrayed her with Lydia. Georgiana could not possibly wed him now. But slowly, she was realising if she flatly refused, it would not go over well. She had not mistaken the potential for violence in him tonight as she had finally ceased to be mollified by his lies. If Lydia were party to George's feelings, likely she was gaining some monetary reward in return for delivering Georgina's fortune to him. There was no reason to hope the coachman, hired by Lydia to preserve their secrecy, would now abet an escape. Georgiana had become the foolish girl from every cautionary tale, willingly placing herself into the power of those who would use her, exploit her, and ruin her future for their own ends.

How to stop them? How to escape?

She had allowed herself to be put to bed like a great baby, but it did not matter. It behoved her to let them believe she was still their puppet.

Lydia had taken control of the funds they had with them for the journey, but Georgiana had a little. How much would fare returning to London cost? How much would be the cost for a fare to anywhere, anywhere at all? It was an unacceptable notion—to arrange to travel, *by herself,* on a common conveyance with all manner of *strangers*? But her fear and disgust were crushed by her aversion to a meek acceptance of her fate.

Their current inn, The Crown, was a fine establishment beyond the bustling town of Wetherby—unlikely that the post stopped here. How to find the nearest stop?

Pinning her plaits up was easy, but dressing herself took a great deal of bother, and she was not sure she managed every button, tape and hook; she forgot her hat entirely. But finally she threw her fur-trimmed pelisse over the whole thing and called it good enough.

Her eyes fell upon her pearl ear bobs, which could be worth money to someone. As quickly and quietly as possible, she gathered up anything of value that would fit into the pockets of her carriage dress. She stuffed such wardrobe items as could fit into her valise, as there was no way to manage the trunks without the fuss of hiring help to carry them and leaving behind witnesses to her departure. And for the first time in her life, the expense concerned her.

All was quiet; Lydia often went out after Georgiana was abed. Or to George's room, perhaps? Or was she just next door, listening even now to ensure her idiot charge did not flee in the night? Georgiana's belly roiled.

From her window, she could see the dark, quiet yard bathed in moonlight. Wetherby was perhaps a mile distant. Her plan was simple: slip down the servants' stairs, out the back, and walk to Wetherby. At the first civilised establishment, ask about the post and hope one was leaving soon, going anywhere except north, from someplace nearby. And hope there were no thieves or ravishers on the road between here and Wetherby. And hope no one at The Crown saw her leave. And hope Lydia and George were not waiting to pounce even now, preventing her departure. And hope she had enough money to reach safety.

So many hopes. So many fears.

Stupid, stupid child. She forced herself to leave the temporary haven of her room.

Doncaster, Yorkshire County

Doncaster was a bustling metropolis, with a population of nearly seven thousand. It supported several posting inns and the famed annual St. Leger races. Lizzy looked around with interest, as this would be the longest stop on the entire route. While other passengers traipsed into The Little Red Lion for a meal, she questioned the yard's inhabitants, earning suspicion and even contempt—but no new clues related to Miss Darcy.

Since she had some time, she extended her walk along Market Place, where Doncaster's inhabitants had been selling wares out of stalls since medieval times. The pungent scents and noisy chatter of customers blended into a cacophony beating at her poor fatigued brain. Smiling at the absurd thought of an eloping heiress haggling over a mackerel, she asked no more questions and purchased a meat pasty. Just as she determined it time to return to the Little Red Lion, a bright yellow chaise pulled up at an inn, directly in her path.

Lizzy watched as an older man let himself down and then turned to assist two other female passengers. Briefly, she was overcome with envy as she compared it to the impossibly crowded, uncomfortable mail coach.

You mustn't waste time wallowing in self-pity, Lizzy.

As she moved away, her eye caught on an oddity. The younger of the two females' costume was in the latest style, a carmine red velvet pelisse with ermine trim. For all the fashion of her dress, she was hatless—her hair dishevelled, a plaited blonde coronet mostly tumbled from its pins. If her missing hat was an anomaly, her resemblance to the description of the fifteen-year-old Miss Darcy was uncanny.

Her costume met with some mishap.'Tis coincidental that she perfectly matches Miss Darcy's description.

Inexplicably, however, she quickened her pace towards the Yellow Bounder. *I must question her, even though it* cannot *be her.*

Just before reaching the threesome, however, her common sense returned. The girl could easily be Miss Darcy, but her companions, an older couple, were certainly not a rascally bridegroom and Lydia Younge. The girl stared at her feet, her demeanour one of abject misery. The other two maintained a lecturing pose—a mother and father, disciplining their daughter. Probably for losing her hat. Lizzy was growing foolish in her fatigue and anxiety.

Turning away, she had just taken a step towards Church Street and the Red Lion when she heard—very clearly—a masculine voice in a carrying, ponderous tone say, "Hear, hear now, Miss Darcy! Tears will do you no good at all—this day-long silence is ridiculous! You must tell us what you are about, so far from home, unaccompanied!"

Lizzy froze in her tracks, whirling. Miss Darcy? *Miss Darcy?*

Her mind racing at a thousand thoughts a second, she darted towards them—having no idea what she would say—only that she must somehow, some way, protect the girl from bearing the full brunt of her rash mistakes, if it could be accomplished.

Luckily, an idea occurred to her in the very moment she approached. Mimicking Jane's sternest, harshest governess, Miss Persons, Lizzy called out, "Miss Darcy!" imbuing her voice with starchy fervour. "There you are at last. I do not hesitate to inform you Mr Darcy is most severely displeased!"

All three of them turned to her with similar expressions of surprise —none more so than Miss Darcy.

"And who might you be?" the older man asked with suspicion.

But Miss Persons was a past master of that particular emotion, so Lizzy merely mimicked how that governess would reply to such an inquiry.

"Impertinence!" she accused violently. "More to the point, who are *you*, sirrah, and what are you doing here with Miss Darcy?"

"Impertinence?" the older woman gasped while her companions gaped. "If *you* have *charge* of this young lady, why did we find her at an inn, *alone*, some *thirty* miles north of *here*?"

"*I* answer only to Mr Darcy, or Colonel Fitzwilliam," she replied snippily, refusing to be cowed by this valid accusation. "Miss Darcy also answers *only* to those good gentlemen, who are even now awaiting word from me," she added for good measure, because, frankly, Miss Darcy's silence was the best possible response, and Lizzy tried to convey—by a pointed look to the young lady in question—that she ought to maintain it.

The older man sputtered and the woman narrowed her eyes. Miss Darcy, on the other hand, somewhat visibly calmed at the mention of her brother and cousin, though she could not hide the apprehension in her expression.

"Your name, madam," the man insisted.

How to answer him? If she gave the alias, would the rather obvious, indiscreet search of "Miss Jones" come to light? In that instant, she decided the truth would better serve.

"Miss Bennet." Lizzy enunciated, with just enough contempt to be obvious she considered his manners sorely lacking.

"*This* is your companion, Miss Darcy?" he asked the young lady.

Lizzy tensed, but Miss Darcy half-heartedly cast her lot in with the unknown Miss Bennet, hoping for the best. "As she says," she assented.

"I am Mr Rushworth," the man said, condescension dripping from every syllable. He nodded towards his wife. "Mrs Rushworth," he added.

That woman raised her brows and lifted her chin in bare acknowledgement.

"Friends of Miss Darcy's lady aunt," he added.

"Lady Catherine?" Lizzy asked, pulling the name out of her memory.

"Indeed. We dined with her not a fortnight past. And we do not mind telling you, Miss Bennet, we find this whole situation *most* irregular."

"That, my good sir, is because it *is* most irregular. It wants Mr Darcy, as I think you will agree, and *at once*. If you would be so good as to procure lodging for us, I will send for him immediately."

"He is in Doncaster?" Mrs Rushworth questioned.

"He is searching for his sister, of course! I will send expresses to intercept him. I have every confidence we shall quickly do so." *Perhaps not every confidence. I shall also rely upon the power of prayer.*

Mrs Rushworth decided it time to impose her own authority. "It is my duty as a friend of the family to see to her safety and to advise Miss Darcy in this, *ahem*, irregular situation," she lectured. "I hesitate to place her in the care and company of the person who has *obviously* lost sight of her once before."

Lizzy drew herself up to her full height. "Mr Darcy, I trust, will explain to you—if indeed he decides you must know anything about it —the circumstances, which are *not* due to any lack of vigilance on *my* part. Miss Darcy requires a companion, and thus I am obliged to act, and shall not leave her. I, madam, answer to him and only him. Let me disabuse you of the notion that I would violate that trust by abandoning her to the guardianship of others, no matter how distinguished."

Lizzy's sour expression made apparent her personal opinion of the Rushworths's eminence. "Naturally, when he arrives, he may make any other arrangements as he sees fit."

"You are very disrespectful of your elders, Miss Bennet," Mrs Rushworth said.

"I seek only to do my duty by Mr and Miss Darcy," Lizzy replied self-righteously.

Mr Rushworth, however, now interrupted, in a somewhat softened manner—prompted, perhaps, by the frequency with which Lizzy trotted out Mr Darcy's name, or, most likely, so there might be no more delay in sitting down to his next meal. "It is no use standing about in all our dirt, arguing," he pronounced decidedly. "I will see to our rooms. Miss Bennet will wish to send her expresses as quickly as possible." He turned on his heel and strode towards the inn, leaving the rest of the party no choice but to follow.

GEORGIANA DID NOT KNOW WHAT TO THINK AS SHE TRAIPSED UPSTAIRS, Mrs Rushworth in front of her and Miss…um, Bennet as rear-guard. Had Fitzwilliam discovered her absence and hired this…this dragon to find her? She was certainly dusty enough to have been travelling some ways; her clothing was plain, dark, and ugly, as befitting a fusty sort of companion. The kind who might even take a switch to her for her misdeeds. A shiver of fear crept up her spine.

Another alternative, that Miss Bennet was somehow connected to Lydia and George, was equally likely. If so, Georgiana could not risk exposure before the Rushworths, who were well-acquainted with Lady Catherine. The only thing to do was wait and see, perhaps attempting yet another escape.

The Rushworths were well-known at this establishment. With a minimum of fuss, the innkeeper's wife led her to a clean and comfortable room, opening another door inside, a narrow servant's room adjoining Miss Darcy's, for her supposed companion. Georgiana stood quietly as Miss Bennet ordered Miss Darcy a bath and dismissed the woman, who shut the door behind her. And then they were alone.

"Well, that was awkward," Miss Bennet said, heaving a sigh and dropping her pinched manner as she loosed the ribbons of her hat. "I thought Mrs Rushworth was going to order my arrest for misplacing you. Thank you for not explaining I never had you in the first place."

Georgiana nearly gasped in fright at the sudden change from dragon-like to jaunty. This woman *must* be from Lydia!

"Wh-who are you?" she managed, eyeing the door.

"Miss Bennet, as I said. Your brother and I have been searching for you, and a merry chase you've led."

"Fitzwilliam…searched for me?"

"Oh, yes. Unfortunately, you had been gone some days before we discovered you were missing. I, um, assisted Mr Darcy."

Georgiana remained suspicious. Miss Bennet did not look like the sort of person her brother would employ. *Unless* she acted dragon-like in his presence, as she had for the Rushworths.

"Will you send for him?" Georgiana asked tentatively. Plainly, the only way to determine the truth was to see her brother, although the thought of facing him terrified her almost as much as the Rushworths' interrogations.

"I will send an express to your London home," Lizzy answered, her expression serious. "I could also try sending for Colonel Fitzwilliam, if you know his direction."

Georgiana was confused by this information, momentarily forgetting to be frightened. "Wait, I— he—Fitzwilliam—is in London? He is not, um, searching?"

"Oh, he didn't really suppose you'd *left* London. We followed your trail from Ramsgate to town. He believed Mrs Younge brought you to London for amusements and such. I had information from a maid at The Swan that you continued north, and we had an, um, disagreement regarding how to proceed. So he stayed and I kept on."

Georgiana felt her first thread of hope. "Oh...Miss Bennet...is there any way he could possibly, um, *continue* believing that? If you could return me to Darcy House at once and not–not mention where you found me? I vow I would never, ever do such a thing as this again."

Miss Bennet smiled sympathetically. "If only," she said. "However, I sent a letter to him from Stamford—where *I* discovered the elopement. There is a slight possibility he could already have received that letter and even now be on his way north to stop the wedding. Also, there is the small matter of the Rushworths. They do not seem the sort to keep mum. How did you come to be with them?"

Georgiana crumpled into the hearthside chair. "I...I did not want to elope. I wanted to go home. George is not at all how he pretended to be in the beginning and Lydia—um, Mrs Younge—"

"You needn't explain Lydia to me." Miss Bennet took the other chair. "It was my concerns about her that led your brother to investigate whether or not you'd really gone to Rosings Park in the first place. So, how did you get away from her and...George, did you say?"

Georgiana, desperate for a sympathetic shoulder, threw caution to the winds and decided to trust Miss Bennet.

"Yes, George." A stab of sorrow pierced her. "I knew him when I was young and then it seemed he was a friend of Lydia's and I thought...that is, I have since come to realise I was their dupe."

Miss Bennet laid her hand on Georgiana's in mute sympathy, instead of tendering sharp agreement with her conclusions; Georgiana appreciated the gesture.

"I tried to slow us as much as possible. I have never been a great traveller, but I feigned prodigious carriage sickness."

"I thought you travelled terrifically slow. Very clever."

"I do not know what I hoped to achieve by it. I suppose I was miserable and hoped I would gain more courage," Georgiana admitted. "Finally, I could not tolerate another moment and I tried to insist upon a–a real wedding at the chapel at Pemberley instead of—you know."

"I can imagine how well that went over," Miss Bennet said.

"Yes. I finally realised they were—they did not care if I was happy or miserable. And I think—I think they—they…Lydia and George… were…" she trailed off.

"Lovers?" Miss Bennet asked matter-of-factly. "Very likely."

The girl could not help but be impressed by Miss Bennet's candour. She did not speak to Georgiana as if she were a young child to be wrapped in cotton wool. Of course, Lydia had not treated her as a child either, but she mocked and teased Georgiana for her innocence, making her feel ashamed if she was not worldly. Miss Bennet seemed straightforward, but not scornful.

"Yes," Georgiana agreed. "I did not know what to do or how to buy fare or *anything*. I had to get away from there…to–to escape. I knew it was a risk, but I had no choice. I waited until they believed me abed. I left the inn where we were putting up, walking back towards Wetherby. It was perhaps a mile and I was terrified," she continued, remembering how every breeze-blown leaf seemed a ravisher ready to pounce.

"At the first posting inn I came to, I saw the Rushworths. I have dined with them several times while visiting my aunt. I was so relieved to see familiar, *safe*, faces, I simply dissolved in a weeping fit at Mrs Rushworth's feet. Of course, they wanted to know why I was there by myself, but I could not tell them." She shuddered. "They were angry that I would not say anything for myself, and they planned to return me to Lady Catherine, who is in town. I am afraid I feigned carriage sickness *again*, to slow the journey."

Miss Bennet patted her hand. "You did well to escape Lydia and this George person. And it was wise not to admit anything to the Rushworths. They may suspect, but they do not *know*."

This bit of sympathy put paid to the last of Miss Darcy's composure. She wept, while Miss Bennet held her hand and relinquished her last clean handkerchief. The arrival of writing materials, a hip bath, and pitchers of hot water, however, soon distracted the young lady from her tears. While the maid helped Georgiana bathe, Miss Bennet wrote out her express, addressing it to Darcy House in London.

DARCY RODE HELL FOR LEATHER NORTHBOUND BESIDE AN EQUALLY determined Colonel Fitzwilliam. If they made haste for the border, there were still slight odds of overtaking the eloping couple.

And so, it was with a sense of dread that he spied in the distance a dark green carriage exactly like his own—travelling south towards them.

His sharp eyes did not recognise the coachman but knew they had taken a man hired by Mrs Younge. *Oh no!*

"Colonel," he called, slowing his horse and pointing.

Richard drew abreast of Darcy, looking long and hard at the carriage.

"Could be yours," he said sorrowfully. "But if they are returning… we are too late."

"It is not too late for me to run my sword through his treacherous heart and make Georgiana a widow," Darcy pointed out.

"Excellent idea. I say though, you must allow me to do any slaying. After all, I act for His Majesty and Wickham is officially a deserter, who I predict will resist arrest," Richard replied.

"Killjoy," Darcy muttered.

They waited in the middle of the deserted road while the carriage approached. As it drew closer, they could see the coachman put his hand on what was undoubtedly a pistol, but as the colonel was in full uniform, they also witnessed his uncertainty. The carriage halted when they were still some distance away.

"Your name, sir," the colonel called.

The paunchy man opened and closed his mouth, obviously debating speech. Richard put his hand on his pistol.

"Bartles, sir," he quickly replied. "Ollie Bartles. What be the trouble?"

"The trouble is a carriage exactly matching this description has been reported stolen, and its owner's sister kidnapped," the Colonel answered coolly.

Even from where they sat, they could see Bartles turn a deathly shade of pale.

"I d–don't know naught about it, sir," Bartles stammered. "I was 'ired ta take some nobs north, and hay'nt done naught but drive 'em!"

Darcy watched the door to the carriage open, a golden-haired man pushing his way out: George Wickham, wearing an army uniform a bit worse for wear and a familiar cocksure expression. "What in blazes is the problem?" he asked, carelessly holding a pistol.

For just one moment, as he laid his eyes on Darcy and the colonel, alarm was evident. But only for a moment, quickly replaced by his usual smirk.

"Why, my good friend Fitzwilliam," he said. "With company. Lovely."

"Where the devil is my sister?" Darcy snapped.

Wickham's smirk only widened. "Ooh! Swearing from the good Vicar Darcy! My, my, we are in a passion today! Sadly Vicar, your little bird has flown." He made a graceful motion of bird wings flapping with one slim hand. "Changed her mind—prerogative of females everywhere, don't you know. However, for a reasonable sum, I can ensure no one hears about her...flight."

Darcy did not change expression. He glanced over at Richard. "Kill him," he said.

Richard tossed the reins of his horse over to Darcy. "Gladly," he replied, dismounting.

Finally, Wickham's smile faltered. "Wait one moment," he said backing away and raising his pistol.

"Oh, do fire it," Richard said, grinning evilly, still striding forward. "It will look so much better in my report."

"Re–report?" Wickham stuttered, shifting his weight, glancing from side to side, plainly searching for some avenue of escape.

"Yes. The one recounting the capture of a deserter, gambler, and carriage thief who dared fire on a colonel when cornered like a rat," Richard explained. "The report of your death."

At that moment, Lydia Younge poked her head out of the window, hat askew, rouge smeared. "Wickham?" she croaked. "What is happening, darling?"

George used the slight distraction to throw the pistol at the colonel and run, heading for a nearby forested area. But Darcy was ready. Kicking his mount, he sailed past the befuddled Lydia and still-grinning Richard. In seconds he was upon the fugitive, glad now he had kept a whip handy as well as sword and pistols. With one smooth motion he lashed out, the rope cinching tightly around Wickham's left ankle and sending him sprawling face-first into the dirt.

Darcy drew his pistol. "Get up," he said.

Wickham rolled to his front, his mouth bleeding, his two front teeth missing. "Wait...wait," he cried. "I won't say a word. I swear, I will never speak of this! I never touched her, I swear it!" Except with his damaged mouth, it came out sounding like "Way...way, I won shay a wod, I shware, I will neser shpeek ob dis! I nesher tusht her, I shware id!"

Darcy's only answer was the cock of his pistol. Somewhere behind him, Lydia shrieked.

"I shware id," Wickham sobbed, snot and tears and blood mingling on his face and dribbling onto his dirty uniform as he tried to rise. "Arrgh! My ankle…I shink it's broken! Neber say a wod, I shware id!"

"Shut. Your. Mouth," Darcy said, his voice low, red hazing his vision. The pistol's weight felt perfect in his hand. Georgiana was one in a long line of females whose lives the scoundrel had ruined. Bleeding out in this remote Yorkshire countryside was a better death than he deserved.

Evidently Wickham saw the truth in Darcy's rage. His life nearly over, he fell perfectly still.

"Where is she?" Darcy growled.

"I shware I do nod know," Wickham whined. "She ran away 'rom us at Weserby. She was daken up by an older couple, s-shomeone she knew apparendly. Name is…name is–is Rudwey, Russwords, somesing like. Went soud," he mewled, pointing in the southward direction. "I shware, dere's nussing else!"

"Darcy," Richard's voice called from nearby, soft and easy, even jovial, beckoning him back from the murderous edge of fury. "Methinks you have new quarry to trail in these Rudley-Rudworths. Allow me to manage these rogues."

Darcy glanced at Lydia Younge, her expression horrified, peering at them from just beyond his cousin, tears leaving trails of kohl and face powder on her cheeks.

"One word," Darcy said lowly, his voice full of hostile intent. "If I ever hear my sister's name connected to either of you, even one word of scandal, there is no corner of hell where you can hide. I will not care for my life, my fortune, my name, or my honour in this pursuit. Do you believe me?"

Wickham nodded, his eyes showing white all the way around the pupil in his fear.

Lydia was stupider. "B-but *she* may have spoken—these people that took her with them—"

"Pray she does not," Darcy hissed. "And you might yet live." His eyes narrowed on her. "That is my sister's necklace around your throat."

With fumbling fingers, she reached to unclasp it, yanking it off her neck in her hurry to be rid of the thing, allowing it to fall to the ground.

Richard picked it up on the point of his short sword. "Mrs Younge," he said politely. "We have not been introduced, but I believe you know my father. Matlock? Yes? I fear you have not been at all discreet, and you know how he despises indiscretion." Making a tsking noise, he tossed the necklace off the tip of his sword to Darcy, who caught it easily.

Lydia paled. Darcy holstered his pistol and turned to his cousin.

"Will you provide escort to this filth? Perhaps some authority at Ferrybridge can take them. 'Tis but a mile or two, I believe."

"'Two would be my pleasure. We shall send the carriage on," Richard said. "I believe Mr Bartles and I will come to a right understanding about what should and should not be said regarding our little adventure. 'Tis a lovely day for a ramble."

"Walk?" Lydia began in protest, but catching sight of the colonel's maniacally cheerful expression, closed her mouth. He had never resembled his father the earl more than he did at this moment.

"I–I can'd walk," George wailed. "My ankle, I shink id's brok—"

"I would be happy to drag you behind my horse," Richard said pleasantly. "Or perhaps you can walk, after all. Shall we try it, hmm?"

"Stand up, Wickham!" Lydia squeaked. "By all that is holy, *stand*!"

George managed to drag himself up, wincing in pain.

Darcy shrugged and turned away from the pair. "Thank you, Colonel. I will leave word every place I change mounts."

"Godspeed, Darcy," Richard nodded, giving his cousin a small salute as he thundered southward on the Great North Road. Turning to his 'guests' with a mock gesture of politeness, he asked, "Shall we?"

15

Lizzy and Georgiana joined the Rushworths in a private room for the evening meal. Neither anticipated it with any degree of delight, but their hosts were insistent. Lizzy, at least, had procured her trunk from The Little Red Lion, the mail coach thankfully having left it behind. In her cleanest black dress, her hair tightly scraped into her best imitation of a chignon, she braced herself for the encounter.

Georgiana made do with having her only dress brushed and freshened; she felt she would rather starve than face the Rushworths again, but Lizzy was reassuring.

"Simply say nothing," Lizzy cautioned the younger girl before leaving the room. "Answer no questions. Dissolve into tears if you must, but no more stomach complaints. They will assume you are with child, if they don't already."

Georgiana gasped. "I would not—"

Lizzy sighed and gentled her voice. "Truth matters little to gossips. They leap to precisely the worst possible conclusion fitting known facts. Silence is your best friend. Pray keep your mouth closed and disregard them, even if they cut up rough. The *only* person you answer to is your brother. You owe the Rushworths *nothing.*"

"They did rescue me," Georgiana said in a small voice.

"You were a female alone and in distress. They did as anyone with a grain of kindness ought, and your brother will compensate them for any little expense or delay incurred. Simply limit your conversation upon this matter to thanks for their kind assistance and say no more." Lizzy guided the girl through the door, feeling her tremble as she clutched Lizzy's arm.

"I will not allow them to bully you," Lizzy assured. "By using your head for something besides a hat perch, you routed two experienced scoundrels. They did not expect your courage or determination, and thus you are free of them."

"I was more terrified than brave," Georgiana admitted.

"Anyone with sense would be. Thank goodness you had courage to take action regardless. You are safe now, and your brother will be here soon."

"I am more afraid of him, I think, than that long, dark road into Wetherby," Georgiana said morosely.

Lizzy looked askance. "He is the last man on earth to be feared."

"You have never seen him in–in an ill humour."

"Of course I have! Did you think your disappearance cheered him? That knowing his young sister was in the clutches of an untrustworthy companion *he* hired cast him into transports of delight? You cannot always expect a placid pool of calm from a man of such deep passions. Only remember he will do all in his power to protect you, both from the consequences of your own choices and from the Lydias and the Rushworths of the world."

Georgiana stared at her. *Man of deep passions?* Fitzwilliam was cold, strict, and unfeeling! If he protected her, it was due to his fears she would dishonour their name if he allowed her the tiniest morsel of independence or amusement!

Not that I have disproved his supposition. Before she could dispute Miss Bennet's estimation of her brother, they were at the door of the dining parlour.

Watching with something like amazement, her companion transformed from "elder sister" to the dragon-like governess Georgiana had first believed her to be. Miss Bennet's eyes narrowed, mouth pinched, her features firming into a perpetual expression of disapproval before she rapped imperiously on the door.

Who is she? Georgiana followed her into the room.

TWO MORE DISAGREEABLE PERSONS THAN MR AND MRS RUSHWORTH,

Lizzy had seldom met. She assumed she and Miss Darcy should remain at The Crown and Cushion until Mr Darcy appeared. Unfortunately, however, there was *limitless* opposition to this course.

"Of course, *you* may stay and await Mr Darcy's arrival," Mr Rushworth declared condescendingly. "However, Mrs Rushworth and I cannot, in good conscience, depart without Miss Darcy."

"Delaying the reunion of brother and sister is unacceptable. I feel certain he will arrive at any moment!"

"We *cannot* wait," Mrs Rushworth pronounced. "We have an invitation to Lady Rudridge's soirée on Friday. Lady Catherine brought Mr Rushworth's article, published by The British Horticultural Society, to her notice," she added smugly. "She is devoted to her gardens and eagerly awaits Mr Rushworth's advice for successful plantings of *Hydrangea macrophylla*. We expect to deliver Miss Darcy directly to the loving bosom of her *family*."

There was something vulgar about their keenness for the task; Lizzy tried calm rationale and clever argument, but nothing penetrated their determination. It was plain they *relished* serving up this little spectacle to Lady Catherine, raising more than the subject of hydrangeas at the soirée.

Other than a few fine pieces of jewellery, Miss Darcy had even less ready cash than Lizzy. It seemed unnecessarily dramatic to pawn family heirlooms to escape the Rushworths. It would likely be better to accompany them to London, making a push to reach Mr Darcy once there. Surely he could contain his aunt and her cronies? Lizzy would send another express tonight informing him of their route, as well as leaving word at every place they stopped, and, of course, stay alert for any sign of his tall form galloping to Miss Darcy's rescue. It was the best she could do.

Thus, early the next morning, Lizzy found herself seated beside a subdued Miss Darcy, her forward view the twin looks of disapproval on the Rushworths' faces. Given half a chance, they would gladly have quit her at The Crown and Cushion, but she was not so foolish as to permit it; without the incentive of fetching his sister, Mr Darcy would see her rot at that inn, and she hadn't the means to pay for it herself. Besides, there was still a chance any scandal could be contained, if she could concoct a tame story covering all the known details.

The weather was lovely, the rented carriage comfortable, and she was clean and well-rested. Mrs Rushworth disregarded the girls entirely in order to complain to Mr Rushworth about the various imperfections of her neighbours. Absent any conversation from her seat-mate, Lizzy enjoyed the rustic scenery of Nottinghamshire.

It was on a lonely stretch of road in the Nottinghamshire Wolds that all peace was abolished, and hiding Miss Darcy's aborted elopement became the least of Lizzy's worries.

A giant of a man appeared out of nowhere, masked and armed to the teeth, sitting upon his equally large steed, blocking the narrow stretch of road.

"Stand and deliver yer money an' rum goods, or I'll shoot you dead!" he called menacingly.

The postilion reined in his team; Mrs Rushworth screamed.

Another man, also masked, emerged from the woods on foot. Much portlier, huffing and puffing and growling threats, he, too, was fully armed. "Shut it!" he snarled at the shrieking woman, and such was her fear, she actually obeyed.

Lizzy took Miss Darcy's trembling hand in hers. "Be calm," she whispered. "We haven't much. We'll offer it and they'll go away." *I hope.*

The paunchy one approached their vehicle, throwing open the door, while the mounted robber kept his pistols trained on the postilion.

"Hand it all over! Yer money an' yer watch!" he shouted at Mr Rushworth.

Mr Rushworth, though sweating profusely, with Mrs Rushworth's prodding, found courage to mount a weak protest. "Now see here," he began, but the robber shoved the pistol against his breast.

"Alls I wants ta see is yer goods!" he bellowed, withdrawing a canvas bag from his coat. "Into the sack with all of it! Now!"

Thus terrorised, Mr Rushworth made haste to empty his pockets. His watch and what appeared to be a goodly sum of cash dropped into the robber's satchel.

"Pass the sack!" he shouted at Mr Rushworth, who hurriedly obeyed, handing it to his wife. "The rings!" the blackguard added threateningly, and she, too, complied, sobbing with indignation and fury as her jewellery disappeared into the bag. He turned the pistol on Lizzy.

She was ready, quickly emptying her reticule of her meagre store. She had a sovereign in her shoe, and another sewn into the lining of her stays, but as she dressed as plainly as a servant, no more was expected. It pained her to surrender her garnet ring from Mr Wickham, but she pulled the chain from her neck before he could demand it.

Finally he turned his weapon on a shivering Miss Darcy, who was frozen in place. "Yer ear bobs!" he shouted. "*Now!*"

But Georgiana was too frightened to move, staring in horror at the pistol. He repeated the action that had worked to such good effect on Mr Rushworth, jabbing the weapon to her heart.

Unfortunately, not only did it fail to call Georgiana to action, but provoked Mr Rushworth to discover his gallantry at last.

"Villainy, sir!" he cried. "Do you know who you offend? Dare you perpetrate assault upon the sister of the esteemed Fitzwilliam Darcy, whose estate is the grandest in all of Derbyshire! Have you not heard of Pemberley? Does the Darcy name mean nothing to you? The granddaughter of an earl, the niece of the Bishop of Derby, you brigand!"

Lizzy closed her eyes. *No, no, no! Please don't listen to him, please be simple, stupid robbers satisfied with a few pounds —*

"Are ye, now?" the robber drawled, his evil grin—complete with startling golden tooth—pronouncing him every bit as ambitious as Lizzy feared. "Seems we found us a grander booty! Come wit' me, yer Majesty!" With a meaty hand, he grabbed her arm, pulling Georgiana out of the carriage. She stumbled and fell to the ground in a trembling heap.

"No!" Mr Rushworth cried, lunging forward. But the robber turned the pistol towards him and cocked it. Back down went Mr Rushworth, not to rise again. Mrs Rushworth screamed, and the weapon speedily turned on her. It had an extremely quieting effect.

"No cause ta make a fuss," the robber assured smilingly, his gold tooth gleaming. "If this Mister Sir Darcy of Pem-burr-lee wants 'is sister back, 'e can spare a few coins for the fellahs 'oo'll be lookin' after 'er. Tell 'im to leave five 'undred pounds at the north shore of Crag's Lake, midnight, say, three days 'ence. Not so much ransom fer such a pretty leetle piece, eh?"

Wresting the sack from Lizzy's frozen fingers, he began backing away from the carriage. "An' if 'e wants 'er alive, 'e'd better come alone with me winnings!"

"Excuse me," Lizzy said composedly, speaking clearly in her best governess's voice. "If Miss Darcy is departing with you, I shall accompany her."

Mrs Rushworth gasped, and the robber actually laughed. "Beg pardon, precious, but you's not worth a ransom nor the trouble."

"If Miss Darcy's value concerns you at all, you will take me with her. As everyone knows, a young lady is *never* left alone with, ahem, gentlemen." She sniffed, indicating her low opinion of his *gentlemanliness*. "If she is considered ruined merchandise on the marriage mart, her value diminishes. My presence will protect the prize, and thus your investment," she said evenly, as if she were explaining a simple lesson in economics.

The robber frowned. "You 'spect me to b'lieve 'er fam'ly won't pay unless yer stuck to 'er?"

"I am saying she is worth far more if her reputation is safeguarded. She has no father or mother, depending entirely upon her brother's good will. My presence protects *his* philanthropy. It costs you nothing and ensures a happy outcome for your trouble." Lizzy kept her gaze steady and her demeanour confident, as if her plan were the only practical consideration. The robber pondered her words.

Suddenly he laughed again. "She needs a la-dee-da laidy's maid, does 'er Majesty?"

"I am *not* her maid," Lizzy disagreed calmly. Moving deliberately so as not to startle the men with pistols, she let herself down and extended her hand to the girl huddled on the roadside. "Come now, Miss Darcy. There is no need for hysterics. These, hmm, *gentlemen* will take us somewhere safe where we may await your brother's pleasure."

After a suspenseful moment, as Lizzy envisaged the villains shoving her back into the carriage and carting the girl away, Miss Darcy reached up and took her proffered hand. As soon as she was on her feet, she cowered into Lizzy's side, as if she could make herself smaller.

Instantly, the robber saw the obvious—Miss Darcy was too frightened to sensibly follow orders and be an obedient hostage. He would need the other woman to direct her.

"Come on then," he said gruffly, no longer smiling. He pointed the pistols in the coachman's direction. "Be off wit' ya! Get along now!"

The robber's silent companion on the horse moved aside to allow the carriage to pass, and the frightened postilion took his whip to the team. In moments, the two women were left standing on the deserted road, a cloud of dust the only trace of the Yellow Bounder bearing the Rushworths to safety.

In the grey light of early dawn, Darcy reined in his mount in the yard of the Kingston's Arms. He had now spent over twenty-four hours in the saddle. The confrontation with Wickham, his anxiety over Georgiana and Elizabeth, the events of the past few days, his fatigue and soreness, all served to enervate him completely. There was no sign of his sister. He did not know any longer if he was ahead of or behind her. He needed a change of horse, of clothing, and, as much as he hated to admit it, at least a few hours of sleep. In a gloomy fog, he procured a room, left instruction to wake him in four hours, and used the last of his strength to pull off his boots, collapsing onto the mattress in a dead slumber within minutes.

None of the maid's gentle taps on the door a few hours later penetrated his exhaustion. The sun rose higher in the sky, then began to fade; Darcy slept on.

When he finally awakened, he was enraged by the lateness of the hour, and none of the excuses given by the inn's servants appeased him. When a grumbling Darcy was finally clean, dressed and fed, he took the stairs two at a time in his hurry to depart—only to stop short at the inn's entry as he met a vaguely familiar face.

"Mr Darcy!" cried the older man, his mouth open in shock. Beside him, a female, almost certainly his wife, let out a shriek and promptly swooned. Darcy barely managed to reach her before she hit the floor, her husband still staring stupidly.

The innkeeper and his wife both charged into the fray, but the man continued to gape.

"Mr Darcy!" he repeated, in a trembling, hoarse voice. "Mr Darcy!"

In that moment, Darcy placed him. He had dined with the Rushworths at his aunt's home at least twice before. Their shock at this encounter triggered his memory of Wickham's account of Georgiana's benefactors. Rudworth...Rudley...*Rushworth!*

A sense of foreboding filled his heart. Handing over the fainting woman to the innkeeper with a somewhat inelegant shove, he exclaimed, "Where is my sister?"

"I say...you must understand...nothing I could do to prevent—"

Darcy clenched his fists to counteract the urge to grab the man's lapels and force him to *explain*. Still, he was mindful of the innkeeper's wife gawping at them while her husband struggled with the prone body of Mrs Rushworth.

"We require a private place to talk," he ordered the innkeeper. "And to recover."

Moments later, they were alone in a private parlour. Mrs Rushworth lay on a settee, but—having been dosed with salts—was awake, if avoiding Mr Darcy's eye. Mr Rushworth paced agitatedly around the room.

"Where is my sister?" Darcy asked abruptly. "Out with it, man!"

Rushworth quailed at the expression on Darcy's face, but managed —with several stops and starts, and manifold excuses—to tell of discovering Miss Darcy, the chance meeting with Miss Bennet, followed by his sad tale of robbery and kidnap.

"Why did you not remain in Doncaster? Miss Bennet sent for me! A logical course of action would be to *await* my *arrival!*" Darcy promptly disregarded the fact he likely would have missed the express.

"Where was your footman? How did you expect to be able to protect them?" His rage and fear were a weight upon his chest, a tight-ness in his throat, a red haze across his vision.

"We have made this journey dozens of times without," Rushworth sniffed. "Road has always been safe! We, um, had an important event to attend in London, as we explained to Miss B–Bennet! Told her she could stay and wait for you! We could scarcely leave your sister alone with an unknown servant!"

"Miss Bennet is hardly a servant!" Darcy snapped.

"She said she was! Miss Darcy's companion, she said!" He paused for a moment at the furious expression upon Darcy's face, attempting to recall the conversation. "Or at least, she did not correct our impression! W–we determined it best to deliver your sister directly to L–lady Catherine, who is in London even now." Then, like the narrow-minded man he was at heart, he launched his best offensive weapon, his voice gaining assurance. "After all, we discovered your sister *alone*, in Wetherby of all places! Miss Bennet was *alone* in Doncaster! Who can tell how many others also saw them unaccompanied and *wondered* at it! I protected Miss Darcy's reputation by keeping her in our *respectable* company!"

"Devil take her reputation if you could not protect *her!*" Darcy contended. The Rushworths adopted almost comical dual expressions of mixed superiority and fear.

Darcy had made it a habit of many years never to speak a lie; if he could not speak honestly, he would not speak at all. Simply because he was unused to deception, however, did not mean he could not employ the art, and this petty fellow had the power to *ruin* his sister.

After all, it is in my blood.

"You did *not* save my sister. You *took* her from me," he reproved, using the authority-laced reprimand cultivated by his ancestors for centuries. "I travelled through Wetherby with a party that included my sister. Unfortunately, she grew distraught at one point and childishly allowed her anger to overrule her judgment. She fled from our party when we believed her to be abed, and apparently was taken up by you. I and other members of my party, including Miss Bennet and my cousin, Colonel Fitzwilliam, have been searching for her ever since."

Mrs Rushworth chose that moment to give free rein to her rampant curiosity.

"Why would a young girl of good breeding and sense leave her loved ones in a strange town, making herself vulnerable to rogues and strangers?" she asked disapprovingly.

Darcy had known vague assurances would not do, not with such scandalmongers as the Rushworths. He had to give them something more shocking than Georgiana's behaviour or his sister would never be able to hold up her head in society again. With a silent apology to Elizabeth, he handed them the gossip of a lifetime.

"I fear she was deeply upset about my prospective marriage to Miss Bennet," he replied coldly. "We journeyed to Scotland to be wed. I only guess at this conclusion, unfortunately, as you *stole* her from my protection before I could ask her what she meant by it."

Both Rushworths gasped at this disclosure. Mr Rushworth's expression revealed his utter shock; Mrs Rushworth's revealed utter glee at possession of such a thrilling *on dit.*

"Miss Bennet!" Mr Rushworth exclaimed. "You cannot mean *her*!"

Darcy's expression grew so wintry, Rushworth actually took a step back. "I *can* mean it, and I do. As you can imagine, Miss Bennet was deeply distressed by Miss Darcy's flight. Colonel Fitzwilliam and I left her and her maid in Doncaster to continue our search more efficiently by horse. Did you even think to *ask* her what became of her maid? Did it cross your mind to *offer* to secure another servant for her before you attempted to abandon her *alone* in Doncaster?"

"W–we thought she *was* the servant," Rushworth replied weakly.

"Had you only stayed put, as I feel sure Miss Bennet begged you to do, we would not be in this predicament. I am tempted to bring charges against *you* for the abduction of my sister and my betrothed!"

Both Rushworths cried out in instant alarm.

"She did not tell us of–of her wedding plans," Mrs Rushworth protested. "She told us nothing at all!"

"Why should she?" Darcy said frostily, with terrible censure. "Did she, or did she not inform you *I* would explain what was important for you to know?"

"She may have done," Rushworth replied sulkily. "But all of it was dashed irregular, if you ask me. And we had to get to London, and we could not abandon Miss Darcy. Besides, we allowed time at every posting inn for Miss Bennet to leave word for you."

Darcy stared at him with absolute loathing. "It behoves you to listen well now—you took my sister and my betrothed under your highhanded, ineffectual protection and you *lost* them. I accuse you of negligence and hold you to blame. If one word of this abduction reaches *anyone*, including Lady Catherine, I consider you personally responsible. You will protect Miss Darcy and Miss Bennet's reputations as you failed to protect their safety, or you may expect severe repercussions."

"It was highwaymen! They had pistols!" Mr Rushworth shrieked.

"And Miss Bennet had the courage to stay by my sister's side regardless, you prodigious coward," Darcy hissed. "Get out of my sight."

M iss Darcy's shudders were apparent to Lizzy even through the clattering of the cart over the lurching, uneven path they travelled. Not that she could offer much comfort; with her hands tied, it was all she could do to keep herself from jolting out of the wagon. They leaned in, supporting each other, trying to stay upright.

Lizzy pretended to be the most docile of hostages in the hopes their abductors' vigilance would ease, allowing opportunity for escape. Miss Darcy had no need for pretence. *She is as spirited as a plucked weed. Had I been reared by a country gentleman, would I have grown soft and weak?*

Lizzy seldom dwelt on "could have beens" or "should have beens." Her life had not been the easiest, certainly not the comfortable life she imagined for a gentleman's daughter. Nevertheless, she *had* learned to manage bullies and aggressors and all manner of scorn. She also knew she was quick and clever and could get the better of detractors, often before they realised they participated in a contest of wits. These were lessons she could use now.

The fat Mr Gold Tooth led the way on the large horse, while his huge companion drove the cart. From their conversation, Mr Gold Tooth appeared to be the organiser of the criminal operation—at least, he offered commentary upon his own brilliance, while the other only contributed vapid agreement. Neither paid the least bit of attention to the two bound females, which meant they were in a sufficiently deserted area that the criminals had no fear of pursuit—or of their hostages' ability to escape.

If alone, Lizzy would gradually shift over to the open end of the cart until she could roll off. From all appearances, these two louts would not notice a thing until they arrived at whatever destination they intended, and even with bound wrists and ankles, she could eventually free herself. But she was *not* alone, and the whole point of joining Miss Darcy in captivity was to effect a rescue. Somehow.

"'Tis in their best interests to ensure you are well-treated," Lizzy whispered. "Their greed will protect you."

Miss Darcy turned her head sharply. "Will it protect you, as well?" she asked with a quiet note of bleakness. "You have no such assurances!"

"You need have no fears on my account!" Lizzy replied. "I can protect myself."

"You do not know that," the younger woman said. "It is bad enough I put myself into foolish, *dangerous* predicaments. I cannot abide the thought of my stupidity endangering others—you!"

Lizzy, despite the difficult circumstances, found a smile. "You are more like your brother than I first thought. Both of you believe somehow you can control life and fate, and, like gods, feel responsible for the actions of all in your purview. You did not ask me to accompany you, and cannot possibly feel accountable because I chose to do so of my own free will."

"Which was perfectly stupid of you!" Miss Darcy hissed. "If this was fated, it was my fate alone! You ought to have left me to it!"

"I hope you do not believe somehow you *deserved* to be abducted? That is unnecessarily dramatic...another trait you share with your brother."

"You are an odd person, Miss Bennet. I can believe my brother thinks himself a god, but dramatic? He is as dramatic as–as that boulder." She pointed with her bound hands at a large stony outcropping, nearly toppling over in making the affected gesture.

"If size and strength and–and *unfeelingness* are *dramatic*, then so he is," Miss Darcy continued fervently. "*I* am not. I am *pragmatical*. And my weakness has led you into danger, and if I wish to be *deeply* distressed by innocent persons bound and dragged heaven-knows-where by fearsome ruffians, then so I shall be!"

"Please, call me Lizzy," Lizzy replied, in response to that—very dramatic—outburst. "Do you often read novels?"

"Wh–what?"

"I see no fearsome ruffians," Lizzy replied reasonably. "I see two shiftless men, one of them likely an idiot, who stumbled upon an easy way to procure money. They pay us no heed. There is no reason to suppose particular danger until we have more evidence of it, and your distress only blinds you to potential opportunities for escape. Mayhap you have read too many gothic novels, so attempt to transform our tedious journey into a thrilling adventure. Why not keep a happier outlook and predict a happier ending, as circumstances still allow for its possibility?"

Miss Darcy stared at her, and Lizzy plainly saw a resemblance between brother and sister, despite the difference in colouring and gender. It was in the aristocratic profile and dimpled chin and potent gaze. Fortunately, they were both also intelligent; Miss Darcy plainly accepted the sense of Lizzy's words, regardless of her natural inclination to histrionics. She no longer shivered in fear and hopefully would resist the temptation to imagine horrific outcomes.

Finally, she sighed gustily. "I still say you are odd, Lizzy," she said. "Please, call me Georgiana."

AFTER A FEW HOURS, DARCY HAD THE GOOD FORTUNE TO REUNITE WITH his cousin. Richard had received one of Darcy's expresses, begging that he dispose of his prisoners and join him forthwith. Accordingly, the colonel had turned Wickham over to the town regiment for transport back to London.

As for Lydia Younge, she made her escape while Richard was otherwise occupied with Wickham; Richard had allowed it, as he had no real charge against her other than general untrustworthiness and betrayal. He believed her fear of his father would keep her from talking out of turn, and fear of him and Darcy would keep her lying low for some time to come. He was, quite simply, too much concerned with the urgency in his cousin's message to do otherwise.

Quickly, Darcy explained what had occurred, and that they had less than three days remaining to acquire the ransom and leave it in the prescribed area. "The scoundrel was clever enough in his impromptu crime," Darcy said bitterly. "I barely have time to procure the money and return to Crag's Lake in time. The site is close to limestone caves and numerous coal mines, not to mention the heart of Sherwood Forest. Abundant hiding places."

"Time enough to institute a full-out search and deal with the attendant gossip if the rogue fails to honour his end of the bargain, I suppose," Richard agreed. "In the meantime, I will scout Nottingham. You go to Pemberley for ransom, I presume?"

"And for men I trust to return with me. I hope to bring Seth Adams and his sons as reinforcements. As much as I despise the idea of paying thieves and kidnappers, I am willing to do so. I have no assurance that the criminals who have my girls will do as promised once they take possession of the ransom. I intend to have a small force of my own."

Richard nodded. "Adams? Is he a tenant?"

"Yes, as was his father and his father before him. As loyal as they come. He has three sons, all of whom are good, strapping lads who inherited their father's quick intelligence," Darcy explained. "They all ride, and they will hold their tongues."

"'Tis as good a plan as any. I will discover what I can and meet you. Do you have any other information? As I recall, 'north shore of Crag's Lake' is a large area. How will you know exactly where to leave the ransom? How does he expect to collect the money and exchange his prisoners?"

"I must assume the kidnapper has calculated a means." His jaw clenched, his teeth grinding as he tried to swallow down his anxiety. "All I can think is to have the money waiting and hope and pray all will be well. Devil of a thing."

Richard reached out and clasped his cousin's shoulder. "I will learn what I can before you return. Have you any description of the criminals?"

Darcy told him what Rushworth remembered, including the golden tooth. They debated seeking out the area's militia, but Darcy too-well recalled the threat Rushworth repeated—any sign of pursuit, and the kidnappers promised to do harm to their captives. For all they knew, these highwaymen were part of a neighbourhood gang with eyes and ears everywhere. Sherwood Forest was notorious for hiding its thieves.

"I have sent word to The White Lion Inn at Hollowstone to keep a room ready for me. I will meet you there upon my return," Darcy said. The colonel promised to use extreme caution in his investigations, and they parted ways.

WHILE DARCY WAS TOO INTENT UPON HIS MISSION TO PAY ANY MIND TO the discomfort of his posterior, by sunset, the abuse of said region was all Lizzy and Georgiana could think of. Lizzy attempted to note their direction, but the trees were too thick and the path too winding.

"If this wagon would only stop, I am sure I would not care if they shoot me," Georgiana muttered, shifting on her hip in a vain attempt to find a more comfortable position.

"I will beg them to shoot in another minute," Lizzy agreed. "But I believe we slow. Hush, listen."

Mr Gold Tooth engaged in impatient instruction to his cohort as they entered a small clearing. Lizzy noted a rough structure, too crude to be called a cottage, at its centre.

"Keep 'em trussed," Mr Gold Tooth directed. "Water's all they need at present. Don' talk to 'em, don' listen to 'em. Just keep 'em quiet and trussed 'til I return with the swag. Got it?"

Goliath-man appeared to contemplate this. "What if dey 'as to…" He faltered, blushing, and risked a glance back at the captives before continuing in an overloud whisper, "…use a *necessary*?"

"Give 'em a bucket, yeh tom-turd," Mr Gold Tooth huffed, dismounting with some effort from the gelding.

Goliath-man's thick, overhanging brow furrowed. "But dey's ladies. Ladies don' use buckets."

"We don' 'ave no golden chamberpots for 'em!" Gold Tooth retorted, chuckling at his own wit. "Now, who does the thinkin' 'round 'ere? Is it me?"

Goliath eagerly nodded his agreement.

"That's right. You do as I says an' we'll be swimmin' in lard. Now, gets 'em down and puts their royal 'ighnesses in their palace." Guffawing at his joke, he nevertheless watched carefully as his accomplice untied the ladies' ankles so they could walk. With little effort, Goliath lifted them down off the cart and led them into the shelter.

Lizzy blinked, trying to adjust to the dark interior. There were two small window openings but no glass, just rude shutters that could be bolted closed. The floor was dirt; there were no tables or chairs. Directly behind her she heard Georgiana's indrawn breath of anxiety or disgust.

Goliath pointed to the floor and ordered them to sit. Goldtooth watched as he rebound their ankles, tying them all the way to the knees. Then Goldtooth made him bind their wrists behind their backs. When it was done to his satisfaction, they were left alone. The girls could hear every word, however, as Goliath was again instructed not to talk to them or unbind them, but to keep a close watch until the ransom was retrieved.

Goldtooth then took leave of his partner—with a few more admonitions—and shortly thereafter, they heard the sounds of his departure on the gelding.

Judging from the noise, Goliath now unhitched the pony from the cart.

"'Tis not as bad as it might be," Lizzy reassured her fellow prisoner quietly. "Listen to how gently our captor speaks to the pony. He can hardly be too great a scoundrel."

"Some men treat their dogs far better than their wives," Georgiana pointed out. "At Pemberley, the stablemaster was known for his skill with animals. He was said to have the healer's touch, and there were always two or three dogs trotting after him wherever he went. And yet, his wife was known for her bruises and blackened eyes. At least until Fitzwilliam discovered the situation."

Lizzy tried not to press for more information about Mr Darcy, but she could not help herself. "What could he possibly do about such a thing?"

"No one is sure precisely how he managed it," Georgiana shrugged. "His wife would not say, or at least, my maid never did hear. But shortly after Brother called upon him, he stopped indulging in spirits and by all reports remains temperate. Fitzwilliam *can* be terrifying though."

Lizzy remembered how he had dealt with the ruffian at The Swan, and had to agree.

Both girls lapsed into silence. They could hear Goliath moving around as daylight faded and it grew colder. The ground was damp, chill seeping into Lizzy's undergarments. She hoped Georgiana wore more petticoats and would stay warmer; at least the girl was thus far uncomplaining. When a light rain pattered upon the leaky roof, they both shifted their rumps to avoid the portion of the "floor" becoming a large mud puddle.

Goliath entered the hut, quickly holding up an overflowing water pail to indicate his purpose. Clumsily, he brought it to Lizzy's lips; she was too parched to do more than drink thirstily of the stale-smelling water. Georgiana did the same, and he departed once again. Eventually, they smelled smoke, then the mouth-watering scent of roasting meat. Their stomachs growled in hunger, but neither complained and Lizzy thought Georgiana rather a good sport for a spoiled heiress. In time, all sounds of activity stilled and finally came the sound of Goliath's snores nearby.

For a time, they positioned themselves back to back, each attempting to loosen the other's bindings. But the knots were too difficult, and their attempts proved futile.

Idly, Lizzy dug her fingers into the ground beneath her, doing her best to force feeling into her cramped fingers…only to discover the wet dirt floor had the slick, gummy texture of clay-rich soil.

"Georgiana," she whispered excitedly. "I have an idea."

It took hours to create the simplest figure. Digging out enough soil while trussed was an enormous challenge; they forced nerveless fingers to paw in the muddy ground, building a pile of it so Lizzy would have enough material to work. By the time she managed to create a figure she thought would do, her bound wrists were bleeding, and her fingers were half frozen. For some time, Georgiana offered encouragement, but as hours passed and exhaustion overtook her, she fell asleep leaning against Lizzy—which at least lent warmth to her left side, if it somewhat inhibited Lizzy's already minimal sculpting dexterity.

In the dark, Lizzy was no judge of whether the figurine would be acceptable, but finally, sleepy and cold, she finished. Scooting away, she set it against the wall furthest from the puddle and their resting place, hoping it would not crumble to nothing before she implemented The Plan.

It wasn't much of a plan, perhaps, but this small creature she blindly created with numb fingers and bound wrists and the dirtiest of clays would have to be enough to save them both. With a sigh, she scooted back to Georgiana, who mumbled a little, wedging herself as close as possible once more. The floor was damp and hard, the night was chill, Lizzy's trussed limbs ached…but at least she was exhausted enough to disregard most discomfort. Moments later, she slept.

LIZZY AWAKENED IN THE GREY DAWN, COLD, DAMP, AND HUNGRY. ALSO, IT was imperative that she use the dreaded *necessary,* and *soon.* Georgiana had managed to roll into a ball and squeeze herself nearly onto Lizzy's lap.

Turning her head to see how the figurine looked in the light of day, she was pleased to see it hadn't disintegrated in the night. It was certainly far cruder than her usual work and very small, but she hoped it would be a weapon sufficient for its mark.

She waited as long as she could to call to Goliath, as she hated to wake Georgiana from the safety of her dreams. Finally, however, the urgency of other considerations trumped all else.

"Oh, sir," she called briskly. "Sir! It is urgent I use the necessary house, if you please."

The snoring stopped, and moments later Goliath appeared in the doorway, his hair sticking out in all directions. He scrubbed at his eyes.

"Ain't no necessary 'ouse 'ere," he mumbled.

Lizzy noted he would not meet her eyes as he said this. *Excellent. He plainly feels guilty about our accommodations, and is not totally lost to human kindness.*

"But, sir," she pled, adding a strong hint of feminine distress to her tone, "it is becoming increasingly *imperative* we be allowed some relief. Please, kind sir!"

Goliath mumbled something unintelligible that included the word "bucket" and pointed at the pail with which he served them water the night before.

Georgiana chose to inform them all she was awake by bursting into noisy tears. "We *drink* from that pail!" she cried, with a superb touch of hysteria. "Surely you would not have a *lady* drink from a vessel used for *such* a purpose!"

"A person could *die* of its foulness," Lizzy added, managing to squeeze out a tear or two of her own.

Goliath appeared utterly befuddled by this display of feminine histrionics from his formerly tranquil captives. Lizzy understood he was a man who was accustomed to being directed, not forming his own solutions. When she felt he was sufficiently at sea, she provided one for him.

"Is there not a place, private yet nearby, where we might…take care of our needs?" Lizzy asked, giving him a strong hint.

Goliath glanced around at the thick surrounding forest. "Um…aye. Trees," he nodded.

"That would do, in our current predicament. Please, untie me, sir?"

Goliath's expression flared with alarm. "I cain't untie ye. Bert'd kill me if I lettcha go."

"But I cannot manage the task without the use of my hands! My *skirts*! Oh, heavens, *cleansing*! Oh, sir!" Lizzy expelled a few more tears. "Please have mercy, kind, kind sir!"

Goliath flushed and looked guilty, but his reluctance remained obvious.

"Sir, we have no *clue* as to our whereabouts. Even if we somehow managed to flee, it would be *foolish* to leave, only to become lost in this awful wilderness, and likely be torn to bits by wild animals." Lizzy gave a dramatic shiver, attempting to appear terrified by the notion of leaving his fearsome presence.

"Torn to bits!" Georgiana repeated tearfully, entering into the spirit of the thing.

"We know our relations will pay our ransom and we shall soon be returned to civilisation. We know *you* will keep us safe!" Lizzy averred.

"Oh, do, do keep us safe! *Please* say you will!" Georgiana begged.

Goliath nodded, more enthusiastically now.

"This is what you shall do—untie us, but free us one at a time to take care of our…private business. You *know* we would never, ever abandon each other. You may use the one who is within your sight as a hostage for the person beyond it."

Goliath looked confused.

"Neither of us will run away! You have my word as a lady! Now untie me right this moment before I grow *hysterical*!" She pitched the last word as a threat, and Georgiana increased the volume of her already noisy weeping.

Faced with a decision between more feminine frenzy and Lizzy's air of command, Goliath predictably followed orders. He lumbered over, crouching before her to begin working on the ropes, even tsk-ing when he saw the damage to her wrists.

"Ye ought not ta try 'n move yer hands," he scolded. "I gots ta keep ye tied. Bert said so."

"It could not be helped," Lizzy replied. "I am a restless person."

Minutes later, she was free; it was all she could do not to cry out when blood began flowing back into her abused limbs. It took her a moment to stand upright steadily; once she managed it, she summoned a glare.

"Now then, untie Miss Darcy please. I shall return shortly."

After taking care of her 'business,' Lizzy returned to find Goliath had finished untying Georgiana, who was now gratifyingly quiet.

"Thank you for your courtesy, brave sir," Lizzy said, entering the shelter while Georgiana made haste for the trees. "We shall give you no trouble, I assure you. As a token of our appreciation for your protection, I have made you something during my restless night. A little gift."

Goliath looked perplexed. "Made *me* sumtin'? A gift? *Me?*"

Lizzy bent down to the figurine and picked it up. "Unfortunately, it will crumble away. There was not enough prepared material to do the thing correctly. But perhaps you may enjoy it, however briefly."

She presented him with the miniature figure of a mermaid.

Goliath promptly held out his hand, and she set it carefully in his large palm. His eyes widened as he lifted it to eye level.

"Cor!" he gasped. "Ain't it a treat!" He touched a finger to the scaled tail. The tip of its fin broke apart and he gave a cry of anguish.

"As I said, it will not last," she said. "I am a sculptor. If I had full use of my hands and a pail of water, I could make you a mermaid that would last forever. Or—" she paused suddenly, as though a thought had just occurred to her.

"Aye?" he asked, completely enthralled.

"I could make you a *life-sized* one," she said, in feigned excitement.

"Wha—?" he gasped again.

"A life-sized mermaid for your very own." With two hands, she sketched in the air an extremely well-endowed mermaid. "The soil is absolutely *rich* with clay. Of course, we need a vast deal of water and as many containers as possible. Also, a shovel. And a considerable amount of soil will be required to make it large enough."

For a moment, silence reigned. Lizzy felt her own nerves stretch taut as their captor slowly debated. If he refused and bound them again, she could not think how they might escape.

"I gots me one more bucket. An' a water trough. An' I c'n dig," Goliath replied eagerly. "I will gettcha all the dirt in Sherwood Forest! But we gots ta do it quick-like, afore Bert shows t'morrow night. 'E'll take it fer 'imself, 'e will. Bert, 'e's not so good at sharin'."

"Goliath's" name was Fergus, they learned, along with the names of all six of his sisters and much of his life history. As Lizzy suspected, Fergus was one of those whose wits were only half present—on a good day.

"Stand and deliver!" he suddenly shouted, apropos of nothing. "Thas' me line, y'see. I practice it regular. Bert lets me 'ave me own pistols, too. Not loaded, o' course, on account of 'em bein' quick ta pop when I'm 'oldin 'em. So was ye scairt when I said it? Stand and deliver!" he bellowed again.

"Terrified," Lizzy replied drily. "But really, Fergus, it was unkind of you to scare nice ladies. And someone *could* get hurt."

"We don' hurt no one," Fergus defended. "Jest gets us a bit extra so's we can eat good. I usta be fair 'ungry most days afore I met up wit' Bert."

"You mean, as Miss Darcy and I are now?" she asked, her belly rumbling.

"Bert said ta jest give ye water," he answered reluctantly, but she could see his conscience smote him, and he was silent for some minutes, watching as she strained the clay-soil through one of Georgiana's petticoats.

"I don' s'pose it would hurt t'give ye some bread," he said at last.

"Your mother would be so proud," Lizzy said, with only a touch of sarcasm.

Fergus nodded in agreement.

It would take many days to strain enough clay to do a life-sized model but Lizzy cared nothing for the statue's completion. Her purposes included keeping Fergus distracted and to stay free of bindings. In this endeavour, she was wholly successful, their enthusiastic captor even using their ropes to construct a makeshift worktable from branches trussed together and balanced upon two boulders. Additionally, Fergus was industriously digging enough soil to build a dozen models, and as the ground was thick with clay sediment, this was tremendously difficult. Lizzy hoped he would sleep deeply tonight—another important factor in her plan.

Though it ceased raining, the air was chill, and the work at least allowed them to move about; Georgiana kneaded clay to break it into more malleable material, while Lizzy did the straining and sculpting. After straining clay enough from the soil to begin, Lizzy began shaping the figure, beginning work on what was obviously a large, deeply enhanced bosom. Fergus was appreciably enthralled.

Of course, if Bert made an unexpected appearance, it was likely all would be lost, and every now and then Lizzy wondered if they should risk making a run for it. But, for all his ignorance, Fergus never *completely* forgot he was supposed to be guarding the girls, not once allowing them both out of his sight at the same time.

With every passing hour, however, Bert's arrival became less likely, and the opportunity to flee in the night more promising. Unfortunately, her plan required her to hit Fergus on the head while he slept, so they could take the pony without fearing he would awaken before they were far enough away to avoid recapture. Yet, knowing all about Fergus's widowed mother and six sisters, she was not sure she could risk fatally injuring him. And she was quite certain a head wound, even of the non-fatal variety, would not improve his already diminished brain box.

Don't forget Bert. We have no assurance he means to return either *of us once the ransom is paid, no matter how harmless his cohort. He may decide he cannot afford to return us, since Fergus has revealed so much. Your first responsibility is to rescue Miss Darcy. Fergus must suffer the consequences of his actions.*

It was a difficult decision, but there was no choice.

MOONLIGHT SHONE THROUGH THE OPEN DOOR OF THE RUDE SHELTER, gleaming upon Fergus's prominent forehead. His bulk partially blocked the opening—he had left the door open while Lizzy played Scheherazade, her stories easing him into slumber. Lizzy waited until Fergus had been snoring loudly for over an hour, his crumbling mermaid statuette clutched in his arms like a favourite toy. Then, she squeezed Georgiana's hand to let her know it was time. Georgiana squeezed back, and Lizzy risked a whisper.

"Get the horse, now."

Georgiana knew horses, and believed the horse's natural instinct would be to return to its stable—hopefully somewhere beyond the forest. The younger girl was confident she could get a bit in its mouth and ride it even without a saddle. Of course, Lizzy pictured the horse leading them out of the woods like some giant hound dog on a scent for home, not *riding* the beast. But the great thing was to put distance between them and Fergus, while preventing Fergus from catching up to them. Once reaching civilisation, they would find an inn and send for Mr Darcy. They were both filthy, but with possession of a horse, they could claim a carriage accident. Lizzy still had her sovereigns. As a plan, it had weaknesses—but it would have to do.

Quietly, Georgiana slipped out of the hut, stepping carefully over Fergus. Perhaps he was not a heavy sleeper, for though she was almost perfectly silent, his snores ceased for a moment while Lizzy's heart stuttered a frantic rhythm of suspense.

Then he let out another thunderous snore, and Lizzy could breathe again. She tiptoed out quietly, following Georgiana. Making her way to the worktable, she hefted the day's prime achievement—a magnificent clay bosom, heavy enough to make an admirable weapon. Cautiously she returned to the peacefully snoring Fergus.

She stood motionless, poised to strike but paralysed by guilt. Could she do this? Could she truly injure a defenceless man? The next moment the pony nickered, sounding as loud as a gunshot in the quiet night. Fergus's eyes popped open. Conscience vacated the premises in favour of its elder sister, survival, and Lizzy dropped the clay breasts on his head. His eyes closed once again, and Lizzy fled.

THE THIRD TIME LIZZY TRIPPED OVER A TREE ROOT AND FELL TO HER HANDS and previously-scraped knees in the inky blackness, Georgiana repeated her offer.

"Perhaps now you would allow me to take a turn walking while you ride?" Georgiana asked, halting the pony in its tracks.

Lizzy slowly rose to her feet, steadying herself with a nearby tree branch.

"I am well. 'Tis only my pride that is bruised," Lizzy replied. "Your skirt is wide enough for you to sit on the beast, but mine is not."

"Lizzy, we have no audience in these woods to care if your knees show," Georgiana chided.

After a moment, Lizzy said, "I have no skill in horsemanship, and would likely tumble off it. At least I am nearer the ground when I fall off my own feet."

"I believe the horse can carry us both, at least until dawn," Georgiana said, yawning. "Cling to me. I would not let you fall."

"No, thank you," Lizzy said crisply. "Please attend the horse, and I will apply myself to staying upright."

Silence returned, except for the sound of horse hooves on the soft forest floor. Lizzy could not hear or see Georgiana, but she knew she hurt the younger girl's feelings with her brusque tone. Georgiana was being brave for a pampered heiress, but she had little self-confidence.

After several minutes, Lizzy admitted, "I am deathly afraid of horses, as it happens. Truly, I am thankful you are managing the beast."

"You? Afraid?" Georgiana asked incredulously. "You, who faced down armed criminals and—and *the Rushworths*? Afraid of a horse?"

Lizzy smiled ruefully in the dark. "When I was a young girl, a horse took rather a large bite out of my arm. I still have the scar, and the fear. You see how essential you are to the success of our operation. If it were up to me, I would have left the horse behind and we would be aimlessly following paths, likely straight back to Fergus or he would be racing after us on its back."

She paused and added carefully, "The beast does seem to be travelling in some sort of definitive direction, yes?"

"I believe so," Georgiana replied seriously. "I am giving him his head, and it *seems* he knows where he is going. If he were going to circle back to Fergus, we ought to have stumbled upon him by now."

"If the trees were not so thick, we should see the beginnings of a sunrise," Lizzy answered, instilling a note of confidence into her voice.

"This forest seems unending," Georgiana said softly, after several quiet minutes. "I need distraction. Will you tell me about your family, Lizzy?"

Lizzy sighed, as weary as Georgiana of listening for the sound of pursuit or other villains. Lizzy needed distraction too, from the blister on her left heel and the bruises sustained in that last fall...and her own fears of the darkened forest. But she hesitated, unsure what to say on *this* topic, of all things.

"I did *not* grow up in elevated circles," Lizzy said at last, adding lightly, "Your Lady Catherine would have fits if she discovered the likes of me *speaking* to the likes of you."

"The old cat would likely disapprove of me conversing with the vicar's wife," Georgiana said bitterly. "You cannot rule yourself out of countenance on her account. Nearly everyone is too lowborn for an earl's daughter."

Lizzy nodded, then decided it didn't much matter if Georgiana knew the truth about her, since in all likelihood she would never see her again after the—hopefully—successful resolution to this adventure. And it would certainly give her something else to think about besides the dark forest and villains in hot pursuit.

"My father has an estate in Hertfordshire, near the town of Meryton," Lizzy said. "That is all I know of him. We never met, as he left my mother before my birth. I was reared in Ramsgate with my mother and my elder sister, Jane. Jane is the daughter of a baron, quite in love with a sea captain who is making his name capturing purses from Napoleon. My mother..." Lizzy could not think how to finish the sentence. "My mother is not respectable, but she has done her best."

Lizzy almost grimaced, imagining her companion's response to all this. But Georgiana's only reply was almost too commonplace. "Ramsgate? Then we might have been neighbours."

All that potential for gossip and pointed questions, and she only mentions the neighbourhood? How odd! What an un-curious girl!

"We were not, however. My family lives off of Harbour Street, and 'tis a fair climb to Albion House from there," Lizzy explained. *In more ways than one.*

"So...how did you come to meet Fitzwilliam?"

Perhaps not so un-curious after all. "He sought me out with a message from my father's relations. Someone in Hertfordshire discovered my existence, a relation of a friend of your brother's, I believe. But there was, evidently, some muddle, for Mr Darcy believed the Elizabeth Bennet he sought was a young child. He was, uh, surprised, at learning the truth. During the course of our conversation, he revealed that his sister lived nearby in Lydia Younge's care. I wrestled with my conscience, I admit, over whether to tell him he left his sister in the care of a...a—"

"A selfish strumpet?" Georgiana offered.

"Or Cyprian, but, as you say," Lizzie agreed. "I was certain he would not believe me, because, to put it frankly, my mother is a harlot, as your brother is well aware."

Utter silence greeted this pronouncement, and Lizzy assumed she had either managed to shock the girl, or confuse her. *'Tis likely a good thing I will never see her again after this. Plainly, I am no judge of what a fifteen-year-old gently bred girl ought to hear.*

"I am sorry," Georgiana said in a small voice. "I was speaking of Lydia in particular, and did not mean to imply...um, that females of–of questionable morals are any more or less selfish than, um—"

It took Lizzy a moment to follow her, and when she did, she had to smile. "You needn't agonise about sparing my tender sensibilities, Georgiana, for I have none. 'Tis a sad fact of life that a man might have any number of trysts or mistresses and be considered upright, while a female may be scorned or vilified for a simple broken engagement."

"It was one of the reasons giving me courage to flee George. Just thinking about what others would say, how they would be horrified or mock me when they learned of my havey-cavey wedding...it made me ill."

"Society has its uses, then," Lizzy said matter-of-factly. "As the world's standards are fickle, I follow my own judgment in these affairs. My mother is a kind person, for all she is an outcast, and Lydia is a vile schemer, for all she is still received in some of the best homes. There are some, most perhaps, who would not have believed me when I revealed Lydia to be a—ahem—selfish strumpet, simply because of my parentage. Fortunately, your brother is better than that. He believed what I told him about Lydia, and we joined forces to search for you. He really is a most...reasonable person."

Not to mention handsome. Lizzy made a scrupulous effort to push away the memory of him holding her face within his hands as if she were something precious. She would fall on it for sure if she went off into reveries now.

Georgiana sighed heavily, and the pony nickered in seeming sympathy. "I am so weary, I almost do not care that I must face him soon and contend with the scandal and the Rushworths and Lady Catherine and the season I have undoubtedly lost all hope of having. I wish he were here now to make it all...disappear."

Lizzy smiled sadly into the darkness. "I am sure he will do his best. But you will have to find the strength within yourself to face the consequences, forgive yourself your mistakes, and rely upon yourself for happiness rather than seeking it from others. As a general rule, others seldom provide it for long."

"Perhaps you are right," Georgiana answered. "I have a dreadful sense it will be some time before I feel anything close to happiness."

Indeed, it might; the gossip could be cruel. To turn the girl's thoughts, Lizzy offered a private sliver of herself she would not usually share. "It might take some time, yes, but you will find it again. As a young girl, I was terribly hurt by my father's abandonment. I felt he was to blame for all our struggles, and I was angry."

"At school sometimes the other girls could be spiteful," Georgiana agreed. "I tried to stay quiet and unnoticed but was always terrified someone would mock me. How awful it must have been to be at the centre of that sort of attention. I have neither mother nor father now, and sometimes I am angry, too, simply because they are both *gone*."

Lizzy nodded. "I was furious. But one day something happened that helped me move away from the worst of my anger."

"Can you tell me what it was?"

"As long as you promise not to laugh."

"I would never!" Georgiana replied.

Lizzy smiled into the darkness, remembering. "I modelled a seal pup, and as I set it upon our gatepost a nice lady wearing a lovely dress walked by. She exclaimed over it, asking if it were for sale, giving me a whole shilling, thanking me for sharing my talent. I nearly tripped over myself expressing abject gratitude, but she hushed me, kindly saying, ''Twas only a shilling. You have a gift.' Money was of such significance to us, and I could see she was wealthy...but in my childish way, I began to also see there were more important things. And now I cannot imagine being without my art. Its absence would leave me incomplete, restless, with a hole inside my heart I would not know how to fill. In time, I became glad for the life God granted me."

They walked along in silence for some ways. Lizzy stumbled in the darkness, and wondered if Georgiana was dozing, until suddenly she spoke.

"I wanted someone who would love me, who would not ever leave me. I knew George from childhood. I trusted him. I believed if he was my husband, he would always care for me," Georgiana said earnestly. Then, after a small pause, "Though it did not hurt he was the handsomest man I have ever seen."

Lizzy laughed, and Georgiana joined her. Some distance ahead, Lizzy spied greyness, a lightening, a breach in the ceiling of trees. Dawn approached, and the forest was thinning. For the moment, all was well.

THE LONGEST FORTY-EIGHT HOURS OF DARCY'S LIFE WAS PAST, WITH BUT few hours remaining until he could take final steps towards the rescue. He was exhausted, filthy with road dust, sore from the saddle, and yet grateful for those physical discomforts—for they prevented him from fixing on the mind-numbing terror at the captivity of his sister and his…his… Well, he had no title for what Elizabeth was to him, no comfortable set of appropriate adjectives. There was only what he wanted for her and with her, which happened to be the things she had refused—most decidedly. If he saw her again—*when, not if*, he told himself—he would have to rephrase those proposals. And he *must* be more convincing the next time.

He left the Adamses some distance back, spurring his horse too hard in his eagerness and anxiety to finish this last leg of the journey. Every time he slowed, the sluggish speed chafed at his nerves. He heard his father's voice in his mind: *Character is the measure of your self-possession*, and forced himself to slacken the reins. At least he was past Mansfield now, and though it was early, there was the beginnings of traffic on the road. Perhaps Nottingham was not as far distant as he believed.

Not far ahead, in fact, he saw two women, one mounted, one walking beside the horse. Or rather, limping beside it. The mounted one stopped the horse, saying something to the other. A strange feeling encompassed him.

If this were a dream, 'twould be my sister upon that horse, with my Elizabeth beside her. It cannot be. But his heart pounded, and he could not prevent a nearly painful stab of hopefulness as he urged his mount forward.

They were covered in dirt, as if they had rolled in mud. It was everywhere—the horse was the only clean one. The blonde girl on the pony was hatless; the walker's bonnet was limp and muddy, and they were every shade of dishevelment. His heart raced as he drew up beside them, as they turned in unison to peer at him.

"Fitzwilliam?" Georgiana quavered.

"Thank God," Elizabeth said.

Darcy could not speak. For a moment, he thought he might burst into sobs. His eyes took them in greedily; they were whole, dirty, but apparently unharmed in essentials. Dismounting in the middle of the road, he strode towards them. Georgiana dismounted as well, but hesitated, looking up at him uncertainly. He opened his arms.

He finally took a whole breath when she threw herself into his embrace. He patted her back gently as she began sobbing, meeting Elizabeth's eyes for the first time.

She looked at him with grave compassion, relief, and appreciation in her lovely eyes. And something else—approval, he thought, watching her nod and smile. After all of the trouble his sister caused her, he became aware she wanted him to treat Georgiana gently. For some reason, this touched him almost as deeply as had the reunion, and he swallowed another lump in his throat.

He tried to speak, choked, covered it with a cough, and tried again. "Are you well? Were you harmed?"

Georgiana could not seem to stop crying, but Lizzy answered. "We were not harmed, not really. We are filthy, fatigued and much in need of a meal." She gazed at the sobbing girl. "And perhaps somewhat distressed."

"I am so glad you are safe." He looked somewhat helplessly at his weeping sister.

Elizabeth put her hand on the girl's shoulder. "We will remove ourselves from the middle of the road and seek a more comfortable place to unravel, shall we?"

Darcy fumbled about for his handkerchief with one hand, finding it as his sister quieted in response to Elizabeth's gently firm words. Georgiana took it from him and blew her nose in what was not at all a lady-like manner, stepping out of his arms. In the distance, he could see the Adams men approaching.

"The villains who had you," he began. "Are they...?" he peered around, as if expecting to see them behind the road hedge.

"Lizzy hit him over the head," Georgiana offered. "We stole his horse and it led us out of the forest."

Darcy looked at Elizabeth with something approaching awe. "Forest?" he said.

"They left us with only one guard, and he was somewhat simple. It was no great feat to escape him," Elizabeth said.

"Do not listen to her, Brother. She was brilliant, and she saved us," Georgiana insisted, beginning to tear up again.

"Let us go now, shall we?" Lizzy said quickly. "Hopefully to a nearby inn. Where are we, exactly?"

"Somewhere between Mansfield and Nottingham," Darcy replied, shaken. "Had I travelled another road... I might have missed you entirely."

"But you did not. And our plan was to stop at the nearest inn and send word, so you'd have discovered us eventually," Lizzy said comfortingly.

He ran his hands through his hair, attempting to calm himself. The vast number of things that could have gone wrong had not; his girls were here and evidently unharmed. Finding a safe place to recover from the ordeal was the most important task at hand. All else could wait.

"A re you still able to ride, Georgiana?" Darcy asked with concern. "We passed an inn not too long ago. Mr Adams and his sons will be upon us at any moment, and I will send them into Nottingham to inform Cousin Richard, who is awaiting my arrival there."

"Of course," Georgiana murmured. Before he could offer assistance, she remounted the pony in a single graceful motion, rearranging her skirts as the sound of approaching hoof-beats signalled the arrival of the Adams men. Darcy looked at her askance, seeing she rode without benefit of side-saddle. His protective instinct ordered that she dismount at once, so the Adams men did not see her in such an immodest display. But Elizabeth looked at him strangely, as if wondering at his sudden grimness…and blast it, Georgiana was here and unharmed and who in blazes cared about aught else today?

His tenants seemed to think nothing of how Miss Darcy sat her horse; introductions were made and expressions of relief and joy at the ladies' escape were immediately offered. The Adamses *did* seem to notice Elizabeth Bennet, however. Even in her dishevelled state, she was beautiful, her loveliness impossible to mar. He glared at the "ogling" men until they looked elsewhere.

Darcy made arrangements for the Adams men to travel on southward to Nottingham, meet with the colonel, and explain what had transpired. There was talk of vengeance and hunting down the villains; Darcy quelled it, repeating the need for utter discretion.

Only when the other men were off to Nottingham did Darcy fully face Elizabeth for the first time. "Do you ride?"

"I am perfectly happy to continue on foot."

"The first thing I noticed, before even identifying the two of you, was your limp," Darcy said evenly. "I suppose you have more than one blister."

"She is scared of horses," Georgiana offered. "I begged her to take her turn riding, or to ride double with me, but she would not do it for anything."

Lizzy aimed a scowl at the younger girl.

Darcy's eyebrows shot high. The woman who voluntarily accompanied his sister to a kidnapping by highwaymen was afraid of *horses*? But he saw her embarrassment in the delicate pink of her cheeks.

"'Tis no matter," he said. In one easy motion, he lifted her up and set her upon his own mount. She squawked with surprise and clutched his shoulders as if perched above a dangerous abyss.

"Buffoon! Let me down!"

"I will hold you and not let you go," he said patiently, as though she had not just insulted him, but she continued to grip him, squeezing her eyes shut and giving his shoulders a hard shake, full of fury and terror.

"No, no!" she cried.

"Elizabeth!" he said, not yelling, but in a voice of absolute authority. "Look at me now."

She might have disobeyed even so, but the horse shifted restlessly beneath her outburst and she froze and opened her eyes in alarm.

"I will not allow you to fall. You will not be harmed. You are safe with me. I swear."

Slowly, almost one finger at a time, she slackened her grip. "I do not want to do this," she whispered, closing her eyes again, perilously near tears.

"All will be well. I promise you," he replied gently. With the grace of a man who had ridden all his life, he swung himself into the saddle without disturbing her precarious seat. And then he gathered her into him, securing her against his hard chest with one arm while expertly handling the reins with the other.

Elizabeth opened her eyes when the horse moved forward, then quickly shut them again and buried her face against his protective shoulder. Darcy turned back to look at his sister, motioning with his chin.

"Ride on," he said.

LIZZY SHIVERED IN ANXIETY AND HUMILIATION, AFRAID TO OPEN HER EYES and mortified by her fright. She did her best to recast those feelings into resentment towards the man who provoked them.

"Elizabeth, you may open your eyes now. I will not allow anything to happen," Darcy murmured.

"Haven't you ever been afraid, even if it made no sense?" she asked querulously.

"I am certain if I were captured by armed gunmen, I would be terrified. You, reportedly, were undaunted."

"The villain in command departed quickly, leaving us with an easily guided simpleton," she retorted.

"Did you know you would be left with a simpleton when you volunteered to accompany my sister into danger?" he asked coolly.

She gave no reply.

"Thank you, Elizabeth," he whispered. "Thank you so very much."

THE WHITE HORSE INN WAS WILLING AND EAGER TO EARN THEIR CUSTOM, despite the unorthodox appearance of the two ladies. The story of an accident was trotted out, and every sympathy and service extended, with little curiosity. Unlike all of the previous inns Lizzy shared with Mr Darcy, they were no longer travelling incognito, and this one was well-acquainted with the Darcy name. According to the attentive maid promptly assigned to help Lizzy bathe, most everyone in Derbyshire and northern Nottinghamshire knew or knew of them.

"Pemberley be the grandest place in the world," the maid assured her. "'Tis open to visitors. Folks as come through here can't stop talkin' of it after they've seen it. Don't matter how grand *they* are, the Darcys is grander."

After her hair was washed and brushed before the fire, a nightdress —only a few sizes too large—was procured and Lizzy was put to bed on no less than four mattresses. She fell asleep at once and slept for most of the day, only wakening to a soft tap on her door. It was Georgiana and servants bearing trays of delicious smelling dishes.

"My brother sent word we are to eat every morsel of this meal," she said, once the servants departed.

"You have not spoken to him?" Lizzy asked.

"No, thank goodness," Georgiana replied, applying herself industriously to the stew. "He knows we have nothing to wear to a meal, and I, for one, am not anxious to hear what he has to say."

"Surely you can see he is overjoyed at your return. He obviously cares deeply for you," Lizzy felt compelled to remind her.

"Yes, I know. But there is bound to be a long lecture about the Darcy name and the behaviour expected of a Darcy and a reminder that if I am not to be judged for the sins of—" Georgiana broke off mid-sentence and stared at her plate.

"Judged for whose sins?" Lizzy asked.

"I am not allowed to speak of it," Georgiana answered quietly, after a moment's pause. "I wish I could."

Lizzy rolled her eyes. Silly girl, to think her secrets were anything special or scandalous. At times like this, she felt a hundred years older than Georgiana, rather than six. They finished their dinners discussing nothing more significant than the weather. Considering their miraculous reprieve from danger, a vague gloom possessed them both. Neither showed any interest in prolonging the meal.

Alone once more, Lizzy tried to understand her low spirits. Wasn't she safe, and Georgiana as well? Wasn't she well fed and cared for? Didn't she possess almost certain promise of financial reward for her pains, and thus the means to fulfil her dreams? It was only the after-effects of perilous adventure, she told herself, that dulled them in her eyes.

The next morning, fortunately, she felt much more herself. Her energy restored, she called for the maid to inquire about her clothing, which had been taken away for cleaning the day before.

The dress, she was informed, was ruined. Servants had been dispatched to Mansfield to acquire immediate replacement clothing until her trunk could be procured from wherever the Rushworths left it.

The clothing eventually provided must have cost a fortune in bribes to a dressmaker. Delicate unmentionables of linen so sheer they could thread through a ring; chemise, drawers, and petticoats in soft white, with fine silk stockings—in pink!—to match; a collarless round spencer of blossom-coloured, silk-trimmed sarsnet, with morning robe of white muslin to wear beneath. A matching bonnet, half-boots, reticule, and kid gloves completed the outfit.

After dressing in the stylish costume, Lizzy was escorted to a private parlour for breakfast. Georgiana, also elegantly clad and already seated, sat with a bemused expression upon her face.

"Good morning," Lizzy greeted the younger girl. "Did you sleep well?"

"Very well," Georgiana replied. After a moment's pause, she added, "You just missed my brother. It was…passing strange."

"Strange?" questioned Lizzy, placing a roll upon her plate.

"Yes," Georgiana said. "I was uneasy, waiting for Fitzwilliam to begin, um, speaking with me about…" she made an airy gesture meant to convey 'every mistake I have ever made.' "Except he did not say much of anything at all. He seemed preoccupied. We were eating breakfast when a servant entered with an express for him. He read it and…and Lizzy, he *cursed.*"

Lizzy, having heard Darcy curse before, did not find this quite so shocking as his much-sheltered younger sister.

"He then ordered me to be ready to leave within the hour for Pemberley," Georgiana finished.

At this, Lizzy felt her heart sink. What else had she expected? Had she hoped Mr Darcy would want to speak with her, hear the entire story of their capture and escape?

Georgiana can repeat the tale, Lizzy. He thanked you yesterday, before purchasing you a costume fit for a duchess. Did you hope to flaunt your fine feathers? After you rejected him oh-so delicately, the last thing he wishes is more conversation.

All that was needful, she reminded herself, was means for travel and inquiring about Mr Wickham. Depending upon the reply, she would make her own future plans, putting Mr Darcy out of her mind entirely.

Except, perhaps, on the long and lonely nights to come.

"May I write to you?" Georgiana asked. "I know, Lizzy…I have not thanked you properly. What with thinking about consequences and knowing my life is over for the foreseeable future and the postponement of my first season likely until I am an old maid of twenty years. But I am so grateful to you. Truly."

Lizzy, already an "old maid" of one-and-twenty, suppressed a smile at this combination of thanks and drama. *If I had a younger sister, would she be so sweet and silly?*

"You are welcome. Please do write. I will anticipate hearing from you." Farewells were difficult, and Lizzy experienced sorrow all out of proportion to the circumstance; quickly, she cast about for a neutral subject. "Tell me about Pemberley. What is it like?"

Georgiana immediately launched into a soliloquy—having mostly to do with a certain horse stabled there, with little detail about the estate. They had no more finished eating when Mr Darcy entered. Lizzy was surprised at the change in him from the day before. Forbidding, detached except for snapping eyes bespeaking fury or exasperation, he strode into the room with an ill-suppressed air of impatience.

"The carriage is being brought around now. Are you ready to leave?" he asked shortly, addressing Georgiana.

At his obvious coldness, his sister stiffened, all her former easiness gone. She nodded, mumbled something and fled. Mr Darcy turned to Lizzy.

She waited for him to begin his polite goodbyes, but he stared at her. Would he flip a sovereign at her and depart? Uncertainty made her irritable.

"Thank you for the clothing," she said, with not as much graciousness as she ought. "Before you go, if I might ask one or two questions on a different search entirely—"

"Miss Bennet," Darcy interrupted. "You look...you look exceedingly...I apologise. I have received news...I must beg a favour of you, whom I owe so much already. I am trying to think how to ask, and yet you are so lovely, speech has flown."

Lizzy's brows rose in astonishment. "That is not what I thought you were going to say."

Her bewilderment cleared his haze enough that he remembered what she had begun to say before he interrupted.

"A different search? You are hunting for someone else?" he asked.

"I am seeking someone from my past," she said, eager to move beyond the awkwardness his compliment inspired. "What is the favour you would ask?"

He took a breath. "I will, of course, be happy to assist you by any means within my power. As to my favour, this morning I learned I must return immediately to Pemberley to manage um, a situation. I would say much more but I must be quick. I wonder…would you consider accompanying us to Pemberley? If I may only have a bit of time to address my current difficulty, I will then be at your disposal."

The request astonished her. She had thought him eager to distance himself. "That is the favour?" she asked uncertainly.

Darcy was tempted to offer reassurances that he would not repeat the offer she found so distasteful before, but as that would be a barefaced lie, he could not. He needed time, however, to prove he had taken her reproofs to heart, and at the moment, he had none.

"I would be exceedingly grateful," he said. "I know also you have plans and hopes and…and ambitions, and I do not wish to interfere." *Much.* "I vow to address the matter of my debts to you from Pemberley, if you might only grant me time. Please."

Lizzy ought to have refused Mr Darcy's invitation; any unfinished business could surely be carried out through correspondence. But his obvious humility had charmed her, and at any rate, she now enjoyed beautiful views from a luxurious carriage, being carried into Derbyshire and hopefully closer to Mr Wickham.

As Mr Darcy rode, she and Georgiana were left to themselves. She explained that this coach—as well as the several outriders accompanying them—belonged to Pemberley. Plainly he took no chances with their safety, though it was only an easy day's journey.

Something else plain was the ease with which Mr Darcy sat a horse. Lizzy could not help but admire his control of the beast—which seemed even larger than the one he perched her on yesterday— although she did her best to forget *that* embarrassing experience. She tried not to be obvious, pretending admiration of the scenery instead of his form, but Georgiana caught her watching.

"For a person who is terrified of horses, you certainly spend a great deal of time staring at Fitzwilliam's," she said.

"It is the biggest one I have ever seen," Lizzy managed, forcing her eyes away.

"He *is* a beautiful stallion. His name is Mars, and he has sired prime flesh," Georgiana replied, and then she was off on the topic of horses again, certainly a favourite subject.

Lizzy did not mind. While she had little to contribute to the conversation, the scenery was strikingly beautiful, lushly green and hilly. As they pulled into Chesterfield to change horses, Georgiana informed her this would be their final stop before Pemberley.

If the Darcys were treated respectfully in Mansfield, their treatment in Chesterfield was royal. Nevertheless, Mr Darcy's state of mute impatience and dismay communicated itself so loudly to Lizzy, she found herself hurrying Georgiana back to the coach.

Oddly, no one else appeared to notice Mr Darcy's distress. Once they were back on the road, she asked Georgiana her opinion on the reasons for his consternation. The younger girl looked at her with genuine puzzlement.

"I imagine he is occupied thinking of likely punishments for me," she finally answered gloomily.

"He might be pensive, if it were that," Lizzy replied. "To me he seems troubled. Did he give any clue to this business that hurries him to Pemberley?"

"I see nothing unusual about him," Georgiana disagreed, peering out the window at her brother.

"You cannot tell *now*," Lizzy said. "At The Cock and Pymat in Chesterfield, did you not notice his abstraction?"

"My brother never has much to say at the best of times," Georgiana observed.

You likely make something of nothing, Lizzy assured herself, and tried to enjoy the views.

When the coach stopped for no apparent reason, for a brief moment Lizzy feared they faced another robbery. But Mr Darcy opened the carriage door.

"I thought you might like to have your first look at Pemberley," he said, gazing intently at Lizzy. "This is a fine aspect, so I had them stop."

"What a good idea, Fitzwilliam! It is a truly lovely sight, Lizzy," Georgiana agreed enthusiastically.

He handed Georgiana down, and then held his hand out for Lizzy. She took it, recalling another time, another touch. Once down, she let go of him quickly, as though the contact burned, turning away to look out over the valley floor.

Her breath caught.

"Lovely" was *such* an understatement, a frail and hollow descriptor for the sight. The immense, lushly forested parklands stretched as far as the eye could see, threaded through with a ribbon of silvery-blue river. Livestock and deer grazed peacefully, while in the distance, a handsome house reigned as monarch sitting upon its valley throne.

To call it a "house" was even more vast an understatement. It was the grandeur of the Derbyshire countryside moulded into bays and pediments, columns and pilasters, walls and wings—a monument to man's best in art and architecture, fitly placed as the centrepiece of nature's majesty.

"Oh," Lizzy said stupidly, looking up at Mr Darcy. "I didn't dream..."

He gazed back at her, understanding in his eyes, all trace of the anxiety he displayed at the Cock and Pymat temporarily displaced. "I cannot help but have a feeling for the old pile." But he did not look once at the great house, only at her, as if captivated by her awe. And she—she was as drawn to him as to his home. The house *was* him, a part of what made him who he was.

"Well, it is awfully hard to keep it warm in wintertime, but other than that, I like it best of all the properties," Georgiana piped in. "The stables are the finest here, by far."

"I do not think we will convince Miss Bennet of Pemberley's superior attributes by that means, Georgiana," Darcy said, and Lizzy heard the gentle teasing in it.

Georgiana did not. "Oh, Lizzy, I am sorry. I am sure you would love the galleries, though."

Lizzy smiled at her, glad for the distraction of the girl's presence. "Your brother only teases us, Georgiana. Luckily, the view alone is almost enough to convince me. I hope once you've recovered from your adventures, you will give me a tour of it."

"You ought to have Fitzwilliam show it to you. He has committed the history of the place to memory, and can tell you what walls were standing where centuries ago, and which ancestor built what parts," Georgiana replied seriously.

"I would love nothing more than to give you a complete tour, inside and out," Darcy said earnestly. "But such an undertaking wants time, and business calls. I do hope to have things settled in time to join you for the evening meal, and perhaps tomorrow we may at least tour the gardens, if the weather continues fine."

He turned to his sister. "Georgiana, I will leave you both now and ride on ahead. I gave instructions for the Imperial Room to be prepared for Miss Bennet. As you and I are the only ones aware of the great debt owed her, I will leave it to you to ensure she is extended every courtesy."

Lizzy did not take his speech of indebtedness to heart; she assumed instead he made a point with his sister, which was confirmed when he added, "And, Georgiana, you and I will have a serious conversation tomorrow. I promise to make time for that, as well."

Georgiana's shoulders drooped. Mr Darcy bowed to both ladies, remounted his horse, and galloped on ahead.

Lizzy smiled at the younger girl. "He will not beat you, Georgiana. Do not despair."

"How do I explain, Lizzy? What reason can I possibly give for such monumental stupidity?"

Lizzy took her arm as they walked back to the waiting carriage. "Perhaps all he truly needs to know is what you've learned from your ordeal. That is what I would want to know of myself."

Refraining from speech while being assisted into the carriage, she continued once they were alone again. "Your brother has your best interests at heart, naturally, but he can only offer guidance. Only *you* can decide who you wish to become. What decisions will you make now, while feeling calm and sensible, so history never repeats itself?"

"I do not care to dwell upon my mistakes. I hate recalling what a fool I was. Most of all, I despise knowing every word out of George's mouth was a lie, all beautiful lies. I wish they *had* been true, and I wish it still."

Lizzy reached over and squeezed her hand. "Tell me what was best about it."

Georgiana gave her an incredulous look. "What was...best?"

"Yes. Your favourite part of the whole experience. Of everything that happened."

"I cannot believe you wish to hear anything good of my misadventures," Georgiana looked as if she suspected Lizzy of collecting evidence of her misdeeds. "Why?"

"Because, you have to *know* yourself, and until you do, you are doomed to err again and again. In the time we have spent together, I have observed your quick intellect. You are *not* a stupid girl. What did Lydia and George offer that made forsaking wit, sense, and protection desirable? When you can understand that, why, seek it again, but on *your* terms, instead of accepting the false offers of rogues."

Georgiana looked thoughtful, then sighed. "I still dread speaking to

Fitzwilliam tomorrow. He is so…so *perfect*, always doing exactly the right thing at the right time. Even when he is angry, he is only quieter, never losing his self-possession or his dignity. 'Tis annoying."

Lizzy, remembering Mr Darcy having a go at the drunken Mr Smiles, could not help herself, and giggled. "He is but a man, Georgiana. A better man than most, mayhap, but only a man, for all that."

HANDED DOWN FROM THE COACH BY A FOOTMAN IN FULL LIVERY, LIZZY and Georgiana were escorted into an entrance hall so grand as to render Lizzy speechless. Huge, masterful paintings hung on front-facing walls in life-sized glory, while gilded bas-relief sculpture adorned others. Her boots echoed on black and white marble floors, the sound resonating against towering, exquisitely decorated ceilings. Even the carpets covering the curved staircase leading, undoubtedly, to more dazzling splendour, were intricately woven works of art. It was an entry designed to impress kings, and Lizzy's jaw dropped in unconcealed and unashamed fascination. She stood in the middle turning a slow circle, and looked her fill.

After several moments, Georgiana tried to get her attention.

"Oh, not yet, if you please," Lizzy replied abstractedly. "I have to soak in this glory for another minute.

"I forget what it is like to see this for the first time," she said with a laugh. "I suppose it is pretty."

"Pretty? Calling this pretty is like saying the ocean is water—a massive understatement. I am *awed*."

Still smiling, Georgiana said, "I promise you can spend all the time you like studying it very soon, but our housekeeper, Mrs Reynolds, is waiting to show you to your room now."

For the first time, Lizzy became aware of the presence of a woman awaiting her notice. The housekeeper was not so old, perhaps forty, but she wore the dignity of Pemberley wrapped around her like a cloak, and it added countenance, if not years, to her bearing.

"Oh, I beg pardon," Lizzy said. "I was unprepared for such…"— she paused, trying to think of a word grand enough to describe it —"…*magnificence*. It is more glorious with every step."

Mrs Reynolds smiled approvingly at this sign of the house receiving its due honour. "Think nothing of it, Miss. Whenever you are ready."

Lizzy stepped towards an astonishingly lovely painting. She had seen a similar work in a plate reproduction of a famous master. "This is not...not a Rubens, is it?" she asked.

"Indeed it is, Miss. Many of our paintings are wonderful reproductions of the ancient masters, but Pemberley also has one of the finest art collections in all of England. Old Mr Darcy was a collector, and his son after him."

"Collections?" Lizzy murmured.

"Oh, yes, Lizzy. Our walls are filled, but we always seem able to accommodate another," Georgiana effused.

"I am beside myself now," Lizzy whispered, "and I am only in the entry."

"Your room is lovely too, I promise."

Lizzy knew it discourteous to keep them waiting, but found herself exceedingly reluctant to abandon all this beauty in favour of more commonplace matters. Giving one last longing look at the Rubens, she turned with a sigh.

However, before she took a step, a tall, blonde female dressed in the latest fashion darted into the entry through an east-facing corridor, almost as if she were being chased. Though likely in her middle forties, she was exquisite still—in her youth she must have been a diamond of the first water. Lizzy, standing near Mrs Reynolds, heard the housekeeper's quiet intake of breath. Surprise? Shock?

"I will not wait," the woman announced, addressing the housekeeper. "I have been shut in the back of the house like some criminal awaiting the magistrate! Where is Fitzwilliam?"

For several moments, no one spoke or moved, an awkward tableau. Lizzy looked at Georgiana, but the girl seemed confused; plainly, she did not recognise this visitor.

Mrs Reynolds opened her mouth to say something, but nothing coherent emerged, a flush of colour tingeing her cheekbones. Lizzy saw her glance at Georgiana and try again. "If you would be so good, madam, as to—"

The woman's eyes fell upon Georgiana and she gasped, interrupting. "Is this—?"

But before she could finish her question, Mr Darcy entered from the same direction as the stranger. Taking in the situation at a glance, he turned a thunderous glare upon Mrs Reynolds. It was a look the visitor, evidently, had no difficulty interpreting.

"Do not blame Mrs Reynolds, please," the woman said with mocking humour, even as her eyes greedily riveted upon him. "You know I always have trouble doing as I am told."

Darcy's jaw, already clenched tightly, firmed even more. He nodded curtly to the footmen stationed on either side of the front entrance—both adroitly pretending not to listen to every word—and they vanished like smoke.

"Mrs Reynolds, take Miss Darcy upstairs. At once, if you please."

He glanced at Lizzy, something sharp, nearly pleading in it, as he moved to stand beside her; astonishingly, she saw he meant her to stay. The housekeeper unhesitatingly stepped to Georgiana, who gave one more curious glance at the visitor before departing easily. She had no interest in being near her brother while he so obviously seethed in displeasure. Only when Georgiana's footsteps faded away did Mr Darcy speak, addressing himself to the visitor.

"Because you refused to await me where we might have this conversation in privacy, we shall have it near an exit, so you might state your business and be quickly gone."

His incivility surprised Lizzy. *I have seen a displeased Mr Darcy before, but have also witnessed many a coarse innkeeper treated with greater courtesy.*

It affected the woman, for she flinched. But amazingly, she chose to disregard his acute displeasure. Instead, she took a sudden, visible interest in Lizzy, gazing at her curiously, though Lizzy could see her hands shook. She clasped them together in a white-knuckled grip, forcing the trembling into nothingness. As someone who regularly subjugated her emotions, Lizzy felt a sympathy. Whomever this woman might be, this encounter required all her powers of control.

"Who is this pretty young creature, Mr Darcy? Will you not introduce us?" The woman spoke as if she were in a Mayfair ballroom instead of trembling beneath the full weight of the Darcy glare.

Lizzy looked at her, then glanced at Mr Darcy. He hadn't moved, his features as hard as granite. But she felt the hesitation within him, as if he stood upon some precipice of judgment. When he spoke, however, he sounded decisive as ever.

"As you wish. Lady Anne Grayson, this is Miss Elizabeth Bennet, a dear friend of the Darcy family. Miss Bennet, Lady Anne Grayson."

He paused the barest second. "My mother."

Love Wisely but Well

The Perfect Gentleman Volume 2

1

L izzy's brows rose as she stared at him, then again at Lady Anne. For some reason, she had believed his mother dead, though he never said so. There was no physical resemblance between him and the older woman. Now knowing her identity, however, she could see Georgiana was nearly her image. Remembering her manners, she curtseyed. "My lady," she murmured.

"Miss Bennet," the woman replied, inclining her head, her tone gracious despite her unsteady hands. "Are you from this area? Have you known my children long, might I ask?"

But Darcy was finished. "No. You may not arrive unannounced, take root in my entryway, and pretend we engage in a cosy *tête-à-tête* at Almack's. It has been a long, unusually trying week, capped off by *your* arrival. Now, why, pray tell, have you appeared uninvited upon my doorstep?"

More disrespect! Quite astonishing! Lizzy felt her eyes go wide.

"I supposed I was unlikely to receive an invitation," she answered cautiously. "I believed it to be the only w–way."

Lizzy watched Lady Anne begin twisting her hands into the lace of her sleeves, as if in this way she could restrain the trembling.

"You might have begun with a letter," Darcy replied coldly. He was formidably unyielding; in comparison, Lizzy thought him docile and unassuming at *their* first meeting.

"Would you have read it?" Lady Anne asked hopefully.

His inherent honesty surfaced. "I cannot say. Perhaps not."

He held so still, he appeared as if carved from marble, like one of the busts positioned near the massive doors. Lizzy watched Lady

Anne's hands clench still tighter, ruining the expensive material, as tightly wound as her son. Both of them wore expressions of cool indifference. Perhaps there was more resemblance than Lizzy had first detected.

"I hoped to visit, to have an opportunity to know you a little," Lady Anne continued. "I did not realise Georgiana would be here, as I understood from friends that she was on the coast. I dare not come to you in London and cause talk, but my correspondent wrote you left there abruptly on business, so I took the risk."

"I have only just arrived," he replied. "And while I cannot imagine a welcome occasion for your visit, your timing is excruciatingly bad at present. As you have seen, Georgiana *is* in residence, and for you to distress her is unacceptable."

Though it was obvious there was bad history between them, and though she knew she understood nothing of the circumstances, Lizzy watched his mother accept this set-down as the blow it was meant to be. But she revealed nothing in her tone.

"She has grown so tall and lovely," Lady Anne mused. "A child no more, but a young l–lady."

Lizzy finally heard it—the trembling reached her voice now.

"Yes, well, time does not stand still. She is no longer a two-year-old who cries for her mama and does not understand why Mama does not come."

"I suppose not," the woman said, and then, as if her desperation had reached some sort of impossible peak, she threw herself off of it. "But perhaps it ought to be *her* choice whether or not she sees her mama now."

A deep, chilling cold entered the room, emanating from Mr Darcy. Lizzy could almost see the frost settling into his features at this premature suggestion that Georgiana should meet the woman, especially considering the difficult situation they just endured with Lydia Younge. Though it was none of her affair, she felt an urge to calm Darcy, so he need not make decisions while enraged. Beyond this…the lady exuded a wretched bravado Lizzy found oddly pathetic; she could not prevent herself from intervening. Darcy opened his mouth to reply, but Lizzy laid her hand upon his arm. He stilled, looking at her.

"Lady Anne," Lizzy said, "Mr Darcy did not prevaricate when he explained the last several days have been distressing. Miss Darcy is… fragile at the moment. Your suggestion of a meeting is untimely."

"She has been ill?" Lady Anne asked, the note of anxiety obvious.

"An unhappy experience," Lizzy explained airily. "Nothing she won't overcome. It is my opinion, however, that Mr Darcy's nerves are stretched thin, and you are about to send him over the edge. Might I suggest we continue this conversation tomorrow, when we have all had time to settle? Mr Darcy, surely there is somewhere on this great estate where your mother might stay a night without, ah, intruding upon Georgiana?"

Lady Anne looked at her son; her white-knuckled fists betrayed how much she wished for his answer to be a positive one. When he remained silent, she added, "I vow not to seek her out."

He glanced at her sharply. "But keeping vows is not your forte, is it?"

Lady Anne flinched and bowed her head.

Lizzy's hand tightened on Darcy's arm, and sighing, he pulled away and left the room.

An awkward silence ensued.

"That went well, I think," Lady Anne said at last.

Lizzy looked at her, giving a rueful half-smile. "He truly has had a beastly week. You could not have timed your, um, reunion more unfortunately."

"I should have continued waiting for him in the east wing parlour, where they put me after I arrived early this morning, but I did not believe that dragon Mrs Reynolds when she said Fitzwilliam was occupied. After waiting for hours and in my general state of…ah…uneasiness, I began to believe no one informed him of my presence and they hoped I would rot there. I fear my reception would not have been much improved in the best of circumstances, however. Georgiana…she is truly unharmed?"

Before Lizzy could answer, Darcy returned, followed by a footman. "Accommodations are being prepared," he said gruffly. "John will escort you and see your things brought over. You will stay at Holmwood Hall. We will visit you there on the morrow. Please do not test my goodwill by returning here."

Lizzy had opened her mouth to speak her farewells, when Lady Anne surprised her by curtseying to her, very low, in a gesture of deep respect. Lizzy barely had time to return an abbreviated curtsey of her own before the elder lady swept from the room. Despite herself, Lizzy was touched; if she recalled correctly, Mr Darcy's mother was the daughter of an earl, the sister of Lord Matlock. Of course, the lady did not know to whom she curtseyed, and likely would not have done so if she *had* known. Still, it was a lovely gesture of condescension.

FOR A MOMENT, SILENCE REIGNED BETWEEN THE TWO REMAINING occupants of the hall. Darcy appeared disgruntled, and Lizzy wondered if she was now to be lectured for speaking out of turn. She felt she would deserve it—she *had* been rather highhanded.

"I do not have 'nerves,'" Darcy said suddenly.

"What?" Lizzy replied, startled from her thoughts.

"Your description to Lady Anne of my supposed disposition. I am surprised you did not wave a vinaigrette about as if I were a doddering invalid."

Her own nerves easing, she looked at him carefully. His hair was untidy, as if he had run his hands through it, but otherwise he was unrumpled—his cravat perfectly tied, the road dust clinging to her skirt nowhere in evidence upon him. He could use a shave perhaps, but she liked him that way, with a touch of roughness. His eyes though...he gazed at her with a bleakness that broke her heart.

"Perhaps there is somewhere we might sit and talk?" she asked.

"You have not been allowed a moment to recover from your journey," he said gruffly. "I will have someone show you to your room."

Lizzy could imagine how she would feel if she were, without warning, abruptly confronted with her absent father's appearance. "The travel was hardly arduous. Show me your library. If it is as wondrous as your entry hall, I will swoon, and then you'll be rid of me," she said impishly.

He met her eyes. "You must know, Elizabeth, that ridding myself of you is the last thing I want."

She blushed, but before deciding what he meant by it or how to respond, he took her arm and led her upstairs to the library on the second floor of the west wing—one of *three* in the house, he remarked. "Our libraries are the work of generations. Please feel free to make use of them."

"Truthfully, it is doubtful I will remember how to find my way here," she said, not explaining that the loss of her bearings had much to do with the feel of his hand at her elbow.

"One cannot walk more than a few feet in this place without tripping over a footman," Darcy said drily, nodding at one stationed nearby who swept the door open before them. "There is no need to fear losing your way. Everyone will be glad to assist."

He closed the door behind them, but before Lizzy could take in the sheer elegance of the room, he tugged at a nearby pull, ordering tea once a housemaid almost instantly appeared in answer to his summons.

It is entirely inappropriate for us to share a private meal! Lizzy's conscience reminded her.

Shut it! Lizzy told her conscientious self. *This is completely innocuous compared to the previous week's indiscretions, posing as husband and wife. I am in no danger from him.* She was rather surprised, however, that Mr Darcy did not seem to care much for the propriety of the situation, either. Probably he was too much disturbed by the unexpected visit of his parent to overthink rules and etiquette, or even of Lizzy herself.

They shared a comfortable silence while Lizzy gazed at her surroundings. Despite the masterfully painted ceilings, gilt-laden mouldings, endless shelves crammed with every conceivable contribution to literature, three crystal chandeliers, velvet sofas, thick rugs, and the expensive aroma of leather, it achieved an atmosphere of cosy elegance.

Once tea arrived, complete with an assortment of delicate accompaniments, she saw no point in avoiding the topic of his mother's absence.

"When did she leave?" Lizzy asked. "Your...ah, Lady Anne."

Darcy sighed heavily. "When Georgiana was two years old," he replied. "She met someone else and fell in love. Her life was a 'misery' to her unless she could join her lover. Some peer's younger son."

Lizzy nodded. "I imagine there was an uproar when she eloped."

"That is not exactly the situation," Darcy replied. He set down his teacup so he could stand, moving to the window with his back to her —almost as if he could not face her and tell the tale.

"What exactly happened, then?"

"My parents moved to Scotland for several weeks and established residency. And then...they were divorced." He spoke dispassionately, but still refused to meet her gaze.

Lizzy could not help her surprise. "Is that legal?"

He shrugged. "Not in England. In the eyes of English law, most agree my parents remain married, although there are some who argue

—never mind it, it does not matter. Taking it to the courts was never a possibility. 'Twould have been an exercise in futility and expense. She left England permanently to reside in the country more friendly to her opinions."

"I suppose your father could have gone elsewhere as well," Lizzy mused, replacing her teacup on the tray. "If he had wished to remarry."

Darcy gave a short, sharp jerk of his head. "Look around you, Elizabeth. Look at this place. Pemberley has stood for centuries, in one form or another. *This* is what it means to be a Darcy. We are built for holding fast and firm, not for flight. My father, his roots planted in English soil, was doomed to the life of a married man whose wife was a flagrant adulteress. His despair concerned my mother not at all. She and her lover married in Scotland and lived in Glasgow. She took his name and wore his ring and forgot entirely about the family she left behind."

"I am surprised your father bothered with the Scotch divorce."

"If you had known him, you would not be. It was her suggestion and, I believe at first, he went to Scotland, hoping to win her back. He was so often preoccupied with estate business. He was much older than she and had, perhaps, neglected his wife, his marriage. But her mind was made up. There was no negotiation possible. She did not wish to be married to him, and divorce in England is nearly impossible to obtain...so, to the extent he could, he gave her freedom to marry another."

"Not many men would have been so generous," Lizzy replied gently.

Darcy whirled to face her. "He was heartbroken. Such a proud man, humiliated before everyone he knew. He regretted the scandal's cost to his children, tried to mend what he could, in his way. But she did not want him and thus he relinquished his entire life's happiness, for her."

His face was white, painful memories suspending his usual stoicism. Lizzy felt she was seeing, perhaps for the first time, the man beneath the armour constructed to shield himself from sorrow and hurt.

"But he did not surrender his *entire* happiness. He kept you and your sister. I am sure having your love and support meant everything to him. I cannot believe he remained in misery *every* moment, with such a fine man as you for his son and heir."

"Oh, Elizabeth," he said, his shoulders slumping. "How good you are. For me to ever have thrown up *your* birth, *your* mother at you, when mine…"

Lizzy waved this off. "I can better understand now why you have tried so diligently to avoid your own scandals. But it seems Lady Anne did not entirely forget her children."

He sat down beside her on the settee. "Her husband died a few years ago. They had no children. I suppose she is alone in the world and now it is *convenient* to remember us. She has a marriage settlement from my father, to be paid out upon his death, but has never answered my solicitors' letters to claim it, which troubles me. Possibly she wants more…perhaps even to style herself the widowed Mrs Darcy."

"Surely not!" Lizzy cried.

"I hope not. Nevertheless, her presence can only cause a renewal of gossip and scandal. I want nothing to do with her," he said, his tone both stubborn and challenging, as if he expected her to argue.

She looked at him earnestly. "I know how you feel. If Thomas Bennet walked into the room this very moment, the only thing I would wish to do is…is spit in his eye."

Unexpectedly, he smiled. She had never seen him do it before, not fully, with real humour. He was always handsome, but with a smile upon his face he was unfairly so. The previous hint of dimple was wholly confirmed.

"Such a lady," he said, teasing her, making her smile. "Such a fierce lady. Elizabeth Bennet, you are perhaps the only person on earth who knows exactly how I feel right at this moment."

"How do you feel?"

The emotions riding Darcy so hard since his reunion with Elizabeth coalesced with the painful stew of feelings experienced since he received the emergency missive from Mrs Reynolds, informing him of their unexpected visitor. Need and sorrow, pleasure and pain, desire and anger—all cascaded through and overwhelmed his heart and mind.

But he had promised himself if he ever had the chance to be near Elizabeth Bennet again, there would be less kissing and more consideration. He had taken her reproaches to heart; his thoughtless suggestion that she live with the father who abandoned her was even more reprehensible, now that he faced his own bitterness towards his mother. His conscience screamed he provide proof he cherished her, beginning by acting with as much self-possession and sensitivity as honour and respect demanded.

But how could he show her? How would she know?

He took her into his arms and kissed her with a need from the deepest, most primitive part of his being.

The second their lips met, Darcy knew he had made a mistake. He was too unsettled, his feelings too shattered, his customary control gone. Ever since seeing her that morning, the pale pink of her costume emphasising her beauty, he had wanted to kiss her, to hold her, to worship at her feet: his idol beloved. Moving away was near impossible; only his need to show her the honour she deserved stopped him from continuing.

Abruptly, he let her go.

Lizzy scooted to the opposite side of the settee.

"I apologise. You need not fear me. I only wanted to—"

"Wanting is not our problem," she said. "But we *must* be sensible."

Darcy knew he must convince her that together they would be the happiest, most sensible couple in the world. Because he did not have words at the moment, he held out his hand. When she took it within her much smaller one, his joy swelled.

For some time, he dwelt on that simple pleasure. If he could convince her to stay, there would be thousands of opportunities to do this, to soothe the growing ache in his heart.

"**D**earest," he said, "I need your help."

"My help?" she asked with puzzlement. "Have you another missing relation? A cousin this time?"

The force of his dismay lessened in the face of her teasing. "Not that sort of assistance. But before I explain, I would like to know what you wish for most in life...those hopes and dreams I did not think to ask you of...before. What does Elizabeth Bennet require in order to be happy?"

He awaited her answers with bated breath, knowing everything *he* needed was right here in this room, and wondering if it would ever be so again.

"What I need to be happy?" Lizzy echoed, the words she'd flung at him when he proposed returning to her. She had accused him of not really knowing her, of seeing only what he wanted to see. As they still, it appeared, had feelings for each other, it was a legitimate query. And yet...

"Why do I feel as though giving you an answer will place a weapon into your hands?" she asked.

"Is it so obvious? I want to make your dreams come true," he said. "My feelings for you have remained unchanged...no, that is incorrect. My feelings for you are stronger than ever. I cannot accept your refusal without at least *attempting* to change your mind."

"Mr Darcy—"

"Please, dearest...would you call me by my given name, Fitzwilliam? Are we friends enough for that?"

Lizzy placed both her hands upon his much larger one with a sigh. "Fitzwilliam," she repeated.

He leaned over and kissed her cheek, tenderly, sweetly. "I love the sound of my name upon your lips," he said hoarsely.

"That won't survive," she said. "Not once I begin saying it with irritation when I'm peeved, or stridently when I wish you to do something you do not."

"What will you ask me to do, that I will not wish to do?" he asked.

She thought for a few moments. "Receive my sister, for one. I will not live in a home where she is not welcome."

"I would receive your mother if it meant you would accept me."

"You would not! You *could* not!" she said. "Georgiana would be ruined by association!"

He was quiet for some time, staring at their joined hands.

"I know I was cruel," he said at last. "When I told you I would not marry you until Georgiana was settled, I implied you were not worthy of her. It is the furthest thing from my feelings, but I did not think it out properly. I was tired and distressed, although that is never an excuse. If Georgiana could grow to have your strength of character and purpose, I would be a happy man. What I should have said was this— my mother purchased her happiness at the expense of her husband's and children's happiness. I never wish to be the sort of person who would do that."

"But nothing has changed," she replied. "Society has forgiven your family. My presence drags you all through the muck once again."

"Society forgives nothing. For one thing, it is not society's duty to forgive. It is, rather, a personal obligation. But I digress. Georgiana's choices have changed everything. The scandal will greatly affect her future, regardless of what I do or do not do."

"Perhaps no one will discover it," Elizabeth said hopefully. "After all, she was returned quickly."

"I do not believe we can depend upon that. At the least, the Rushworths are unlikely to maintain their silence, despite my threats. Regardless of our efforts at discretion, there are those who might draw correct conclusions. However, I gave the Rushworths an untruth which may mitigate the scandal, or at least, give society a different one."

"What did you tell them?"

"I cannot reveal it until I discover if I have any hope of contributing to your future happiness."

It was Lizzy's turn to sigh. "I sculpt," she said. "I believe I mentioned it once before."

"I do remember you saying something about crafting…er, figurines, or…fish?"

"Well, yes, in Ramsgate, especially during the holidays when tourists flock to the seashore. But my dream is to study with a master, to do more than work with clay. I am…I am good, Fitzwilliam, and possibly I could be more. If I could learn from a master, gain wider experience with other materials, perhaps I could sell enough to go abroad and achieve my potential."

"Go…abroad?" he repeated flatly, his heart tripping over the words.

"That is where, for the most part, the larger community of great artists reside, and where I might find instruction. I understand there to be somewhat less prejudice against artists of my gender."

He was silent for some moments and then, "Is travelling a requirement of your dream? If the master could be brought to Pemberley, would it be just as…nearly as good?"

"Truly? Here?" she asked, sounding hopeful before her voice turned wistful. "Fitzwilliam…I would be a terrible wife. When I am engrossed in my work, I forget to eat and sleep, much less pay mind to the needs of a husband. I should never be the hostess you ought to have upon your arm, or the mistress Pemberley requires. And think of your children! They would be mocked for their odd mother of degenerate pedigree. 'Tis impossible!"

"As a young man, I would not have cared a fig for any of that, if only my mother had stayed," he said quietly. "She was the centre of our home, and when she left, it felt as if she took all our happiness with her. I lost nearly a year of school, at loggerheads with anyone who remarked upon my family's situation, always being sent up to rusticate in punishment for brawling. If we are fortunate enough to be parents, surely we can train our children to value what is important, to appreciate who you are and your great gifts."

He meant every word. He neither knew nor cared whether or not she had any real artistic talent—but her heart, her great and courageous heart, was gift enough.

Elizabeth bit her lower lip. "That is kindly said, sir, but you put the cart before the horse. What we may or may not be able to teach our children, or the art masters you might be able to hire for my instruction do not signify. We do not know each other! You have known me for a week. Seven days! Obviously, there is a strong feeling between us, but I have not an inkling of whether what we have could last. What if you discovered you made a dreadful error in judgment and we were completely unsuited. What would we do? Go to Scotland?"

"If necessary, yes," he replied seriously.

"No!" she said. "That is a *horrible* plan. Do you think I am so cruel as to force such a scandal upon you a second time?" She tried to pull away from him, but he clasped her hand firmly.

"Of course not! I am not expressing myself well, as usual," he said. "Please, let me explain."

She quit resisting, leaning back against the settee. "We need time. I will go back to Ramsgate, to my family. You may write."

"I need to tell you the lie I gave to the Rushworths," he said cautiously. "I told them that we—you and I—were eloping to Gretna Green, and Georgiana accompanied us along with my cousin the colonel. That Georgiana broke away from us in Wetherby because she was so upset at the idea of our marriage."

On hearing this, Lizzy firmly pulled away from him; he let her go, watching as she paced the room in distress. "You are mad. They could not have believed it."

"But they did," he said, standing. "Evidently nothing either you or my sister said to them contradicted my tale."

Lizzy shook her head in disbelief. "Why would you lie about such a thing?"

"It just…came out of my mouth. But as soon as I said it, I knew I wanted to make it truth. I realise you have not long known me, and you do not love me. However, I am certain of this—I can earn your respect, I can help you find happiness, and I can worship you with my heart and mind and body until death do us part. I will be faithful." He paused until she met his eyes, willing her to see the strength of his devotion.

She halted where she stood, meeting his gaze; it slayed him to see her lost expression. He stepped closer.

"I will give you all the time you need to accept me, to know me better. If you do not wish to make it a marriage in *fact*, I will wait," he promised. "And if, after some period of time, you decide you cannot tolerate being my wife, we will go to Scotland. I will see you well provided for, and you may lead whatever life you wish abroad."

Lizzy gaped. "I cannot believe you would condemn yourself to your father's life."

"I am willing to take the risk, with one caveat. If children do come, it changes everything. I will not agree to any separation if we have a family together."

She turned away from him again, slowly walking the circuit of the room, deep in thought. When she finally spoke, she did not say any of what he expected.

"Have you ever heard of a man, a land steward, by the name of Mr Harry Wickham?" she asked.

"Yes," he answered slowly. "Why do you ask?"

"I knew him, long ago. He...he did me a great service once. I have always wanted to thank him, but I know only that he was a land steward somewhere in Derbyshire." Her voice was quiet. He wondered if perhaps his offer was so unattractive, she had already dismissed it, moving on to other concerns. A wave of sorrow washed over him, but he pushed it aside. He had made the best offer he could; there was naught else he could do, except begin planning an extended tour of the Continent for himself and Georgiana.

"Mr Wickham served as my father's steward. An honest, hard-working man. Unfortunately, he died several years ago," he answered quietly.

"Dead!" she cried, staring at her feet. "I did not expect that, I suppose."

"Riding accident," he clarified. He waited until she met his gaze. "His son, George Wickham, is the man who attempted to elope with Georgiana."

"Good heavens!" Lizzy gasped. "I expected that even less. She said she had known him as a child. I didn't ask his surname—but of course it is a common one. What an odd coincidence." She gave a deep, shuddering breath, pushing away the sadness of knowing her childhood friend was gone, and the sorrow that his son had caused such pain.

"George holds me to blame for many of his own troubles," Darcy continued. "My father felt somewhat responsible for Mr Wickham's death—he was investigating a property line dispute between two of our tenants when injured, and...it was not an easy passing. Father saw to George's education and would have given him a living, if not for the unwed mothers he left in his wake. I only hope Georgiana is telling me true when she says he did not—" He ended the sentence abruptly.

"I sincerely believe your sister to be as innocent as ever," Lizzy said, moving closer to him again so she could lay her hand upon his stiff shoulder. "He wooed her as a young girl wishes to be wooed, with posies and poetry."

He could not help it, covering her hand with his. "How do you wish to be wooed, Elizabeth?" he asked, his voice low and dark.

Her grin was impish. "I would likely swoon if you recited poetry."

"I think we have established that I prefer you awake," he replied. "But I am certain I could arrange for a posy."

Elizabeth could not keep from twisting her hand around so he held it clasped within his large one, and when he drew it to his cheek, she had to stifle a sigh. What to do? What was best for all?

No longer could she hold out a vague hope of Mr Wickham's patronage, and only now, upon the verge of momentous decision, could she see the many weaknesses in her plan. There was no reason to think he would have wanted anything to do with her; she likely represented an embarrassment. She could admit, now, it had been a plan born of desperation.

But as plans born of desperation went, it was no more unlikely than Mr Darcy's! *Marriage*! A girl of no fortune or family, wed to the master of Pemberley!

"I do not understand why you offer for me," she said, her voice tinged with disbelief. "Surely, you can find someone within your own circles, who would understand her duties to your house and name, someone devoted to being the mistress of all this," she said, gesturing with her free hand.

He took both her hands in his. "You mean, as my father did? My mother brought the correct pedigree, and it all came to naught. I want to marry someone for whom I have feelings, a passion. I want her to be strong, courageous even, and have something in her head besides shopping and soirees. I want her to be honest, faithful, and practical. I want her to be a friend and good example to my sister. I want her to be *you*. I know not how else to explain it, my dear."

"Aren't you concerned…coming from the family I do…if I would be true to our vows?" she asked, her voice low.

His voice was firm in reply. "No. I believe you are *more* likely than most to be true. Not because of family or blood—but because of who you are. And because I know I will never neglect you or give you cause to look elsewhere for happiness."

Lizzy heaved a great breath. "I need time. I know you must think me foolish to look such a gift horse in the mouth."

Darcy drew her in close, allowing himself the luxury of her nearness, trying to take heart in the fact that she had not absolutely refused. "If you are comparing me to a horse, I fear I will have to work much harder."

She looked up at him. "Fitzwilliam...you've spent your whole life *restoring* your family honour. Marrying me may undo all your sacrifices. How will you feel when the whispers grow loud, or worse, when the room quiets as you enter and people you have known your whole life, even family members, cut you dead? What of the marriage portion your bride ought to have contributed to replace Georgiana's?"

"Then I shall hope you are as great an artist as you believe...else you had best pay close attention to those masters I hire," he said, his eyes alight with good humour. "Pemberley requires a very healthy income. The footmen's livery alone will oblige you to be most industrious."

She frowned at him. "'Tis not a laughing matter," she replied.

He brushed her cheek in a soft gesture of caring. "Darling, some will be doing and saying those same things about Georgiana as soon as tales of her misadventure spread," he said, moving an escaped curl behind her ear. "Which they will, if we do not marry. I am fully confident that I, however, can bear society's scorn. My income allows me to marry where I please, without harm to our children. Furthermore, not everyone is of my uncle's stamp. Upon consideration, I see I took his defection too much to heart," Darcy said.

"I would have taken it the same way. Family is...family *should be* loyal above all things," Lizzy averred.

"And you wonder why I want you?" he asked, pulling her close. He laid his face against her hair, breathing in the faint floral scent, allowing it to soothe him. "You know, it may not be as awful as you say. Some of my friendships are not wholly of the first circles, and those friends will not run at the thought of a little scandal. In fact, my friend Charles Bingley—whose father began life as a hewer—wrote the letter bringing me to you in the first place. His father's second wife is your father's sister. She is good. Had she learnt of you sooner, I am certain she would have wished to know you."

"She is the one who sent you to…to investigate my home?" Lizzy asked tremulously.

"Yes. I do not know if she believes you to be a child or if that was my friend's misunderstanding…or if his abysmal handwriting led *me* to misunderstand. I left the letter in London."

"Speaking of letters, I must write to my mother and sister and assure them I am well. And somehow, impress upon my sister she is not to allow my mother to make rash decisions about her future. Mama is *not* very sensible, which becomes obvious when she chooses a new protector. I usually—" With chagrin, she realised what she had been about to admit, and clapped a hand over her mouth.

Darcy cocked his head. "Do you select your mother's *protectors*?"

Lizzy looked at him carefully, trying to ascertain if he would believe a half-lie. "Um…no? Amongst her preferences, there will be some who are more practical, less temperamental. I…I claim rights of refusal when a suitor is *entirely* inappropriate, and she trusts my judgment. As it were. 'Tis not as though I *enjoy* knowing aught about her *affaires d'amour*—"

Darcy pulled her in tightly again, his smile apparent in his tone. "Only you, my darling. Please, tell your mother her monetary concerns are finished. Henceforth, her bills are to be sent to me. There is no need for you to act as procuress ever again."

"How you tempt me," she said. "But Fitzwilliam…truly…I do not know if Mama will ever be…virtuous. Even if she no longer needs a man to pay her bills, the truth is…she likes men. She…she requires…affection."

He took her hands in his again. "See if you can speak with her about the concept of discretion. Tell her I am willing to be generous in exchange. But even if she is not, you cannot live her life for her. We already know there will likely be rumours, but Pemberley is a long way from London, and further still from Ramsgate."

"I cannot believe you are willing to overlook so much," she said.

"I have spent the last few days wondering if those villains who had you would hurt you or–or worse. I thought it even odds I would never see you alive again. Once one experiences that sort of distress, one's perspective is forever changed. I would do anything for your sake, dearest. *Anything*."

"If I were a better person, I would tell you to go to blazes," she said.

"But, I fear I am just unscrupulous enough to agree to be your wife, Mr Darcy, if you are imprudent enough to ask."

"Fitzwilliam," he reminded. And then, with a sly grin, recited:

> *"Then plainly know my heart's dear love is set*
> *On the fair daughter of rich Bennet:*
> *As mine on hers, so hers is set on mine;*
> *And all combined, save what thou must*
> *combine By holy marriage: when and where and*
> *how We met, we woo'd and made exchange of*
> *vow, I'll tell thee as we pass; but this I pray,*
> *That thou consent to marry us today.'"*

She shook her head despairingly. "Unfair, sir. Plying me with Shakespeare instead of posies." She grinned. "I cannot find it in me to do as I ought and refuse. But please, call me Lizzy. All those dearest to me do."

"Lizzy," he said, and crushed his mouth to hers.

3

L izzy looked distractedly about her exquisite room. It featured hand-painted walls and silk brocade coverings with rich velvet hangings, a room fit for royalty. If she were in her right mind, she would be overwhelmed.

Of course, she was not in her right mind. Had she accepted an offer of marriage from the owner of all this magnificence? What had she been thinking?

Dazed, she nodded as a helpful maid pointed out the writing desk. "And here's the bell pull, Miss," the girl said. "If you need anything at all, give it a tug and someone will be here in two shakes."

"I thank you." The maid curtseyed and left Lizzy to her disjointed thoughts.

Sighing, she seated herself at the mahogany writing table, withdrawing a piece of the fine parchment. As she stared at its blank surface, she wondered how she could possibly explain this whole situation to Jane without sounding completely mad!

Nevertheless, a greedy, uncontrolled sliver of her soul danced giddily about the room. For so long, the sum total of her hopes and dreams had been a great deal less than Fitzwilliam offered. A master! How did one go about hiring one? However, the man who undoubtedly hired drawing and dancing and music masters for Georgiana must know how it was done. And she had no doubt he would find the best.

Dearest Jane,
'Tis no longer necessary to borrow Mama's silver combs to create
mermaids.

She needed a kiln capable of firing larger pieces. And marble! 'Twas so expensive, but now, perhaps, within reach. She had tried her hand at sculpting in stone, but with only inferior materials and without the proper tools, her crude attempts were dissatisfying. A set of fine chisels would go a long way towards rectifying any deficiencies. Would Fitzwilliam consider an engagement gift?

Was the decision to marry made out of avarice? Or was she foolish, imagining she would truly be allowed to fulfil a dream and yet be the kind of wife Fitzwilliam expected and deserved?

By the time the maid appeared to help ready her for dinner, nothing else was on the paper.

DINNER WAS SERVED IN A DINING ROOM MADE TO COMFORTABLY SEAT forty. The formal room matched the expressions of both Darcys, though Georgiana could see her brother appeared easy in his posture and appearance.

"At least they did not seat you at the head of the table," Lizzy said to Darcy. "I would have to stand upon my chair to be heard."

"Now, now," he replied. "I am sure a good shout would do just as well."

Georgiana looked askance at both of them. And then Fitzwilliam winked at her. It was most disconcerting.

As they proceeded through the courses she grew increasingly bemused. Perhaps it was Fitzwilliam's unusual cheerfulness. He had never been what she would call jovial—and in recent months he had grown positively grave. But tonight, he was jesting. And winking.

Her feelings about her brother were muddled. She had struggled with anger towards him for a long while. After Papa died, Fitzwilliam —always protective—had grown more difficult, refusing to allow her to do anything amusing, even after she put off her mourning. Not knowing which girls to trust at Lydia Younge's very exclusive school he had reluctantly allowed her to attend, she had not made friends. She had been angry with those girls, too. They all spoke unceasingly of their parents escorting them to this or that event, and of their mamas taking them shopping and planning their wardrobes and their seasons. Her anger seemed odd now; she felt a certain hollowness without it.

She glanced at Lizzy—still in the same dress she wore that morning —suddenly recognising that the lady had no other.

I have dresses she could wear. She and Lizzy were much of a height, although Lizzy had much more in her upper half than Georgiana. She felt embarrassed she had not seen to it earlier, but she would talk to the housekeeper immediately.

"Lizzy, I have some dresses that could be easily made over for you," she blurted. "Until your trunk arrives."

Both Fitzwilliam and Lizzy looked startled at the abrupt change in topics, but Lizzy recovered first, and smiled at the younger girl.

"Why thank you, Georgiana," she said. "That is most gracious."

"I sent word for your trunk to be retrieved from Newark, where the Rushworths left it," Fitzwilliam put in. "It should be here tomorrow."

This was dispiriting, but Georgiana persevered. "I would still like you to have them. The dresses…I have too many, and one trunk cannot hold much." *And I want you to stay for a long while*, she silently added.

"You are correct," Lizzy said with a laugh.

Pleased, Georgiana smiled upon her serving of roasted venison. Perhaps…perhaps after she demonstrated she was not a stupid goose, despite her recent actions, Lizzy would consent to act as companion. It might take some time for Fitzwilliam to agree to allow her to have her own household again, but…just look at him! He smiled at something Lizzy said! Fitzwilliam never smiled! Plainly, she was a good influence upon him. Surely, she could help him realise his younger sister was no longer a baby and should be allowed certain privileges and amuse-ments. She and Lizzy could go, back to Ramsgate perhaps, and this time instead of Lydia's falseness and dangerous romance, Georgiana could have a real friend. Maybe Lizzy would show her how to work in clay, and they could have long walks and talks and read books and shop and all the things Lydia never had been interested in doing, not with Georgiana. And eventually, Lizzy could talk Fitzwilliam into allowing her a season, mayhap before her twentieth birthday.

While Georgiana made these plans, the meal and conversation moved forward without her attention. However, she did notice once the dessert was served Fitzwilliam's solemn expression returned as he sent the footmen from the room.

"Georgiana," he began.

She turned to face him, willing herself to meet his gaze. Was he going to take her to task for her mistakes now, at the dinner table?

"I have excellent news," he said.

Good news?

"Elizabeth has agreed to become my wife."

Georgiana's jaw dropped in astonishment, and the recently dissipated anger reappeared with impressive force. Fitzwilliam was selfishly taking her friend for himself! And Lizzy—of course she had chosen the eligible, wealthy bachelor over a stupid fifteen-year-old girl! The betrayal of it all nearly choked her. And was she supposed to offer congratulations? Before she humiliated herself by bursting into tears, she pushed back her chair and hastened from the room.

"Georgiana!" Fitzwilliam called after her, but she paid him no heed.

DARCY STOOD AT ONCE AND MADE TO FOLLOW. HE HAD WITNESSED THE hurt expression cross Lizzy's face at the signs of Georgiana's obvious displeasure. Had he dreamed she would behave so boorishly, he would never have told her in Lizzy's presence. But until this moment, Georgiana seemed to genuinely like Lizzy; she had just been offering dresses from her own wardrobe, devil take it!

A hand upon his arm halted him before he reached the door.

"Fitzwilliam," Lizzy said, and the sound of his name upon her lips caused a shiver of pleasure, despite his anger. "Wait one moment. What do you intend to say?"

"I do not know," he said gruffly. "Perhaps I will skip words entirely and go directly for the birch rod, as my father would have done, had I ever behaved so insolently." Noting the look on Lizzy's face, he added, "I have never laid a hand on the girl and would not. Nevertheless, I will be having words with her. By the time I finish, she shall regret her conduct tonight."

"No."

"No?" Unused to being crossed, his expression darkened.

"I fear we are about to have another disagreement." She sighed.

"If you believe this behaviour is acceptable, I fear you are correct. Should I permit such unkindness, especially towards you, whom I esteem above all others?"

"Girls can be difficult to understand," she began.

"What she needs to understand is that you are always to be treated with respect! Can she have so quickly forgotten she owes you her life?"

"An overstatement. Listen to me."

"Not an overstatement, not by half! You threw yourself into the lion's den—for her! I have not yet learned all the details of the escape, but I do not have to be told you engineered it! And this is how you are to be repaid?"

"Listen to me!" she said earnestly. "What I did for your sister, I did as much for you as for her. So if it is gratitude that prompts your anger, stop blustering for a moment and listen."

He quieted then, looking into her eyes. "It is gratitude and much more," he growled, "as I think you are aware." Placing an arm on either side of her, he trapped her against the wall.

"Are you trying to intimidate me?"

"I am listening to you now," he replied, nuzzling her throat.

"It doesn't feel as though you're listening," she whispered.

"How does it feel?" He kissed her.

Lizzy allowed it, but before they could forget themselves, she lightly pushed at him.

Of course, he was a large and solid male—had he not acceded to her wishes, she would have had as much success in moving him as in moving the wall behind her. But he retreated easily, only leaning in again to press his forehead against hers, his breathing not quite steady.

"It feels as though you try to distract me," she said, a rueful tone in her voice.

"It is possible I have wanted to kiss you all through these past several courses, and used the first excuse to take advantage," he admitted. "But I am listening now. Tell me why I should not beat my childish, discourteous sister?"

"You said you would never beat her," she chided.

"Perhaps not. But I am at my wit's end with her behaviour. I cannot let this go."

Closing her eyes, Lizzy leaned back against the wall and tried to explain. "Early in our misadventure, I discovered Georgiana was wretched that her poor choices had involved me in danger. This is not the thinking of a selfish girl. I do not question your right to correct her. I only ask you to first discover why she needs correcting."

Perhaps noticing her unsteadiness, Darcy led her back to her chair, this time seating himself beside her and taking her hand in his. "I am to discover why she behaves abominably," he said, placing a kiss upon each finger. "Understood."

"Except," she added, "even if you ask her why, it is possible she won't be able to tell you."

At this he put up his head, though he did not let her go. "Then what is the use of asking?"

"Once I dumped an entire pot of ink on Jane's new gown. My mother was beside herself. 'Why, Lizzy?' she wailed. 'Why would you do such a dreadful thing!?' I refused to answer. I knew shouting, 'Because I hate her!' would only get me into more trouble. I was too young to understand the jealousy I bore because she had a father who bought her pretty new clothes and I did not. I suppose I would not trouble to ask Georgiana for whys. Perhaps...instead of asking 'why,' just talk to her. Hopefully you can discern her reasoning."

Darcy kissed her hand once more. "I will buy you a hundred pretty new gowns," he said, hating her struggle with such unfairness as a child.

She laughed, and it did something to his insides.

"I wasn't abused, you know," she said. "I could be a horrid little beast and was often a trial to my poor mother. My punishment for damaging the dress was to rise extra early and build the fires in every room each morning for a month. Jane felt sorry for me, so she did half of them herself, and this even though she had to embroider dozens of flowers over the ink stains to protect me from her father's wrath." She cocked her head and grinned up at him. "Her exquisite embroidery made the dress even lovelier, and I had to bite my tongue and endure all the compliments she received for it."

He smiled. "Your sister sounds like an angel."

"Oh, she is. 'Tis why I wish so much for her to have everything she wants. Truly, Fitzwilliam, will you be patient with Georgiana? Even if she is behaving badly?"

Sighing, Darcy pressed a kiss to her furrowed brow. "I will try," he said. "Do you wish to retire now? Or would you rather wait up?"

"I don't fancy staying downstairs alone," she replied. "But come with me to the library first, and show me where you've hidden the trumpery novels. You must have an Ann Radcliffe or Clara Reeve tucked in there some place."

"I will have your pudding sent to your room," he said, kissing the tip of her nose, "and you may indulge all your vices while I, like Job, suffer in the pursuit of virtue."

And the staid and impenetrable master of Pemberley had to stop himself from whistling while he led his betrothed to a library in search of literary guilty pleasures.

THOUGH IGNORANT OF THE VOW GEORGIANA HAD PRIVATELY MADE, DARCY saw, by the sullen expression on her face, she was not in any better frame than the hour before. While it might be better to interview her tomorrow, he had a journey to undertake and was anxious to start first thing in the morning. Besides, he was in as good a humour now, fresh from an extremely agreeable good-night kiss, as he was ever likely to be.

They stared silently at each other from across his desk, the tick of a clock the only sound. As time passed, however, he recognised this was not new—especially since Father died. Even when she was not angry with him for refusing some request or another, they did not converse easily. His successes at any sort of fathering were trifling at best, and he wondered why it had never occurred to him that she needed one, still.

He also remembered sitting in the exact chair in which she was seated, not much younger than she was now, waiting for his father to take a strip off of him for fighting at Eton.

And yet, Father only conveyed his disappointment without destroying my pride. How had he managed it? Never had Darcy missed him as much as he did at this moment.

"I owe you an apology, Georgiana," he said finally.

Georgiana looked up sharply in surprise.

"When I sent you to Mrs Younge's school, then hired her to be your companion, I believed her to be of excellent character. Obviously, I was misled. Will you accept my apologies for putting you in her care?"

Georgiana nodded, but showed no sign of softening her posture. His anger surged—she should be begging his forgiveness for accepting Wickham's illicit proposal! She knew better! Especially as he had opened the door by making the first gesture of contrition. Only the vision of a stubborn adolescent Lizzy, hiding her hurt behind defiance, gave him pause. Finally, at a loss for any other topic that might open conversation, he broached the subject of the kidnap.

"I have not yet heard the details of how you managed escape from those scoundrels. Will you tell me how it was accomplished?"

This query, it transpired, was a stroke of brilliance on his part. She soon forgot she was the injured party, enthusiastically revealing the particulars of their adventure. She told of how relieved and yet terrified she was when Lizzy insisted upon accompanying her, how Lizzy had never been afraid for one moment and, finally, about the creation of the clay "bosoms" (whispered with a blush) and their ultimate fate. Throughout the tale, it became clear that Georgiana held Lizzy in the highest esteem...which made her decided rejection of his offer more confusing.

By the time she finished, at their reunion upon the Mansfield-Nottingham Road, Darcy was utterly flabbergasted.

"I knew Lizzy was remarkable almost from the beginning," he found himself revealing. "I was most discourteous at our first meeting. We had a misunderstanding of identity. I thought she was her mother, and, um, I..."

He found himself at a loss as to how to explain the story without indiscretion regarding specifics he and Lizzy had not yet discussed.

"Oh, Lizzy told me about her mother, that she's, um, not respectable," Georgiana put in.

"Ah. So this is why you are upset about my forthcoming marriage to her."

"'Tis not!" Georgiana cried fiercely. "I would never! I am the last person to judge another for her mother's actions, especially considering mine!"

He was chastened by Georgiana's response, particularly since his own initial actions towards Lizzy had not been so humble.

"Well said. But since Lizzy knows you are aware of her upbringing, I am sure she assumes you do not want her in our family for that very reason."

Georgiana looked stricken. "I was disappointed!" she burst out, tears filling her eyes. "I wanted her to become my new companion, and then you said you were marrying her, which means she will want to be with you instead of me and then she will have babies and they will need her and I...and I..." she trailed off, tears trickling off her chin and dripping onto her lap.

Darcy found his handkerchief, using the action to cover his bewilderment. As he pulled a chair close to hers, he searched for words;

nothing wise occurred to him. Handing the linen over, he tentatively placed his arm about her shoulders.

To his surprise, she turned into him, burying her face in his shoulder. So, he awkwardly put his arms about her, embracing her. For some minutes she held the position, and he was ashamed to realise that—with the exception of the moment of discovery upon the Mansfield-Nottingham Road—he had not hugged her since their father's death. She had always been such a loving child; Father had practised no economy with his hugs and kisses, even though he was not by nature demonstrative. How she must have felt Father's loss, perhaps even more so than Darcy! How simple it must have been for the likes of Wickham to take advantage of this affection-starved girl!

"All will be well, my dear," he said, patting her back. "All will be well."

When, finally, he was sure her tears finished, he tilted her chin up to meet his gaze. "Sweetheart, you do realise that companions may come and companions may go, but sisters are family?"

She bit her lower lip and dropped her eyes. "I suppose I did not think it out," she admitted.

He made an admission of his own. "I asked Lizzy to marry me before we even found you," he said. "Except I botched the thing royally. She rightfully refused."

"Y–you did?" she sniffed. "She said no? How did you change her mind?"

"When the Rushworths asked me why you were alone in Wetherby, I told them Lizzy and I were on our way to Scotland to be wed, accompanied by you and Cousin Richard, that you—upset by the elopement, had run from us in Wetherby in a hysterical fit—after which they whisked you away before we could retrieve you. I fear Lizzy is marrying me to save your reputation."

Georgiana went wide-eyed at this recital, all tears disappearing. "Oh, my," she said. "She does not care for you?"

He sat back in the chair, looking thoughtful. "I would not say that," he said at last. "We have a certain, um…" he began, blushing faintly. "Rather, we are compatible, and I believe she is beginning to care for me. However, she struggles with trusting people, especially men, I think. I fear she has not met the best of my sex, nor ever met her father."

Georgiana nodded. "There are many men in the world like George

Wickham, I suppose. But Fitzwilliam, you would never behave badly. She is safe with you."

He was touched by her defence of him, but looked Georgiana directly in the eye. "You do realise my marriage saves your reputation in one sense, but sullies it in another? There are some who will not tolerate any connexion to someone with her relations. If you wish to make the most advantageous marriage possible, you should live with Lady Catherine and distance yourself from us."

There was a long pause. "What...where do you wish me to live?"

Darcy longed for the wisdom of Solomon, weighing what was in his sister's best interests against the wishes of his heart. And yet, there was only one answer he could give with any degree of honesty. "Why, I always want you with me, Georgie-my-girl," he said, using her child-hood nickname, and taking her hand.

She sniffed again but did not weep, her eyes now shining. "I wish to live with you, too."

"Are you certain? There will likely be repercussions that will seem harsher in the future, when you seek a husband. The bluest bloods may not consider you eligible."

"Brother, I nearly eloped with a penniless soldier. One can expect I will become more selective as I grow older, but it is probably imprac-tical to assume too much improvement."

They both smiled.

"I leave tomorrow for Derby, to visit Uncle Darcy. I hope to obtain a common licence so we can dispense with the banns and be wed imme-diately," he said.

"Oh–h," Georgiana said apprehensively. "I do not envy you. You know Uncle will ask every detail of Lizzy's people, and he is so...so—"

"Yes, I know. But we must marry immediately if the wedding is to be of any use to you, and I do not fancy a trip to Scotland. However, I will inform him if he does not produce the licence swiftly, we will do exactly that. He will want to avoid an elopement at all costs, I am certain." He pressed his sister's hand. "You will look after Lizzy while I am away?"

"Oh! Yes, of course! That is, if she will accept my apology for my behaviour tonight."

"I am sure she will, and happily. She will need your friendship. The news we would be married by licence as soon as I could procure one from Bishop Darcy was startling—much quicker work than she expected."

Georgiana nodded. "I think it wise. Hurry her to the altar before she has too much time to think." She laughed, and after a moment, Darcy joined in.

4

Lizzy awakened disoriented, not quite sure of her whereabouts. Once she remembered, the feeling of stupefaction remained. Pemberley. In a grand room, sleeping on layers of downy mattresses covered with silk and fine linen.

She had stayed awake far too late reading a suspenseful novel, then hearing sounds that may or may not have been ghostly whisperings, creakings, and groanings. In the daylight, however, the room's beauty returned, with a cosy fire baking away the morning's chill. She sat up, then—remembering Fitzwilliam was away acquiring a licence from his uncle—fell down again. His uncle, the Bishop of Derby.

What do you think you're doing here, Elizabeth Bennet? It was madness. What she ought to do was gather her things and set out for Ramsgate. For home, her true home.

But what would such an action mean for Georgiana? A valid justification was needed for the girl to have been on the road to Scotland, and her brother's wedding would answer.

Yet, it was also likely Georgiana's future needs were ill-served by a marriage to Lizzy...which obviously occurred to Georgiana already, judging by last evening. If they undertook a wedding on her behalf, her views on the matter ought to be considered. Lizzy felt a tinge of bitterness that once again, she had been judged and found unworthy.

Could Fitzwilliam possibly truly love me? Or has he mistaken his first infatuation for something deeper?

"I won't think on it for now." For today, she had different designs in mind.

She had given some thought to Lady Anne's presence, feeling she could justify interfering. As Fitzwilliam's betrothed and Georgiana's potential sister-to-be, her protective instincts were raised. Mr Bennet abandoned Lizzy sight unseen; Lady Anne, however, had known exactly whom she forsook, which seemed even more hurtful. For her to appear, desiring reconciliation with the children she had discarded, was incredible. Before she could cause more trouble in the lives of her offspring, her departure should be encouraged.

And yet, Lizzy could not help a deep curiosity. The beauty of this place was astonishing and Fitzwilliam and Georgiana could never have done anything to warrant desertion. However, she had little idea of old Mr Darcy's character. Fitzwilliam respected him deeply, but had also admitted his father's neglect of his wife. How far had that neglect extended?

The summoned maid offered timid congratulations regarding Lizzy's imminent nuptials to the master, which news had evidently been announced to the household at large this morning. Lizzy's belongings had been delivered, and Susannah had taken the liberty of freshening the dresses; however, a number of frocks belonging to Miss Georgiana were also at her disposal. Though Susannah was respectful, it was plain what the maid thought of Lizzy's wardrobe by comparison.

I suppose I should meet Lady Anne as the future Mrs Darcy, not the humble Mrs Jones.

And so, much to Susannah's approval, she chose a delicately embroidered India muslin round gown with a lovely cashmere shawl. The kid boots were from yesterday's provisions, but silk stockings and dainty petticoats were donations from Georgiana's own wardrobe. Lizzy puzzled at the generosity—an apology for the dinnertime fracas, or Fitzwilliam's insistence?

She would ponder later. Her object now was to leave the house before Georgiana awakened.

IF THE EXCESSIVELY HELPFUL PEMBERLEY HOUSEHOLD HAD OBJECTIONS TO her destination, they were far too subtle for Lizzy to note. Though the Hall was less than a mile away, yesterday's elegant carriage accompanied by no less than three footmen was provided for her transport.

Holmwood Hall was a three-story Elizabethan country house situated on a hilltop, and though well out of sight of Pemberley, its six pavilioned towers announced its importance to the countryside. It was not on the scale of Pemberley, but Fitzwilliam had hardly tucked his mother into some anonymous cottage. Would her presence here cause talk? He had not seemed concerned about it yesterday, but rather happily put off the matter until his return.

A maid curtseyed low in response to her knock—could the Holmwood Hall servants already know of their engagement? Lizzy had no calling card, but the impropriety was disregarded. Whisked into a tastefully decorated parlour, she was informed Lady Anne would be notified immediately of her arrival.

Lizzy prepared for a long wait, as it was far too early for callers, gratefully accepting a tray of tea and scones. However, only half an hour passed before Lady Anne appeared. If she had hurried her toilette, it did not show in her impeccable appearance.

"Miss Bennet," she said, "I hope I did not keep you waiting long. I received a note from my son indicating he would be unable to attend me until tomorrow or the day after. I did not expect visitors."

"I apologise for the early hour, ma'am," Lizzy replied. "I was anxious to call before Georgiana begins her day. Fitzwilliam is away, as he informed you. He has no idea I call. I thought to speak with you privately regarding your intentions."

Lady Anne bowed her head. "My intentions?" she asked slowly.

"What you hope to accomplish by your visit."

"Am I allowed to ask...who are you, Miss Bennet?"

Lizzy hesitated; it was a reasonable question. "Fitzwilliam and I have an understanding," she stated firmly. In truth, she understood little, but she wasn't going to broach it with his estranged mother.

Obviously Lady Anne wished to ask more questions, but Lizzy pressed forward with her own.

"Why, after all this time, have you come?" Lizzy asked. "You must know your presence distresses your son. To hear nothing of you for what...thirteen years?"

The older woman sighed. "I have wished to write for many years. Possibly not the first year I left, and had you known me then, you would not have wanted me to. My regrets built as slowly, I suppose, as my stunted character. It was Georgiana's fifth birthday when I truly comprehended the full measure of what I sacrificed to be with Alex. And from that moment on, I grieved."

"It took three years to miss your children?" She tried to keep contempt from her voice, however unsuccessfully.

Lady Anne stood abruptly and went to the window, staring out. It was so like something Fitzwilliam would do when deeply upset, Lizzy's brows raised.

"I shall be honest with you, Miss Bennet. Most of what I reveal does not paint me in an especially good light. Of course I am not, in too many ways, good, but I am honest. I have struggled to become honest with myself. I have no intention of sharing much with Fitzwilliam, for I have not come for absolution. I would never attempt to defend my actions, nor cast aspersions upon the father he loves. I only wish to tell him...of my regret, perhaps, and to...to apologise in person." She toyed with a tassel dangling from her shawl, twisting the thing until Lizzy wondered if it would pull off the fabric's edge, adding, "However, I have the very strong impression that if I cannot convince you I deserve a hearing, I shall be turned away."

Lady Anne paused, as if expecting Lizzy to answer that charge. Lizzy remained silent. She had no idea whether her influence extended to convincing Fitzwilliam to change his opinion on this matter, or any other. However, Lady Anne was correct in one sense—if Lizzy determined his mother was up to no good, she would do her best to be rid of her.

Lady Anne sighed quietly, continuing to address the window. "I was married to George Darcy when I was seventeen. He was thirty-seven. Elderly, I thought then. Though I am of excellent birth, my portion was not large. I did not want the marriage, but Mr Darcy took one look at me in my first season and wanted me. What did my feelings upon the subject matter? It is an old story, and not a particularly interesting one, so I shall not bore you with the particulars of my objections to the match. Mr Darcy was a kind, if distant husband. Within a year, I had Fitzwilliam, and he was pleased. So was I. But then there were three other babes, none who lived, each one twisting a knife in my heart. I became...afraid. Afraid of losing more children. And so I distanced myself."

"You refused your husband your bed," Lizzy stated frankly.

"You are blunt, Miss Bennet."

"My mother is a courtesan," Lizzy replied, seeing no reason to prevaricate. "According to her, this is a common reason why men like him go to females like her." Fanny had explained several methods of preventing pregnancy to her daughters, hoping to avert similar difficulties with their own husbands.

Lady Anne blinked. "Ah. And your father?"

"I believe you were explaining your story," Lizzy replied succinctly, half-expecting the interview would come to an immediate close.

"So I was," Lady Anne agreed with a wry smile. "You are correct. But the distance was not just with Mr Darcy. I also tried to distance myself from Fitzwilliam. I grew convinced he would be taken from me too, and at the time, I was incapable of appreciating the...the blessing of each day God permitted us to have together." She shook her head. "I was reared to believe myself very grand, Miss Bennet, but foolishness was my defining quality."

Lizzy shook her head. "It does seem..."

"Stupid? Cruel?" the older woman asked.

"I would say impossible. How does one distance oneself from one's child?"

Lady Anne grimaced. "In our illustrious household, 'twould be an easy thing, one would think. Nursemaids and nannies and tutors and, eventually, Eton. But Fitzwilliam did not permit it. I had not begun soon enough. 'Mama, let me show you,' he would say, and share with me his treasures and secrets. I could never resist his sweetness. He let himself inside my unwilling, withered heart regardless of my maternal deficiencies. I kept a reserve, though, trying to protect myself, should illness take him. Finally, however, it was school that took him away. I was desolate."

Lizzy snorted. How could the woman squander half of Fitzwilliam's life repelling him, and then be crushed by his absence?

Lady Anne shook her head, as if impatient with herself. "I do not blame you for finding me unreasonable. I was a spoiled looby, who could not value my true treasures. Nevertheless, with Fitzwilliam gone, my life seemed a vast wasteland. The season was empty of entertainments and every amusement dulled. I decided I wanted another child. Mr Darcy was elated."

"I rather imagine so," Lizzy said drily. "It was quite the, ah, long drought. Unless he went elsewhere, to a mistress."

"I do not think he did," Lady Anne remarked, after a moment's surprised silence. "I have considered the question and I believe he was never unfaithful. However, he was a very private man. I was, I felt then, such a small, inconsequential part of his life, I did not believe he noticed much whether I was there or not. In retrospect, I believe I failed to give him any sign I wanted more attachment, and perhaps he felt he behaved according to my wishes. At least until I demanded the divorce. But I am getting ahead of myself."

She seated herself and poured a cup of tea, adding sugar and lemon. But she did not drink it, only stared silently into the cup, as if there were answers in the leaves. Lizzy waited, saying nothing.

"I became pregnant with Georgiana, but instead of jubilance, all my trepidation returned. It was a difficult lying in, likely made more so by my fears. By the time she was born, I was terrified, for her and of her. I told myself she was Mr Darcy's child, to be a comfort to him in his old age. Eventually I left her with nursemaids and went to London, where I could not hear her cries, with her little needs I could not meet."

Lizzy felt Lady Anne was hardly remarkable amongst the haute ton in leaving her child to be reared by servants; what was rare was her apparent guilt for having done so.

"I was in London when I met Alex, and I fell in love for the first time in my life. He was handsome and dashing, a younger son of the Marquess of Abington. He loved me, in return." She set down the untouched cup of tea.

"But could I have fallen in love with a man about town? Oh, no! I was married, and Alex had scruples. He would not take another man's wife. I was thirty-one years old and newly in love. I was wilful and spoiled. I would not accept that I could not have him. I convinced myself Fitzwilliam no longer needed a mother, and I was too afraid to be one to Georgiana. For months, Alex resisted me and my wiles. But I was the pitiful, lonely lady whose dreadfully cold and elderly husband stayed buried in the country, caring nothing for her. And, as I said, Alex loved me, and hated that I was so unhappy."

She spoke in measured tones of contempt, without a hint of self-pity, but finally, Lizzy felt something besides disdain. Lady Anne drew a clear portrait of herself as an overindulged woman who abandoned her family while turning to another man. However, her loneliness and unhappiness were obvious in every detail. Why had her husband left her alone for so long? And why the devil had he taken her as his bride in the first place? Hadn't he cared that she was unwilling?

Perhaps not. Too many were entirely disinterested in a female's feelings in these matters, and an earl likely cared less than most. Likely he had presented his daughter as agreeable. She wondered, however, if

George Darcy had bothered to ask, or if he arranged it with her father like the business transaction it had been.

"I concocted the scheme for a Scottish divorce," the older lady continued. "I acknowledge now, I was only appeasing my own needs, that it was no help for my husband's. But I convinced myself he had no feelings for me, that I was merely an inconvenience. That as long as he had the children, he had everything he wanted."

"This was not the case?" Lizzy asked, after a long silence.

Lady Anne gave one sharp negative motion of the head. "I asked him for the divorce. He went with me to Scotland. He begged and pleaded with me to change my mind. He promised he would do anything in his power to make things at home different, that he would become a better man, and that he loved me. But I had decided my needs were more important than his. I refused him utterly."

"That...was cruel," Lizzy said. "And very sad."

"I warned you I am not good, Miss Bennet." The tassel finally gave up the fight, ripping free from the shawl's edge. For all her self-discipline, the older woman did not appear to notice she had torn her clothing. "I relive his despair in my dreams now. But such was my desperation then, I steeled my heart against him. I never told Alex any of this. He died thinking Mr Darcy let me go willingly, or at least, willingly enough." She put one finger upon her chin, her gaze turned inward and contemplative. "I understood, inside, that Alex would not have taken me if he had known. I wanted him, and so I got him."

"Was the marriage happy?" Lizzy asked, sipping her own cold tea for the sake of something to do with her hands.

Lady Anne laughed, the sound more self-mocking than humorous. "If this were a child's tale, it would have been miserable. The moral would have our selfish love destroying both of us, turning to hatred in the end. But Alex was warm and wonderful and wise. He was patient with my childishness and never allowed me to put him off. From him, I learned, for the first time, how to love and how to show it and share it with others. Eventually, I even put aside my fears of having more children. Sadly, it never happened. We both grieved over that, but..."

Lady Anne returned to the window, staring out.

"I also began grieving over the children I cast aside. Ironic, is it not? There is certainly no pleasing Lady Anne Fitzwilliam of Matlock!" She said it with contempt but there were tears in her voice.

"It sounds more pitiful than ironic."

Lady Anne glanced briefly over her shoulder with a brittle smile. "Pitiful. Yes, that is apt. As soon as I learned to love, I learned how much I once had. I wrote letters to the children, nearly weekly, although they were never sent. I promised Mr Darcy, you see, I would stay out of their lives. It was the one thing he insisted upon. As guilty as I felt over him, I decided I could not break my vow in this matter as I had in so many others."

"That seems heartless to his poor children."

"No, George Darcy was not a cruel man. I am certain it was the scandal. He wanted to distance them from their wicked mother, for their sakes, I am sure. But perhaps I only make excuses for my own cowardice. Perhaps I did not send those letters out of a selfish fear of rejection. I am certainly weak enough for that to be the case. Regardless, I held to my promise."

Lizzy was unsure how to respond. Lady Anne's actions had been pathetic and destructive and selfish...and yet, the picture in Lizzy's mind was of a girl, not a woman, certainly not the woman standing before her now with equal parts self-possession and self-disgust. It was of a girl, a spoiled, lonely girl who hadn't learned any means of coping with loss and grief, until the wrong man taught her how. "'Tis a sad tale for everyone," she said at last.

"It is generous of you to see it that way. Not entirely sad, though. As little as I deserved them, I had eleven wonderful years with Alex. Of all my many regrets, I do not regret him."

"I would not expect you to," Lizzy replied, and cocked her head inquisitively. "Mr Darcy has been dead for a year and a half, as I understand," Lizzy said. "Fitzwilliam says you have not claimed your settlement nor answered his solicitors. Why have you come now?"

"My usual correspondents were neglectful. I did not learn of his death until six months after the fact," Lady Anne replied. "Whatever you think of me, I would not dream of taking an inheritance meant for a faithful wife. I do not wish to argue with lawyers. If I do not answer them, they cannot pay it. But of course, with Mr Darcy gone, I was no longer bound by my promise not to see the children. I knew they would need at least a full year of mourning before they would even receive a letter from me. It seemed disrespectful to intrude earlier. I have written so many letters since then! But I could not send them. Each was too full of either justifications or pity or a love that would utterly disgust them. I know they must hate me, and I understand. But

I felt…I still feel I have to try to–to confront their contempt directly, and doing so in person is the…the honourable way." Her shoulders hunched, gathering the shredded scarf more tightly.

For many minutes, the only sound was the crackling of the fire in the hearth. Neither spoke, but it was not precisely an awkward silence.

"I will take my leave now," Lizzy said at last. "I have no idea what to say to Fitzwilliam. I do not believe he would read your letters, much less receive you in…sympathy. However, I will say nothing to discourage him from doing so, and if he wishes my opinion on the matter, I will tell him…I like you. For whatever it is worth." She could not help feeling compassion for this woman who asked for none.

"It is worth much to me, Miss Bennet," she said in astonishment, turning to face her. "Thank you for listening to an old lady's tale of idiocy, and for not…not saying everything you must be thinking."

"I told you my mother is a courtesan, and you kept your thoughts to yourself," Lizzy replied wryly.

"The days when I counted myself better than any other are long behind me," said Lady Anne softly. "I have learned a few things, you see."

Lizzy walked partway to the door before looking back. "If you had to do it all over again, would you change it? Make different choices?"

Lady Anne smiled sadly. "Ah, that question. The problem with it, Miss Bennet, is all of my choices made me who I am now. If I were to go back in time and undo them, I would still be the selfish, spoiled Lady Anne Darcy, who understood so little. She both craved love and thrust it foolishly away. I do not believe I can give you a satisfactory answer."

"That one will do. And please, call me Lizzy."

ON THE JOURNEY BACK TO PEMBERLEY, LIZZY CONTEMPLATED LADY Anne's tale. There was certainly blame to spare. Some belonged to the old earl of Matlock, no doubt, for forcing the mismatch in the first place. Lady Anne shouldered considerable blame, but it also appeared George Darcy could have prevented some of the disaster their marriage became, had he tried sooner to mend the breach. Had he mourned those lost babes too, with no idea how to aid a young wife's grief? It was all too sad.

Suddenly, she wished fervently that Fitzwilliam were not so

distant. She could not reveal much of what she had learned from his mother—and after all, she would not welcome another telling her how to feel about her own absent parent. Still, she would welcome assurances that her marriage to him would not suffer the same fate. At least, unlike Lady Anne's marital beginnings, they wanted one another. For now. But how many of her mother's liaisons had been with men who had wanted their wives, at first?

As the carriage pulled around the circular drive at the front of the stately home, Lizzy spied Georgiana at the top of the front steps. Oddly, the girl's hands were clasped together almost as if she were wringing them.

Nearly as soon as Lizzy alighted from the carriage, Georgiana dashed down the front steps towards her.

"Oh, Lizzy," she said, somewhat breathless from her exertions, "I am so happy you returned. No one could say where you went and I was afraid…well, that I had made you feel unwelcome. Nothing could be further from the truth!"

Lizzy smiled and took Georgiana's arm, leading her back up the steps. "I went for a ride along your beautiful countryside." She paused a moment and added, "I thank you for the dresses and things. You were exceedingly generous."

Georgiana made a deprecating wave. "I am happy you like them. This looks well on you." She blushed. "I am sure Fitzwilliam will think so."

Lizzy sighed. "We need not marry," she said quietly. "Perhaps a solution…more suitable…could be arranged."

"I am so sorry about my behaviour, Lizzy," Georgiana replied gravely, halting at the top of the steps and turning to face her. "Please agree to be my sister. I did not think clearly last night, and you make Fitzwilliam so happy. And me. Please, if you could disregard my lapse in manners, I would be ever so grateful. Again."

This pretty speech lost its intended effect when Georgiana added, "No…no, no, no. Anything but this!"

Lizzy looked up sharply, but she saw Georgiana was looking past her at the drive, where an elegant black carriage pulled up behind the Darcy vehicle.

"Who is that?"

"Oh, oh dear. Oh, no! 'Tis my aunt's coach. Lady Catherine…she is here!"

"Ah, Lady Catherine," Lizzy said. From everything she had heard, there was no reason to suppose this visit would be a pleasant one.

"Oh, I do wish Fitzwilliam were not in Derby today," Georgiana wailed.

"That might be easier, yes," Lizzy said, as a woman emerged and studied her surroundings with the air of one making notes on needed improvements. "But remember, you have faced highwaymen. I doubt your aunt is armed."

"Her tongue is a dangerous weapon and she wields it like a lash," Georgiana murmured.

As they watched, another female, much shorter and stick-thin, stepped out of the carriage.

"And Anne, her daughter," Georgiana whispered. "Aunt wants Fitzwilliam to marry Anne. Papa also wanted him to marry her, they used to row about it. I was not supposed to hear them but I listened at Papa's study door because Papa never shouted, but he did that time. The more he shouted the quieter Fitzwilliam became so I mostly could not hear. But Fitzwilliam did apologise for calling Anne a milligrub, because of all her sham illnesses, although he still refused to marry her."

The approach of the great lady meant no more time for Georgiana's hurried explanations, but as hurried speeches went, it revealed much.

Lady Catherine addressed her first remarks to Georgiana, wasting no time on preliminaries. "I see you look none the worse for your misadventures, young lady. I received the extremely brief note from your brother, informing me you were unharmed. Fortunately, I was already packing in my haste to be with him during this terrible time. Where is Fitzwilliam? It is imperative I speak with him. At once, if you please."

Georgiana floundered. "Um. He–he is not here. Not...not until tomorrow, my lady." She gathered her courage. "Might I introduce you to Miss Bennet?"

The imperious woman barely deigned to notice Lizzy. "Georgiana, please show Anne inside to the green parlour. Not the yellow parlour, as the windows in the yellow parlour face full west and she suffers from the headache."

Georgiana blushed at her aunt's ill-mannered disdain, somehow finding strength within the insult to attempt a diversion. "You–you must be hungry after your journey," she said. "We could have refreshments served if you would care to join us...in the green parlour, of course."

"Nonsense. I never eat so much as a crumb between breakfast and tea, and I suggest you do not either, to prevent dyspepsia and flux of humours." Her voice grew aggressive, her tone a demand brooking no refusal. "Miss Bennet, I should be glad to take a turn in the nearest of Pemberley's renowned gardens, if you will favour me with your company?"

"I will," replied Lizzy, disliking the gleam in the older woman's eyes upon her discovery of Fitzwilliam's absence. She tried to convey in her smile to Georgiana that she was perfectly able to manage any number of overbearing aunts. Nevertheless, Georgiana continued to look anxious as she led away the silent Anne.

Lady Catherine was a handsome woman, though her eyes were too small and her chin too ignoble to be any competition to her sister's beauty. She maintained a brisk pace towards one of the estate's fine gardens; plainly, the walking stick she carried was an affectation.

Lizzy had little time to enjoy the beds of blooms before the woman began in strident tones, "You can be at no loss, Miss Bennet, to understand the reason of my journey hither. Your own heart, your own conscience, must tell you why I come."

"I would suppose you have spoken with the Rushworths, learning of my forthcoming marriage to your nephew," Lizzy answered calmly.

Lady Catherine whirled so fast upon Lizzy she had to stop herself from taking a step backwards. "Marriage! It is a wicked lie! Miss

Bennet, I am astonished you would dare aspire to such a connexion! Who are your people? Who is your mother? Your father? How could you agree to this mismatch?"

Lizzy nearly laughed—she knew better than to indulge that particular line of questioning. "As to my parents, they are no one you might know," she answered. "I may as well ask who is Mr Darcy's mother. However, Mr Darcy is not marrying my mother nor am I marrying his. Therefore, I expect we shall be solely and independently responsible for our happiness, and not rely upon our parents to provide excuse for any absence of felicity."

The elder woman narrowed her eyes. Her voice lowered to a threatening pitch. "Let me be rightly understood. This match, to which you have the presumption to aspire, can never take place. No, never. Mr Darcy is engaged to my daughter. Now, what have you to say?"

Lizzy raised a brow at the lengths to which the woman was willing to perjure herself. "Do you accuse your nephew of attempted bigamy? It seems a harsh allegation, especially since your own sister might also be thus accused. I am comforted to disbelieve him guilty of the charge, and those who love him might behave better than to cast such aspersions."

"Miss Bennet!" Lady Catherine gasped furiously, her face flushing with anger. "I know your sort! You have cast your arts and allurements, throwing a net of deceit over a man's duty towards his family! Perhaps you have successfully turned his head—but I am here to prevent further scheming! I tell you, there will be no marriage! His mother is dead to us, but his remaining relations will not allow his descent down the slippery slope of depravity. He has a duty to Anne and, I assure you, his own sister's future depends upon him fulfilling it!" She stamped the point of the walking stick into the ground for emphasis.

Lizzy, if it were possible, grew even calmer in her fury. The only difference she could see between this bully and the ones she rebuffed on the streets of Ramsgate was the cost of Lady Catherine's costume.

"First bigamy. Now, a blackmail," she said sardonically. "In the few minutes I have enjoyed the dubious pleasure of your company, you have both threatened and offered bald-faced lies. If there is conversation needed for a depraved soul, you may wish to arrange it with your own vicar. On the chance your hearing is as defective as your morals, let me be clear—your wishes shall be of no consideration to my future plans, or to Mr Darcy's."

Lady Catherine's eyes flared, and for a moment Lizzy wondered if the older woman contemplated whacking her with the walking stick. Finally, however, she took apparent refuge in her own superiority, drawing herself up with lavish disdain.

"Very well. You have insulted me in every possible method, and I shall know how to act. If Miss Darcy can never hold her head up in polite society again, you need only blame yourself. I return to the house now. It has been an arduous journey, and I shall require Mrs Reynolds's personal attendance. At once," she ordered viciously.

"One moment, Sister," sounded a melodious voice from behind them. Its owner strolled out from behind some foliage moments later, in the person of Lady Anne.

Lady Catherine froze for a moment as if seeing a ghost, her jaw dropping open in astonishment. "You!" she gasped.

"Lovely to see you, Catherine. However, you are much deluded if you think to threaten with impunity and expect us to offer hospitality. Think again."

"Never mind that," Lady Catherine hissed. "I would not stay in the same country as you, much less the same household. I see Fitzwilliam has fallen further than I thought possible!"

"Oh, dearest sister, he can fall beyond this, I assure you. If you have no intention of supporting Georgiana's interests in society, he shall not have any desire to pay for the upkeep of your London town house. Likewise for the 'assistance' he currently lends to rescue Rosings Park from the disaster you and the baron made of it. If you desire his support, you shall ensure he can hold his head high wherever he goes in this country. Otherwise you shall never see another penny. I vow it."

Lady Catherine actually began sputtering. "He–he would not! His honour—his duty—"

"I see your mind has grown disordered since last we met," Lady Anne said evenly. "You have him confused with his father, who made those promises of financial support and rescue. But Fitzwilliam is *my* son, Catherine. Mine. And you know how little I care about appearances or honour. You either earn his support with your loyal devotion to his interests, including his marriage to Miss Bennet, or you will find yourself another champion. Are we understood?"

Purple with rage, Catherine turned on her heel and stalked away.

Lizzy watched her depart. "My. What an unpleasant person, your sister," she remarked.

"Quite so," Lady Anne said. "But she was reared by unpleasant parents, and married to an unpleasant husband. I suppose the odds of becoming unpleasant herself were dreadfully high."

"Be that as it may, I am grateful for your interference. How do you know Fitzwilliam supports her?"

"Oh, that," Lady Anne made a disparaging motion with her hand. "I have any number of correspondents, most of them willing to rub my nose in all I miss by living in sin and shame. I do have a few genuine friends, however." She smiled at Lizzy's continued puzzlement. "The de Bourghs lived on credit for years. The baron was a fool, and my sister has always been better at spending money than managing it. Rosings Park was crumbling around Catherine's head. Shortly after Sir Lewis—her husband—died, Catherine suddenly began employing her high stickler friends to ensure Fitzwilliam would be received. She opened her London town house for the first time in years, and there is word of parties at Rosings Park again. Most understand Mr Darcy paid her bills in return for her support of his children."

Lizzy shook her head. "If the scheme is so deliberate, I am surprised she was able to successfully manoeuvre her nephew back into the best circles."

"I am sure they would not be accepted by everyone, but all who Catherine could blackmail or bully was sufficient to gain entrée to Almack's and a full social calendar. Not to mention, Fitzwilliam is a well-heeled bachelor of aristocratic birth, which is enough for most. He has been sought after at all the best events of the season for several years."

Lizzy was thoughtful. "If his father promised his support, Fitzwilliam likely will believe himself bound, also. He feels his obligations deeply. Perhaps even if Lady Catherine no longer offers hers."

Lady Anne shrugged. "Mayhap. But she will not risk it, the greedy cow. Power equals two elements—influence and money. Without both, she is only half a person. She required a reminder."

Lizzy shook her head at the workings of society. "How odd. I have neither power nor money, and yet I have always felt whole."

The other woman gave a sigh. "The rest of us should aspire to your self-possession, Lizzy. 'Tis a gift."

Lizzy smiled wryly. "Thank you. But how did you happen to be here for so timely an intervention?" she asked curiously.

"Ah, that. First, please know I had no intention of interfering with anyone. There is a lovely path between Pemberley and Holmwood Hall, from the days when Mrs Henry Darcy—Mr George Darcy's mother—lived there...it was her dower house. I thought to see my gardens—I planned them, you know. At least, most of those nearest the house. I expected changes, but no...they are exactly as I left them." She paused, and Lizzy, hearing the tiny shudder, purposely looked away while Lady Anne collected herself.

"I planned to remain unseen, and turn away if sighted. But I heard the distinctive dulcet tones of Catherine's voice, and I was in a quandary, I admit. Had it been Georgiana, I am unsure I could have walked away. Since it was you, I did not mind meddling."

Lizzy took a deep breath. "Well. I do thank you again. I will go back to the house and make sure she departs."

"Oh, she will. She will not sully herself by remaining near me. As long as no one informs her I stay elsewhere, you are safe."

Lizzy put her hand forward, and Lady Anne pressed it. "Please, enjoy the gardens," Lizzy said. "But you cannot allow Georgiana to see you, under any circumstances. Only Fitzwilliam can permit that."

Lady Anne nodded her understanding. "Thank you."

Lizzy turned back once, just before she entered a courtyard which she hoped would return her to the house proper. Lady Anne stood near where she'd left her, staring out at her gardens. Her loneliness was palpable, and Lizzy felt a surge of sympathy. With a sigh, she pushed the thought aside, in search of the correct path to the house.

"HER LADYSHIP WAS IN A PERISHING HASTE TO BE OFF," MRS REYNOLDS commented.

"Yes, well, I do not suppose she was happy to hear what I had to say," Lizzy replied as they made their way to the green parlour, where, evidently, Georgiana was still to be found.

The housekeeper tsked, the most displeasure she would express. "I suppose it best she took herself away, then. If I might say so, Miss Bennet, we are all pleased to hear the master be taking a wife. I've been in service for twenty years and housekeeper for fifteen. He was always a fine boy, and now a fine man. We wish him happy."

Lizzy raised a brow, glancing at the housekeeper once more; Mrs Reynolds must have become housekeeper at an unusually young age. Then she smiled to herself, realising the woman had not offered unqualified felicitations. The message was clear—they were willing to be happy for the master but were taking *her* under advisement.

"I do as well. By the way, I left Lady Anne in the gardens. I will steer Georgiana to other pursuits, but if she does express an interest in visiting them, please send someone to warn her ladyship. She has promised to depart immediately if she sees anyone, but I would rather not have any more surprise encounters today."

Mrs Reynolds sniffed and said she would take care the girl never caught sight of, as Mrs Reynolds put it, "trespassers."

GEORGIANA EXPRESSED NOTHING BUT RELIEF TO SEE LIZZY UNSCATHED from her confrontation with Lady Catherine. Seated together in the grand parlour, she breathed a dramatic sigh. "Of course, Anne is my cousin, and Papa always said I ought to be kind, but I never know what to say to her. She prides herself in saying nothing unless she has something particular to say—so one might ask how she fares, and receive dead silence in reply. 'Tis very unsettling and I begin babbling to fill in the spaces of the conversation."

"I do not suppose we will see much of her, or her mother, in the future," Lizzy interjected. "Lady Catherine was not precisely taken with me."

"Do not feel slighted," Georgiana remarked. "She likes very few, only her old cat friends, and their main form of entertainment is outdoing each other for meanness. She swooped in saying, 'I am sorry for you, young lady. *Such* a household!' and took Anne away. I was so relieved! I thought for sure she would settle in at Pemberley and we would have the devil's own time ridding ourselves of her!"

"Please, no cursing, Georgiana. You know every indiscretion you commit will be blamed on my poor influence, and I plan to have enough of my own sins to atone for without adding yours," Lizzy said wryly.

This, evidently, gave the girl pause. "Oh! I never thought of that!" She squared her thin shoulders. "I know I have not shown much sense yet, but I have taken what you said to heart. I will try to...to understand myself, as you said. I will do my best to be a credit to you. And Fitzwilliam, of course."

Lizzy reached over and put her arm around the girl, who leaned her head on Lizzy's shoulder. "I could do much worse for a younger sister, even if you could do much better for an elder one."

The day passed surprisingly quickly. Georgiana took her duties as hostess seriously, and while she did not give Lizzy a complete tour of the house, she helped her find the rooms she would use most often, including all three libraries, the three dining rooms, and several receiving parlours and day rooms. The green and yellow parlours were reserved for the "grandest" visitors, and were deeply formal, while others were cosier and less like museum pieces; all were beautiful. Georgiana said Mrs Reynolds would want to introduce her to the servants, including Cook, and was probably waiting for Lizzy to indicate an interest or for Fitzwilliam to arrange it.

Lizzy sighed, knowing the mistress of this household would be kept busy with the domestic matters alone. How much time would there be for her art if she fulfilled her duties as they ought to be executed?

The next morning, Susannah informed Lizzy that Mr Darcy sent word he would arrive by the afternoon, with a guest in tow; Bishop Darcy was coming to Pemberley.

This news had the household in an uproar, which Lizzy found slightly absurd. Pemberley was a superbly run establishment not requiring uproar to achieve perfection. Hers, however, was a minority opinion.

Georgiana, who was quiet with nerves, tried to explain that a guest's impressions of Pemberley were tied to the honour of the Darcy name, but Lizzy just rolled her eyes.

"This is the loveliest house on earth, in the loveliest setting in England. If the Bishop cannot find something nice to say about it, he suffers from dyspepsia and should forfeit midday meals," Lizzy said drily, making Georgiana giggle for the first time that day.

Lizzy wore another of Georgiana's dresses, Susannah having a good hand with a needle. Lizzy realised that unless she wished to be clothed in a profusion of pastels and girlish designs, she would have to visit a dressmaker soon. Still, this one was, like all of Georgiana's apparel, beautifully made of the finest fabrics, and suitable for introduction to a bishop.

She did her best to disregard her feelings of anxiety; she had never even seen a bishop, much less met one. Had Fitzwilliam changed his mind after speaking with him, coming to his senses? The thought made her heart ache, though she told herself it would be in his best interests and possibly hers. Attempts to distract herself with the beauty of the paintings in the family wing were unsuccessful, as the autocratic features on too many of his ancestors stared back in varying degrees of disapproval. Since there were so many about busily dusting, waxing, lugging carpets in and out, and mopping every surface, she decided to count servants instead, and was up to forty-eight by the time word came that the Darcy coach had pulled into the drive.

GEORGIANA AND LIZZY WAITED AT THE TOP OF THE FRONT STEPS FOR Fitzwilliam and his uncle to emerge from the carriage. The bishop himself was rather impressive, Lizzy had to admit. Tall and silver-haired, she immediately saw the resemblance between him and his nephew as they climbed the steps to greet the ladies.

Fitzwilliam's eyes glimmered with cheerful good humour as he made introductions, but of course circumstances dictated the most sober behaviour. Still, he pressed her hand tightly and she squeezed his in return.

Bishop Darcy was a man of few words. After acknowledging the brief introductions, he merely nodded in agreement to Fitzwilliam's suggestion they briefly refresh themselves and re-adjourn in the summer dining parlour for a light nuncheon.

Whatever hopes Lizzy held for a moment alone with Fitzwilliam before the meal were quashed when Georgiana joined her to wait for him. He could do no more than take Lizzy's hand once again.

"How have you fared?" he murmured.

"Missing you," she whispered, barely having time to get the words out before Georgiana jumped into the conversation, peppering him with questions about Derby.

Bishop Darcy joined them before ten minutes passed, and they made their way into a light, airy dining parlour where a cold collation had been laid. Conversation was overformal at first, but as Georgiana revealed Lady Catherine's visit in response to her brother's questions about their time apart, the bishop sat straighter in his chair.

Lizzy braced herself for a reiteration of Lady Catherine's opinions and wondered if she had the courage to castigate a bishop, if it came to that.

"Matlock's entire family is seriously deficient in character," Bishop Darcy remarked. "Lady Anne was the best of the lot, and is not that a sorry commentary on the Fitzwilliam moral fibre?"

Lizzy saw Fitzwilliam's shoulders stiffen, and Georgiana slumped, as if to make herself smaller. While Lizzy was relieved the bishop was no great admirer of Lady Catherine, she could see such open insults upon Lady Anne were hurtful to her children.

She had grown up hearing insults directed towards her mother. Each one seemed a burr in Lizzy's stockings, and the truth of the accusations only made the bite of the burr work in deeper. Bishop or no, this man could not be allowed to demean his niece and nephew at their own table.

"I strolled in the gardens yesterday. I understand Lady Anne designed them herself. The lady must have had an artist's soul, for I have not seen such beauty elsewhere. Have you, sir?"

The bishop's eagle eyes turned upon her abruptly. His heavy brows beetled.

Lizzy made her expression a calm pool, meeting his sharpness with polite interest. Fitzwilliam watched them both warily.

"How did you find your travel from Derby today, Uncle?" Georgiana asked, a strained note of desperation in her voice.

Bishop Darcy glanced at his niece and subsided, answering her question about the journey.

Lizzy decided perhaps her efforts to make Fitzwilliam and Georgiana feel more comfortable had not been an unqualified success. The meal continued, but she caught the elder man's gaze upon her more than once.

Finally, the bishop pushed back his chair. Ignoring convention, he said, "Miss Bennet, I wonder if you would be so good as to show me these distinctive, artistic gardens?"

Fitzwilliam's eyes widened. "What an excellent idea, Uncle," he said. "I would not mind a stroll myself."

"I would enjoy it as well," Georgiana piped in.

The bishop put up one hand in a halting motion. "There is no need for all of you, if you please. Come now, Fitzwilliam, surely you do not expect me to perform your marriage ceremony without having one private conversation with your bride beforehand? Unless, Miss Bennet, you object?"

It was nothing less than a challenge and Lizzy knew it; however, her courage, as always, rose up to meet it, and she flashed the older man a brilliant smile that briefly seemed to take him aback.

"Not at all," she said, and made a pretty curtsey to Fitzwilliam and Georgiana before allowing the bishop to lead her from the room.

6

Bishop Darcy was not at all loquacious. For some minutes they strolled in silence along the naturally carved pathways of the lovely gardens. *Perhaps he believes I quake in fear and trembling, awaiting his righteous anger. Or, more likely, he waits for me to confess my sins.*

The thought made her smile slightly. In truth, she would be content to continue the walk in silence amongst this beauty all day long.

"What do you think of Pemberley?" the bishop asked suddenly.

"'Tis lovely," she replied unthinkingly, startled he would deign to make small talk.

"Lovely," he repeated, as if she were a remarkably slow student. "Lovely." He stopped and shook his head.

Since she had no intention of attempting to guess which adjective he preferred instead, she remained silent.

"What I see, what I experience when I come to Pemberley, is history. Achievement. Hard work. Sacrifice. The lifeblood and sweat of generations." He waved an arm towards the house, the surrounding lands.

Lizzy steeled herself to hear she deserved none of it.

"My brother George was eleven months my senior. Not even a full year. Was he possessed of more intelligence than I? Did he love Pemberley more than I did? No, and no. But he was the heir, and so it was his. Perhaps you believe I begrudged him. You would be wrong. My father explained it to me as soon as I was old enough to understand—to divide Pemberley would be to destroy it. George, you see, was required to spend his life in service to the place. That was his sacrifice. I was required to surrender it entirely—that was mine. We both did what was needed to assure its survival, and young Fitzwilliam will do the same."

Lizzy felt puzzled at his words. Was he leading up to the sacrifice Fitzwilliam must make in choosing a more suitable bride? She was not a required participant in this little sermon, so she nodded in agreement and kept pace as he resumed walking, his arms clasped behind his back now, his tone lecturing.

"The wife of the master of Pemberley necessarily has sacrifices required of her, as well. Fitzwilliam cannot spend most of the year in town and leave the place's management to stewards. Even when he is in London, there are solicitors, men of business with whom he must meet—and other properties that must be managed. He must dine with politicians in their clubs, ensuring they do not send the country to the devil and the largest landowners with it. 'Tis a good life, but once pleasure becomes more important than the labour of estate management, the death knell of Pemberley rings," he said with conviction.

"One need not be concerned I will beg Fitzwilliam to attend the season's latest parties," she replied, as he seemed to be waiting for some response.

The bishop nodded. "You are no Lady Anne, requiring frenetic action and the London crush so you need not ponder your misery," he agreed, and then held up his hand at the expression upon her face. "Nay, do not take me to task for criticising her, though why you would defend her is beyond my ken. She was good to and good for Pemberley, for as long as she lasted. She is precisely my point. She was unhappy here, and yet there is no changing what is required of Pemberley's mistress. So she flung herself at life's rules and broke herself against them."

Lizzy felt it unfair to blame the setting. Lady Anne made grave mistakes, yes, certainly. But she did not feel Pemberley was responsible, nor country living and duties to the estate. The Darcys' marriage would have been troubled wherever they lived.

"Perhaps if her husband had been more attentive," she began carefully, wary of criticising his brother, but wishing blame could be apportioned in a more balanced manner.

"George could not bend, not with Pemberley on his shoulders. He needed a partner in his labours, not a distraction from them," the bishop replied sternly.

Lizzy decided her opinions were of no interest; it was no use offering them up for the sacrifice-happy bishop.

He looked around him, as if searching for the lingering ghosts of Pemberley's past inhabitants, until his gaze fixed once more upon Lizzy.

"This is what young Fitzwilliam needs. A…partner, for lack of a better word. He tells me you are an artist. Will not say a word about your people, or how he took up with you in the first place, which I suppose says enough. He says you helped Georgiana out of her foolishness and then out of danger, and the family owes you. I believe his pledge that you are of good character. He is not stupid. I am prepared to give him his licence, as he swears there are no impediments. None he knows of, at least. But are you prepared to do your part, even the parts you despise? Will you learn what you do not know and never wanted to know? Or will you leave him to carry the burden of the place alone, as Anne did George? Because I tell you, 'tis a heavy weight, a lonely one, and a *severe* impediment to his future happiness if you cannot find it in you to partner him fully. If you care for him at all, I beg you to consider this…*before* you say those vows."

Lizzy did not know how to reply. Bishop Darcy had honed in on her own fears and concerns from a direction she hadn't anticipated, with the accuracy of a well-aimed blade to the heart.

"You are far more dangerous than Lady Catherine ever was," she muttered.

He let out a dry bark that might have been laughter. "He lasted longer than I thought he would," he said, pointing his chin towards the direction from which they'd just come.

Fitzwilliam strode towards them, and Lizzy's heart lifted…so strong, so confident, the breeze ruffling his dark hair as he came to her rescue, so much who she wanted and, yes, needed at that moment. Could she possibly be who he needed her to be? Could she want him enough to sacrifice? And what, exactly was required? It seemed she had better speak with Mrs Reynolds and find out.

DARCY LOOKED AT LIZZY AND HIS UNCLE, TRYING TO READ THEIR expressions. His uncle's demeanour was placid; Lizzy, however, had bolted the shutters on her inner self. Of course, he wanted nothing more than to wrench them back open and let himself in. She had missed him, she said. If he kissed her, he might discover a re-entry point. Loosing the passionate woman she protected so scrupulously, setting her free, again and again…this was to be his new life's work. But first he had to discover what damage, if any, his well-meaning uncle inflicted.

"May I join your excursion? It has been too long since I took the time to view the gardens."

The bishop smiled good-naturedly. "It has been a tiring day. I find myself wishing for nothing more than an afternoon nap. If you would excuse me, I shall see you both at dinner." Bowing politely to Lizzy, he left them alone in the garden.

Fitzwilliam stared after him. "I did not expect he would…give us privacy so easily."

Lizzy sighed. "I believe he feels we have much to discuss."

Stiffening, he said, "If he uttered one word implying you are unfit to be Mrs Darcy, I shall—"

"No, no," Lizzy interrupted, laying her hand upon his arm. "He would never employ the crude tactics of Lady Catherine. And, unlike her, I truly believe he has your best interests at heart."

Darcy's brow furrowed. "I think I will be requiring a far more comprehensive accounting of your conversation with my aunt. However, if I judge correctly, 'tis my uncle's words which upset you. Please, Lizzy, tell me what he said."

"May we walk?"

The gardens were laid out in a formal French style, natural pathways making use of dappled shade from abundant trees, thus creating the impression of wilderness—albeit a safe and beautiful one. Between the shady paths, beds of snowdrops, daffodils and primroses flourished.

Darcy nodded, willing her to share her thoughts at her own pace, and, taking her arm, led them along the path. For several moments, they walked in silence. For Darcy's part, he enjoyed the closeness, the gentle weight of her hand upon his arm. They passed one elderly gardener fussing with a bed of roses. The old man bobbed his head in greeting and, clipping one slender stalk, efficiently denuded it of thorns and handed it over with a little bow to Lizzy.

"Thank you, Jackson," Darcy said approvingly.

Lizzy blushed disarmingly at the courtly gesture, murmuring her thanks. As they walked on, they heard the gardener mumble something.

"What did he say?" Lizzy asked when they were further away. "I could not quite hear."

"I doubt you were meant to," he replied, shaking his head. "I believe it was something to the effect of, "'Tis high time.'"

"You have grown elderly, Mr Darcy," Lizzy teased, "if your servants worry for your marital prospects." But her lovely smile dimmed. "However, if the household is hoping for a proper mistress at its helm, I fear it is doomed to disappointment."

"Not true, Lizzy. You are as gracious, intelligent, and capable—"

"I know that," she interrupted. Then she grinned. "I do have a rather high opinion of myself, don't I?"

"Deservedly so," Darcy agreed, his face sombre but his eyes smiling.

LIZZY DIDN'T WANT TO SEE THAT SMILE FADE. BUT HER CONCERNS WERE real and prohibitive: she did not know if she wished to devote her life to Pemberley's interests above her own. And surely, if she sought to truly love him as he deserved, it ought to be an easy decision?

I need more information. This conversation can wait.

"I saw your mother," she said.

His smiling eyes disappeared and she felt his arm stiffen. "And what did my mother have to say?"

"In point of fact," Lizzy answered carefully, "I last saw her here. She walked over from Holmwood Hall to see the gardens. I believe she was happy to see them unchanged."

"She ought not to be this near the house. I will send word she is to keep away." His voice was harsh and unyielding, but she heard the painful edge in it.

"Actually, 'twas a good thing she decided to make the walk, in this particular instance," Lizzy said, and gave him a detailed account of the confrontation with his aunt. As she suspected, it distracted him utterly from thoughts of the more recent one with his uncle.

"The devil you say!" he swore. "How dare Catherine speak to you in such a way! Wicked lies! I have never been promised to Anne. Never! I admit she and my father spoke of a match. My father believed the marriage to be the best means of easing our way in society. But I refused, and while she hints she is still amenable to the arrangement, I have always rejected it outright."

Lizzy put her other hand upon his arm, a calming gesture. "I believe you, Fitzwilliam. I am certain you would never propose marriage bigamously. I am afraid I may have called the old holier-than-thou a liar. And possibly accused her of a blackmail."

"Did you now?" he said, his tone lightening several degrees. "Blackmail?"

"Yes. She threatened to ruin Georgiana's chances if you did not marry Anne."

"She did not," he said, his voice cold once more.

"Oh, but she did," Lizzy said. "However, your mother appeared like a cool Adrestia, 'she whom none can escape.' 'Twas quite something to watch her put Lady Catherine in her place so easily, reminding her what she owes you. I did not know of her dependence upon your support—but Lady Anne knew, and did not hesitate to flog her with it. Lady Catherine was furious, but completely thrown. So, she gathered up Anne and flounced away...and good riddance, I say!"

He was silent for some moments before sighing heavily. "I am sorry my relations have been so beastly to you."

"Not your mother," Lizzy disagreed softly. "She was very kind."

"Likely she is attempting to insinuate herself," he said gruffly.

"And if she is?" Lizzy replied gently. "It is one of my many failings. I have an unfortunate degree of compassion for Females Who Make Terrible Mistakes. Could you bear it if I find myself liking her?"

There was a silence while he considered it. "I am not sure," he replied at last. "'Tis not very good of me, but I would rather you be on my side of the fence."

"I am," Lizzy said. "Unequivocally I am, first and foremost. It is only...I believe she is, too."

"Am I supposed to accept that she has suddenly suffered a massive episode of regret, now that she finds herself alone and friendless?"

"Don't you think she ought to feel regret? She failed her wonderful son and her beautiful daughter. If I lost you, I would regret it every day of my life." She felt the truth of her words. If she did as Bishop Darcy no doubt hoped and reconsidered marriage, life without Fitzwilliam would unquestionably bring her deep and abiding grief.

Darcy paused a moment, staring intently, then steered her down a different path, his pace no longer aimless.

Once they rounded a bend, his destination became obvious. A folly sat upon a hilltop, a glorious Romanesque structure of Ked brick, leaded dome, and carved stonework.

"Grandmother Darcy had it built," he said as she halted to take it in. "Winter was her favourite season. She loved the snow and the sight of snow-capped peaks surrounding her from this spot."

They continued onward, climbing the steps to the building's arched entry. The windows bore heavy velvet drapery, keeping it cool inside, and dim after the bright sunshine...but not so dim Lizzy could miss the painted interior ceilings and walls, full of cherubic angels and Roman gods on nearly every conceivable surface, including the high-domed ceiling.

"Oh, my," Lizzy said, bemused. "'Tis...impressive."

"A bit overdone for my tastes." Darcy shrugged. "Rumour has it, Grandmother Darcy was taken with the Italian artist who carried out the commission. He stretched it out for all it was worth."

Lizzy raised a brow. "How scandalous! Have not all Darcys prescribed to the motto of 'Death Before Dishonour'?"

The corner of his mouth lifted with that hint of a grin, which on another man might be full-on laughter. "I am sure my grandmother did not stray," he said, pulling her close. "For a time, however, she may have enjoyed the view inside the folly slightly more than the view of the mountaintops."

Lizzy looked up at him, struck by how handsome he appeared and how much she had missed him. "If your grandfather resembled you, I am sure the view at home was sufficiently gratifying." She gazed up at him. "Very gratifying, indeed."

Darcy stared into her eyes, all hint of a smile gone up in flames. "I missed you, too," he said, and took her lips in a feverish kiss.

Since arriving home, he had wanted to pull her into his arms, to kiss into her smile, to hold her tightly, and never let her go. All during lunch he had struggled to pay heed to the conversation, day-dreams of plucking out the pins from her hair and seeing it down once again preoccupying him. It was a devil of a thing to obsess on in company with his cleric uncle and his sister, and he was sure his uncle had looked at him a few times in consternation and suspicion. Possibly not, however, since the bishop had foolishly left him alone with the most desirable female in all of England.

The feel of her in his arms was everything he longed for. Doing his best to control himself, he centred his attention, noting what made her shiver. He kissed his way down her jaw, finding the spot behind her ear that had caused her to tremble once before. It still worked, filling him with curiosity.

What else would she like? How could he make her want him the way he wanted her?

His practical knowledge of sexual congress was limited. He knew the essentials, of course, having been around livestock all of his life, not to mention in possession of multiple artworks featuring the nude female form.

His father, of course, had spoken to him about it, albeit obliquely. He had been adamant the Darcy seed was never to be sown unto any female under his protection, which included Pemberley or his several other lesser properties, and that a man bedded one woman in his life, and only after he gave her his name. He also was careful to enlighten his son as to the various diseases females selling favours might pass along to their clientèle. His father's description of the pox alone was enough to cause Darcy to forswear the idea of paid companionship, even had his clergyman not already put the fear of damnation into him for any illicit inclinations.

At Eton, of course, there were boys who were obsessed with females, and set their sights on gaining intimate experience and then speaking of it to anyone who would listen. And many did listen, but not Darcy. For one thing, the young men were exceedingly crude, speaking as if the females they "tupped" or "swived" were merely vessels for their ever-plentiful seed. For another, listening to their ribald tales set him up for powerful yearnings of his own, hungers he was aware must yet exist for some years before assuagement was possible. Paying them any mind was an exercise in frustration and futility.

All this ran through his thoughts as he kissed and held the female whom he hoped rather desperately to wed, and soon. His wants and needs, years in the making, swelled to fever-pitch.

Breaking away from her, he strode towards the observation area and pressed his heated forehead against the cold glass. His body screamed in protest at moving away from what it wanted. He thought his heart might never return to its usual beat.

It was perhaps ten minutes before he risked turning to face her. She was seated, half the room away, in one of the comfortable chairs placed near the small, empty fireplace where a fire was kept burning during the long winter and early spring, protecting the folly's paintings from the damp. She stared into the cold, black hearth, her thoughts impenetrable. Perhaps she was confused or upset or disgusted.

He made his way back to her in a slow and measured step, trying to think of something to say that did not include the words, "I beg of you, allow me more," and "I am dying of want." In the end, he knelt at her feet and pressed his forehead upon her knee. After what seemed an endless minute, her hand reached out to toy with the overlong hair at his nape.

"My uncle agreed to marry us on Friday next," he said at last. "Would you be amenable to that?"

"I do not know," she said, and his heart sank. He had offended her, pushing her towards intimacies only a husband had a right to demand.

"I need to speak with Mrs Reynolds," she continued. "I must know what Pemberley requires of its mistress, unless you think I ought to speak to your mother instead."

"No!" he said, over-loud. He gazed up at her, softening his tone. "That is, Lady Anne has not had the responsibility of the place for many years. Mrs Reynolds would be the best person to speak with. But surely you do not doubt your ability to fulfil the duties of mistress?"

"I do not doubt myself, no. I feel as though I ought to know…well, know more. Understand it all."

"I apologise for taking advantage," he said, confused at her mood and placing blame for it on his own shoulders. He stared at the floor. "I should not have."

"Do not," she said. "Do not apologise for kisses we both wanted. I agree we ought not to do anything…more…until I am certain we are set on the right course. But perhaps you should be mindful that you have asked for the hand of a female who happily submits to kissing in a garden folly. It might reflect badly on the future dignity of Pemberley."

"Ah," he said, meeting her eyes directly, his barely-there smile in evidence once more, feeling heartfelt relief she would tease him. "I, for one, cannot think of a better use for this folly, nor a better avocation for

Mrs Darcy. You will not find that duty, mayhap, in any list of Mrs Reynolds's. But please know it is a high priority of the master's. The second highest, perhaps."

"Oh?" Lizzy asked, unable to restrain her smile. "And what is the first priority of the master of Pemberley?"

"The happiness of its mistress," he said, drawing her hand to his lips and placing a reverent kiss upon it.

C harles Bingley's usual good nature was severely taxed. Firstly by Netherfield's drainage issues, and next, by Mr Bennet's indecision upon whether to die or to linger endlessly, half alive. Not that he begrudged the man his need of care, but fiend seize him, his sister needed rest!

A servant interrupted him.

"Sir, an express arrived for you."

Charles swivelled to face a footman proffering a thin envelope. A distraction! Just what was needed! Accepting it with a grateful smile, he seated himself at a nearby desk to read the letter. It was from his friend Darcy, and as he comprehended its contents, his brows rose almost to his hair. Upon finishing, he looked up at the servant, whom he had failed to dismiss.

"There will be a reply, John. For the nonce, give the messenger a meal and a bed, and have the phaeton brought 'round," he said. "I am for Longbourn."

LIZZY AWAKENED EARLY FROM FORCE OF HABIT, AND NOT BECAUSE OF A restful night's sleep. Last night's dinner had been quiet; fortunately, horse-mad Georgiana had not seemed to notice, preoccupied with her raptures over the birth of a new foal in the Pemberley stables. Several times during dinner, Lizzy noticed Fitzwilliam staring at her...but, even more often, she caught herself staring at him.

What was this obsession she had with him? She tried to imagine leaving Fitzwilliam, forcing herself to picture him with another female as his wife, looking upon someone else with that almost-smile.

She rolled over to smother her groan in the pillows.

A maid chose that moment to quietly enter, building up the fire so when Lizzy deigned to place her toes to the floor, no draught would touch her.

It was not as though it would precisely be a torture to live here. But neither did she wish to marry because she hadn't thought of a more comfortable plan for her life.

Fitzwilliam wished to take her on a tour of the house, which would mean precious minutes alone, or relatively alone with him. However, Lizzy needed no assistance in becoming *more* addicted to his presence. What she needed was to use her mind for something besides day-dreams. And that meant learning more about what was expected of Pemberley's mistress, other than receiving kisses from its master.

With a sigh, she followed an assigned footman to the housekeeper's office. It was pin neat, as one would expect. Ledgers and journals lined the shelves along three walls, and reference manuals along the fourth. Lizzy paused to read one of the titles—*Dr Buchan's Domestic Medicine: Or, A Treatise on the Prevention and Cure of Diseases, by Regimen and Simple Medicine, to which is Added Characteristic Symptoms of Diseases, from the Nosology of the Late Celebrated Dr Cullen of Edinburgh, With the Addition of Short Corrected Treatises viz. The Cow Pox, Hectic Fever, Water Brash, Madness, and Dance of St. Vitus.* Evidently Mrs Reynolds truly believed in being prepared for anything.

"Mr Darcy said you ought to see anything you wished" the house-keeper was saying, "so I have set out the account books for your inspection."

There were three large tomes positioned neatly in the centre of a worktable in the middle of the room.

Lizzy attempted objectivity. Upkeep of three household account books was not too onerous a task. Even if the books were dreadfully thick. She smiled and sat, gesturing to them. "I appreciate you taking time from your many duties to show me."

Mrs Reynolds nodded in her formal manner. "'Tis no trouble, Miss Bennet. Anything I might do to help, you need only mention it. I have had the full running of the household for many years. If there is aught needing change, I hope you will inform me."

Lizzy wondered, not for the first time, about the woman's age. With her hair pulled back tightly in the severest of styles, her expression and reserve gave the appearance of someone in her fiftieth year, but her complexion was youthful. Lizzy concluded she must have been young indeed when she rose to ascendency over the house. "I cannot imagine suggesting any changes to such a well-run establishment."

Mrs Reynolds nodded again, as if expecting this. "Nevertheless, the books show every detail of what is required. Of course, old Mr Darcy did not entertain, and I suppose we can expect adjustment. We will begin a new set of ledgers to accommodate that eventuality, of course."

"Of course," Lizzy murmured.

"I assure you I am more than happy to answer to a mistress and review the accounts with you regularly, daily, if you will. There is so much you likely wish to learn."

The woman looked at Lizzy expectantly, and Lizzy hastened to agree. "Yes, I am sure. Filling these three great volumes with the year not yet half gone, much attention is needed. But perhaps daily review might be excessive."

Mrs Reynolds unbent enough to smile at this. "Oh, my dear Miss Bennet. The volumes before you are only for the month of May. The balance of this year is contained on the shelves directly behind you."

Lizzy peered at the shelves. At least twenty enormous volumes resided there, squatting like fat basilisks ready to devour every minute of her day. Dread flooded her heart and Lizzy turned her back on them to face the ones on the table. She opened the nearest, beholding a list of transactions and notations. Apparently, no expense was too small to be insignificant, no point of usage too trifling.

"Such detail," she murmured, turning the pages. "I only had charge of a much smaller household. Nothing on this scale. Even so, I did not record a hundredth part of what is listed here."

"'Tis the only means of preventing theft," Mrs Reynolds said. "We must know, mustn't we, exactly how much of each item the household uses in order to avoid ordering too little, or heaven forbid, determining someone orders too much—either wasting or even selling the balance. It happens. Mayhap a cook will make arrangements with a merchant, who charges more than usual and splits the difference. 'Tis difficult to prevent pilfering, but anomalies might be detected if we completely understand consumption and costs. And if we do not keep track of dairy production, how do we know if the dairymen are not selling a portion of our milk and butter and failing to report the sales?"

"Dairy?" Lizzy asked faintly.

"Yes, we have a fine dairy providing the house with milk, butter, cheese and eggs—after which we sell excess, if any, to neighbouring estates or in Lambton. We also have the laundry and the conservatory that serve the household and the neighbourhood. Pemberley is likewise known for its ale production. We sell as far away as Manchester."

"The household is run like a business, then," Lizzy said.

Mrs Reynolds replied, "It is run with respect and devotion, Miss Bennet. If there is hunger or need amongst the tenants, Pemberley provides. But our inventories must be flawless, and we must know exactly how much we require and how much ought to be charged and how much our price to sell. Mr Darcy and his steward keep the accounts of the farms and the mill, the orchards and the herds, all of the outside custom, not to mention the lesser properties and their various households. The mistress has charge only of Pemberley. But 'tis a great house, and a great responsibility." She said that last almost wistfully, smoothing a hand lovingly over the leather cover of the nearest ledger.

Lizzy opened the middle volume. It seemed to be an inventory of certain linens, by size and colour, listing wear and mending required.

Mrs Reynolds glanced over and nodded approvingly at the page. "One must grasp what refurbishing and mending are necessary in all the house's textiles and linens. Otherwise, the laundress might request sixty hours' worth of darning labour, when actually only hiring forty-five. She pockets the additional fifteen hours' pay. You see?"

Lizzy suspected admiring the efficiency of the laundress was not the point of this exercise.

"You do a magnificent job of managing it all, Mrs Reynolds," Lizzy said sincerely, even as her heart beat leaden in her chest. "I do not know of any man who could do better."

"Nonsense," Mrs Reynolds answered, her tone brisker than ever. "I merely do my duty, nothing more, and I won't be unhappy to share the responsibility. And if you don't mind my saying so, Miss Bennet, this house needs a mistress. I can teach what is needed regarding management of the accounts, but accounts do not make Pemberley a home. That requires a nursery full of children and babies."

The housekeeper glanced at Lizzy's belly and silence hung in the air between them.

Children. Lizzy wanted children, truly, but...she had naively thought to have both, her art *and* children. She might, until they came along, be able to fit in the occasional afternoon with a master, in between remembering the cost of sugar and the receipt for perfect ale and the number of eggs produced daily by Pemberley's hens. But children would need her. Any time not required for the management of this massive household rightfully belonged to them.

A vision of the future formed in Lizzy's mind, of spending years bent over these tomes, the only legacy left to her progeny being volume after volume of inked transactions, her life's creative works reduced to household inventories and the prices charged for damask.

Even if she weren't the one who recorded each line, she would be responsible for it all. If Pemberley caved in upon itself, the victim of countless opportunities for fraud and deceit, it would be all her fault. Mrs Reynolds had certainly served her time...how much longer would she be willing to keep at this all alone, as she had been? No longer, it seemed.

Lizzy abruptly stood, needing escape before she burst into foolish tears. "I thank you for showing me. I know there is more—I cannot—I must—that is, if you will please excuse me—" She fled.

DARCY LIFTED HIS HEAD FROM THE LETTER HE PERUSED WHEN HE HEARD A soft knock. "Enter," he called.

He was surprised to see Mrs Reynolds; he had been informed that Lizzy was meeting with her, and the two of them would be occupied all morning.

"Sir," she said, looking uncharacteristically concerned, "I fear I've blundered."

"Blundered?" he repeated. "How so?"

"I met with Miss Bennet, as I told you. I opened the books to her for the running of the household. I am not sure what exactly, but something I said appeared to upset her."

"What did you say?" he asked sternly.

Mrs Reynolds did not flinch. "I was explaining to her the importance of the house accounts, sir. I may have edged too near the personal, as I did mention my hopes for a full nursery. I swear I meant nothing by it, sir. Nothing at all."

Egad, she believes Lizzy is with child and that is why we hurry the wedding.

"I hardly think a mention of our *distant* future family would upset her," he said, the closest he would come to explaining anything so personal to a servant. "What else did you say?"

"Why, just about the books, and ways to prevent theft and excessive spending. Truly, sir, we talked for under a half an hour. We hadn't even got to the menus, when suddenly she up and says she cannot, and runs neck-or-nothing out the door."

"Cannot?" he said, turning the full force of the Darcy glare upon the hapless housekeeper, but seeing nothing within her expression except puzzled concern. Whether or not Mrs Reynolds was responsible for Lizzy's distress, she plainly had no idea what she had said or done to cause it.

"Yes, sir, that's what she said. And I could be wrong, but she looked near tears."

Devil take it! "Where is Miss Bennet now?"

"She is somewhere in the gardens. Should I send Andrew? I thought you would rather, but—"

"No, no. You did right to inform me. I will find her."

First, he went to the folly. It was private and there were seats where one might comfortably indulge in a fit of the blue devils. But the building was empty. He left quickly, before he could remember what occurred the last time they were there together and commence wondering if it would ever happen again.

But he was not successful elsewhere either. Two of the gardeners had seen her, and each pointed her direction. However, the gardens were so extensive, with multiple intersecting paths, he somehow missed her completely.

Lizzy's words to Mrs Reynolds, "I cannot," echoed in his head. She had gone to the housekeeper to get an idea of Pemberley's management. And she said, "I cannot." Which was impossible, of course, because Lizzy could do anything she set her mind to. Had she meant, "I will not?"

He was beginning to wonder if he shouldn't gather a search party when he came upon, not Lizzy, but the last person he wished to see.

"Fitzwilliam!" Lady Anne said, startled. "I was just walking...I thought I was far enough away from the house, I promise I had no intention of nearing..."

He waved away the excuses, fighting off a surge of guilt that she sounded so uneasy of him. "No, no," he said, unable to keep impatience from his voice. "I am looking for L—Miss Bennet. Have you seen her?"

"No, I have not," Lady Anne replied. "I would be happy to assist in the search, if you are concerned?"

His willingness to reply was a sign of his increasing agitation. "She was meeting with Mrs Reynolds, receiving training in the duties of mistress, and suddenly departed in the middle of it. Mrs Reynolds was concerned, and so I...what do you mean by that look?"

His mother's face wiped smooth, but he had distinctly perceived an expression of aggravation. Was he now supposed to guess at her thinking? What an annoying female!

"I apologise," she said. "But if Miss Bennet met with your devoted servant, 'tis no real surprise if she was overwhelmed. Reynolds is a rarity amongst housekeepers."

"What? Why? Mrs Reynolds is of excellent character!"

Lady Anne waved away this statement. "Of course she is. Perhaps 'tis the difficulty."

His irritation increased. "Come to the point. What is the problem, specifically?"

"Mary Reynolds is like no other housekeeper I have hired before or since. Zealously devoted to Pemberley's interests, she has a very mathematical, very organised mind. Also, her attention to detail is flawless. She is a jewel. Whatever you pay her, you ought to double it."

Darcy lifted a brow. "I never used to think you precisely fond of her."

"Oh, well, no, one is not fond of her. She does not want your *fondness*. She wants your perfection. She wants you to care—passionately—about the upholstery on the divan nearest the pianoforte in the music room...and to understand the cost of recovering it, and if one decides against reupholstering, to know when one will be inspecting it again to reappraise one's decision. She repeats this passion for every stick of furniture in the house, every rug, every linen and drape, every teacup in the pantry and piece of silver in the chests. Let us not even consider the orange trees in the conservatory or cows in the dairy!"

He frowned. "This is why I pay her—to care for these things. The mistress must oversee, yes, but to be involved in such minutiae would be unnecessarily tedious," Darcy replied, trying to imagine how Lizzy might have responded to the housekeeper's point of view. Still, surely common sense dictated what should be a mistress's duties, as opposed to a devoted servant's?

Lady Anne chuckled. "I vow, had Mrs Reynolds a criminal bent, she would be a master thief. By the time she has finished explaining to you the number of ways in which you might be stolen from or taken advantage of by servants and tradespeople, one begins to see a potential for villainy in every person one meets. Sometimes I wonder if she is not tempted, and thus keeps careful records to stop herself."

"I doubt that," he said disapprovingly.

She sighed. "Fitzwilliam, please. Try to imagine you are a young girl who has never had any experience in the management of a grand household. And the person introducing you to it shows you only the most difficult, tedious parts, after which explaining in painstaking detail how any lack of devotion might lead to ruin." She sighed, remembering. "Mrs Trimble held the position when I commenced my initiation to Pemberley, and she was much less, ah, vigorous in her views of a mistress's duties, as was my own mother, who shared expectations of me nearly from my cradle. I elevated Mary Reynolds to housekeeper after Mrs Trimble's untimely death. Despite my experience, at times I wondered at how…keen she was for her duties. Might not Lizzy be feeling, naturally, somewhat overwhelmed?"

A short silence followed. "Did she give you leave to call her Lizzy?" he asked abruptly.

Lady Anne blinked in surprise, then bowed her head. "She is an exceedingly kind, extraordinary young lady," she said finally.

He ran his fingers through his hair in a gesture of either dismay or distress.

"I must find her," he said. "If you will excuse me." He gave the very shallowest of bows, and walked away.

"Fitzwilliam!" she called to his departing back. He paused mid-stride, not turning. "I know you do not want me near, and I swear I am not trying to infringe…but please know I would do anything …

anything in my power to assist Lizzy in her duties, if it would help. I once...I once was good at them, long ago. So...anything at all."

He held still for another moment, then continued on without acknowledging her words.

"Good afternoon, Mr Bingley," Margaret said, sitting down gratefully on the comfortable settee in Longbourn's front parlour. "I hope Mrs Hill has not neglected you. I am sorry to keep you waiting. Thomas was having a bad spell."

"I suppose that answers the question of how he fares," Charles said sympathetically.

"Sometimes I believe he is rallying, and then..." Margaret gave a sigh before taking advantage of the tea tray Hill had left for Mr Bingley, pouring herself a cup. "How fares Netherfield?" she asked.

Charles shrugged. "I have much to learn, still, as becomes more obvious daily. But I did not come to bother you with my troubles." He leaned forward, and for the first time Margaret noticed his animation. "I have received a letter from Darcy," he said.

She was fatigued enough that she did not immediately comprehend the implication. In the two weeks since they last spoke of Thomas's daughter, Margaret's nursing duties had been so compelling that she set the matter aside.

"About Elizabeth Bennet."

Margaret felt her fatigue nearly melting away, so great was her interest in Mr Bingley's words. "Yes?" she asked, setting down her cup.

"It is the da—, um, oddest thing," he said. "Did you know the girl is not a child, but over one-and-twenty years?"

She cocked her head inquiringly. "Why of course! Did I neglect to mention her age?"

Charles laughed. "Either you neglected to mention it or I neglected to listen! I sent Darcy to look after a young child!"

Margaret put a hand over her mouth to prevent similar laughter. It should not be amusing to imagine how flummoxed the sober Mr Darcy must have been once he realised the error.

"But it gets better," Charles announced, almost bouncing in his seat. "You will never believe this. No, never."

"Mr Bingley! Do not tease!" she cried.

"He plans to marry her." Charles made his announcement with unrepressed triumph.

Margaret stared. "Surely…you have misunderstood," she said at last.

Charles pulled a letter from his coat pocket. "I have to say, 'tis not written in his usual style," he said. "Of course, his usual style has more to do with crop yields and—"

"Mr Bingley, please!"

"Oh, right. He does not spend any time on the niceties, you will notice. And I apologise if he is somewhat, um, unkind towards Bennet—"

"Mr Bingley!"

"Very well, very well." He opened the letter and began to read.

Bingley—

I have been to Ramsgate and met Mrs Bingley's niece. You had her age wrong—she is one-and-twenty years, you noddy, a lady grown. A lady like no other. As a matter of fact, I have asked for her hand.

If her bacon-brained father yet lives, might there be an attempt at reconciliation with his estranged wife, for the sake of Elizabeth's name and reputation, before he is planted?

FD

"What do you think, Step-mama?"

"Oh," Margaret breathed. "Oh, my." The letter was hardly civil, especially considering Mr Darcy's renowned politeness. However, when she took into account those heartrending letters a young Elizabeth had written to Thomas, she could hardly blame him. It had been a remarkable child—who had, apparently, matured into a remarkable young lady—who penned those letters. And Mr Darcy seemed to have fallen rather instantly in love with the girl. How marvellous!

"I must travel to Ramsgate and speak to Mrs Bennet," Margaret said. "But I cannot leave Thomas! I just know if I go, he will take the first excuse to 'shuffle off this mortal coil.'" She sighed. "And I refuse to let him die before he rights this wrong! I do not know if it can be righted, but Mr Darcy is correct—Thomas owes his daughter some measure of respectability. Oh, if only he had answered her letters!"

The two of them sat in silence for some minutes, both contemplative.

"I have an idea," Margaret said at last. "It may even stand a slight chance of success, at least for a time. Of course, if Mrs Bennet will not have anything to do with us, that is that. If only I could leave at once!"

"Might I offer my services?" Charles asked. "I am happy to abandon all matters associated with drainage in the north field in order to play Cupid for my friend. If, of course, you would please tell me exactly what I ought to say to Mrs Bennet! I dare not bungle it!"

izzy sat on the bank of the pretty stream, playing in the mud. Or, more accurately, playing with the mud.

She had discovered a clay deposit that, while crude, didn't quite melt into sludge. She had managed four vases, though one of them looked more like a misshapen rock with a hole in it. Too much soil. If she used her petticoat, she could strain and purify the clay...but it was one of the new, fine ones from Georgiana. On the other hand, the mistress of Pemberley could ruin mountains of undergarments without remorse. Hah!

With a swipe of her arm, she backhanded the lopsided mound into the river, where it drowned with a satisfying splash.

"Lizzy."

She heard the relief in Fitzwilliam's voice, and wondered why. Mrs Reynolds, she knew, would not have hesitated to hurry and report his betrothed was a flibbertigibbet, who fled when faced with a bit of hard work. She knocked the second vase into the river.

"Lizzy," he said again, this time crouching within her line of vision. He was perfectly turned out as usual, with snowy white cravat, pale beige buckskins, blue coat, and boots shined to a mirror finish. She glanced down. Not only was her dress wet and splotched with mud, but her hair was escaping its pins; she looked like a slattern. She contemplated chucking a sloppy vase at him.

"Sweetheart," Darcy said gently, "won't you tell me what is wrong?"

Lizzy looked away, facing the river instead. What was she

supposed to say? That being the mistress of the vast business that was Pemberley was the last thing on earth she wanted? That he came with too many burdens attached? That she wanted to run, far and fast? It would all be true. Yet, she knew with a feeling of near despair, she would never willingly leave him. Could never do it, not without regretting it every day of her life. The thought of doing so killed any desire to create, to sculpt, a great wall of despair and sorrow that would crush her.

Pemberley might achieve the same end, however.

"I need time," she said quietly, swallowing down her misery at last. "I learned many years ago life is not always…easy."

"Can you talk to me about what is upsetting you?"

You have assumed these responsibilities from boyhood; you would not understand. "I am learning what…what marriage to you means, for me."

"I know Mrs Reynolds is very…zealous," he said carefully. "It does not have to be quite as onerous a burden as she perhaps implied."

How to explain to him? Lizzy had dreamed of becoming as great in her sphere as he already was in his; however, her talents were as yet untested, her skills mostly untried. What she wanted to do with her life was a great unknown, an experiment almost. And yet…she had so wished to make the attempt. "You said you would hire an art master for me," she began.

"I have already made inquiries," Darcy replied quickly.

"I do not think you understand. It is not like hiring a dancing master, who would come for an hour or two for three afternoons per week until I can flawlessly execute a reel."

"He can live here, and work with you daily."

She sighed. "What if…what if our situations were reversed? I realise this sounds absurd, but what if you, the master of Pemberley, had to become a sculptor so we could be wed?"

She could hear the smile in his voice as he replied, "I would hope inferior art becomes popular."

"But it will not!" She twisted around to face him. "You cannot. You must become the most expert sculptor in the kingdom. It is expected, the honour of the family requires it. And what is more, you are still master of Pemberley, 'tis still part of you and important to you, even if no one else cares, and thus you must devise a means of shoving everything being its master entails into a few hours per week. Because if you marry me, being the master of Pemberley becomes a...a diversion. An amusement for you, entertaining you during the few hours you are not..."

"Sculpting?"

Her shoulders slumped and her gaze dropped. She was being stupid; the two things were not at all similar. Hundreds of lives were affected by his every decision. In comparison, she was a whining ninny. She knew that, waited for him to point out the many flaws in her metaphor. In herself.

Instead, she gave a startled shriek as he scooped her up, wet, filthy dress and all, striding away from the riverbank.

"What are you doing?" she cried. "I'm muddy! You will ruin your—"

He bent his head until he met her lips, covering them with his in a firm, demanding kiss. When she softened in response, he lifted his head. "I could not care less about a bit of mud, but I do not wish to sit in it while we discuss what distresses you. I care about you, about adding to your happiness, not destroying it. I cannot believe you find that so difficult to understand."

He continued his ground-eating stride. She looked up at his set jaw, bemused by his forcefulness. His cravat, exquisitely knotted, now had ruddy flecks on it. He carried her as if she weighed nothing, though she was not a small woman. He was angry. But about what? Life, she knew, seldom gave one exactly what one wished, and there was always a price to be paid. That was all she meant to convey.

They hadn't gone far when they reached a copse of trees surrounding a small grassy knoll. He eased her down and sat beside her, leaning up against a tree as if he hadn't a care in the world.

And yet, she knew he had more cares than most men in the country. The fact that he executed those burdens so well was a testimony to the strength of his character and backbone. Oh, why did she act weak, wasting time snivelling about her fate? He was a wonderful reward for sacrifice and hard work.

"I will marry you on Friday," she blurted.

He glanced at her, brow lifted. "Throwing yourself upon the altar of self-sacrifice?" he asked sardonically, doing a fair job of removing anger from his voice.

She heard it regardless, and leaned back so her shoulder touched his. "Throwing myself at you, rather," she sighed. "I needed time to accustom myself to the idea of...all this," she said, gesturing to the lovely scenery surrounding them. "I am not afraid of hard work. I suppose Mrs Reynolds holds no great opinion of me. I behaved like a goose."

"What I think is, Mrs Reynolds believes you with child, and her comments regarding filling our nursery set you off," he said drily. "Fortunately, your 'condition' will excuse much in the way of, hmm, heightened sensibility."

Lizzy clapped her hand over her mouth, giving a surprised laugh. "Oh, dear." She eyed him slyly. "Your housekeeper doesn't have much faith in your powers of self-discipline."

He shrugged. "I believe it is more the case of knowing I am irresistible."

She turned her head sharply and saw the smile he tried to hide behind his usual mask of stoicism.

He captured her chin. "It was a jest," he said.

"A truth," she countered, and laid her head upon his chest.

DARCY WRAPPED HIS ARM AROUND HER, IDLY PLAYING WITH HER HAIR, plucking the pins from it though he was only half-aware of doing so. His thinking was muddled, too many feelings fighting for attention. Desire, of course, because he was never able to be near her without it to one degree or another. Joy, because she wanted him and had agreed to marry him. Anger, because she felt it was a sacrifice to do so.

He wanted to quash the anger, because it was likely unfair of him to feel it, but devil take it! Why could she not trust him to ensure her happiness? His mother's pleading expression flashed into his mind's eye, doing nothing for his humour as he reconsidered Lizzy's exasperating little simile, attempting to understand. Not that one could compare a piece of art, even a lovely piece, to Pemberley. The two things were not at all analogous.

"Your brow is furrowing," she said. "Why?"

Unbidden, her question elicited a long-ago memory. He had come home from Eton to the terrible news his mother was gone, that she had left them permanently. "Why?" he had cried. "Why?"

His father had turned away, his shoulders slumping. "I have not the first idea," he said. He meant it. George Darcy never understood what destroyed his marriage, why his wife had turned to someone else. Of course, there was never a good excuse for betrayal of such an honourable man and yet...

"I met my mother in the garden while I was searching for you," he said. "She seems fond of you."

"And that is upsetting to you?"

"No. Yes." He sighed. "Devil if I know." Above all things, he did not want history to repeat itself. If he could not learn to understand this female, they might both end miserable. Miserable and alone.

"My first loyalty will always be to you," Lizzy said softly. "If you do not like it, I will cease the...friendship, or whatever it is, Lady Anne and I have begun."

Her hair was gorgeous, the stuff of his dreams. He had let it down now, so it trailed over her shoulders, cascading down her back, his fingers weaving through the thick tresses. "A friendship," he said breathlessly. "Is that what you and she have? If it becomes known you are friends with her, you will be tainted with her brush."

"I am already tainted," she said softly. "I have been since before birth."

"No!" he protested. "Certainly not."

"Most would not agree with you, although truthfully, I think as you do. I do not feel tainted. But I warn you now, I will never choose my friends based upon what the haute ton deems suitable. I am too used to thinking for myself. Your mother knows who I am and what is more, she knows exactly who my mother is and she...she likes me. Such acceptance is a gift, and I treasure it. Nevertheless, it concerns me more what you think, and I would not be disloyal. If we are to be a family, your feelings on this matter must come first."

Your feelings must come first. Darcy heard her words resounding with truth. Lizzy had no friends here, excepting himself and Georgiana. If he rightly understood what little she revealed of her life in Ramsgate, Lady Anne's acceptance was a rare thing—but she would discard it, for his sake. She had offered to essentially discard her sculpting, which he did not understand but which she cared about, for the same reason. His parents, obviously, failed to put each other "first" at critical junctures in their lives. It was probably as simple and as difficult as that.

But he could not trust his mother. It was awfully convenient that she developed this sudden friendship with Lizzy, so useful for insinuating herself into his household.

"How do you know Lady Anne truly accepts you? She comes from a family for whom intrigue and plotting is second nature. She could be..." He did not finish his sentence, not wanting to hurt Lizzy's feelings by stating his aloud.

"Simply using me?" Lizzy finished for him. "I allow it is a possibility. But I am not so good as you. If I were the one who destroyed my connexion with you, I would humble myself before the devil to be near you again. I count that particular ambition as a point in her favour. However, I am confident in my powers of judgment. I think she finds me...refreshing. And...well, likeable."

Of course Lizzy was likeable! A person would have to be a fool to *dis*like her. But for some reason Lizzy liked and at least tentatively respected Lady Anne's motives in return. He wanted Lizzy to trust him; did he trust her?

"What if..." he cleared his throat, finding it difficult to speak these words. "What if I allow Lady Anne into our lives and she...she hurts Georgiana?"

"Your mother," she said in a gentle voice, "is a person with deep regrets. Of all the things for which I blame her, and there are many, for this one thing I do not blame her—desperately wanting to have a...a link with the two of you. She does not deserve one, but I do not blame her for wishing it. Neither would I blame you for denying her, as is your right. She made choices long ago and lives with the consequences, as we all must."

"I was taught, from my earliest years, of man's personal obligations in regard to practicing forgiveness. But mine is a resentful nature," he said gruffly.

She gave a low chuckle. "I am not proficient at the practice, myself."

Oh, but he loved the sound of her laugh. He loved *her*.

"You forgave me my first, crude proposal," he said, his voice slightly lighter. "I suppose I could attempt to follow your example. As I understand it, management of Pemberley's interests would hamper your ability to achieve your promise with...your art."

"I said I would accept that," she countered.

"It would interfere, then, with your happiness."

She was silent—answer enough, he supposed.

"And hiring others to manage Pemberley's work for you would be objectionable, because you do not have the trust in them, or the skills as yet to know if they might take advantage."

"Exactly," she agreed.

"Do you trust my mother?" he asked, speaking more quickly, as if he had to hurry and get the words out. "Do you trust her to help you with the household, in selection of servants, and to teach you to oversee things well enough until you are confident in the running of the house without being overwhelmed with minutiae? Such training could occur over a...a period of time, even."

Likely several weeks. But Lizzy had been clinging to the notion of an artist's life for so long, it would take time to realise he was here to support her now; she no longer needed to dream of opportunities to take her far away from Ramsgate and the humiliation of her experiences there.

She did not fully trust him yet—and how could she, with years of inconstant men as her examples? Once she saw how comfortable and...and, well, perfect their life together would be, once she truly trusted him to care for her as no one ever had, she would not require the crutch his mother might provide. Not so long a time, surely.

"I...I do trust she is an honest person. Brutally honest, in fact." Lizzy turned so she could see his face. He gazed at her, his earnestness plain for her to see. "But Fitzwilliam...you should not do this if—"

"Lizzy," he said, "I told you I would do anything to have you, and make you happy. I meant it."

Wearing an expression of pure joy, she flung her arms around his neck and pressed kisses to his cheeks, his nose, his chin. As he tilted his head just so, their lips met in perfect accord and rich, sweet heat.

"Never have I been brought to my knees with desire, never until now," he said, his eyes searing. "Yet, your trust is more important than my desire."

She smiled up at him, loveliness personified. "I trust you. 'Tis just... I cannot help but fear I delude myself. You, sir, are too good to be true."

"I am not good," he said. "I am a man, with a man's weaknesses. I know I dare not stay out here alone with you much longer. As Heaven is my witness, I cannot imagine wanting any female more than I do you at this moment, and I want you to trust me, always, Lizzy. And that is why, even if you will wed me on Friday, we will wait. We will take the time to know each other better, as you wished. If and when you take me as your husband in all ways, it will be because you want all the things I want. And you will be certain I will care for you always, and never leave you or betray you. You will trust me."

C harles Bingley hoped Darcy would approve of their plans, but decided he could not wait on his permission. If Margaret Bingley's plan was to be effective, they had a limited window of opportunity. He carried with him a letter to Mrs Bennet, hoping against hope she would agree to read it; by the time they rolled into Ramsgate, he was anxious enough that he barely noticed the lovely seaside views.

The home was nicer than he expected. A clean, respectable looking maid answered the door, allowing him entry after he presented his card and asked to speak with Mrs Bennet. He sat down and looked around at the fashionable drawing room where he waited, aware of a slight disappointment. As a den of iniquity, it left something to be desired.

A lovely female entered the room. As he stood, he noted she was the comeliest girl he had ever seen, and his first instinct was to charm. But Margaret Bingley had repeatedly rehearsed to him how young ladies were likely to raise their hopes on the smallest evidence, and until he was certain his interest was fixed and reciprocated, it was critical he maintain a more formal aspect. If he had ever cause for uncertainty regarding his interest, this was the time. Still, he made her quite the pretty leg, if he did say so himself.

"Charles Bingley, at your service."

"I apologise for keeping you waiting, sir," she said, her dulcet tones tinged with the faintest tone of distress. "But Mama is not feeling well and…you did tell Mary you were here with reports of Lizzy? That is,

Miss Elizabeth Bennet, my sister? We are all at sixes and sevens, wishing for more news of her. Please, do be seated again."

Sister! Interesting! This, then, was the natural child whose existence had crushed Mr Bennet's marriage. He realised he had no idea how to address her. Had she taken the Bennet surname? As the elder sister, was she to be addressed as Miss Bennet? Actually, though, Elizabeth would correctly be "Miss Bennet" as the only true Bennet! It was a conundrum, as she had not given him any name at all.

As he re-seated himself, he asked, "You have not heard from your sister, then?"

She sat down on a chair near the settee, her hands clasped nervously in front of her. "We have received one letter from her, only a few days ago, after an absence of more than a week! Of course, we knew she was taking a journey, but instead of returning, she sent a letter. And it said...well, it was a most extraordinary letter, and Mama is especially unnerved. There is going to be a wedding, we understand, and yet we do not know the bridegroom."

Charles smiled amiably. "I, too, was surprised when I received a letter from my good friend, Mr Fitzwilliam Darcy, announcing his engagement to your sister! Very out of character for him to jump in feet-first, so to speak."

The young lady looked up at him hopefully. "So...your friend, Mr Darcy...he is...a kindly gentleman?"

Charles's brow furrowed. "Hmm. Kindly. Well, 'tis not that he is unkind. A right honourable gentleman, he is, but I do not know a more awful object than Darcy, of a Sunday evening, when he has nothing to do." His brow cleared. "Fret not. He is the busiest of men, terribly industrious, always doing three things at once. Excepting the Sabbath, of course. Which is why, if restlessness takes him, it happens then."

"Oh, my."

He saw he had not achieved his object, which was to give a confident report of Darcy's character. "Truly, ma'am, he is a splendid fellow." He continued with a convoluted tale of how Darcy had walloped a regular bell swagger at Eton, thus rescuing the much younger Charles Bingley from a terrible drubbing. He noted she did not look much reassured, though he thought it a grand tale, himself.

"I say, don't get yourself in a pucker," he soothed. "I promise Darcy does not make a habit of getting himself yoked. He has had many an opportunity too, for he is known as one of the finest catches on the marriage mart. His uncle on his mother's side is an earl, and the one on his father's is the Bishop of Derby. No fears he cannot support her, what?"

"Oh, my," she murmured again. "'Tis worse than I thought. I mean...not worse, precisely, but...our household situation is not quite..." She trailed off, plainly at a loss.

Charles was certain he knew the cause. "Darcy knows all about, um, your family history," he said, unable to prevent his blush. He hurried on to the part of the plan he had practiced. "I have a letter here, from my step-mother. She is the sister of Thomas Bennet, which makes her Miss Elizabeth Bennet's aunt, see?" he said eagerly. He withdrew the parchment from his inner coat pocket. "I was to give this to your mother, but perhaps you might like to read it to her, instead?"

The young lady cautiously accepted the folded parchment, and smoothing it open upon her knee, read:

Dear Mrs Bennet,

I send you the greetings of a long-lost sister. It grieves me to admit I only learned of your marriage to my brother a few weeks past. The cause of said acknowledgement being a sad one, as Mr Bennet is ill, nigh unto death, and his marriage and most especially, his daughter, weigh heavily upon his conscience at the crossroads of his own mortality.

However, God works in mysterious ways. My step-son, Mr Charles Bingley, upon hearing the tale of your star-crossed marriage, sent his friend, Mr Fitzwilliam Darcy, who has relations in your city, to discover how you and your daughter fare.

Through some circumstance—the mystery of which has not been fully revealed—Mr Darcy had the opportunity to become acquainted with, and be utterly captivated by Miss Bennet, and he wishes, as you have no doubt heard, to make her his bride.

I cannot say enough favourable regarding Mr Darcy. He is a prosperous gentleman, a great landowner, and true and faithful friend to my son since their days at Eton. At my husband's recent passing his condescension was such that he offered every condolence and sympathy of kinship.

The situation is delicate. We would both, I am sure, wish to avoid any gossip attending the wedding of your daughter to such a great man as Mr Darcy. I feel confident Mr Bennet, were he well enough to understand the particulars, would acknowledge Elizabeth as he ought to have long ago. But he is not able to do much at present and it is left to us to settle what ought to be done now.

I beseech you: pray, come to Longbourn. I would beg a sisterly indulgence, except I have no right. I am sure you have suffered much as a result of my brother's pride, but I will not hesitate to petition your mother's heart, where pride has no place when it poses a barrier to the happiness of our children. Bring any and all members of your household, of course. But come quickly, for I know not how many hours Mr Bennet has left in this mortal realm, and I am certain reconciliation ought to be the dying wish of a father and husband.

Hopefully, Your Sister,
Margaret Bingley

Jane carefully refolded the letter. "Oh, my."

THE BISHOP DID NOT REFUSE TO PERFORM THE CEREMONY, AS LIZZY HALF-feared he might. If he was not precisely content with Fitzwilliam's choice of bride, neither did he state any overt objections. He was "concerned" at the brevity of their courtship, according to Fitzwilliam's brief summary of the bishop's protracted private remarks; but the wedding day arrived without any disavowal on his part. Evidently, he decided to leave those concerns in God's capable hands—and Fitzwilliam's.

Her hands, clasped in his, felt petite and feminine; his touch anchored her in the shifting sands of her new life. From almost the age of twelve years, she had been the most...capable person in her household. It was humbling to learn how limited her experience, but then Pemberley was beyond the realm of most people, she supposed. With assistance, she would do well enough.

The gown she wore was a new one, Fitzwilliam having performed another miracle to procure at least a partial trousseau for his new bride. The figure who peered back at her from the looking glass this morning was beautiful, an adjective she had never before used to describe herself. It was just as well, since she clung to her confidence like she clung to Fitzwilliam's hands, taking her eyes off Bishop Darcy in order to steal a look at her future husband. He wasn't watching the bishop at all; his eyes were only for her. Those eyes were hot and intense, the look he had given her in the garden.

"...not by any to be enterprised, nor taken in hand, unadvisedly, lightly, or wantonly, to satisfy men's carnal lusts and appetites, like brute beasts..."

With a guilty flush, she turned her attention to the ceremony.

"...ordained for a remedy against sin, and to avoid fornication..."

Fitzwilliam had said they would wait, but did she wish to? After all, as the bishop so helpfully stated, their union had the blessing of the church and the protections of society. Whether or not they actually participated in the most tantalising benefits of marriage, in the eyes of God and country they were permanently joined. So why abstain from the (hopefully) most rewarding parts of the business?

Lizzy held her breath as Bishop Darcy spoke the "if any man do allege and declare any impediment" clause, but Lady Catherine did not leap out of the woodwork to put a stop to the ceremony. And then Fitzwilliam gazed at her with almost unbearable intimacy as he vowed to love, honour, comfort, and keep her, forsaking all others.

For many, these vows were merely a means to an end, an ancient tradition and not a personal requirement. They so often meant so little. But Fitzwilliam was a man of his word and kept his promises. She was very sure of this.

"I will," he vowed, and she felt his assurance down to her toes.

And then it was time to make her own promises. She was proud of the way her voice sounded strong and sure despite her fears. Fitzwilliam smiled at her, fully and deeply. He was so beautiful when he smiled! Oh, how she wished him happy!

"Who giveth this woman to be married to this man?"

Colonel Fitzwilliam stepped forward, having agreed to stand up with her as a favour to his cousin. Whatever he thought of this union he kept to himself, but he was kind. He winked at her, his blue eyes twinkling.

A flash of colour in the choir loft caught her eye. She had met with Lady Anne thrice this week, in the early mornings while Georgiana was still abed. True, thus far Lady Anne had mostly shared stories of Fitzwilliam as a young boy, with little attention devoted to the supposed topic at hand—how to integrate Lady Anne into the household management while keeping Georgiana ignorant—an impossibility as far as Lizzy knew. But Fitzwilliam escorted her to and from Holmwood Hall, greeting and taking his leave of his mother courteously, if formally. And he agreed that she could watch their wedding ceremony from the privacy of the loft, as long as no one noticed.

How she wished Jane could have been with her! But time was of the essence. The notice of their marriage had been sent to the London papers and should appear today. She had written to her mother and Jane, and they would be surprised by the suddenness of the nuptials, likely upset; she had received no reply.

Thoughts of the situation with mothers and sisters fled as the bishop instructed Fitzwilliam to take her right hand. As he pledged his troth, she could almost feel him willing her to believe in his sincerity. How could she not?

Unfalteringly, she repeated her own pledge, which was immediately rewarded by another of Fitzwilliam's rare smiles.

He placed a lovely ring upon her fourth finger, saying, his voice low and solemn: "With this Ring I thee wed, with my Body I thee worship, and with all my worldly Goods I thee endow: In the Name of the Father, and of the Son, and of the Holy Ghost. Amen."

The look he gave her was beyond his smile or even his eagerness; it was his offering of not only his worldly goods, but also all of his good and pure heart.

And Lizzy prayed she could trust him with all that was in hers.

THE ENTIRE ESTATE CELEBRATED THE DARCY NUPTIALS. AS MR AND MRS Darcy emerged from the chapel, they were met with cheers and applause and an open carriage. Of course, the liberal number of coins Darcy tossed to the crowds as they drove away did not harm the celebratory spirit. There were tables set up on the south lawns groaning under the weight of meats, pies, breads, and cheeses, for the Pemberley kitchens had outdone themselves in honour of the occasion.

Those who attended the wedding breakfast were few in number but jolly in disposition. Georgiana was beside herself with joy, which Lizzy found touching. She also had the opportunity to witness Colonel Fitzwilliam's easy friendship with both Darcys. Lizzy, who had heard stories of the notorious Earl of Matlock for years, saw no resemblance in his genial son. Then again, she doubted he would be close to Fitzwilliam if he were anything like his false, lascivious father.

The past three days had been a whirlwind, full of preparations and legalities—and fabrics! She had been measured and fitted within an inch of her life. Lizzy might have eschewed pretty things in the past for practical reasons, but with no such limitations, she enjoyed choosing amongst the many fabrics and patterns from a celebrated dressmaker who Fitzwilliam imported from London, along with a roomful of seamstresses.

The solicitors had been another matter entirely. Fitzwilliam, determined that she be cared for in any eventuality, created a settlement so far beyond generous, Lizzy was appalled.

"Your lawyers must think me a fortune hunter!" she said, after he explained the terms.

"In all the world, I care most for you and for my sister. My sister has been provided for. What kind of man would I be if I neglected you?"

"You could do much less and still be an excellent sort of man."

He hadn't replied in words, only taken her hand and pressed it to his cheek.

Since that devastating morning in the garden he had not kissed her, determined, she supposed, to prove his flawless restraint. But somehow, his little touches managed to convey his longing for her all the same.

He cleared his throat, and she realised her mind had wandered entirely out of the room. Georgiana and the colonel had disappeared.

"Oh!" she said, looking around. "Where are—?"

Fitzwilliam smiled. His smiles were growing more and more common, but never commonplace. "Richard is taking Georgiana out on her horse," he said. "A nice, long ride, to give us some privacy, I believe. They have gone upstairs to change."

Foolishly, she blushed.

"Come with me," he said eagerly. "I have waited this age to show you something. Had quite a time talking Georgiana out of doing it, because she has wanted you to see it since your first day here."

"Intriguing," she said, and placing her hand in his, allowed him to lead her from the room.

"I've only seen two footmen in the house thus far," she said, after they had walked up two floors. "The place feels almost empty."

"Most of the servants have the afternoon off, to celebrate. We are making do with a skeleton crew."

"Making do. I see," she teased. "If I had done a single thing for myself today, I would feel very self-sufficient. Alas, I did not. Soon I will not remember how to tie my own garters."

He gave her a sardonic look, but she saw a wash of colour at his cheekbones and she smiled to herself.

"Here is what I wished to show you," he said, throwing open a set of doors.

Lizzy gasped.

"The Pemberley Sculpture Gallery," he said. "The largest room in the house. We believe we have one of the most significant private collections in the country."

Lizzy found herself speechless.

For some time, he was her guide, speaking of the history of each piece, when the house had acquired it and from whom. Many of the works his father had procured.

"Mr Harry Wickham's maternal relations—"

"Were Italian artists," she murmured. "I remember."

"I do not know about that, but he had well-connected uncles and cousins, who could procure very fine pieces," Darcy said. "My father took full advantage, even sending Wickham to Rome—twice, I believe."

"His mother," she said. "His mother was an artist."

"Did you know him well?" he asked curiously.

She shook her head. "I was a girl and he was kind. He built me my first kiln. My only kiln."

"Ah," he said. "He was…a friend of your mother's?"

"Yes," she replied shortly. "But thanks to him, I never again became acquainted with any of her…friends. He made me promise not to."

"God bless him, then. It could have been dangerous."

"Yes," she replied again, and, wishing to change the subject, pointed to a statue of a seated woman with a young girl. "My goodness, that looks very old."

"Truly ancient. It was discovered a hundred years ago, but is well over one-thousand years."

Lizzy studied the folds of the statue's carved chiton, admiring the intricacy of detail. "'Tis hard to imagine something this beautiful surviving the passage of time."

"Ah, but it is much younger than this piece," he said, pointing to what looked like an Egyptian goddess. "This one is thousands of years old." He told her which goddess and when she had been created, details of its composition and what was known about her. He spoke with the same confidence in answering her every question, his breadth of knowledge as impressive as many scholars.

Lizzy was overwhelmed by the scope and beauty of the collection. There were marbles and bronzes, terra cotta and granite, ancient and modern. They studied the many displays for over an hour and yet had barely begun.

"I HAVE A SURPRISE FOR YOU," HE SAID, ONCE THEY HAD REACHED THE END of a passage.

"I cannot comprehend a much finer surprise than this one," she replied, smiling up at him.

His gaze remained serious. "I mentioned Harry Wickham earlier because I have been in touch with his cousin in London. He recommended a master, a man who, he says, is a fine artist and the best he knows amongst those who are willing to take female students. At least, in England. He said the man is somewhat temperamental, but his skills are unsurpassed, and as long as you have talent you will learn much. However, this Signor Benenati has a high opinion of himself. If he does not think enough of your work, he will not stay. I have debated whether or not this was acceptable, for I cannot suffer any disrespect towards you. Ultimately, however, I decided the choice must be yours."

In actuality he hoped he was not erring; perhaps in this instance, "the best" was not ideal. He preferred someone who could nurture his wife's talents at whatever level they might exist.

Happiness lit her from within. "Oh, yes! Tell him yes! All I want is an opportunity. If I am not good enough, it is best to know, isn't it?"

"I cannot agree, for one man's opinion might be faulty. Men are ruled by their tastes, sensibilities, experience, and even their jealousies. It would not do to allow Benenati to be the sole arbiter of your future. If he will not stay, we will find another," he replied seriously. He could hardly bear the thought of someone hurting her, and it went deeply against his grain to take the risk. While he could care less whether or not she was a prodigy as long as the exercise fulfilled her, she obviously cared deeply. But he had promised her the best, and in the end, had been unable to justify breaking his word.

"Very well," she smiled. "But when, Fitzwilliam? When will he come?"

"He can be here within a few weeks," he replied. "I think we had better wait until he arrives to begin construction of your kiln, so we can take advantage of his training in its design. But I vow to put up the biggest and best of its kind."

Lizzy threw her arms around Fitzwilliam's neck. "You, sir, are the best husband I have ever had." She moved her lips to his.

He returned the kiss, adjusting the fit of their mouths together so they could kiss more deeply. This was what he had waited for—the right to kiss her as he longed to do. If it was not everything he wanted, it was more than he had ever had, and he prepared to enjoy every second of the freedom to feel it.

But he underestimated how liberating the taking of those vows would be to the dammed-up emotions he kept tightly tethered. Even though he knew her responses were founded in gratitude, that he had not yet achieved the closeness he had planned upon before pushing for intimacy, he was unprepared for the onslaught. His heart beat in a primitive, pounding pulse: *mine, mine, mine.*

"I WANT YOU," HE SAID. "ON THE LONG ODDS YOU COULD NOT DEDUCE that for yourself." He scooped her up, skirts and all, surprising her.

Lizzy thought, for a moment or two, he meant to carry her to his rooms. She would not have protested, though perhaps his back might, hefting her in such a manner. But he moved instead into an anteroom off the gallery, through which another parlour was tucked away. His knowledge of Pemberley did come in handy, for there was a nicely sized chaise longue in its furniture arrangement. Rather than set her down upon it, he sat himself, keeping her (with her voluminous skirts trailing upon the floor) upon his lap.

"I notice you are awfully fond of carting me around," she said, grinning.

He looked at her through lazy, hooded eyes. "Does it offend you?"

"I like it," she whispered.

The kisses grew deeper, and she rejoiced in their freedom to explore. After all, she had given herself to him in explicit vows: To have and to hold, from this day forward, for better, for worse.

This was definitely the better.

"What a good husband you'll make," she said, as he found a very sensitive spot where her shoulder and neck met. "An excellent husband. The very best." He loved her, and she knew it—knew it by the discipline he exercised, by the vow he upheld to prove restraint—all the while doing everything in his power to show affection and adoration. She looked up at his dear, dear face and knew the right thing to do, at least for them. "Will you make me your wife in truth? I want you to...so much."

Darcy stared at his new wife for a moment, hardly comprehending the words she had just uttered. His wife! The person whom he had, only hours before, vowed to love, to cherish, to honour, all the days of his life. Evidently, she meant him to begin these precious duties immediately.

Abruptly he stood, lifting her again into his arms. She liked it, she had said. He felt strong enough, currently, to carry her to his rooms. Devil take it, he felt strong enough to carry her all the way to Lambton. Manchester. The moon, if need be.

From this moment forward, he silently repeated his vow, *I plight thee my troth*.

10

Fanny Bennet did not look at all as Margaret had expected she would. But then, her step-son's only partially legible letters had largely fixed upon the splendours of the other daughter, Jane. As Jane was not a member of the party now arriving at Longbourn, Margaret was unable to perceive exaggeration.

Fanny must have been a true beauty as a girl and was a handsome woman still. The laugh lines at her eyes and mouth did not at all detract from her good looks. Her travelling dress was stylish but not flamboyant, her manners impeccable while Charles made the introductions.

"Mrs Bennet, my step-mother and Mr Thomas Bennet's sister, Margaret Bingley. Mrs Bingley, Mrs Bennet."

"So good of you to ask me here, Mrs Bingley," Fanny said, curtseying prettily. "So exceedingly kind. Please, do call me Fanny."

Margaret went to her at once, offering her hand. "Thank you for agreeing to come, Fanny. I am Margaret to you. My apologies if we seem a bit topsy-turvy. The household has been much affected by my brother's illness."

Fanny took the offered hand. "Mr Bennet...is he...?"

"Holding his own," Margaret replied.

"Thank goodness," Fanny said, startling Margaret by dropping suddenly into the nearest chair and fanning herself vigorously. "I have prepared myself for the worst, but truly I do not know how I could bear it, had you been forced to say otherwise. I have depended upon Last Words, you see. He would apologise for his Pitiless, Callous conduct. I would grant him my Forgiveness. I have imagined

268

it all in my mind, and would be cruelly disappointed were we denied."

Margaret could hear the capital letters in Fanny's voice. She and Charles exchanged a look, but she read only amusement in his.

"My brother is not of a sentimental disposition," she said carefully.

"So many men are not," Fanny replied, continuing to fan herself. "If they only understood how a female heart melts before True Emotion, and how Tenderly we might reward even the smallest bit of despised sensibility with our Fondest Affections, they would take More Care." She ceased fanning and speared Charles with a look. "Young man, take Heed."

"Yes, ma'am," he said quickly, appearing fascinated.

Margaret blinked. "Oh, ah, yes...that is to say...I would not want you to suffer any further disappointment. Mr Bennet is rather a... curmudgeon, I am afraid."

Fanny surprised her again by smiling fondly. "Bless his heart. He always was devoted to proper conduct. He has been alone for many years." She lowered her voice confidentially. "If a man finds no release for his ill-humours, he becomes dyspeptic and unreasonable."

Charles made a choking noise, quickly disguised as a cough, but Margaret could see he was in danger of going off into whoops.

"Poor Mr Bennet, to have suffered so." Fanny fanned herself again, and then looked at Margaret hopefully. "May I see him? Sit with him?"

Margaret bit her lip. "He is often insensible," she explained. "None of the medicines have done any good, and I will not have the leeches. I stay by his side and prevail upon him to drink barley water whenever possible, but nursing him can be demanding and, um, untidy—"

"I can do it," Fanny interrupted eagerly. "I nursed both of my girls myself whenever they took ill. Of course, two healthier children there have never been, but Janey had a Terrible Fever once at twelve years, and I never left her side, except for the times Lizzy prevailed upon me to rest."

"I am not sure how he will respond to...to you," Margaret warned. "He may be too ill to notice, but then again..."

"If he grows distressed, I will call for you," Fanny averred. "But Margaret, you must be spent, having cared for him all this time. Allow me to spell you, at least until he gains health enough to request my departure." Her big blue eyes filled with unshed tears. "I can do this much, I promise."

Margaret found herself somewhat bewildered. She had invited Fanny Bennet here to ease the way for Thomas's daughter. If a reunion took place there would be fewer to challenge Elizabeth's history. Margaret knew if Fanny was at Longbourn before Thomas died, an announcement of reconciliation could believably be spread to the neighbourhood. She would give out a story of Thomas marrying a widow with one child in his youth, having a daughter with her, then parting over a misunderstanding. She would tell everyone the pair reconciled at long last upon Thomas's deathbed. She would settle a healthy sum upon Fanny, in exchange for her promise to live discreetly thereafter.

She had been prepared for Fanny's bitterness over the rejection of herself and her daughter so many years before. She had been prepared to pay Fanny handsomely to play the part of Thomas's soon-to-be bereaved widow. She had been prepared to be tolerant of uncouth conduct and persuade the woman to act respectably while here and hereafter, for her daughter's sake. She had been prepared for Fanny to refuse to come at all or to be openly hostile if she did.

She had not been prepared for Fanny's apparent true affection for Thomas. She had not been prepared for Fanny's obvious generosity of spirit. Not at all.

"Step-mama," Charles said, clearly happy Margaret might at last be receiving real help. "You are so weary. A rest from your labours would do you wonders."

"Are you certain?" Margaret asked Fanny. "Many have died from this fever, including my husband. Thomas may be contagious. And he is not always an easy patient."

"I am certain," Fanny answered resolutely. "A wife should do for her husband."

"Mrs Hill," Margaret called, being certain the servant was just beyond the door, attempting to eavesdrop.

"Yes, madam?" Mrs Hill said, appearing at once.

Margaret sighed. This might be a mistake, but she was almost too weary to care. And she may as well let the rumours of reconciliation begin, and what better way? "Put Mrs Bennet in the mistress's room," she said to the wide-eyed servant. "See she has everything she needs, and then show her to her husband's rooms. She will sit with Mr Bennet while I rest."

"Yes, madam," Mrs Hill replied, eyes alight with curiosity. "If you will follow me...Mrs Bennet."

After the two women departed, Margaret let out a heavy sigh. Even with a nurse watching her brother at night, she was so fatigued, she could almost have fallen asleep right there in the parlour. With an effort, she transferred her attention to Charles.

"The elder daughter...Jane? I thought she would accompany her mother?"

"I had hoped to bring her with us. Mrs Bennet feared taking her anywhere near the fever. The girl protested, and I believe she might even have prevailed, as Mrs Bennet is not one to maintain strong opinions in the face of opposition...but...enter Mr Fitzwilliam Darcy." Charles sighed heavily.

"Mr Darcy? How so?" Margaret asked.

"Yes," Charles said, a slight indignation entering his tone. "Two beetle-browed solicitors with tall black hats, spectacles, and great stacks of legal documents appear on the Bennet doorstep, full of speeches regarding settlements for the angelic Jane, and she is in raptures as how the gingerbread means she shall marry some sea captain and move to Dover as soon as may be!" He covered his eyes in rueful dismay. "I fear Darcy has separated me forever from my one true love, blast him."

Margaret laughed. "Language, Mr Bingley. Oh, poor you. But do not despair. You shall be falling in and out of love many times before you need fix your interest." She grew pensive. "Have I made a mistake? Bringing Fanny here? Allowing her in with Thomas?"

"I like her," Charles declared firmly. "She is awfully quick to tears and over-fond of mawkish sentiment, but she seems a good egg. And she's no Drury Lane vestal, whatever Bennet believes. Besides, you need help and there is no one else. She is his wife and ought to be here, is what I think. But you ought to have seen her eldest daughter. Loveliest girl I ever met. Perishing waste of beauty on some old sea captain, if you ask me," he said, shaking his head. "Curst Darcy and his curst settlements!"

LIZZY GIGGLED. "PUT ME DOWN, SIR! IF YOU HURT YOURSELF, I WILL—"

But Darcy did not hear what she would do if he were hurt, because he had stolen her words in yet another heated kiss.

The important thing was to get her to his rooms quickly.

He was out the door and halfway down the corridor leading to his apartments before he lifted his mouth from hers. At this moment, he could not care less if the servants saw him kissing his bride.

"Wait," she said, once she had breath.

He did not wish to wait. "Waiting is a terrible idea," he said.

"I want to wait to have children," she blurted.

He froze. Her words acted as an ice bath, his passion-clogged brain clearing. Well. At least there were no servants in the immediate vicinity to learn his wife had no wish to bear his child. He gently set her down.

"Can we discuss this?" he asked, trying to keep the hurt from his tone. *I offered her time. But why did she asked me to make her mine in all ways, only to withdraw her permission as fast as it was given?*

"Apparently we must," she replied, sighing.

At least he could now bring her to the privacy of his rooms. It had, perhaps, been foolish to order her things moved to the mistress apartments so quickly. It would be hellish knowing she was sleeping just beyond his door and yet, untouchable. But it would have looked odd to the household had he not, and…he sighed, opening his door.

Lizzy took in Fitzwilliam's apartments with no small curiosity. They were, naturally, massive…a full sitting room, an enormous dressing room, and finally, a grandiose bedroom fit for a king. The four-poster alone required a set of steps to get into the thing. The décor was mixed…rather than a particular style, it appeared a mish-mash of furniture and paintings from different eras, as though he collected only his favourites for this private place.

It was surprisingly well done, though. Unlike the priceless formality of the other rooms, this area was lived-in and almost… homely. Comfortable furniture of soft leather surrounded a marbled fireplace; she could just see Fitzwilliam seated there, his nose in a book, his long legs stretched out before him. She could envision herself, her own book in hand, reading while tucked beneath his strong arm, his hand idly playing with her hair. The vision was so clear she caught her breath and looked to her husband.

He was at the window, staring out. How was she supposed to discuss something so delicate with his back to her? She sat down on the leather sofa.

Finally he spoke, but to the window, not to her.

"Why not children?"

"Can you sit over here?" she softly inquired.

Slowly he made his way to the sofa, sitting on the opposite edge. Still distant, almost unreachable.

"I do want children...in the future," she said carefully. "Just...not immediately. I've only known you a few weeks, Fitzwilliam. I have so much to learn. And I would like to study with Signor Benenati for a period of time before I become...indisposed."

"How long?" Darcy asked gruffly.

Lizzy felt frustrated. He had, before the nuptials, offered her time to come to know him before sharing their night-time life, as well as the day. It was possible she hadn't thought this all out sufficiently. The man was, plainly, anxious to fill his nursery; she had grown up in a household with the opposite concerns.

"A year or so?" she suggested tentatively.

"A year!" he cried hoarsely.

"Perhaps it sounds like a long while, but in the meantime we shall come to know each other better and I will feel more comfortable, hopefully, with the running of the household and everything attendant to those duties."

"An entire year," he groaned. "You shall have to visit me in Bedlam."

"That seems extreme," she replied, puzzled.

"Extreme? I have always thought myself a gentleman. Now I realise what I mistook for goodness was in truth only an absence of temptation. It shall be devilish difficult to keep away from you for an entire year!"

Suddenly Lizzy realised he had not understood. "I did not mean I would not share your bed, Fitzwilliam. I simply ask that we use preventatives. Children may come even so, of course, but usually they help delay conception."

There was a moment of dead silence. He took a deep, shuddering breath.

Finally, he turned to her fully, his gaze sharp, and scooted closer. "Oh. Preventatives," he murmured. "Where do we procure these, do you know?"

"Lady Anne has already done so for me. I hope you do not mind that I went to her, as I did not know where I might find—"

He had her back in his arms between one breath and the next. "For once, I find I do not mind my mother's intervention at all," he said, and his lips met hers in a devouring kiss.

When he allowed her to speak again, she said archly, "You were awfully upset, while our agreement was to wait to consummate our vows until we knew one another better. Did you lure me into matrimony with scurrilous promises, sir?"

"I did warn I would try to change your mind," he reminded, kissing her forehead, her nose, her cheeks. With an almost painful effort, though, he moved his head back. "However, if you have changed yours about today, it is your prerogative. I cannot swear patience for a wait of years, but I promised you time, and my word is still good."

Lizzy could not help but believe most men would never consider her feelings over a husband's rights to her body. She took a good, long look at the man who owned those rights. He was still perfectly turned out in his wedding finery, his blue superfine with velvet collar unrumpled, his snowy white cravat knotted into impossibly complicated folds. The silver embroidery and jewelled buttons on his waistcoat were exquisite. His trousers were perfectly pressed. He was an exquisite fashion plate.

She wanted to *wrinkle* him.

"Yes," he said, and she realised she had spoken the thought aloud.

Smiling, she began unwinding his neckcloth, the dratted thing that hid so much of his neck from her. "Your valet will wish me to Hades once he sees what I've done to your fine clothing," she said, finally able to toss it aside.

"Perkins will suffer in pained silence as he always does," Darcy said, assisting her in shrugging out of his coats. "If he has forgiven you the river mud, he will forgive you a few wrinkles."

"I daresay you haven't given him enough to do, spending so much of your time standing about in all your perfection." She unfastened his shirt and he helpfully lifted his arms so she could draw it off. "That's better," she said with satisfaction.

He was far more ruggedly fashioned than the statue of *Sleeping Endymion* in his gallery. Broad of chest, wide-muscled shoulders, tapering to a narrow waist.

"I would like to sculpt you someday," she said, her voice coming out in a breathless hush.

"I would like you to touch me now," he replied, a mixture of good humour and urgency in his eyes.

Lizzy wanted to, very much—but she wanted to be closer to him when she did so. "Perhaps I should go to my rooms—"

"No!" he cried.

She grinned. "Patience, dear sir. I meant only that I ought to go to my rooms and ring for Susannah to help me out of this gown. It has an absurd number of buttons."

"Absolutely not. You are not leaving my sight," he insisted. "I will happily play lady's maid."

Lizzy smiled, adding quietly, "I want you to know—if I were unhappy to have your child, I would not have married you. I do want more time before it happens, but there is always a risk. I will rejoice in any child who comes to us, whenever they come."

HE GAVE HER A LONG LOOK. HE KNEW HE HAD BEEN AGGRESSIVE AND obnoxious and nearly thrown a tantrum when he thought he was not going to have his way. She maintained her patience, no matter how he acted. He had barely spared a thought for the risks of birthing, but she would be taking all of them upon herself while he merely enjoyed the taking.

Carefully, he held her face within his hands, and kissed her gently, tenderly. "Is the risk acceptable?" he asked. "Are you certain? I will understand, if it is not. I may not be happy, but I will understand."

"Oh, Fitzwilliam. You needn't be so perfect."

He smiled at her. "It does not have to be all or nothing, Lizzy. I have many...*im*perfections I would dearly love for you to explore."

"I believe I wish to do...everything," she said. "So if you count disrobing ladies amongst your many talents," she teased, giving him her back, "I would like to proceed, if you please."

She took his breath away. So generous, so giving.

"I live to serve," he replied, kissing her nape. While he was, of course, anxious to rid her of all her clothing, the momentousness of what they were doing together made his hands shake. He had been waiting years for this; he did not wish to hurry through it like a green boy, and Lizzy deserved every attention.

He took his time. There was no ripping fabric nor hasty hands. Finally, he went to his knees to remove her slippers.

"Fitzwilliam," she said softly, touching his hair.

"I want this to be wonderful for you," he said, meeting her eyes as he stayed, kneeling, and clasped her hand.

"I have heard the first time is not always easy," Lizzy said, smiling down at him. "But I am not worried, and I do not wish for you to be, either. This is the start of something wonderful. I know it."

Darcy was touched. He was concerned, having heard the same information regarding a first time for a woman. And here Lizzy was, comforting him. Willingly sacrificing, again. He vowed to make it as good for her as was possible for him to do.

"Oh, Lizzy," he said, reaching up to touch her soft, sweet cheek. "How I love you."

MUCH, MUCH LATER, LIZZY WITHDREW TO HER ROOMS, TO A WAITING BATH and the faithful Susannah.

Darcy knew Perkins was likely on the edge of his seat with impatience, wishing to prepare the same for his master. Yet he could not help basking here for a few more moments, savouring sheer and utter contentedness.

Those idiot boys at Eton understood *nothing*. In grabbing for only their own pleasures, they completely missed the joy of giving a woman hers. He felt as though he had discovered the lost treasure of the *Flor De La Mar*. Or something better still. A great deal better.

Smiling, he rose and reached for the pull to summon Perkins. And then froze, seeing a smear of blood upon his sheets, a sign that she was forever his. He wished he could, somehow, give his blood to her in exchange. But he could not.

The sacrifice, as usual, had been all one-sided.

L izzy woke in the night, the unusual sensation of bumping up against another person rousing her from a sound sleep. Silver moonlight from the open curtains shone dully upon a square of carpet near the bed, but the room was mostly in shadow. Some would argue it cool enough for a fire, but Fitzwilliam thought it too warm, and had opened a window.

He was in shadow as well, but she could hear his soft snores. He had kicked the covers away, even as she drew a blanket further over her own shoulders.

'Twas so odd…he was hot, and she was cold, polar opposites in the matter of interpreting temperatures. Perhaps it was because he was a product of the rugged Peak District and its much harsher weather, while she was a child of the temperate seaside. Perhaps this was one argument favouring maintaining separate bedrooms. She could build up a cosy fire in hers while he slept in icy comfort. For that matter, if she wished to use a chamber pot, she could hardly imagine using the one behind the Chinese screen in direct line of sight from his bed.

On the other hand…here he was, right beside her. She could reach out a hand and touch him, any time she wished. She smiled. He was so, so dear. He had been so gentle with her, undressing her slowly, even her slippers. It was not what she had been reared to expect from men, in general, nor what any would expect from *this* man, in particular. He had knelt at her feet, and yet he had never looked stronger. It had reassured her; he would be careful and she was safe here, with him.

Then, after, he had ordered an entire dinner served in his sitting room, where they dined alone, feeding each other titbits, laughing at silly jokes and telling each other stories of their pasts, talking for hours. When they had at last retired, it seemed the most natural thing in the world to turn to each other, to stay together rather than to separate.

He had told her he loved her, many times now. Was that what this was? If he truly believed it at this moment, would he continue to feel so in one year, or two, or twenty? If she kept her own room, her own private spaces, would she perhaps be able to protect herself if his feelings changed?

On the other hand...if she kept him close, right beside her, should a distance between them begin to grow, she might recognise it more quickly. She might, perchance, reach out a hand to touch him in the night, to tell him that she still wanted him, needed him. She could order shawls of cashmere and thick, warm dressing gowns against frigid temperatures and chilly night air. Private evenings together meant more private conversations, new private jokes. She had only to look at his mother, who in making the decision to fiercely protect her heart, found it broken instead by the walls she erected around it.

Lizzy laughed at herself then; Fitzwilliam had not indicated he wished to share a chamber on any kind of permanent basis. Likely it had not occurred to him to think beyond their wedding night. It was much more usual for the husband to visit the mistress's chambers so he could depart at will to his own private spaces, his private life. She could now do the same.

Instead, she scooted over onto his side of the enormous bed. Immediately, in his sleep, he wrapped his arms about her and held her close. He was warm as a hot stove against her chilled flesh.

This is what I want. To be held, just like this.

Something anxious inside her calmed, and she quickly fell back to sleep.

HER HUSBAND HAD NOT BEEN ENTHUSIASTIC ABOUT VISITING LADY ANNE today. Lizzy knew he barely tolerated his mother, and she promised herself she would not press him to change that view. After all, Lizzy was not the young boy who had been dreadfully hurt by Lady Anne's desertion; the girl wounded by her own father's rejection would never blame him for his justifiable anger. But after three wonderful days in which they barely emerged from their rooms—days of discovery, of passion—the real world intruded in the form of an important, unavoidable meeting with his land steward and some bickering neighbours. She decided to make use of the necessary time apart to become more confident in her household responsibilities, and of course it made best sense to do so before the arrival of Signor Benenati. Today was also the colonel's last day at Pemberley before returning to his regiment, and thus the final day Georgiana would have an amusing companion to divert her attention away from goings and comings between Pemberley and Holmwood Hall.

So much time spent in their rooms made the walk a delight. Lizzy was tempted to fling off her hat and hold her face to the sky, but she contented herself in holding Fitzwilliam's hand and breathing in the early summer breeze.

"'Twould be so much faster to go on horse," he teased.

"I told you I needed no one to accompany me," she reminded. "Now you will have to walk all the way home and be late for your meeting."

Darcy smiled at the easy way she referred to Pemberley as "home." "If we had left the house when I first suggested, I would not be late."

"La, sir, spare me your regrets now for failing to refuse me then," she answered unrepentantly.

"Perkins is confused by why I ruin so many cravats. He mentioned he ordered more from the tailor."

"'Tis sad, that a man in his prime should be so clumsy with his hands." She sighed, her eyes twinkling.

"Clumsy, am I?" he growled, quick as lightning pinning her against a nearby tree and showing her exactly how nimble his fingers could be. Several moments later, her hat was on the ground and Lizzy was alight with laughter and desire.

"I take it back; I take it back!" she cried, giggling.

He kissed her, all teasing gone, until she was breathless.

"You will be late," she whispered. "Everyone will think me a terrible influence upon you."

"No," he said tenderly. "Everyone will think me a man in love, who cannot keep his hands off his wife." He kissed her nose and the delicate shell of her ear.

"Anyone would think you deprived," she said, tilting to give him freer access.

"They would be so wrong," he answered roughly, "but the more we are together, the more togetherness I want." With a groan he pulled away.

"We do not have any preventatives with us."

He grinned at her. "*That* is your objection to letting me have my way with you in the out-of-doors? Zooks, but you are an agreeable wife." He bent to pick up her hat, dusting it off before handing it back to her.

She did not put it on, though, just held it by its ribbons and reached again for his hand as they began walking once more. "I think it would be wonderful," she said contemplatively. "Especially if we were sure to be private. Someday, I should like to be with you by the seaside. There is nothing so romantic as the sea, though I am certain excessive sand would be very inconvenient. So untidy, you know, and getting into places one would never wish sand to intrude upon..."

His laughter rang out across the clearing. "Come along, minx. I shall have to take a horse from the Holmwood stable in order to return timely as it is." He pulled her hand to his lips and set a kiss upon it, then smiled slyly. "We shall make seaside plans *later*."

DARCY GREETED HIS MOTHER WITH COLD, POLITE FORMALITY, HIS USUAL manner whenever he was in her company. He only stayed for the briefest moment, hardly pausing to accept her congratulations upon the occasion of his wedding before taking his leave. Lady Anne remained still for a moment after he departed, watching him go. She sighed.

"I wonder if there will ever be a time when he can stand to be in my presence above a quarter-hour?" she asked sadly.

Lizzy, who had already seated herself on the dainty settee and poured a cup of tea, snorted.

The other woman turned to her sharply. "What was that noise for?"

"Nothing. Nothing at all," Lizzy replied blithely. But of course she lied. Perhaps because she and Fitzwilliam had shared every minute together of the last days, she felt especially protective. Or perhaps her wedding vows to honour him had sunk deeply into her soul.

"You plainly have something to say, Mrs Darcy. Please, speak freely. I quite depend upon your courageous ability to say aloud what most dare not even think."

"I am afraid that was the sum total of my commentary," Lizzy replied earnestly. "You know the rest. Most men would not have received you at all, much less politely. Most would not see you beautifully housed but a mile away. Most would not agree to have you as a part of the household, however removed, as he has done, not to mention the opportunity to be a part of his future, or at least the future of his children, should we be so blessed. He has put no obstacles in the way of our friendship, and he has not completely rejected the possibility of allowing you to meet Georgiana someday. While it may not be all you wish, you have a great deal more than most."

"I know, I know. I am impatient. I wish he would see me as I am now, not as I was then."

Suddenly Lizzy wondered: what would it be like for her if Fitzwilliam were passing the day with her father? Would she feel betrayed by that friendship? Likely so, and yet he so generously allowed it, recognising her need for Lady Anne's help, never expecting her to share his feelings. Still, she was his wife; she had an obligation to promote his interests wherever she went and with whomever she might be in company. What would she have him say to Mr Thomas Bennet, if their situations were reversed?

"But have you bothered to see him as he was then? You wish for the man's forgiveness, but you have not asked the boy. And 'tis the boy who is still bitter."

"I cannot ask him to forgive me. I wish to apologise, but—"

"No, you cannot. But do you even understand that for which you apologise?" Lizzy's voice remained quiet and non-accusatory, but also steady and determined. "Do you know what he experienced? The fisticuffs with classmates who were formerly his good friends? The malicious remarks, the overt rejections, the humiliation? The pressure he brought to bear upon himself to behave ever-so-perfectly afterwards, for years and years, so Georgiana might experience as little as possible of what he endured? The cold feeling in the pit of his heart insidiously whispering that if his own mother could not love him enough to stay, there must be something essentially unlovable about him? Have you asked him about any of it?"

Lady Anne stared at her, horrified. Her hand clasped her teacup in a white-knuckled grip, and for a moment Lizzy wondered if the delicate porcelain might shatter. But Lady Anne was an earl's daughter, after all, and following a longish pause, she gently set the cup down. If it rattled in its saucer, they both overlooked it.

"No. You are correct. I have not said anything he deserves to hear. He cannot bear to be near me above a few moments as it is, so I try to avoid offending him by saying as little as possible. Heavens, my very presence is an affront to him. I am here on sufferance."

Lizzy nodded. "And you know why it is so. But if you ever do have the opportunity, you ought to be prepared. You caused him much pain, many years' worth. If he has to shoulder it, you need to acknowledge it, at the least." She took a deep breath. "Now, what do you think of Reynolds's method of inventorying? And how might I verify the totals without re-counting every piece myself?"

'TWAS NEARLY NIGHTFALL BY THE TIME DARCY WAS FINALLY ABLE TO extricate himself from estate business—angry neighbours, confusing boundary maps, and bridge-building agreements. The first hours of engagement, he felt the same as always—the sense of fulfilment as he applied his mind to difficult problems, as he worked towards finding resolution of those problems, and as discussions took shape that affected the future and growth of Pemberley.

But as the day dragged on, and especially as some of the participants showed no interest in the common good, but only in advancing their own particular schemes, he became aware of a new feeling: impatience.

The feeling dogged him, reminding him he could be with Lizzy now, instead of wasting fruitless hours with bickering, short-sighted individuals. Only a week ago, matching wits and emerging triumphant against them on all counts would have energised him. But now he was forced to re-appraise the importance of certain topics of discussion, to wit: would argument about this particular item be worth the time spent away from his wife? Unfortunately, on several topics of discussion, the answer was affirmative. He could not justify diminishing Pemberley's water rights for any reason, regardless of how much he desired to be with Lizzy. But there were some particulars that, in the larger scheme of things, he could and did let go, which made the difference between ending the discussions today rather than continuing them into the morrow. At least all had now departed, each anxious to arrive home before dark, and he had not had to host another meal for them.

And tomorrow was now free, about which he could feel satisfied. He could spend it with Lizzy, perhaps taking a picnic lunch and retiring to a private corner of the estate…

"Fitzwilliam?"

He shifted guiltily away from planning private meetings with his wife, and greeted Georgiana.

"You startled me, Sister," he said, hoping the dim lighting covered his faint blush.

"Oh, I apologise…but Fitzwilliam, do you know where Lizzy is?"

Darcy froze. He had counted on returning for Lizzy hours ago, before the matters under discussion grew so complicated. He had sent a note to Holmwood informing them of the delay and the time to expect him, but had not thought to come up with some excuse to Georgiana for Lizzy's long absence, or to send the Pemberley carriage to collect his wife and bring her home. He was surprised Lizzy had not summoned it, as she was usually so considerate of his sister's feelings; likely she had assumed his cousin would keep her amused.

"Where is Cousin Richard?" he stalled.

"He received an express from London and had to take his leave this afternoon," Georgiana replied. "I have been trying ever since to find Lizzy. Mrs Reynolds said she was out walking, but I have looked everywhere I could think of and could not find her, and no one seems to be at all concerned that she is alone somewhere and—"

"She is well, Georgie-my-girl," he interrupted, his guilt deepening.

"But…where is she? Did she leave?" Georgiana asked, sounding frightened.

He remembered that feeling, the feeling that one's whole existence depended upon the decisions of others, and at any moment those others might decide you and your feelings were entirely inconsequential. He sighed heavily.

"No, dear, she did not leave. I am off right this moment to collect her, and as soon as I return, I will explain. But nothing is the matter, and you are not to fret. Understood?"

"Yes, Fitzwilliam." She nodded obediently, but still looked slightly alarmed.

Please, dear Lord, let me think of an explanation that will suffice, he prayed silently as he called for his carriage. Anything but the truth.

When Darcy entered Holmwood Hall, Lady Anne greeted him from her usual receiving parlour. But she was alone.

"Where is my wife?" he asked, after the briefest possible greeting that could still be termed civil.

"She should be here shortly. She seemed fatigued, and I entreated her to rest. She must have been more tired than I supposed, even, for she has been asleep several hours. As soon as you were announced, I sent someone to wake her. I hope that was acceptable."

Darcy's ears burned. They had not exactly been sleeping overmuch. His fault; he had exhausted his wife. He nodded shortly in embarrassment.

For several moments, neither moved nor spoke. Darcy shifted uncomfortably.

"What was it like for you?" she blurted suddenly. "After I left England. What—what happened?"

He turned his glare upon her, a reminder he preferred she not speak to him at all, much less regarding anything personal. "Excuse me?"

"I would like to know what happened to you as a result of my decision to leave."

"Nothing happened," he said shortly. "As you can see, I am perfectly well."

She closed her eyes. "You are indeed. No thanks to me."

He had nothing to say to that.

"I want to apologise," she said tentatively. "I am so sorry for the pain I caused you. I know that words are never enough but—"

"You are correct," he interrupted. "Words are pointless. The past cannot be changed. I recommend we behave civilly towards one another for the duration of your stay, but I can offer nothing else."

Lady Anne looked at the stiff, broad shoulders of her son. He would never meet her eyes, in fact, tried not to look at her at all—when the only thing she wished for in all her life was that he do so. That he see her.

Lizzy's words to her regarding the pain Fitzwilliam endured gnawed at Lady Anne's heart. She wanted desperately, somehow, to apologise. Since returning to Pemberley, she realised her sins were too awful, the wounds too entrenched, for mere words to suffice. But words were all she had, and perhaps belated words were better than leaving everything unsaid.

But what else could she expect? She had run away from him thoughtlessly, cruelly. Unforgivably. Of course, her regrets did not matter, but what had Lizzy said? That while she was away learning how to feel, how to love, he was being beaten, rejected...that her sweet, loving little boy—the first person in the entire world who had ever loved her purely for herself—had wondered if he was loveable. It was intolerable, and the stupid, useless tears she shed after Lizzy had gone to nap would not help him at all. *Come to terms with it, Anne. Face up to what he bore so that you could be happy.*

"Please," she said. "When I left...I did not think. I did not consider. I regret how it was for you, regret it deeply. Tell me what happened to you."

Why was she doing this? Darcy wondered. What did she expect to gain from useless, painful reminiscence?

"What do you want from me, madam?" he hissed, his expression thunderous.

"I want to know," she insisted. "I thought your father did not need me, would hardly even notice my absence. After I had decided my course, he told me I erred, but by that time, I hardly believed him. Was it true?"

She finally discovered the chink in his armour—his beloved Papa.

"How can you even ask?" he said, nostrils flaring. "How can you have doubted him? You broke him! He was the strongest man I have ever known, but you left him barely a shred of dignity! It was a year before we saw him smile again! A year in which he grieved and bore society's scorn and aged ten! How could you? What could he have done to deserve it?"

"Nothing," she said, her voice almost a whisper. "He did not deserve that. What did you not deserve, Fitzwilliam?"

Darcy knew he ought not to have answered her. It was all over and done, and it did no good to unearth it all, to relive a past that could not be changed. But the memories she stirred, of his father's pain and his own, poked at a wound covered by only the thinnest layer of scar tissue.

"What I did 'not deserve'?" he cried, incredulous at her doggedness in provoking this conversation.

"Yes," she persisted. "Tell me."

He was not proof against the unhealed hurt and fury, and he turned upon her. She was a tall woman, but he towered over her, and his voice rose to a roar.

"Did you believe I would not notice you were gone? I will let God decide what was or was not undeserved, but I will tell you what I did deserve from you—one blasted letter of explanation! One letter saying you thought of your children even once over the years! One bloody word of farewell before you abandoned us! Even one!"

Her eyes filled with tears and contrarily, it made him even angrier. He had to leave here, take himself away from her, and he whirled angrily...only to come face to face with a wide-eyed Lizzy.

Lizzy, his light, his life, who had just witnessed him cursing at his mother, raising his voice, throwing a tantrum, whining like a child over bygones. It was not to be borne. He stalked out.

12

"Fitzwilliam!" Darcy heard Lizzy call. With every fibre of his being, he wanted to disregard her cry. But it was full night now and though he could easily find his way by moonlight, he could not have her chasing about in the dark.

With a sigh he halted, allowing her to catch up to him on the moonlit garden path. He waited for her to say something about his evil disposition, terrible manners, or resentful, unforgiving nature.

"I am sorry," she said, and threw herself at him so forcefully, it knocked him back a step or two. "I am so sorry, darling. I ought to have kept my tongue between my teeth."

His arms immediately and instinctively wrapped around her, but it took him a moment to understand her words as he regained his balance.

"Lizzy," he interjected softly. "It was nothing to do with you." Her hair had worked free of its chignon, and he smoothed the escaping tresses back from her face.

"But it was," she said, shaking her head in fervent disagreement. "Most of the time I can separate the person your mother is now from who she was then—when she left you. But I had just left your arms and was feeling…oh, perhaps, protective, I suppose, that she dare have expectations of, well, anything from you too soon. I suggested she was largely unaware of the adversity her departure caused, and having any kind of amicability between the two of you would take time, if it could happen at all. At least, it was what I meant to suggest. But she must have felt my intention was she should instigate a conversation with you immediately, one you were unprepared to—"

"Lizzy," he interrupted. "Hush." He bent to kiss her and, at her immediate response, his antagonism towards his mother faded. This was what he wanted, what he had needed all day. Her, in his arms, allowing him to hold her. For long moments, he lost himself in her sweet, giving nature, her warmth drawing the coldness of dissension from his bones. Before he could become carried away, though, he let the kisses gradually lighten into brushes of his lips over her cheeks, her forehead, accepting her easy and generous affection as a balm to his sorrows.

She looked up at him. "I promise not to mention anything relating to you, nothing personal, not ever again. I shall keep us wholly in the present."

He sighed, half-smiling. "Do not make promises you cannot keep, my love. I know you are incapable of remaining silent if you feel the need to speak. And…I think I am not as sorry as I ought to be for what I said to her, although I wish I had shown more restraint in the saying. However you instigated the conversation, you were not entirely wrong to do so."

"Oh," she said, surprised.

"Perhaps next time, you will speak to me first."

Her brow furrowed. "I prefer not to speak of Lady Anne in any detail, for I know it upsets you. I feel guilty I rely upon her guidance for the household as it is, knowing it causes you pain."

He brushed a stray curl from her cheek. "My love, I can endure her presence in my life for a few more weeks as long as I know she is helping you. She is helping, is she not?"

Lizzy opened her mouth to speak, then slowly closed it again. "Yes, Fitzwilliam. Yes, she is helping me."

"That is good then," he said. "That is what is important."

LIZZY RESTED HER HEAD AGAINST HIS CHEST, HER HEART BEATING WILDLY in hers. Somehow, when Fitzwilliam said she could have his mother's assistance over a "period of time," she had misunderstood. She had not questioned what he meant by it, only assumed it would be up to her own judgment. Three years, four…maybe five years? Forever? But of course, for him, anything beyond a few days must seem endless. She had not missed the pain and fury and anguish in his eyes and voice as he shouted at Lady Anne. His very act of losing his precious self-discipline spoke volumes.

You knew he wanted her gone immediately. A week must seem like a year to him, a month an eternity. How long could you live with Thomas Bennet as your nearest neighbour and your husband's closest friend? Wrong-headed, selfish girl.

"How..." she began, then had to swallow and begin again. "How much longer do you think you can bear to have her near?"

He took a deep breath. "As long as you require, Lizzy."

Because she was in his arms, she could feel his body stiffen. He was bracing himself, she realised. Bracing himself to endure more, to suffer more, for her.

Briefly, regret seized her, but she drove it back. No one forced her to speak her vows; she wanted Fitzwilliam and she had taken him, recklessly perhaps, but it was done and she would not undo it. And so she made herself speak.

"Do you think...can you bear it until summer's end?" she asked hesitantly. *Three months. Dear heavens, only three months until I am left alone with Pemberley. Pemberley and Mrs Reynolds.*

"If you need that much time, you have it, my love," he answered quietly. Firmly.

That much. Well then. She could do this. She had misunderstood, but she was intelligent and had already learned many things.

"I am sure the summer will be ample," she made herself say brightly. "She has already taught me much. I may always write to her, and I am certain she can continue guidance from afar."

DARCY FROWNED. THERE WAS SOMETHING FALSE IN LIZZY'S DETERMINED tone. A moment before, he had been grudgingly agreeing to a summer's worth of his mother's company, but he found himself saying, "If you need more time than the summer, it can be arranged. I was thinking if she was gone before mid-August when most of the neighbourhood returns for the grouse, there might be less opportunity for rumours. All of the leading families hereabouts are in London at present," he finished.

"Of course," she agreed vigorously. "It makes perfect sense."

Too vigorously. She did not sound...herself.

"How long a visit did you foresee?" he asked.

She shrugged. "I suppose...I suppose I did not precisely plan an ending date. I wish I felt more devoted to the running of the household than I do, so I could convince you I do not need her at all. But having her here through these next weeks is more than generous. You are correct in that we must think of Georgiana's reputation and the potential for rumours. And I know it is painful for you to have her nearby."

Darcy was about to deny this, but at the last moment, held his tongue. She was not exactly wrong, he supposed, though he hated pigeon-holing his feelings for his mother as...painful. He preferred not to think about her at all, pretend she did not exist. After all, his mother had successfully forgotten his existence! So why should he—

He broke off this line of thought. Very well. He had to admit her presence was a problem for him.

He had meant to lead Lizzy back to his waiting carriage, but instead he plunked himself upon a nearby bench. For a moment she stood and looked at him before seating herself beside him.

"Feelings. Bah," he said bitterly.

"I am sorry," she said quietly.

"No, not your feelings," he said. "Mine. I do not like experiencing them. I prefer to disregard such things."

She snuggled up to him and he put his arm about her shoulders, enjoying the sensation of her pressed near.

"But," he continued, "I am afraid I have been ignoring them too much. Even now, Georgiana is likely anxious. I did not think to supply a good excuse for your absence today, and I believe she thought I might have chased you off already." He informed her of his cousin's sudden departure, and his sister's search.

"Oh, dear," Lizzy answered, half-laughing. "We must think of something. I ought to have returned home when I received your note saying you would be longer than we'd supposed. But I was so tired and Lady Anne suggested a nap and I am afraid I leapt at the suggestion. I did not mean to sleep so long."

"I have not let you rest much these past nights," he murmured lowly. "I am sorry."

She lifted her face to him, and he kissed her, fully and deeply. She nestled even closer. "I do not accept your apology, lest it lead to a change of behaviour."

She saw the white of his teeth as he smiled, but moments later he frowned again.

"There is one apology you must accept, and it is one I shall also offer to Lady Anne. I ought not to have raised my voice in anger to her, or cursed at her. Whatever else, I believe...no, I know...my father would want me to treat her respectfully. He would not be pleased, had he witnessed the dramatics in her parlour. I disappointed myself, and I am ashamed you witnessed it."

She lifted up to kiss his cleft chin. "Apology accepted," she assured. "I completely understand. She caught you unawares, which was my fault. I am sure you need say nothing to Lady Anne. You were provoked. She must discover a way to address those wounds without aggravating them."

"No matter the provocation, there was no excuse for that churlish display. I do not care for histrionics, least of all from myself."

"I feel exactly the same. My mother is always so...so nervous. She makes a fuss easily, which I always found difficult."

"Do you miss her?" he asked.

"Well...yes, I suppose I do. I do not precisely miss being responsible for her," Lizzy said. "But I admit I am somewhat anxious about her. Hopefully Jane will exert herself to be a more substantial influence than is comfortable for her, although I expect to hear very soon of wedding plans, now that you have so generously dowered her. I can only hope Mama will make good decisions without me there to make them for her, but she is so very...persuadable."

He nodded, making a comparison he once would have scorned. "The girls I met in London were the same. They seemed to have no thoughts or opinions of their own."

She fiddled with an engraved button on his waistcoat. "I presume they were trying to impress you with displays of feminine helplessness. Mama always said most men would be put off by my capability, and that I should learn to appear meeker and more biddable."

"Very practical advice. Thank heavens you did not listen," he said agreeably, pressing a kiss to her forehead.

"Mama could be practical about men, in her way. It was the one thing she studied—how to be most pleasing to a man—so she knew whereof she spoke. But somehow, all that studied helplessness became part of her." Lizzy sighed.

"I was eleven years when I first disputed her management of our household expenses. By my twelfth birthday, I found myself responsible for the budget and the household. I was young and made errors, but someone had to be in charge. Had I left Mama to it, she would have bankrupted us or chosen the worst lovers possible."

"She was fortunate in her daughter, I think," he said, a little dazed by how young she had been for such cares, and how quickly she must have learned to "manage" the only adult in her life.

"Jane supported me, which helped," Lizzy added. "I would play the part of stingy ogre, and sweet, gentle Jane would offer a compromise involving concessions we had already decided upon. In that way, we would often prevail."

He did not have to ask who devised the tactic. His wife was clever.

"But such methods are exhausting. If I'd had age and maturity, I could have told Mama how it would be. I believe it part of my bitterness towards my father. It was his responsibility to manage her, but he left it all to me."

Darcy nodded. At least his father had continued to uphold his own responsibilities until his illness necessitated Darcy assuming them. Means enough to live had, of course, never been a problem, much less the more deeply personal matters Lizzy muddled through.

"But I am thankful I was not kept so protected and sheltered that I failed to learn important lessons about taking care of myself and others. From what your mother has told me, her upbringing contributed much to her sense of helplessness and despondency. I do not defend her actions," she said as she felt him stiffen, "but it explains some of why she behaved as she did."

"I cannot pretend to understand that," he said tautly.

"I think I do, at least partly," Lizzy said quietly, thinking of the portions of the story it might help for him to hear. "I do not agree with her choices, but I believe I understand them."

"Then I wish you would explain them to me," he snapped.

"Did you know about the babes she lost?"

He was silent for long moments, his displeasure subsiding as childhood memories were replaced with adult understanding, as he remembered a doctor's presence, his father's distraction, and a maid carrying blood-soaked towels.

"Perhaps...yes, I can think of one."

"There were two others. Two girls, and one a son."

"You two speak of this?" Darcy asked incredulously.

"Yes," Lizzy said. "Amongst many other things. Losing those babes did something dreadful to her nerves, and also to her marriage with your father. And...I do not believe...they knew each other well, despite how many years they were together. They certainly did not discuss their difficulties."

After a few moments he said, "Father was very stoic. He did not believe in airing grievances. Pemberley was his answer to every complaint. He loved this place, and he gave it his all."

"It shows," she said steadily. "But Lady Anne had no such outlet. In her way, I believe she was as helpless as my mother. I suppose 'motherhood' was to be her Pemberley, but she was frightened, afraid to be hurt again. She...connected your father to the deep hurt, and she ran from it, and from him. But, like my mother, she still sought a man to tell her what to do and how to cope. Later, after she had been away long enough to regain some equanimity, she could see her thoughtlessness. But she had promised your father she would not write to either you or Georgiana, and so she kept her word, though she bitterly regretted it."

"What? He would not—" Darcy began. But then he remembered how sensitive his father had been regarding the scandal, how irritable he could be at its mention. "He had our best interests at heart," he said gruffly.

"Doubtless," Lizzy said gently. Her breath was warm upon his chest, even through the layers of his clothing. "He was a good father to you. You are a lucky man, Fitzwilliam."

Darcy remembered she hadn't any father at all, and her mother could be more child than woman. "I know that," he said, pressing a kiss to her hair.

"Have you decided what to say to Georgiana about tonight?"

"I suppose you believe I should tell her where you were. That I should allow them to meet," he said, his voice chilling a few degrees.

"Unnecessary. You could always say I was visiting tenants. Acting lady of the manor and all that."

"She would wonder why you did not take her with you, and it is several hours past the time for polite visits."

"So tell her I was lost."

"I already told her I knew where you were."

"Do you truly care whether she believes you or not? Georgiana is told what you think she should know and little else."

"It is called protection," he snapped back, annoyed, as though she were criticising. "I realise you had none, but I hardly wish to subject my sister to situations which she is ill-prepared to face."

"You talk as though I am coercing you to introduce them," Lizzy said with puzzlement. "I have never offered my opinion on the subject. I would not. 'Tis not my place."

He made no reply, and Lizzy spoke again. "Two more weeks," she said. "Give me two weeks with Lady Anne. I will come every day and ask every question I can name. I will write down everything she says. And then she can go. We can tell your sister that…an old friend of mine from Ramsgate is visiting and we are putting her up at Holmwood. Because she—she took sick, and Georgiana is not to be exposed. That would do."

Darcy sighed heavily. There was no mistaking the unhappiness in Lizzy's voice when she spoke of sending away Lady Anne, even as she offered him the perfect excuse and means to rid himself of the entire muddle.

"You," he said, not bothering to disguise both his admiration and frustration, "are dreadfully devious, my love."

"I know," she nodded against his chest. "It was required for survival before. But I have not been Mrs Darcy for a full week, and I expect it will take some time for me to drop the habit of it."

"I do not want Georgiana to grow to be…helpless," he blurted.

Lizzy nodded again. "Somewhere between the way I was reared, with too-heavy burdens on my shoulders, and all those society misses at Almack's with whom you could not hold an intelligent conversation, there must be a happy middle ground."

Darcy noted she did not again mention his mother's upbringing, and how it had contributed to their difficulties. She would not. She was doing it again, putting aside her own needs in favour of others' wishes. Specifically, his.

"There could be personal consequences to Georgiana knowing Lady Anne. In…in receiving her. Should Georgie decide—not too soon, of course, I could not even consider the possibility for another two or three years, at least—but should she have a London season, distancing herself from her mother would be the wiser course," he stated, struggling to be matter-of-fact.

"Very true," Lizzy agreed. "All the more reason for Lady Anne to leave at once. Perhaps two weeks is too long. I—"

"That is not what I meant!" he interrupted. "Please, let me think."

Lizzy sat up, lifting herself off his chest, and Darcy immediately felt the chill of night air where she once sweetly rested. Devil take it! He was going about this all wrong, but dashed if he could say all the correct words when...upset. Feelings! Bah!

"I meant that as Georgiana will be involved in the consequences of whatever decision is made, she should perhaps be involved in the decision itself," he heard himself say more calmly. "I promised you Lady Anne's assistance and guidance, and I mean to keep my word. Georgiana may decide she wants nothing to do with her mother. If so, keeping her at Holmwood might be...difficult."

"This decision should not be entirely up to me, not at your sister's expense. I completely agree that her feelings on the matter should be a consideration," Lizzy said quietly, trying to put her own selfish interests aside.

He made a noise of frustration. "If I know my sister, 'twill be more likely she will want Lady Anne to stay permanently."

"At least then, Georgiana would know she had a choice, that you felt she was old enough, and mature enough to participate in its making. But your feelings are important to your sister and me, to both of us. We will be unhappy if you are made unhappy by Lady Anne's presence."

"I am..." He inhaled deeply, then began again. "I am...angry at her. I am angry at my mother."

Lizzy scooted in close again, burrowing her hands under his coat. "Yes," she said equably. "I would be, too."

Darcy wrapped his arms around his wife, the chill at his side diminishing. "But I am not as angry as I was a few weeks ago. Or even...as I was an hour ago, I suppose. It helps to know she would have written, had she not promised."

"'Tis because you are annoyingly perfect," she said mischievously, smiling up at him in the moonlight. "If our positions were reversed, I am sure I could maintain my antipathy for much longer and much more unreasonably."

His smile gleamed in the moonlight. "Perhaps you could educate me in...a few of the more forward-thinking, progressive misdeeds. After all, you have had the advantage of a superior education, as it happens."

"Well..." Lizzy began slowly. "There is one thing I have contemplated. But perhaps…" She lifted her mouth to his ear, whispering a suggestion.

Seconds later, she found herself scooped up in his arms, Darcy striding at a pace that could only be termed "brisk" towards the patiently waiting carriage.

"It is past time we returned home," he told his giggling wife. "We can speak with Georgiana over dinner, and then, madam, you are in for it!"

As he held her close, Darcy made a new resolve. Despite her generous offer, he knew Lizzy wanted Lady Anne's help and friendship, at least at present. He also knew he must relinquish his resentment, which might take a concerted effort on his part. But the husband of Mrs Elizabeth Darcy must have such extraordinary sources of happiness necessarily attached to his situation that he could, upon the whole, have no cause to repine. Lizzy's happiness was his. He would do whatever it took to ensure it.

13

So hot. So thirsty.

Those two sensations endlessly ruled Thomas Bennet's existence. It was as if there had never been another life beyond this heated, dry wasteland where nothing grew or changed, never any relief from the interminable flames.

Hades. It must be where he was. He had died and gone to the devil.

Where was Margaret? Margaret would give him a cool drink, easing him for a few seconds. Not that he could swallow enough for a lasting effect.

But Margaret was not here. Good, kind, fair-minded Margaret would never be in Hell. He was alone. Thomas avoided thinking of his sins, but they were difficult to evade when one was damned, the flames flicking his feet. His abandonment—he hated the word, but the flames insisted it was the correct one—of the girl. He told himself she was not his, and thus was not his responsibility.

Except she was. For he had married Fanny, the beautiful, laughing Fanny. Given her his name, accepted, at the time, his babe in her belly. For his four months in Ramsgate, he devoted himself to the young "widow" day and night. There had not been anyone else then. Anything planted in her belly had undeniably been planted by him.

Fanny lied! he cried to the flames.

You abandoned your wife and child! the flames cried back.

His was the greater sin, he knew it. He was reared a gentleman, had spoken vows. Even despising her, he owed Fanny and the babe his support. If the child died on the streets…his fault. The innocent words of her letters mocked him.

Dear Papa…

Dear Papa…

The conflagration threatened to incinerate him. So many times, he felt the relief of death waiting to claim him. He had balked. Knowing Hades to be his destination, his only reward for a life poorly lived, was the impediment to acceptance. But somehow, Hell had come regardless. Perhaps he should allow the bleak flames to consume, accept his fate of eternal inferno.

"There, there now, Thomas," came a voice, vaguely familiar. Not Margaret's. "Try to drink, dearest?"

He tried opening one bleary eye, but there were only shadows in the hot, dark, airless room. It must be a demon, taunting him with drink he was too weak and helpless to ingest. The liquid refreshment mostly spilled down his front, mocking his avid thirst, as demons were wont to do. To his surprise, the demon tried again, and his parched, charred tongue was carefully wetted. Again and again, a damp rag dribbled precious, delectable fluid into his mouth, so slowly he did not choke or vomit.

"'Tis awfully warm in here," the voice chattered sunnily while imparting the priceless drops. "I suppose your doctors prescribed the room be overheated. Whenever the girls or I were sick, our doctor insisted the good sea air was curative, and had us open wide all the windows. Since none of us have ever died, I believe he knew whereof he spoke."

But you must be dead now, he wanted to tell the chattering, friendly voice. *Since you are with me in Hades.*

But the voice plainly had not yet realised its fate, for it rattled on cheerfully.

"Of course, you have no sea air, more's the pity. Still, even if it's not quite so bracing as the seaside, it surely could not do any harm, don't you think? 'Tis a lovely day out—one could wish for more of a breeze, but perhaps as the day wears on?"

Margaret was quiet, never given to mindless babble; in this way brother and sister were much alike. This angel-demon could not be silent to save her soul. Everything entering her head flowed out, and not as the carefully measured drips of barley water upon his greedy tongue, but in a steady, unwavering flow. Once upon a time, the sounds might have annoyed the devil out of him. Before, of course, he had learned the devil's voice, an endless dissonance of regret and shame.

In contrast to his dark thoughts, the sunny voice spoke of cheerful, harmless things: the weather, pretty dresses for someone named Jane's trousseau, the astonishing marriage of another girl called Lizzy, and her curiosity about a man named Mr Darcy. Darcy? Surely the faultless gentleman from Derbyshire would not be spoken of in perdition? Never mind; Thomas's desperate conscience grasped the voice as a lifeline and held tight, clinging to its simple, earthbound feelings.

Cool air brushed his cheeks, a feeling so delicious, he wondered at it. Could there be breezes in Hades? Perhaps to taunt one with the loss once they were taken away? That would surely increase the torture. And then the area was suffused with light. The angel-demon had opened a window in Hell, giving him a glimpse of heaven.

Heaven was Longbourn in early summer, the tree-tipped edges of Oakham Mount just visible in the distance. It was the view from his bedroom window.

Was it possible? Could this angel have rescued him from the flames, dragging him back from the fiery brink?

It was too bright, and the angel only a shadow. He shut his stinging eyes against the glare.

Tears fell from them regardless.

"Now, now," the angel said, close by his side again. "You will be well, Thomas. All will be well." A deliciously cold cloth bathed his heated face.

"Don't leave me," he croaked, forcing his rough, cracked lips to move. "Please, don't leave me."

A cool, soft hand clasped his hot one. "I will not leave," the angel promised. "I am here now, and will not leave you, my dearest."

A PERPLEXED GEORGIANA GREETED HER BROTHER AND SISTER UPON THEIR return to Pemberley. As their highly talented but extremely volatile Cook had already held dinner for a quarter-hour there was no time for private conversation.

But once the meal was finished, they adjourned together to the music room. Georgiana was a talented musician but indifferent in her practice; still, she played when her brother encouraged her, and he and Lizzy both complimented her performance despite its several errors.

Lizzy noticed her husband had grown quiet, as he played absently with her hand, twisting her wedding ring upon her finger—a lovely band of gold adorned with sapphires and diamonds.

"Do you play, Lizzy?" the younger girl asked.

"I am an undistinguished performer," she laughed. "My sister, Jane, is far superior. Of course, her father hired a music master for her, which was always my excuse for any failings in comparison. Truthfully, though, my preference was for sculpture."

"For which you shall have your own master soon," Darcy interjected. "I have received word from Signor Benenati. He will be here within a fortnight."

Her eyes lit, and discounting all etiquette, she threw her arms around him while Georgiana laughed in scandalised delight. His sister's eyes widened further when he put his arm about Lizzy's shoulders rather than completely quitting the embrace, wanting the strength of her nearness.

"Georgiana," he began carefully, "I would like to talk to you about where Lizzy spent the day."

"I wondered," she said, equally careful and apparently puzzled by his sudden change of tone.

"She was at Holmwood Hall, where we have a…guest."

"A guest?" she repeated.

"Yes. Lady Anne Darcy. Your—our mother." He had sought in his heart what to call her, but the fact remained, according to British law, her second marriage was illegal. While she might favour the name of her lover over that of their father's, he would never use it again.

"Oh," she said in a small, bewildered voice. "What…what does she want with us?"

He struggled to keep his expression neutral. "I believe…she would like to meet you. And spend time coming to know you. But, Georgie-my-girl, this was her idea, to come and, ah, visit. You need not."

"The lady on the day we arrived…the one looking for you—was it her?"

"Yes," he said tersely.

Georgiana bit her lip, staring down at her lap. He could not tell her thoughts.

"What would you like for me to do?"

Of course she desires my opinion. She is only fifteen years. But he did not want her to become one of those vapid girls he had danced with at Almack's. Or heaven forbid, her mother.

"I would like you to think carefully about what you wish to do," he answered at last. "Obviously, her reputation is not, ah, respectable. I do not think there is much risk of public censure as long as you are at Pemberley, for here the Darcy name will protect you from open scorn. However, you must bear it in mind if you wish for a London season someday. The more who know, the more the rumours, the more who will not know you by association, who might perhaps cut you. Vouchers for Almack's might be withheld. If she departs soon, I think it unlikely any rumours would continue to circulate. If she remains too long, we risk outright scandal."

He looked at his sister's bent head, at her golden curls gleaming in the candlelight. She was so young. He wanted nothing more than to keep her safe and well.

She lifted her head, her expression serious and thoughtful. "How do you think Papa would have wished for us to act?"

"Papa," he began, shaking his head in remembrance. "Papa hated scandal."

"Do you believe he hated scandal more than he loved Mama? Would he have received her if she had come home?"

Darcy blinked in surprise at her unexpected question. Would he have? Had he cared for Lady Anne enough to do so? He would not have liked how Darcy had spoken to his mother earlier. Would he have gone so far as to allow her to come home?

Yes. Darcy's heart echoed with the answer. Yes, he would have wanted it.

"I believe he might have," Darcy admitted a little hesitantly, glancing at his wife.

Lizzy heard all the words he would not allow himself to speak, and could not stay quiet in the face of his reluctance. "Even so, it does not mean you both have to welcome her with open arms," she interjected. "Meaning no disrespect, but it is your lives that would be affected by her return. Perhaps you would like to begin a correspondence first, if anything. There is nothing saying you need have her stay in the neighbourhood to become acquainted."

Her husband shot her a relieved half-smile.

"And yet I have always wanted to meet her," Georgiana said, fretfully. "I wish, Brother, you would decide what is best for me."

Darcy knew he and Lizzy had given her good guidance; she needed to learn confidence in herself. "I would be glad to do that for you, if it is truly what you wish," he said carefully. "Still, I feel you are old enough now to make this decision yourself. I am certain if you consider the situation carefully, you will be able to do so. There is no reason to decide tonight, however. Think on it for as long as is needed."

Georgiana sat up a little straighter, smiling at her brother. "Thank you, Fitzwilliam," she said, her anxious mien clearing, and Darcy knew he made the correct decision in encouraging her to make her own choices. She turned to Lizzy. "I would like to know, as you have met her and spent at least a day with her. What do you think of her? Do you like her?"

Lizzy looked at Fitzwilliam, but his expression now gave nothing away. "I do like her. But my liking her will not change the conse-quences of you knowing her."

Georgiana nodded and turned back to her brother. "Did Cousin Richard see her before he returned to town? Did he speak of it?"

"I know he intended to pay a call at Holmwood on this visit, but he did not discuss it with me. I do not know what he thought of the meet-ing, or if he even did so," Darcy said.

"He did. Lady Anne described the visit as exceedingly pleasant," Lizzy offered. "She thought him far wittier and more charming than his fa—, um, she thought him an agreeable person."

Darcy's impassive expression broke, and he again gave Lizzy his half-smile. She felt it in her toes.

"He is," Georgiana replied loyally. "Cousin Richard is wonderful. He rode Brimstone—he is one of Fitzwilliam's worst-mannered stal-lions—and took him over jumps as though he were riding a cloud."

Thereafter followed a description of Cousin Richard's exploits on their riding course, a clever and difficult arrangement of a dozen jumps throughout forest and field, none of which, apparently, presented the least bit of difficulty to the colonel. Finally, however, she quieted on the subject of horses, and excused herself to reflect upon the situation with Lady Anne.

Once Georgiana departed, Lizzy laid her head upon Darcy's shoul-der, and he tucked her in more closely. He surreptitiously breathed in the smell of her, a light, clean lavender. Through some strange alchemy, her scent meant peace to his soul.

AT BREAKFAST THE NEXT DAY, GEORGIANA WAS QUIET—UNUSUALLY SO. OF course, the news of her mother was bound to be unsettling, so Lizzy's voice was gentle as she addressed her younger sister.

"Georgiana, are you anxious about meeting Lady Anne? Because you needn't meet her at all."

"Oh," Georgiana said, startling from her thoughts. "No, I am sorry. I am not distraught, although it is all I have thought about since you told me she was here," she admitted. "I believe...I believe I do wish to meet her."

Darcy stared at his plate, the hearty breakfast suddenly less attractive. He had known this might be the case when he offered it. And so he said in as enthusiastic a tone as he could muster, "I will take you whenever you are ready."

"Perhaps tomorrow or the next day," Georgiana said. "I am in no particular hurry. I have gone around and around in my thoughts, because I do not want to be a disappointment to Papa. I believe you are correct, and he would have wanted us to have...a connexion with her if she returned. But Fitzwilliam, I do want a season in London. Papa always planned I should have one, and...and Mama did leave us. And Lizzy said we all have to bear the consequences of our choices—is that not so, Lizzy?"

Darcy glanced at his wife. Did some of the brightness in her eyes dim? But she answered his sister unhesitatingly. "Yes, Georgiana, very true."

"So I do want to meet her. And I would promise to write her but... Fitzwilliam, if it is truly my choice, I hope she departs before everyone comes home for the grouse! I do not believe we can afford the scandal of her and Liz—, um, what I mean to say is—"

"No, you needn't mince matters," Lizzy interjected. "Fitzwilliam's hasty marriage is likely to cause sensation, if not outright scandal. Lady Anne's presence here will exacerbate gossip at best, and be injurious to your reputation at worst."

Darcy rose immediately, and stood behind Lizzy, his hands upon her shoulders. He did not care for any talk impugning his wife.

But Georgiana was not finished. "Since I am responsible for your hasty marriage, I promise not to complain if scandal results from that —especially since we are much happier with you here, Lizzy. And

Fitzwilliam, if you wish for Mama to stay, I shall not object. But you have asked how I feel, and so I have told you." She sighed resolutely.

Darcy did not move, unsure of what to say. He had assumed Georgie would want to know Lady Anne; she had always been curious about her mother, and never experienced the worst of the acrimony associated with her departure. Well, he supposed, the meeting would take place.

Afterwards, however…his heart lightened at the thought of Lady Anne's departure. His anger was dissipating, but this did not mean he enjoyed the woman nearly living in Lizzy's pocket.

But what of his wife? He had promised her she could have his mother for as long as she needed. Knowing Lizzy, she had been planning yuletide activities!

He need not have worried.

Lizzy's shoulders were stiff beneath his fingers, but her voice was decisive as she said at once, "Then, Georgiana, she will be gone by August. We shall tell Lady Anne."

After much thought, Darcy decided to have Lizzy escort Georgiana over to Holmwood Hall to pay a call upon her mother. Firstly, he did not want his sister's opinions affected by his own. He owed Lady Anne an apology over their confrontation, but he had not yet come to a conclusion as to what sort of association he wished to have with her, once her visit ended. More time of contemplation was needed.

Possibly because he understood that she had wished to write to them, but also because things were easier now that there was a definite departure date, he began to have questions and feelings which had nothing to do with anger…curiosity about her former life with his father, and speculation regarding her life in Glasgow. He remembered her as having a kind of straightforward charm and making friends easily. Perhaps when the ladies returned from their visit, Georgiana might change her mind about desiring Lady Anne's imminent departure. He did not know how he would feel if that were the case.

However, the visit was not a particularly long one. Well before expected, a servant entered with the news of their return—as he had requested to be notified. He found Lizzy alone in the conservatory, the air inside thick with summer's weight and the scent of orange blossoms. She sat upon a stone bench, looking…lonely. But when she heard his approach, she lifted her head and gave him a heart-stopping smile.

"Lizzy dearest," he said, "might I join you?"

She scooted her skirts aside to make room for him on the bench. "I wish you would," she replied, leaning into him as he placed his arm about her. They sat together for some moments in silence.

"It is a lovely dress you wear today."

"Thank you," she replied. "I wondered if the colour was too bold, but Lady Anne thought—," she broke off mid-sentence. "I think it turned out well," she finished.

He shifted his body upon the bench so he could face her. "I am glad she advised it," he said gently. "It becomes you." Tucking a stray curl behind her ear, he asked, "How was the visit?"

"It was more awkward than…one could wish," she answered gravely. "Your sister was not her usual self and Lady Anne seemed struck by the same discomfiture. We only stayed as long as was strictly polite."

In truth, after the visit's conclusion, Lizzy finally made herself face the inevitable. During the course of it, Lady Anne made a heartfelt apology to her daughter, and Georgiana timidly accepted it. But the fact remained: they were strangers to each other. Georgiana could no more wave away the years of separation than Fitzwilliam. The damage was done, and it would take time—and possibly a miracle—to foster reparations. Lizzy's tiny, greedy hope that mother and daughter would instantly strike up a friendship dwindled with every awkward, uncomfortable minute.

"I am sure it was exactly what one could expect, after…everything."

Darcy took his wife's hand. He was beginning to understand that Lizzy had thought to depend upon his mother far more and longer than he had ever dreamt. However, she had not yet understood this dependence to be unnecessary. Lady Anne's intervention was superfluous.

"My love, all will be well. I know you wish to be an excellent mistress to Pemberley and you will be. Mrs Reynolds has been handling matters by herself for several years, and she is hardly ready to be pensioned off. You may do as much or as little as you need to in the way of supervision."

Lizzy nodded, staying silent. While she appreciated his indulgence, she had no illusions about Mrs Reynolds's opinions on the matter. The woman already pushed for her to become the Mrs Darcy her beloved master deserved, and a different one than Lizzy wished to be. Nevertheless, she had decided this was something they would have to face, coping with expectations a day at a time. For now, Lizzy listened carefully to Mrs Reynolds and formed her own ideas of what truly needed her touch, as Lady Anne recommended. There was still much to learn and much to observe. While she would miss her discussions with the older woman, she understood this was as much because of their friendship in the midst of an oft-bewildering collection of rules and responsibilities, someone with whom she could test her thoughts and ideas and receive practical, good-natured advice in return. Lizzy could not imagine bothering Fitzwilliam with most of it. No, she would make do, as she always had, and there was little cause for complaint.

"You are quiet," he said gently.

"I...I am missing Jane," Lizzy replied. She had been feeling lost after the uncomfortable visit. The thought occurred to her, if Jane were not already settled in Dover, Lizzy would have loved to invite her to Pemberley for a nice, long stay.

Darcy tipped up her chin. "You miss your sister? Or you anticipate missing my mother?"

"No, not precisely. Just a little blue-devilled," Lizzy protested, taking a deep breath. "'Tis of no concern. I should probably return to the house. Georgiana is to accompany me on a drive into the village this afternoon. We feel a need to remind the good citizens of Lambton the importance of our custom."

"Lizzy," he said. "Tell me what is wrong."

She looked him in the eye. "Not a thing. Yes, I shall miss Lady Anne's friendship and tutoring, just as I miss my sister's companionship and encouragement, but I was not wallowing in those feelings, I promise you. Neither shall I complain to you of that which cannot be changed. I am no Grumbletonian."

"It is not in your nature to complain, but is it to sit here alone, giving every appearance of unhappiness?" he asked, and the concern in his tone touched her heart.

She reached out to caress his firm jaw. "I am not unhappy. I am accommodating my new life. At times it might require some reflexion. Please try to understand—your life has been Pemberley and then Eton and London and house parties all over England, and managing the lives and livelihoods of hundreds. For me, there was only a little seaside town where I was not even respectable, with my mother and sister and some half-formed dreams. 'Tis a dizzying difference." She lifted her face for his kiss; it was the one thing she could count on amidst this strange new world—his affection and care. She needed those now for, despite her brave words, she was full of astonishment at all the changes in such a short period.

"Oh, my dear," he said gently as his lips met hers. He kissed her thoroughly, firmly, and she felt how much tenderness he meant to convey in that connexion, and some of the uneasiness of the morning disappeared. He ended the kiss, looking into her eyes. "I wish you would come to me when you are feeling…dizzy. I shan't accuse you of complaining. I want to provide the encouragement and friendship you would seek from your sister…or my mother."

She smiled. "It comes as no surprise to you, I hope, that the first friendship I form as Mrs Darcy is completely inappropriate."

DARCY GAZED AT HIS WIFE, AT HER GOOD-NATURED SMILE AS SHE POKED fun at herself. His marriage had given her wealth, security, and standing—but divested her of the only home and family she had ever known. Was it enough? He could only hope so, but was not above sweetening the pot, and not only with kisses.

"I have a surprise for you," he said.

Her smile turned questioning.

"Come with me."

They walked hand in hand, while she tried, unsuccessfully, to pry hints from him. From the conservatory they took a path leading through the gardens—but, he assured her, there was a less roundabout route from the east wing of the house.

"Perhaps I shall build a covered path so you will not have to battle the elements in winter," he said mysteriously.

At last they reached an outbuilding whose purpose she could not guess. It was constructed with both simplicity and grandeur, giving the appearance of a Hellenic temple.

"It was once a banqueting house," he answered her unasked question. "It has a kitchen in its basement, but has not been in use for some years now, and I had alterations made."

They climbed a set of steps, walking through an impressive Ionic-columned portico to reach a wide door, which Darcy threw open. Curiously, Lizzy walked inside, unsure what to expect. Nothing could have been more stunning to her than what she found.

It housed a large, brightly lit open space, lined with shelves along two walls, as well as easels, tables, pedestals, and various supplies and tools Lizzy immediately recognised. Her heart pounding, she hurried towards a worktable displaying the finest selection of chisels she had ever seen. Mouth agape, she turned to her husband.

"There are more tools in there," he said, pointing to the tall chests behind her. In awe, she slid open drawer after drawer of chisels, rasps, rifflers, hammers, knives, and brushes of every size. She hardly dared touch them, but once she did, she saw how beautifully they were made, how light and true. The least of them was finer than anything she had ever used. On the top of one chest sat a superb set of brass scales for weighing the clay. Not only were there tools for use on clay, but it appeared nearly every tool one could possibly need for fine stonework had also been provided. Her eyes filled with tears. She was speechless in the face of the exorbitant generosity. Almost blindly, she fingered the fine parchment sheets lying upon the nearest easel.

Fitzwilliam opened his arms and she went to him gladly.

"Thank you," she whispered around the lump in her throat. "Thank you, so very much."

"Signor Benenati gave me to understand you were in need of a number of items. We are building the kilns as he has instructed. They are in the basement."

"Kilns?" she whispered. "As in, more than one?"

"Yes. As I said, it once was a kitchen beneath us, so constructing them there made sense...just new sorts of ovens, so to speak. There will be two of them ready by the time the Signor arrives, though they are not yet complete. As for all this, I gave him carte blanche to procure what is needed and have it sent here. I hope all meets with your approval."

She sniffed, trying to contain her emotions. "Fitzwilliam, I have never seen such beautiful tools. I have been known to use my mother's knitting needles and kitchen knives, whatever I could find. I have never possessed such fine papers and pencils. Thank you, thank you for your unexampled kindness. I can never repay—"

"Hush," he said brusquely, plainly uncomfortable with her outpouring. "You are my wife and I wish only for your happiness, not your gratitude."

"May I not be both grateful and happy?" she asked, pulling his face down so she could kiss him, so he would know how fiercely joyful her feelings. He responded immediately, both of them expressing what had no words.

"When will you trust that I will do anything for you?" he asked, looking down upon her, eyes fiery with need and emotion.

"Anything?" she asked, a little slyly.

He grew suspicious immediately. "Within reason," he added quickly.

"No, no, you have already given your word as a gentleman," she teased. "'Tis too late for qualifiers."

Darcy raised a brow and regarded his wife sternly, but in truth he was too relieved to see her as she appeared now—utterly delighted, such a contrast from her lonely mien in the conservatory—to make his expression too severe.

"What is it you wish?" he asked.

"I want to sculpt you," she whispered. "You would be the most perfect specimen—"

"No," he interrupted. "'Tis out of the question."

"But how can I expect to sculpt the human form if I cannot use an actual model? I have only attempted the female figure in the past, but I am itching to do both." She looked up at him pensively. "I do understand, however. You are busy, and posing would require many more hours than you likely have. I will have to make do with willing volunteers from the village or from amongst the servants."

His brow furrowed and he looked at her darkly. "Certainly not. I forbid it."

Her brows rose. "I do hope you are not forbidding me from sculpting the male form."

Darcy hesitated. That was definitely what he meant.

Would she so easily bring scandal down upon our heads, after the risks we have already taken?

However, his conscience reminded, Lizzy's little pastime was unlikely to come to the notice of London or even Derbyshire society, and it was hardly more scandalous than the mermaids she had already confessed to selling through some small trinket merchant.

Except, of course, the thought of her staring at partly-clothed bodies of other men is the single most reprehensible idea I have ever considered.

"Over my dead body will you be sculpting the bodies of other males," he pronounced, preparing for the argument to come.

To his surprise, she merely laid her head upon his chest, holding him more tightly. "Of course. You are too good. We can work together in the evenings, after your other duties are complete."

She was attempting to manage him, obviously. Twisting his words around to a meaning he had not intended. He opened his mouth to protest when, unbidden, a vision of the two of them flashed before his eyes: Lizzy, at her easel, peering intently at him while he stood before her. Being the whole recipient of her undivided attention, as he watched her watch him. At this unexpected thought, the weakest part of his character voted for allowing it. Perhaps immediately.

He cleared his throat, attempting to regain control of the situation. *Her little artistic pursuits plainly are of great import to her, and mayhap posing for her is the only means I will have of sharing it, he reasoned.* And so he did not protest.

"I shall consider it in the future," he said instead. "But in the meantime, perhaps you can find other, more benign subjects for your models."

Lizzy lifted her eyes to his. "I am expert at several different aquatic species, but I have resolved to never sketch, draw, sculpt, or paint another fish as long as I live."

Darcy looked pained. "Surely in the range of God's creations between mackerel and strange men, there is *something* of interest to you?"

Lizzy immediately felt repentant. She could not imagine the cost of these fine supplies, and already she complained. His apprehensions regarding the viewing of men as subjects for her work were understandable—it was shocking if one did not consider it from an artistic, almost scientific point of view, and he had not definitively refused to pose. In time, he would see she attempted to create beauty in the same calibre of the works in his own gallery. For the nonce, she was privileged to study those works at her leisure.

"Of course. I feel I am the most fortunate female in England to have the opportunity to do so."

He looked relieved, and she smiled broadly, adding, "I hope, however, you will forgive me if I take advantage of private opportunities to study you, during those moments when we find time for... research?" she asked, a finger twining in the hair at his nape.

"Research?" Darcy muttered.

She trailed her hand down the finely tailored fabric of his coat sleeve. "Examining you," she persisted. "Very, very closely."

He could deny her nothing.

"Now?" he asked.

A FORTNIGHT LATER, THE MORNING HAD NOT BEGUN AUSPICIOUSLY FOR Mary Reynolds. To begin with, Cook's pastry crust burnt, for which the big oven and young Davy—who had the job of watching it—were blamed. Cook had an impassioned fit, throwing the entire kitchen into an uproar. By the time she settled him, it was time for her morning meeting with the mistress, always a challenge.

Mrs Darcy was intelligent, but Mary despaired of ever successfully conveying the utter magnitude of her responsibilities. Without exactly dismissing the housekeeper's concerns, Mrs Darcy managed to communicate a certain...frivolity regarding their import. Her contributions, when she made them, were succinct and sensible and Mary felt relieved whenever she took the trouble. However, such contributions were irregular and the list of details for which Mrs Darcy refused to so much as offer an opinion grew daily.

Not that Mary expected her to show proficiency at once—plainly, the mistress had not much experience with the running of a great house. But Mary was ready and willing, nay, anxious to instruct her in the vast storehouse of knowledge required for the perfect organisation of Pemberley. Much of it, Mary had herself learned through trial and error...so many errors, especially in those early years directly after Mrs Trimble died so unexpectedly, and Mr Darcy had taken a risk in allowing young Mary to replace her. Lady Anne had expressed her doubts, but old Mr Darcy insisted she be allowed a trial.

Mary had worked day and night to learn, to study the household books and records, to make changes for the better, to prove and improve herself, and never once had old Mr Darcy's confidence faded. Even Lady Anne soon admitted that Mary's efforts were more than acceptable. Of course *that female* hadn't stayed much longer, fleeing to London, utterly abandoning Pemberley.

The other servants of the household, now, they'd given her trouble enough; the older ones looked askance on young Mary, at only five-and-twenty, ruling the roost. But she had outworked and outmanoeuvred and finally outshone them all, earning her place as if born to the position. Her pinnacle occurred the day old Farragut was pensioned off; he always treated her with contempt, even after ten years in service with her. She never bothered hiring another butler after his departure, so little did she need one, so ably had she seen to the fulfilment of his duties herself. It was a point of pride with her that he had never been missed.

Oh, the trouble Mary could save Mrs Darcy, if only she would take heed! If only that awful Lady Anne hadn't been given the opportunity to sink her idle claws into the young mistress! But of course, the master was cut from the same tender-hearted bolt as his father, and hadn't been able to give *that female* the cold exit she deserved.

How *that female* could have been miserable, married to such a fine, handsome and superior gentleman as old Mr Darcy, she would never understand. Mary had done her best to make his home the smoothest running household in all of England, to make him happy.

It was to be her gift to his memory, that she train up the mistress so Pemberley's legacy would continue for his children and grandchildren and great-grandchildren. It was to be hoped, once Lady Anne departed the mistress would grow more attentive. More…responsible.

Alas, Mrs Darcy had been less manageable than ever this morning! In a passion, all because of Signor Benenati's expected arrival. Such a fuss over a silly art master! Mary felt uncharitable towards him before he ever showed his face.

Therefore, it was, perhaps, not entirely Signor Benenati's fault that Mary Reynolds took exception to him upon arrival. For one thing, though he was every bit of fifty years, he was too…exuberant. His eyes, piercing and intelligent, disconcertingly looked at her directly instead of over or through her, as did most of the well-bred. He had a full head of silver hair, a neatly trimmed silver beard, a deep, richly accented voice and the most impertinent manner Mary had ever encountered!

She had taken his card herself—because he was an honoured guest, even if he was a foreigner—and then, before she could escape to fetch the master and mistress, he had taken her hand…and kissed it! Such brazenness! Uttering ridiculous compliments! As if she were some addlepated housemaid, willing to permit such goings on!

Pish! Honoured guest or no, Mary made sure he knew that disrespect to herself, or any female under the Darcy employ, would not be tolerated. Had he shown proper chagrin for his roguish behaviour? No! He apologised for being transported by her beauty! Gammon!

I will watch over you, Mrs Darcy, Mary vowed silently. *I shall make it my duty to ensure that foreigner acts respectably. Old Mr Darcy's tragedy shall never repeat itself while I safeguard Pemberley!*

BERT BUNCH PICKED HIS TEETH WITH AN IVORY TOOTHPICK. USED TO BE, HE had to use his knife, but since his new partnership, he had come up in the world quickly. Those first days after losing Fergus he had a few bad moments. After all, Fergus was devilish frightening.

Bert was bemoaning his ill-usage at the Cock & Crow after Fergus's desertion, when another man sympathetically offered to stand him a tankard. He accepted with suspicion, for generosity was not a byword at the Cock & Crow, especially from one dressed so fine. But several ales later, his fortunes were on the mend. The nob offered him an irresistible proposition: stash a few goods, make a few deliveries, transport a few valuables, deliver a few letters, earn a few coins. If some deliveries were men in various states of consciousness, if the letters were needed in the dead of night, it was none of his affair.

Yes, Bert was a fortunate man. It was devilish good luck, losing that idiot Fergus. After all, his new partner was rum gentry with ten times the brainbox.

Bert inspected his reflection in his new looking glass, grinning at his gold-tinted smile—and tapping the tooth for luck. After all, hadn't his partner declared this very tooth to be a sign they were meant to be confederates? Besides his fancy speech and fine manners, Mr George Worthy's smile possessed two grand, gleaming golden teeth!

F rom his first day, Lizzy held Signor Benenati in what seemed to Darcy to be an unnatural awe. Darcy supposed—at least as far as artistic technique, history, and knowledge—the man was respectable enough. Not only was the signor's skill significant, but he could boast of close associations with the likes of Nollekens, Bartolozzi, and the recently deceased Joseph Wilton, a founding member of the Royal Academy. His works were impressive even beyond those of his friends; after all, Darcy hired him for precisely these reasons.

Upon his arrival, they took the signor through the sculpture gallery. Almost immediately, he began instructing. He pointed out various weaknesses in a painting by Thomas Procter, and the strengths of a bust of Sir Isaac Newton by his former mentor, Wilton. And because he knew these artists personally, he could speak anecdotally, infusing interesting detail. Darcy's education was not insignificant, and, as a lover of art and beauty, he was as well-versed artistically as any layman…and yet he could not speak the same language as Signor Benenati, one shaded with the intimate brushstrokes of nuance as well as expert methodology. Skilled instruction on anatomy, modelling, and drawing was only the half of it; in comparison, Darcy was merely hoi polloi.

Lizzy, naturally, was entranced. Fascinated. And shortly thereafter obsessed.

Darcy wanted her to be happy. But he could not convince himself it was healthy for Lizzy to be fixated upon her pastime—and one man's opinions. As evidence, after a mere month of Signor Benenati's residence, Darcy lay in bed with his wife, the early morning sun luminous upon her tresses and one pale, perfect shoulder, and yet, was he awakening her with kisses? Did he anticipate a prelude to amorous pleasures? No! Instead, he was hurting his head attempting to think of how to persuade her to take a day away from her artistic pursuits, readying arguments for the protests bound to follow.

Even before he could open his mouth, however, Lizzy was slipping out of bed—moving quietly so as not to waken him. Stealing away at the crack of dawn! Or at least half past seven.

"Where are you going?" he asked, as if he did not know.

She turned back to him and smiled widely, as if he hadn't caught her in the act of sneaking away from their bed. "Good morning," she said. "I apologise for waking you."

"I was awake," he replied evenly. "Come back."

"I wish for an early start," she explained. "I would like to be at the studio without delay, as I promised to take Georgiana to visit Lady Anne this afternoon."

"I have not had my morning kiss," he complained.

"Your evening kisses lasted until well into the morning," she answered severely, and, blowing him an impudent kiss from where she stood, escaped to her rooms.

Sighing, he threw back the covers. "'By long forbearing is a princess persuaded, and a soft tongue breaketh the bone,'" he reminded himself, shrugging on his banyan and ringing for Perkins.

However, Darcy's early morning concerns persisted throughout the day. He reminded himself he should be grateful Lizzy found her little artistic pursuits so engrossing. At least she no longer seemed quite so anxious about his mother's now imminent departure.

He had not, as yet, proffered his apology to Lady Anne. Urgent estate business, seeing to the completion of the studio refurbishment, and enjoying the company of his wife and sister all managed to be of greater import than seeking out a private moment with his parent.

Lady Anne, of course, never expected him to call. Today he had received from her a largish packet of letters. Included at the top was one addressed to him:

Dear Fitzwilliam,

It was extremely kind of you to allow me these weeks at Holmwood

Hall. I am full of appreciation for your forbearance. I thank you with all my heart for allowing me to know Georgiana and Lizzy.

Before I take my leave, I hope you will forgive the impertinence of penning what I originally believed better addressed in person—that is, the apology you are due. Especially have I regretted the crudity of my first attempt. I once felt an appropriate apology required an opportunity to reject it.

Consigning a letter to the flames seems somewhat less satisfying, to me, than rebuking the offender aloud—but then, I am a Fitzwilliam, and we were always a bloodthirsty lot. Your sense of honour, however, comes from the Darcy side (thank the Almighty).

Still, before I leave for Glasgow on the morrow, I wish to deliver a better apology than the one I first offered: There are no words to express my regret for all the ways in which I failed to be the mother you deserve. If it were possible to undo my mistakes, the person I have since become would make the attempt. Unfortunately, no amount of wishing can rewrite the past, as we both know. I am, and will always be, grieved by how my choices injured you.

As to the offence you have laid to my charge, regarding my failure to write to you, please allow me to express that there were honourable, if misguided motives. It was decided, so that my sins should not attach themselves to my children, I should sever all connexion. Although its intent was borne of love for you and your sister, I add this neglect and pain to my long list of wrongdoings.

However tardy, here are most of the letters I wrote, but failed to send. I do not expect you to read them, and only submit them as evidence you were never forgotten. Use them as kindling if you will!

In closing, may I be allowed to express my deep pride in the man you have become? In every way, you have fulfilled your early promise. Your tenants, your servants, and your family have nothing but good to say of you. I have every expectation of your continued prosperity, in your future as in the past.

I will only add, God bless you.
Anne

P.S. If you have a preference as to what surname I ought to take, please make it known. If you find it distasteful for me to use Darcy whilst in England, I shall not. Neither would I wish use of the Grayson name to stir up old scandal, and I am willing to abide by your wishes in any case. Unsure how to style myself, and unwilling to provoke, I have closed this letter plainly. I mean no disrespect.

Darcy was surprised by the sheer number of letters included. He opened one, dated eleven years prior, describing a cold winter day in Glasgow and full of questions about his school and interests. Another was primarily to Georgiana, telling her how beautiful a baby she had been, and full of apologies. He folded the letters, replacing them in the bundle. He felt no real desire to read them at present, but it was warming to recognise they did, indeed, exist. Through Lizzy he understood it was his father's decision for there to be no communication, but Lady Anne did not blame George Darcy, and, without dishonesty, took responsibility.

It was not in his nature to avoid that which needed addressing, as he had been avoiding his mother. And, he recognised, he could indeed accept her apology. The past was over and done. He was uninterested in continuing animosity. He admired her courage and plain speaking. He could even admit he…liked her.

He rang to have his horse saddled. A farewell visit was in order.

LADY ANNE TREATED HERSELF TO A FINAL WALK THROUGH THE GARDENS AT Holmwood. They were not as beauteous as Pemberley's, but they were lovely in their own right, and she did enjoy the feel of the sunshine upon her face—as well as the peace within her heart. Sending the letters to Fitzwilliam felt right, just as taking her leave now seemed a good choice. She had never meant to stay so long, and was grateful for the unexpected blessing. Indeed, they had said she might remain until mid-August.

But now that Lizzy was busier with her artistic pursuits and seemed to be settling in at Pemberley, Anne understood it was best she absent herself, long before the neighbourhood first families returned from town. She had accomplished what she set out to do, apologising to her children. If Glasgow would never be home at least she knew she could expect letters from Georgiana and Lizzy, far more acknowledgment than she had ever dared hope. The burning feelings of anxiety and distress urging her to Pemberley in the first place were gone, and it was time for her to be as well.

She could not have been more astonished to see her son striding down the garden path towards her. Were Lizzy or Georgiana, perhaps, dawdling behind him? But no one else appeared. He was alone.

"Fitzwilliam!" she said, startled. "I did not expect to see you."

He gave her a considering look. "I do hope you meant to take leave of your family before your departure," he said evenly.

"Georgiana and Lizzy visited me earlier today, so we have already said our goodbyes," she replied, her heart racing. "And I sent you a letter."

"I read it," he said, giving her no clue to his feelings. At least he had not hurled the older letters at her; she had known he would not, being too much a gentleman. He would dispose of them privately if he so chose. On the slim chance he might actually read them, she removed any which mentioned numerous topics best let alone.

"Thank you," she said, unsure how to respond. "Thank you for not ejecting me when I arrived, as I deserved. Thank you for allowing your wife and sister to–to know me."

"I owe you an apology," he said, rather abruptly.

She drew back. "I am certain you do not."

"On the occasion of our last private conversation, I raised my voice to you. I cursed at you. It was conduct unbecoming a gentleman, and I am sorry for my boorish behaviour."

His tone was formal, but sincere. "'Tis forgotten," she whispered. "Please, do not give it a second's thought. What were meant to be expressions of regret...well, they were very crudely done. I have often wished them better said, if not unsaid completely."

She thought he would take his leave then, but he only nodded.

"Are you anxious to return home? To Glasgow?" he asked, almost conversationally.

"I would not say anxious, no. But I wish to depart well before the Harpers and the Mumfords return from London," she replied, naming two of the leading families hereabouts.

He nodded again, looking uncomfortable. "I appreciate that. Because of my wife and sister, you understand."

"I do understand."

"But there is a matter we have yet to address…you have dower properties. In England. All a part of your settlement, as you must remember."

She bit her lip, once again surprised by her son. "No, actually. I…I was young when I wed your father and…and I did not pay attention as I ought to have. But, Fitzwilliam, I must forfeit anything of that nature, as I was not a good—"

"No," he interpolated. "Father did not divorce you legally, and in any case, I know he would not have changed those settlements if he could have. You have a home in Brighton and a residence in London, as well as an income. You ought to read those letters from my solicitors more carefully."

She shook her head. "I cannot take these things. Perhaps, if there are legalities involved, I can sell everything back to you for–for a guinea. I will sign anything you wish. 'Tis not right."

"This is pride speaking," he said. "I beg you to consider what is best for your daughter. If you take up residence in Brighton and style yourself Lady Anne Darcy, the scandal of your other marriage will eventually be reduced to whispers. In time, all will be almost as if it never happened."

"But it did," she insisted. "My sins will never be forgot."

"You give yourself too much credit. As an exciting on dit, your disgrace is somewhat lacking. The high sticklers will never forget, certainly. The patronesses of Almack's will send no vouchers. But consider the situation frankly—years ago, you took up with a man not your husband and lived abroad with him. Your husband never repudiated you. Both men are dead, and you returned home to live quietly in Brighton. How dull. It will become known, eventually, that your son and daughter receive you. Lady Catherine understands, as well, 'tis in her own best interests to promote your reputation. You are the daughter of and sister to an earl. That one fact matters more than an old and lacklustre scandal."

"My presence in town might harm Georgiana's future."

"Georgiana will not be coming out for two or three years. The best thing for her, the ideal, is for you to achieve some level of acceptance, and there is ample time to discover how it will be. But my prediction is that you will gain friends quickly in Brighton, should you reside there, where society is not so rigid. There will be invitations from those new friends and, I daresay, some old ones, when you next visit town. As long as you live quietly, and presuming you and my wife's mother do not decide to, say, open a brothel together, you ought to weather any whispers admirably," he finished drily.

Lady Anne smiled at his little joke, studying his impassive features. It was difficult to know how he truly felt. "I will do whatever you wish, of course," she said at last. "I will admit to homesickness for England. But please, Fitzwilliam, tell me what it is you want most. Perhaps you offer this because you feel in some way responsible for me. Please know I have more than enough to live on without it. You did not have a choice when you were a boy, but you do now. I will gladly remain in Scotland if you would be happiest to have me away."

He met her open gaze. "I have considered this carefully. What I wish is to leave the past behind. I wish you would accept your settlement and take up residence in Brighton as Lady Anne Darcy—if you believe you could be happy there. And once you are settled…I wish you would write, upon occasion, and tell me how you get on."

She did not burst into tears; she was the daughter of an earl, and could maintain her dignity even in the face of overwhelming joy. But it was a very near thing.

A BEAD OF SWEAT TRICKLED DOWN LIZZY'S FOREHEAD, BUT SHE WAS TOO intent upon her task to wipe it away.

A hand. A blasted male hand.

She attempted to model a hand that might pass the rigorous appraisal of the signor. How naïve she had been, to suppose he would allow her to immediately begin plying her new tools on blocks of marble! She understood her drawing skills were weak, but she had always been able to "see" with her hands, in modelling and moulding clays. She was prepared for harsh critiques of her drawings, of course. She agreed with every abrasive opinion he gave on them.

"Give me clay," she had said. "Let me show you what I can do in three dimensions."

After a few weeks, the signor allowed it. She decided to be bold, but clever. She would model a mermaid, an object she could sculpt in her sleep, but which would display her talent. She made it bust-sized, taking her time with it. It was easily the best mermaid she had ever created.

She held her breath as she unveiled it for him, prepared for his approval.

"*Immondizia.* Unacceptable," he pronounced.

The worst of it was, once he pointed out the many flaws in perspective, detail, structure, and finish, she could see them too.

To say she was discouraged was to understate the matter.

Signor Benenati had seen her despair. "Bella," he soothed. "You are a child without training, without the discipline. You have the talent, of course you do. I will help you to, how do you say, grow it up."

It had helped to hear he thought she had any talent at all, but beyond that, he essentially proffered a challenge, and everything within her soul rose to meet it. Whatever he asked of her, she answered with more. She knew she was consumed by her need to do well; feeling her creative essence overflow was addictive. The only thing she loved more than the hours in her studio were the hours alone with Fitzwilliam. In one sense, it was the same thing—both her art and her love for her husband tapped into a deep well of pure, undiluted passion, and exploring it in one way or the other was equally fulfilling and rewarding.

She straightened, her muscles stiff and sore with hours spent bent over her worktable, and rubbed her aching back. Critically, she looked at the hand she laboured over. There was something wrong with it, but for the life of her, she could not define its problems.

The signor was downstairs in the basement with the kilns, but it was time to get his advice. Of course, this meant she would have to listen to him enact an operatic tragedy over her errors, as was usual for him but eventually he would calm and explain how to fix them. And the next hand she modelled would be much better, although he would likely discover a whole new round of blunders. One day he would not find anything to criticise.

Perhaps he'll put me to modelling noses after this. It did not matter. Whatever it was, she would master it.

The sense of liberation Darcy felt upon taking his leave of Lady Anne was invigorating. Finally, he felt as if he and his mother were on a solid footing. Long ago, he had deeply loved her, and it was somehow a great relief to feel able to…to care about her once again. Not only that, but he felt his father would be pleased as well. Naturally, the first person he wanted to share this surfeit of feelings with was Lizzy; he knew she would be in the studio again, after having taken time to visit Lady Anne, and he ought to wait until she returned to the house. But that was hours away, and he longed to see her now.

Allowing his impatience to have its way, he made for the studio, climbing the broad stone steps with anticipation. Just beyond the door, however, he was surprised to hear the sound of an angry male voice. He opened the door slowly, curious.

Once inside, it was unmistakeable: this was a tantrum…in Italian.

"No, no, no!" Signor Benenati cried, followed by an incomprehensible outburst. Darcy moved further inside, so he could see what was happening.

Neither Lizzy nor the signor paid him any mind. Their attention, instead, was upon a small sculpture of a hand.

Darcy did not speak much Italian, but even he could translate the torrent as criticism. By the look on her face, he knew Lizzy could as well. He caught the word "deplorevole"…deplorable? Surely not.

He looked at the offending modelled object. It looked like what it was, a hand. If it was not, perhaps, the work of another Michelangelo, neither was there anything obviously wrong with it, certainly nothing deserving of this bombardment of censure. He realised Lizzy had sculpted it…and this…this beast dared criticise! A great swell of rage nearly overcame him.

"Quiet!" he roared. "Signor! You will desist this minute!"

They both turned to him, startled.

"Fitzwilliam, please, no," Lizzy began, but he was too angry to pay heed to her words. He proceeded with a stern lecture explaining exactly how respectfully his wife was to be treated.

Signor Benenati drew himself up, full of offended dignity. "Perhaps *il Signor* Darcy would prefer to discover another, less truthful tutor for his pupil."

"Gladly!" he countered, affronted by the man's insulted demeanour, by the claim of higher ground—that he was honest instead of degrading and disrespectful.

Benenati gave a sharp, stiff bow to Lizzy, turned on his heel and walked out the door.

Darcy turned back to his wife, who gaped at him.

"I am sorry," he said more softly. "I ought never to have hired such a—"

"Fitzwilliam!" she cried. "Bring him back!"

"What? You cannot mean it!"

"Mean it?" she cried, her voice rising with panic. "Of course I mean it. You were insulting! Please, please, you must apologise!"

"Apologise?" he asked, astounded. "Never! You are owed the apology! He was the churl who—"

But Lizzy ran out of the studio, chasing after the signor, leaving Darcy alone with his anger.

DARCY STRUGGLED WITH HIS RESENTMENT FOR THE REMAINDER OF THE afternoon, imagining in his mind the things he ought to have said, had he not been so astonished and disgusted. None of those conversations involved apologies to ill-mannered lackwits who had forgotten themselves.

As it happened, he did not see Lizzy until just before they went in to dine, when she quietly informed him she had convinced the signor to overlook his interference and asked him to please, in the future, discuss his criticisms with her rather than directly with Signor Benenati.

Darcy fumed. He had not anticipated his interference would be discounted in any way. Lizzy was, obviously, bullied by this foreigner, and either too cowed to regard it or else her early years of disrespectful treatment accustomed her to insult. It made him all the angrier, knowing his wife was unused to the consideration she deserved, and a man he hired perpetuated the offence.

There were times when a husband knew best, and plainly, this was one of them. However, the dinner table was no place for a private conversation. For his part, he was too out of sorts to pretend an interest in polite chit-chat, but Lizzy was able to draw Georgiana out upon her opinion of a new colt, and they somehow survived the meal, and the remainder of the evening.

But that night, for the first time, Lizzy did not come to him. At first, he thought she was delayed; then, as time passed, he began to seethe. Would she truly choose her loyalty to the art master over her husband?

It seemed the answer to that question was *sì*.

16

Lizzy sat before the fire in her seldom-used sitting room, staring unseeingly at the flames. Every time she remembered Fitzwilliam's anger, her feelings veered wildly in opposing directions. Annoyance, of course, as well as panic at the thought of losing her instructor. Those emotions vied with affectionate despair at his pure motive in defending her, whether or not she required his protection.

The look on his face when she told him she smoothed over the disagreement with the signor! She guessed he would not like it, but had not fathomed how much he would detest being countermanded. It made her feel ill to remember it.

You had a choice, she reminded herself sternly. *You knew when you married him that your art would come second to his requirements.*

But he promised I could have both! her soul cried in response.

At least now, before there were children who needed her, and while he was so busy giving Pemberley its due, this was to be hers. She tried for balance; she made time for Georgiana and visiting tenants and the vicar. Lady Anne informed her calling cards would soon arrive, and Lizzy ought to return the visits, leaving her card, followed by formal calls to be made in person. But the neighbourhood was still in London, and Lady Anne departed tomorrow. Even with the ritual of formal calls, Lizzy was unlikely to achieve even cautious acceptance in the community for some time. This meant there were still many hours to fill each day. Hours, perhaps, other ladies might use to maintain a large circle of family and friendships. Hours that for Lizzy would be empty, had she not this new instructor with his fascinating insights.

Of course, Pemberley would be happy to steal those hours. Lizzy knew it, could feel the pull of its needs, so carefully and consistently presented by Mrs Reynolds. Lizzy resisted many of the housekeeper's delicately worded suggestions that she do more; she knew she ought to, but she wanted, so much, to devote the time to her artistic studies. Once she accepted the harness of estate duties, there would be no relief.

Am I being selfish, to insist upon what was promised? To share duty with dreams?

The result of her introspections was no result at all. Go to Fitzwilliam while he was so angry and possibly have an argument she desperately did not want? Offer to relinquish her instructor, despite how much it would hurt? How could she convince him of her deep desire to continue studying with the signor, despite the man's flaws? And could she even assume Fitzwilliam would *want* her to come to him tonight? She had been disrespectful, refusing his protection, failing to even acknowledge his rights. She was miserable at being a wife. It was certainly true she had thought only of what she wanted instead of considering his feelings. Perhaps he would even prefer her to stay away.

In her hands was a good-sized ball of clay, which she alternately formed into random shapes before crushing them into nothingness. But her befuddled brainbox could not settle. Every time she tried, her mind's eye reverted to the memory of Fitzwilliam's unhappiness; for the first time in her life, she turned to the clay and found no answers, no comfort, no reprieve. She may as well tell Fitzwilliam to send the signor away; she could not work if her husband hated her. Nevertheless, an aching bitterness tried to bloom; he had promised!

If I am not an artist, who am I?

Abruptly, she became aware she was no longer alone. Fitzwilliam stood in the doorway, his expression as hard as it had been all evening long. Even in his banyan and little else, he exuded authority and power. The words she ought to say knotted in her throat. Words of apology. Words of resentment. It was as if she were two people, neither achieving dominance nor permitting speech.

After a few moments, he seated himself on the settee beside her. His long legs stretched out in front of him in a nonchalant pose, though he was anything but.

"You interrupted the signor as he was about to explain what was wrong with it," she said softly, at last, the resentment winning when it became obvious he was not going to do anything except glare.

"He explained enough, in my view," he grumbled.

Guilt filled her again. She ought not to have accused when, to be sure, Signor Benenati likely had been cursing her work, her antecedents, and his own lucklessness in having such a bacon-brained pupil.

The fact that she understood little of it removed most of the sting for her...but if Fitzwilliam did, then much of his anger with the signor was understandable.

"Do you speak Italian?" she asked.

"No."

"I do not either," she said. "The signor knows he can say whatever he likes in that language. I do not care, as long as once he begins speaking English, he explains the problems with my work."

"There was nothing wrong with your work," he bit out. "Nothing."

She let out a sharp bark of mirthless laughter. The sound surprised Darcy so much, his glare turned to puzzlement, and he shifted sideways to face her.

"I saw the hand you created," he persisted, frowning at her. "It was perfectly acceptable. If there was some small flaw, it certainly was undeserving of the sheer hostility in his harangue." He paused for a moment. "I do speak French. I recognised some of the words he spoke. The fellow should be tossed into the nearest river, and you tell him to disregard me, as if I am the buffle-headed cretin who would speak so to a lady!"

He threw himself off the settee, moving away from her to stare out the dark window.

"I appreciate that you thought the piece well done. However, I knew something was wrong with it when I brought it to his attention." Lizzy could see he would not accept this. The rejection of her words was in his very posture. He could not believe her. The hand might be better than anything she had ever done, but it was not perfect. She wanted it to be perfect, if such a thing were possible. She tried again, to explain.

"To him, I was very provoking. He tells me and tells me and tells me how something ought to be done. But I cannot understand what he means. I have to do it myself, and do it incorrectly. Then I begin to see, and after he gets off his high ropes, he will show me exactly what is wrong. He is a very good teacher, Fitzwilliam. If he curses me in Italian, I do not mind it, I promise. I can disregard it."

"I cannot, because it is wrong. If he cannot instruct you without cursing you, he is a fool. He does not have my permission to do that."

Lizzy felt torn. On the one hand, she knew the irascible signor was first and foremost a brilliant artist. He accepted this private situation due to the incredible amount of money her husband offered, but it likely dented his pride to take on such a raw pupil. After only a handful of days, she knew that had he truly decided she was talentless, he would already be planning his departure, regardless of the loss of income.

On the other hand, Fitzwilliam cared about her and how she was treated, and his money had procured the signor's talent in the first place. He likely would not allow his horses to be cursed, much less his wife. He was master here, and both she and the signor, to his way of thinking, defied him.

Her pride chafed. A rebelliousness long contained wanted escape.

But the simplest truth of the situation was this: if she had not wished to deal with a proud aristocrat, she ought not to have married one.

She went to him and wrapped her arms around his lean waist, leaning her cheek against his back. He stiffened in her embrace, and it hurt her to feel it, but she would not let go.

"Have you ever wanted something so much you were willing to tolerate…well, nearly anything?" she asked wistfully. "Foreign insults. Passionate tirades. I do not care, Fitzwilliam, because I want what is in his mind. I want it so much, I cannot tell you. Please, allow me to take it."

He turned within her grasp so he faced her. "I do not like him."

"You do not have to like him. I do not have to, although I actually do. I am sorry he can be ill-mannered. I wish he were not, because it upsets you—but not because it upsets me. It is within your rights to expect improvement in his behaviour, but usually, he is amiable and, as I have said, very instructive. I learn from him, and this is what matters. To me, at any rate."

For a long moment, he stared down at her, the fire's flames reflected in his eyes. "Yes," he said lowly. "Yes, there is something I want so much I am willing to tolerate nearly anything." He held out his hand.

Lizzy took it willingly enough. It might be a surrender, of a sort, to his pride and to his anger. And yet, the feelings in her heart would not let her see it as such. Perhaps she had difficulty putting words to what she felt for him—but showing him was, thankfully, a gift always within her power.

As he entered the breakfast room, he watched as la Signora Reynolds peered right through him as if he were *un fantasma*. She thoroughly snubbed him with silent insults raining down upon his head while maintaining her demeanour of respectable servitude, as only the best servants could do. Emilio Benenati was a proud man, but he cursed himself anew. Yesterday he made the error, angering *il Signor* Darcy. Today, all the servants knew exactly what happened although there were no witnesses to the conflict.

At the outset, he had resisted this appointment with great energy, having lived long enough to understand if something sounded too good to be true, it likely was. The money offered for this position was suspiciously high. He would either not be paid or the student he was hired to instruct was a madwoman, *una demente, una pazza*.

The humiliation of instructing a female, one of little or no artistic experience! He was no mere tutor, to be pawned off on the education of an amateur! They ought to seek a governess to teach her to paint tables, or net purses...but never Emilio Benenati!

However, his most lucrative patron had recently died; with the country at war, commissions were not thick on the ground, despite his excellent reputation. He was not a man to save what he could spend and he needed the income, but even so, had not a trusted friend insisted he cultivate this opportunity, he might have refused it.

It had not taken him long to recognise Elizabeth Darcy's genius. No training, true, and she had much to learn, but even so, her gift was obvious— *la femmina* or no. Someday she would be *magnifica*. This is why he grew frustrated when she did not follow his instructions... although to be fair, she did not repeat her mistakes. And she understood he meant nothing by his somewhat belligerent reproofs; she had already grown dear to him, *come una figlia*, like a daughter. To be paid to impart his knowledge to her was a stroke of the best fortune.

But the husband, he did not know this. *Il Signor* Darcy, he only acted the part of the good *marito*; no worthy husband allowed his wife to be treated with disrespect.

I was in a fury when Darcy began bellowing, but my guilt made me rash when I said I would leave. There are so many reasons to stay: il denaro, il talento, e la comodità — the most comfortable situation I have ever known.

But while he would feel regret for the loss of these things, Emilio was not in the habit of worrying over money, and he had talent of his own, enough to earn a good situation elsewhere eventually. Elizabeth was dear, and he would miss her, but...no, there was only one true reason for sorrow if he had to make good on his threat to leave Pemberley. One real, irreplaceable loss.

L'amore.

He glanced again at the indomitable housekeeper, who determinedly paid him no heed, her proud chin in the air. Mary.

His heart burned within his chest.

FANNY BENNET TENDERLY FED THOMAS ANOTHER SPOONFUL OF BROTH.

"No more of this pap, Fanny. 'Tis not fit for a puling babe," he grumbled.

"You know the doctor's instructions," she said patiently. "Nothing but beef broth and new wine until he's certain the fever will not return."

Thomas did know, and while he despised feeling weak, each passing day he was able to sit up a bit longer, do a bit more. He gave a careful sideways glance at Fanny, trying to study her without appearing to do so.

The years had been kind. She did not have, perhaps, the youthful fairness she once possessed, but there was no doubt that she was still an exceedingly comely female. She chattered unceasingly, which should have been intolerable. Had she talked so much when he knew her long ago?

No matter. He had nearly met his Maker long before he was ready to depart. If she talked incessantly, he also acknowledged her speech centred around simple, quiet things—the loveliness of the summer day, the excellent scones they had for tea, the graciousness of his sister Margaret, her pleasure in his increasing strength. He did not pay much attention to the words, but he allowed the easiness of it to flow over and around him.

Since he was so much improved, Margaret had gone home to Netherfield, leaving him in Fanny's care, along with two new servants she had finally been able to hire. Fanny held Margaret in the greatest respect, a shining example of kindness.

Yes, his sister was kind. But so, too, was the woman he married and then abandoned long years ago. He had treated her abominably, and yet here she sat, spoon-feeding him. Since God had seen fit to spare his life, he knew he had much for which he must atone. Much for which he could never atone. And yet, he could not help but chafe at the thought of how Fanny had supported herself and her children. He knew, of course he knew. When he decided to determine if Fanny had a son by him, he had discovered more than he wished to know about her livelihood. His thoughts ran hither and yon, his pride warring with regret. He tolerated one more mouthful of soup.

"How much longer will you stay at Longbourn?"

Fanny shot him a look. Her expressive, open face reflected some emotion before she schooled it into her sickroom demeanour. Was it dismay? Or did she hide an impatience to return to Ramsgate and her life there?

"How much longer do you wish for my assistance?"

"Dashed if I know," he muttered, struggling to sit up. She moved to readjust his pillows into a more supportive arrangement.

"I shall leave at once should you no longer wish me to stay, of course," she said, in as quiet a tone as he had ever heard from her. Her head was bowed so he could not even attempt to read her expression.

"'Tis not a matter of wishing you away," he began. There were so many things that ought to be said: apologies, discussions of the future, discussions of their past. But Thomas Bennet had ever avoided confronting difficult things, especially where his feelings were concerned, and he told himself he was too weak, too ill as of yet, to broach them now.

"Oh?"

"Gads, Fanny, are you so eager to be gone?" he asked querulously, as if he had not been the one to bring up the topic.

"Of course not, Thomas."

But Fanny, weary of wondering what she ought to do about her future, went on. "But if I am to stay, I will need to send for the rest of my things and have someone close the house in Ramsgate and pay off the servants."

"Perhaps it could be leased," Thomas said, nodding in relief, as if everything between them were settled. "That's as well, then."

Fanny smiled to herself. "So…I shall remain at Longbourn…and be introduced as your wife?"

"I just said so, did I not?" he retorted, as if he had actually enunciated this conclusion.

Fanny nodded agreeably.

His brow furrowed. "I say, Fanny, I will not wear the bull's feather," he asserted, by which Fanny understood he would not stand to be known as a cuckold.

"Of course not," she replied. A year ago, she would have left it at that. *But*, she reminded herself, *I am not alone any longer. Lizzy's husband has offered a satisfactory allowance. I can live well enough with or without Mr Thomas Bennet.*

However, Mr Darcy had also given her to understand—with extreme delicacy and civility of expression, of course—the most beneficial thing she could do for Lizzy was to conduct her own affairs with the utmost discretion and restraint.

And then he provided Jane with that wonderful settlement! She had immediately taken a house in Dover, and Fanny received a letter from her just this week describing the simple wedding ceremony to her captain and Jane's unending happiness. There was no question that both of her daughters, though well-settled with good men, would benefit from the respectability only a resumption of Fanny's own marriage could provide.

She stole a glance at Thomas from beneath her lashes. He was awfully pale and skinny from his near fatal illness, but his very survival spoke well of his natural strength. She could imagine him clean-shaven and returned to his common robustness. It would be a treat indeed, to have a companion so nearly her own age.

All of these considerations made her willing to forgive Thomas, but not at the cost of her rather unsteady, newfound confidence. She would never again be alone and desperate, no matter what happened with him, and so, she cleared her throat and continued speaking.

"I would give you one caution, husband. If I am to stay, I will not have the past thrown up at me. I say this once only, and expect you to pay heed—I was faithful to you from the time we met until long after Lizzy was born. I know I did wrong, not telling you the truth of Jane's father, but I feared what the truth would bring and could not bear to lose you. Even after you left us, I loved you and believed you would return until the three of us nearly starved. Then...I did what I had to, and until I learned to harden my heart, I suffered for it."

She straightened the pillows and fussed with his coverlet, giving him an opportunity to speak; he looked at her solemnly, but said nothing.

"I did wrong...but you did, too. We can only be happy together if we forgive each other for our mistakes. I am willing to forgive you, if you will do the same. I...I am a good person, Thomas, and you will either treat me with respect or I will go home to Ramsgate."

THOMAS LOOKED AT FANNY IN ASTONISHMENT. THE PRETTY, RATHER flighty young female he married would never have spoken it. He had always felt he had done her a rather large honour in marrying her in the first place; he was a gentleman, and she was the daughter of a solicitor. One thing was certain: she was no longer that girl. But then, he was hard pressed to call himself a gentleman.

He regarded her silently, wondering about this new, bolder Fanny. Since her return, he had felt guilt, gratitude, and jealousy. He became aware of a new feeling added to these: longing, as a husband for a wife.

"As you say, Fanny," he said at last. "As you say."

T he day after Lizzy's row with Fitzwilliam, Signor Benenati apologised to her for his behaviour, paying her several extravagant compliments, which she did not take much more seriously than she took his tantrum.

It was a busy day. Not only did she spend several hours in the studio and visit three tenant wives who were increasing, she received two letters: one from Margaret Bingley, and another, in a handwriting she could not recognise, with Fanny Bennet's name upon it. Of course, without Jane to transcribe, Fanny had obviously employed another to write on her behalf. Lizzy had written several letters, with only one reply, and none since Jane departed for Dover. After dinner, she and Fitzwilliam retired to his large sitting room together; while Fitzwilliam attended to his own correspondence, Lizzy first opened the missive from Mrs Bingley.

It was not Lizzy's first communication from her aunt, who had sent a gracious letter and lovely wedding gift. But the news in this letter she found shocking.

Lizzy's mother and father had reunited. Mrs Bingley's words were warmly encouraging of this event, and, ever so delicately, gave Lizzy to know Mr and Mrs Bennet's long estrangement and Fanny's subsequent life had been glossed over and explained satisfactorily to the neighbourhood. The gossip, acute in the beginning, had subsided as Thomas threw open Longbourn. The neighbourhood now looked upon Fanny as a welcome addition.

With a feeling of near dread, she opened the letter from her mother. As she feared, Thomas Bennet formally introduced himself, calling it a "pleasure" to act as Fanny's scribe. In the rest, she could hear Fanny's voice but Lizzy's own delight in the letter was diminished by the presence of his careful hand.

"Devil take it," she said aloud.

Darcy looked up. "Troubles from your mother?"

Lizzy sighed. "No, at least, not from her perspective. She has, apparently, reunited with my—with Mr Bennet," she said sourly. "He has fully recovered from his illness."

"Surely that is good news?" he asked, not sounding the least bit surprised.

"Yes, but...did you have something to do with this?" she asked suspiciously.

He shrugged. "It was your Aunt Bingley's idea, but naturally I approved. She felt if some sort of public reconciliation took place, all would go more smoothly with your acceptance as my wife. Of course, no one thought Bennet would live, and according to Bingley, all were astonished when your mother stayed on to devotedly nurse him."

"That surprises me not at all," Lizzy said, pacing the room in frustration. "Her heart is soft. But how, pray, can she simply...continue where they left off? How can she pretend he did not abandon us! We could have starved to death!"

"Lizzy, surely you can see it is for the best if they reconcile. If anyone questions your family, your parents living quietly together on a country estate is an agreeable substitute to the truth of the past," he said, his voice rising.

Lizzy's voice rose as well. "And surely, you, of all people, can understand why I have trouble accepting him. I want nothing to do with him, and now, if I ever wish to see my mother again, he will be there!"

"At least you can entertain your mother again, safely," he said firmly. "Besides, you were the one who advocated reconciliation with my mother."

Lizzy opened her mouth in surprise. It felt to her as if she sacrificed Lady Anne's friendship in order that he, and Georgiana, should be comfortable.

"And you were correct to do so," he continued, his voice gentling. "I spoke with Mother yesterday and we shall leave the past in the past," he said, with what sounded like condescension to Lizzy. "We agreed to write. She will be moving to Brighton rather than returning to Scotland, and re-establishing herself in society. In time, I am confident we will be able to receive her."

She closed her mouth. This was good news, of course. "I am happy to hear that," she said, swallowing her resentment. It had taken months for his reconciliation to take place, even with his mother's abject apologies...but he seemed to expect her to welcome "Papa Bennet" into the family bosom without qualms, although the man had not mentioned regrets.

I needn't, though. Mama is happy, and it is her life to live as she chooses. She is safe, which is my largest concern, and her actions will not reflect badly upon Georgiana.

"I think you can see, in this case, it is best to let bygones be bygones," Darcy said.

More condescension, it seemed. But he was correct that the reconciliation would make all easier, for Georgiana and for herself. Fanny's quieter life in the country would contribute greatly to the death of gossip.

"My, this is good advice," she replied pointedly. "I am sure you, also, will be happy to hear that the signor apologised profusely for his words of yesterday. He assures me it will not happen again."

"I do not think we should be so forgiving, in his case," he answered stiffly. "He was unconscionably vulgar. It is a bad example I set if I allow you to be spoken to in that way and do nothing. If we wish for the servants to respect you, we must make certain we have no tolerance for disrespect."

"He is an artist, Fitzwilliam. I am not excusing his behaviour, but he is hardly a servant to be dismissed without a reference. Please, I ask you to forgive it this once. His apology was sincere."

"Of course it was. He would not like to lose his comfortable situation," he replied coldly.

Lizzy felt hurt at this implication that the only reason the signor would stay was for a salary, but more than anything, she wanted the conflict resolved.

"No, I am sure he would not," she agreed, forcing herself to patience. "But he is also an excellent teacher and I have learned much. I would be so pleased if you would visit the studio again. I promise to be much more welcoming. I would like to show you that I do not waste your resources and the signor is worth your esteem."

"I will not turn him out, since you insist," he said, containing his anger with effort.

"Then you will visit the studio tomorrow?" Lizzy asked, determined to disregard his ill humour.

"I have several important meetings tomorrow. Call of duty, you know."

Lizzy struggled to overlook his lacklustre enthusiasm. Fitzwilliam was still upset. He would see, over time, the signor's promise to speak respectfully. This would blow over, and all would be well.

George Wickham sipped the glass of fine smuggled French brandy while waiting for his partner.

Partner, indeed.

The man was a weasel, his rooms reeking of unwashed body mixed with a heavy cologne—as if a bought scent could disguise the odour of sweat, urine, and other unpleasantness. At least his brandy was acceptable, and only because George provided it. The cur had helped George's fortunes rise sufficiently to make breathing in his ugly smells bearable while awaiting the results of tonight's treachery. But where was he?

At last, he heard the rattle of the door as Bert Bunch opened it, his usual heavy step loud upon the wooden floor. Naturally, he remained foolishly unaware of his surroundings until George had his arm wrapped around Bert's throat, knifepoint pricking the flabby folds of his neck.

"Orf!"

"You are late," George hissed.

"Awwh, it's you, Worthy," Bert huffed. "Warn a fellah, why doncha?"

George, sick of the overpowering stench, shoved him away. Bert stumbled a step or two but righted himself, leaning heavily on the desk and loosening his neck cloth.

"Where have you been?" George demanded. "You ought to have transferred the package by nine o'clock and returned an hour ago."

"I hadda make sure I weren't bein' followed, din't I? An' dat package was an 'eavy one. Dead weight, 'e was, an' wore me out gettin' 'im delivered. I needed a drink or two ta refresh meself after."

"Drink on your own time, you addle-pated fool. Where is it?"

With much grumbling, Bert fumbled about in his pockets for the leather wallet provided by Mr Worthy's mysterious consorts. It was a dull sheaf of papers after all, to Bert's disappointment. Jewels and gold were much more his idea of proper payment for services rendered.

To his surprise, however, Worthy merely stared at his outstretched hand.

"Where the blazes did you get that?"

Bert frowned. "From yer blokes what took da, um, package," he replied with confusion.

"Not that, devil take you," he swore, squeezing Bert's outstretched hand so tightly the man cried out in pain, dropping the wallet heedlessly to the floor. "The ring. Where did you get it?"

THE LARGE GARNET CROSS ON THE RING'S FOREGROUND GLEAMED IN THE candlelight, the surrounding diamonds sparkling like stars. "I gots it 'afore I started workin' fer ye. I din't diddle you outta nuffin'. Just a bit of da blow from me last job. It were too small, an' I 'ad me pal fix it fer me finger. Fine, ain't it?"

A fury such as he had never known filled George's head. Before Bert could utter a protest, George had his neck in a twist, his knife out again—this time, nearly pinning the man's meaty hand to the desk.

"That is my father's ring, you bleeding cheat. Tell me, who had it?"

Bert tried to free himself, but he was caught tight and could not escape the depraved strength of the other man. Wickham pushed the knife down upon his hand, just hard enough to draw blood. Bert shrieked.

"Tell me!" George screamed.

In the rage ruling George's every thought, he saw Bert no longer, but only his father as he had that last time at Pemberley, in an elegant room smelling of illness and death. He had been fetched to the side of his dying father, and even then, Harry looked upon his only son with disappointment, comparing him to the odious Darcy. Though only eleven years of age, by then George had hatred enough of Fitzwilliam Darcy to last into eternity.

George sat at his father's side for hours, waiting for him to die; he felt empty, miserable. His mother was gone; she had hated Harry Wickham and taught him to do the same. And yet, he wanted time to prove he was worth ten Darcys, to show his father how wrong he was.

Harry woke, and reached for George's hand. He reluctantly took it; only then did he detect the ring's absence. George could not recall the last time he noticed it upon his finger. A gift from his Italian grandmother, he knew his father treasured it. George had once asked Harry what a jeweller would pay for it, only to receive a scathing reply—even though he had merely been curious.

"Where's your ring, Papa?"

But Harry, feverish and incoherent, could not reply. Over the next hour, George tried again and again to ask after its whereabouts. It seemed vital to know. At last, Harry opened his eyes.

"The ring, Papa," George said again, urgently, half-desperate, somehow believing if only he could find the thing, all could be made right. "Where is your ring?"

Harry's rheumy, exhausted eyes wavered. He looked at their joined hands and then past him, seeing sights George could not.

"Left it for..." Harry muttered. George leaned closer to hear the almost-whisper, "...for the son I never had." And then he stilled. He gave a last, breathless sigh, and saw nothing more.

The son I never had. Those final words had haunted and taunted George throughout all the years since. He had sworn that once he found his ring, he would kill whoever had it—certain it was Darcy.

He threw a regular dust-up over it to old Mr Darcy, who remembered the ring but insisted neither he nor his son had it. The old man dragged out everything in the vault to prove it; it wasn't there. Privately, George hunted for the piece in every possible hiding place Fitzwilliam might have. Finally, he had to accept his father lost it somehow and was out of his mind upon his deathbed.

These memories crashed in upon George at the sight of the long-lost article, all in the space of a moment.

"Tell me!" George screamed again. Blood leaked from the point of the knife where it broke the skin of Bert's hand.

"I nabbed it on the toby months ago!" Bert cried, trying frantically to think what he could remember about his last job as a highwayman. He recalled the female from whom he stole the ring, but what did the looby think, that introductions were performed before he grabbled the bit? Worthy was dicked in the nob! Panting heavily against the choking hold at his throat, with winded desperation, he screeched the only name he possessed from that party of travellers. The one who was supposedly worth a ransom, a ransom stolen from him…and now perhaps worth something after all.

"Darcy!" he cried. "The name was Darcy!"

DARCY WAS UNSURPRISED TO FIND LIZZY HAD ALREADY BROKEN HER FAST and left for the studio by the time he reached the breakfast room. He quelled the familiar surge of dismay.

She made only the barest ventures towards acceptance—the return of a few formal calls the extent of her exertions. No efforts were made to plan entertainments whereby Pemberley might introduce her to the first families, although Mrs Reynolds had offered again and again to assist her with arrangements. His tenants liked her, fortunately, and the vicar extolled her virtues, but she made almost no progress in assuming her rightful place in the community. Lizzy did her best to attend to the most important of her duties, but she was on her feet from dawn until dusk. Her lovely hands were rough and scratched, and she looked pale and tired.

At least weekly, Mrs Reynolds revealed another grievance—usually having to do with the wretched art master whom Lizzy chose over her own husband. When would she realise she no longer needed to pursue a goal wherein only an extraordinarily talented few knew success? He would support her, and in a style far greater than even the most accomplished artist could expect!

He refused to encourage her in it and waited for her good sense to prevail, for her to leave off dabbling and fully commit to him and to their life together. If not for her ready passion at night, he might have despaired. Her husband only had a part of her attention—the husband who had never heard the words "I love you" from her lips.

If only he had not hired the despicable Italian! Darcy had promised Lizzy the indulgence, of course, and his word was law. He hoped, however, she would soon outgrow it. In the meantime, he put off Reynolds's complaints and possessed himself in patience.

Georgiana was present in the breakfast room, despite the hour. He kissed her on the cheek and went to the sideboard to fill his plate.

"You are keeping early hours," he remarked as he seated himself.

Georgiana frowned at her kippers.

"Is there something the matter with them?" Darcy nodded at her plate.

"What? Oh, no. I was only thinking."

"About accompanying me and Brimstone out for an early ride?" he asked hopefully.

"What would you think about hiring another master?"

This was certainly not what he had expected her to say. While he had, of course, made sure Georgiana was provided with instructors appropriate to her station, she was not, as a rule, fond of lessons. Of course, her education had been neglected shamefully while at Ramsgate with that worthless companion, who had not done a thing to encourage appropriate interests, and he had not yet brought himself to the point of hiring new instructors. Evidently, it was time for that to change.

"What did you have in mind?" he asked carefully. He made a brief motion in the footmen's direction, and they silently exited the room.

"I would like you to hire a music master for me."

"I shall indeed do so," he agreed enthusiastically. "And drawing and dancing masters as well."

"No!"

He raised a brow.

"What I mean is…I would like to study music seriously."

"I am afraid I do not completely understand," he said, puzzled. "Why would a drawing master prevent your serious application to music?"

She sighed. "I have had, in the past, opportunities I have squandered. My instructors have complained to you that I have not applied myself. And yet, they came each week, wasting their time with desultory instruction and an indifferent pupil. Why?"

Although perhaps the question was rhetorical, he answered it. "Because they were well-paid to do so, of course."

"Exactly!" she said, beaming at him. "That is not the…the sort of instructor I hope for."

"I shall be hard pressed to find an instructor who teaches for the excitement of it," he said sardonically.

"Fitzwilliam," she said, "this time I would like a truly excellent music master—one who is as…as astute in musical instruction as Signor Benenati is for Lizzy's lessons."

Georgiana's expression was cautious; she was aware her brother disliked the signor and Darcy was familiar with her admiration for Lizzy's growing proficiency.

"I know I have skill at the pianoforte, despite my lack of practice. The notes come easily to my fingers. The music remains in my head. In the past, I have failed to…to sit still and keep at it. To improve. Instead, I wanted…other things."

She looked at him, sincere regret obvious in her expression. Darcy knew what she had wanted. To fall in love, she had thought, but mostly, simple attention from him, or from anyone. She had been lonely, grieving, and restless, and was hurt because of it.

My fault.

"Some days, I go to the studio with Lizzy, as you know."

Yes, he did know. She loved Lizzy, and he wanted them to spend time together, even if it was there.

"I watch how…how diligent she is. How much time she takes. I have seen her destroy something that took hours to create because it was not good enough."

"I am not sure this is necessarily a…beneficial practice," he said, reluctant to say anything critical of his wife. "Perhaps much good is destroyed because of some little flaw or impossible standard of perfection."

"I am not expressing myself well," Georgiana sighed. "I have been practicing my music, and finding much comfort. I know you do not like the signor, but I watch him help Lizzy, when I, like you, thought her effort flawless. He points to something, makes some little adjustment, shows her so patiently until she can see. And then she either fixes it or begins again. When she is finished, even I can see it is better than the first. This is what I want, Fitzwilliam—someone who can help me to become better than I can possibly become on my own. A master who will leave if I am wasting his time, because then I am also wasting mine."

Darcy frowned; he wanted Georgiana's happiness, but he was afraid Lizzy's compulsions might influence her in ways not for the best. Nevertheless, her desire for excellence was logical, as well as suitable to her station.

"Very well," he said at last. "I will begin a search at once."

The unimpressive papers so recently and nefariously procured by Mr Bert Bunch were, in fact, very important, and worth much more to George Wickham than jewels or guineas. In exchange for a certain member of the criminal classes—whom George had lured, entrapped, imprisoned, and conveyed to his enemies by means of Bert's delivery service—he received a dispatch purloined from a particularly high-placed War Department official. This memorandum contained secret information on troop placement in the coming spring—information the French would dearly love to obtain. One sale, and he'd be in clover; the time grew near for him to leave England forever.

He had one little task to complete first.

It was time to revenge himself upon Fitzwilliam Darcy. To his mind, the man had stolen so much from him—his bride and her thirty thousand, his living, his father's respect, not to mention his father's life… even his own front teeth! He could not forget their last encounter, armed only with an unloaded pistol, humiliated and helpless before his worst enemy. The ring gleaming from its rightful place upon his finger was a sign from the fates of what Darcy was due.

Death.

George had been hiding on the grounds of Pemberley for several weeks. They would never capture him; he knew the place like the back of his hand, and the old gamekeeper, who ought to have been pensioned off years ago, would never go looking. The chilling air did not bother him, but even should it snow, he would find a way to take his vengeance. He stayed in a hut belonging to a previous gamekeeper who, being of hermit-like temperament, lived tucked away in the midst of the forested acreage. It had been sealed up for the season; none would discover him. Being so near the home of his youth rewarded him with many memories, useful for reviewing all the inequities of his life, feeding his rage, sharpening his ire. But he would not be hurried.

He was an excellent shot, and he weighed the loaded pistol in his coat pocket as he surveyed the surrounding countryside. Because the weather held, Darcy frequently took his favourite stallion on his riding course; near the last hurdle was a perfect stand of trees. He could hide at near range, and when Darcy stopped to rest his mount, as he usually did, could pick him off his horse. It would all be over in an instant, with none the wiser. The site was far enough away from the house and stables, no one would ever hear the shot. He could escape scot-free to his waiting life on the continent. Perhaps a poacher would be blamed.

There was one singular flaw with the plan; Darcy would never know. Would never know George was responsible for the end of his reign of arrogance and privilege. It was important Darcy recognise his judge, that he pass his last moments horrified and afraid and repentant. What good was justice if his enemy never realised from whence it came?

So he bided his time. And waited. And watched.

EMILIO HAD NEVER WORKED SO HARD IN HIS LIFE TO WIN A FEMALE'S regard. Mary rebuffed him as often as she was civil; at times, he told himself he was finished, her prejudice too great. She thought him some sort of foreign Don Giovanni, and would not believe he was serious in his courtship. He had buried two wives, and both of them together had given him less trouble than Mary. And then she would do some little thing giving him hope—such as a few weeks ago when she allowed as how he might use her given name when they were alone—and all of his dreams would flare to life again.

Just this morning, she laughed at a quip he made, and he was afire with optimism.

You are an old fool. But he followed her into the empty still-room regardless.

"Mary," he said, certain she knew of his presence, though she did not turn around nor interrupt her preparations of some herbal potion.

"I have work to do," she said at last.

"Yes, you are very busy. Do you wish to know what I think?"

"Not particularly."

But the rebuff sounded more habit than reproof.

"I think you are busy so you will not have to think about your lone-liness," he said gently.

She whirled on him. "I am busy because I have many responsibili-ties! Do you know how much work is required to keep Pemberley operating smoothly? I do more in a day than you do in a month!"

He nodded. "I know you do. I also know Mrs Darcy would never refuse you if you wished to hire more help, so you might not be quite so, how do you say, occupied."

"No, she would not even notice...because she is too busy with you, amusing herself, instead of taking up her responsibilities!" Clearly scandalised at her own indiscreet outburst, she clapped a hand over her mouth.

He moved in close, anger written across his face. "Mrs Darcy *è la femmina più brillante*," he thundered. "She has *un talento*, a gift. Can you understand that? Can you comprehend something without a price in shillings or guineas? She is to be encouraged, not criticised by *sciocchi*, fools who cannot see beyond silly inventories or the silver polish. Your work, madam, as expertly as you might perform it, will not last beyond the next week or month, while hers will be extolled centuries hence!"

Embarrassed, Mary said, "I ought not to have criticised. 'Twas not my place."

"No, it was not," he said, frustrated because she plainly missed his point. He knew she was of the earth, earthy. Hers was not an imagina-tive perspective. But loyalty was her byword, and the fact that she had shared her frustration with Mrs Darcy told him more than she would wish about her feelings for him. Also, he'd moved in so close their bodies almost touched, and she had yet to storm away—another clue. She had definitely softened.

"Mary," he said, more gently, "leave Mrs Darcy be. She is doing as she ought. Can you see there might be a higher calling than mistress of Pemberley?"

"No," she said, utterly bewildered, her eyes wide.

It made him smile. He put his arms around his poor, puzzled Mary, and to his infinite satisfaction, she did not move away—only continued staring at him with wariness and yes, longing.

As gently as possible, he bent to kiss her. He did not need to be told it was Mary's first kiss, for she was awkward and stiff, her lips closed. But he was patient, and tender, and it was not long before she allowed him to draw her in closer, to deepen it.

Ah! This was why he persisted, unable to admit failure! Her feminine allure, her ardour, all were trapped behind a wall she built to prevent the world from seeing her magnificent feelings. He had loosed them, and marvelled at her *passione*.

Suddenly, a small, surprised, shriek interrupted the interlude and they jumped apart. A kitchen maid stood with her mouth agape, astonished beyond comprehension to see this infraction of Pemberley's moral code by the last person on earth suspected of possessing human frailties.

Mary stared at him with complete and utter panic.

"I apologise," he said at once, shouldering the entire blame for the benefit of the kitchen maid. "My behaviour, it was *imperdonabile*."

"Signor Benenati! You will pack your things and be gone from Pemberley at once!" Mary cried. "I will see to it! Go! Go now!"

Because he could see she was distressed, and because the kitchen maid was agog over the entire exhibition, he decided discretion was the better part of valour. He had no intention, however, of packing anything. He gave her a look that said, plainly: We are not finished.

"*Al nostro prossimo incontro*," he said. "Until later."

He bowed in his most courtly manner, and left for the studio.

LIZZY PASSED A CLOTH OVER HER MARBLE SCULPTURE. SHE HAD COMPLETED it far sooner than she ever expected. There were no miscues, no false starts, no errors. Her vision of what lay hidden inside the marble block remained true through every cut. And now Jane's face, as she imagined it through an incandescent bridal veil, stared back from the stone.

"*Bellissimo*," the signor said from behind her. "Your sister, you say?"

"My sister Jane. She wed some months ago...I was not there but I imagined it as if I was. She said she wore a veil with a wreath of flowers, and this is how I pictured her."

"Your marble, it is exquisite, as if she is here in the room with us. She looks very *contenta*. A happy bride."

"I made it for...to give to my husband. He dowered my sister so she could marry the man she loves. Her happiness is due to his generosity and goodness. I thought I could give this to him, and he could see how much I..." She trailed off, unable to complete her sentence.

"How much you what?" the signor asked, one brow raised. "How much gratitude you have for his money, that he could pay for your sister's contentment?"

"No! I mean, I am grateful but..."

"But what? To show him he does not squander his money on costly instructors and all of this?" he waved an arm to encompass everything surrounding them.

"Oh, perhaps that is part of it," Lizzy said, annoyed. "I do want to show him he is not wasting his fortune. I am grateful to him, for everything. But this is more than gratitude."

Signor Benenati looked at her with deep sadness in his eyes. "Bella," he said gently, "you are a great artist. It is a privilege to work with you. But life, it is not only in the stone. He will need the words. Me, I can see you have made this with love. But unless you tell him, he will see your talent, perhaps he will even see your affection for your sister, *e niente altro*...nothing else." He made a slicing gesture with his hand.

Her brow furrowed. "The words do not come so easy as the stone. Not for me."

He only looked at her sympathetically.

"In my home...my mother...she said these words...to many," she said, inexplicably compelled to explain herself. "She said them easily and often, but we understood. My sister and I knew it was not real. It was a...a role she played. To each other, however, we did not use these words. Not ever." She looked at the signor with pleading in her eyes, hoping he could somehow understand. "I do feel them, and I know he wants to hear it and yet...my throat closes."

The signor patted her shoulder and shook his head. "Open your throat, Bella. Life is too short to keep the silence."

He left her there, looking at The Bride. Lizzy knew the signor was wise, and she was a coward. Superstitiously, perhaps, she had feared cheapening her feelings if she gave them words. But what she had with Fitzwilliam was permanent, the foundation of her life, bearing no resemblance to the flawed transactions in which her mother once participated. Sighing, she moved to a stack of parchment. Perhaps, this first time, it would be easier to pen the words so difficult for her to say.

"MR DARCY," MRS REYNOLDS SAID, PEERING AROUND THE DOOR OF THE study with a timidity unusual for her. "I wonder if I might have a word?"

Darcy looked up from his papers, sighing inwardly. He had not spoken with Reynolds so much in the past twelve years as he had in the past twelve weeks. To be fair, she couched her grievances cautiously; they were mostly to do with Signor Benenati, and all were minor. A part of Darcy collected these complaints against the day Lizzy came to her senses and began to question the signor herself. Because the criticism validated his own opinions, he had not discouraged Reynolds, as perhaps he ought, from sharing trifling reproaches.

"Of course. Come in, Mrs Reynolds," he said politely. "Please, sit down."

"I regret I must give you my notice, sir," she said, perching on the edge of the hardest chair in the room.

"What?"

"I cannot work in such close proximity to him any longer," she said. Although her words were as cool as ever, he saw signs of discomposure; her usual "not a hair out of place" neatness was ruffled, and her eyes were wild. "I cannot work here if he is here."

"He? Do you mean Signor Benenati?"

"Yes, yes. Signor Benenati. He is…he is intolerable!"

"Intolerable? What has he done?" Darcy gasped, alarmed.

The housekeeper stood. "It is not…it does not matter. There is a conflict. I will stay the month, and train—"

"No, Mrs Reynolds. He will go, not you. He will leave immediately. I will see to it."

For a few moments it looked as though she might argue. She nearly vibrated with the emotion she withheld. But at last she only said, "Thank you, Mr Darcy. Thank you." She appeared near tears, which he found more alarming than ever.

"No thanks are necessary. Please, go and…and rest. Calm yourself. All will be well. I will see to everything."

After Reynolds departed, Darcy paced his study for several

minutes. He was angry, to be sure. He did not know what Benenati had done, but could guess. The man was prone to abusing women; Darcy had instructed Peter and Edmund, the footmen assigned to work in the studio, to tell him at once if they witnessed any untoward behaviours. Although they had never reported anything, plainly Benenati preferred to act "intolerably" where there were no witnesses.

Lizzy would not like it. But if she could stand for the abuse of his servants, he could not. He strode to the door and spoke to the waiting footman.

"James, ask Mrs Darcy to come and see me. As soon as possible, if you please."

The footman hurried away to do his bidding. Darcy waited, growing more upset with every passing moment.

LIZZY APPROACHED THE STUDY DOOR WITH PUZZLEMENT. NEVER HAD Fitzwilliam sent for her in the middle of the day, and she was unsure what to expect. She felt a little as if she were a child being summoned for discipline, which, she told herself, was foolish.

There were much cheerier reasons for such a meeting. Perhaps he, too, was feeling the distance between them of late? And wanted to–to spend time with her?

James returned her smile as he opened the door for her. Fitzwilliam did not. He looked grave, almost foreboding. And very tall and imposing as he turned to greet her.

"Fitzwilliam," she said, her smile fading as the door closed behind her, "what is wrong? Has something happened?"

"Yes…that is, nothing which cannot be put right." He hesitated, hating to see her happiness fade, knowing this would be difficult for her to face. "I regret to inform you, Signor Benenati must be let go."

"What?" she cried out. "But…but why?"

"There has been an incident. Involving Mrs Reynolds. It was a choice of either losing her or Benenati," he said firmly.

"What could he possibly have done to Mrs Reynolds?" she asked, her heart pounding hard within her chest.

"As to that, I am unsure. She would not say."

"She would not say," Lizzy repeated, trying to follow this incomprehensible state of affairs.

"No, she would not. But I have known her for many years, and do not question she was deeply upset."

"Surely you will first speak to the signor to see if he can explain?" Fitzwilliam must know how she felt about the signor; the man was a mentor, but also a–a father, of sorts. She loved him like family, regardless, and it appeared Fitzwilliam had not even attempted to discover details of the housekeeper's displeasure before pronouncing judgment.

"I will not. I have had enough of the man and his ill-humour!"

"He has made a concerted effort to discipline his tongue, which never amounted to much more than grumbling, in any case," Lizzy said, doing her best to control her own. "Ask Edmund or Peter. They are near him all day. He is quite amiable."

"I have seen for myself his lack of amiability. Even so, the incident I witnessed is not the only complaint I have received," Darcy retorted.

"What else has he done? You have not mentioned any problems to me."

"Some weeks ago, he was consorting with a housemaid," Darcy said, naming the first offence coming to mind.

"Oh, surely not! And if so, why did you not have him removed immediately!" Lizzy cried, with horrible disappointment. She was only too aware of how vulnerable lower servants were to predators of the male variety, and assumed Pemberley was made safe for them.

"Well...it seems that particular incident was a misunderstanding. Rosa, the cookmaid, is Italian, and from a village near his birthplace. They were speaking in Italian and the conversation was misconstrued. Still, Rosa had no business chatting with the signor while she ought to have been working." He scrubbed his hands across his face, remembering the countless times he had listened to Mrs Reynolds's diatribes about the signor. "The fact remains, he is too familiar with the servants, often keeping them from their duties with endless chatter. He also encourages a lack of discipline and loss of dignity reflecting poorly upon the reputation of the house."

Lizzy grit her teeth to keep from losing her own discipline and dignity. "Pray tell, what was he doing that insulted the pride of Pemberley?"

Darcy, for the first time, looked uncomfortable. "Singing," he muttered.

"Singing is not allowed?"

"It was not simply singing. He attempted to organise the servants in a performance of *Le nozze di Figaro*. Cook was in a pelter because his figure was judged too, hmm, rotund, to play Figaro. Do you not remember when we were served almost nothing but beef tongue hash for three days running? The entire household suffered. And so of course he had to be given the part. The rehearsals were ear-splitting, and individuals were distracted. The kitchen, I am told, was a cacophony."

"Fitzwilliam," Lizzy said, struggling for patience, "none of this is relevant and all of it is harmless. You must see that."

"What I see is I have not had any peace since he arrived! If it is not one thing, it is another. Reynolds was profoundly disturbed by whatever it is he's done this time. I cannot have my housekeeper upset, my household in an uproar, and my wife—" He broke off mid-sentence.

"Your wife? What about your wife?" she asked warily.

"He fans the flames of my wife's unhealthy obsession with a...a hobby-horse!" he sputtered.

"Hobby-horse," Lizzy said, turning pale. "A horse that goes nowhere. I see," she said, her voice a whisper. She made for the door.

"Lizzy, I did not mean it that way," he said, much more softly. "I ought not to have said that."

She paused in the doorway. "You are entitled to your opinion," she replied, holding back her tears with effort. "I only wish you had bothered to...to glance at my work before deciding it holds no promise."

"I have not decided anything...Wait, where are you going?"

"I need to walk."

"It is cold out today," he said, panic possessing him. He wanted to take her in his arms and undo this entire conversation. He felt eerily as though she had already left the room, however. Her body was still present, but some essential part of her had abandoned him. Again.

"It does not matter," she said in a frozen voice.

"Take along a footman," he called helplessly as she exited the room. "James," he addressed the footman standing suspiciously close to eavesdropping territory, "see that Mrs Darcy is accompanied on her walk."

Lizzy neither paused nor acknowledged them as she swiftly retreated. James looked at her in surprise and then at the master; Mrs Darcy was usually of a very friendly disposition.

"Get her cloak," Darcy said abruptly, shutting the door in the footman's face.

Darcy did not send for the signor, as he ought to have done. Instead, he told himself he could not settle domestic matters until he finished the important document from his solicitor he had been scrutinising when Mrs Reynolds interrupted. At the end of the hour, he was still on the first page. His mind fixed on the expression upon Lizzy's face. It was the look she wore whenever she hid her thoughts from him. And she hid from him whenever the subject of her art came to the fore. Was it any wonder he hated it?

He could not stay in this room a moment longer. Brimstone undoubtedly needed exercising, and so did his master. He threw open the study door just as Georgiana approached. Inwardly he groaned; he could tell by the look upon her face she had caught wind of at least some of the troubles brewing.

If I were to catalogue the topics I least want to discuss with my sister, "My marital difficulties" would surely top the list.

"I am taking Brimstone out," he said shortly, giving her the barest excuse for a bow. "You may join me if you wish." His expression was at its most forbidding. Once she would have run scurrying in the opposite direction at the very sight of him in such a state.

"I do wish," she said unhesitatingly. "Give me ten minutes to change. And do not dare start without me, Fitzwilliam Darcy!"

19

Lizzy was not on the grounds for many minutes before she was in George Wickham's sights. Because she was quite a distance away, even with the aid of his finely made monocular, he could not ascertain the identity of the female. A footman trailed her, and her full crimson skirts and stylish hat were no simple maid's costume. At times he lost sight of her, but was able to gauge from her direction and the path she was upon where he would next pick up her trail. Finally, he obtained a good enough view to determine she was not Georgiana.

Ah. The wife again.

Before coming to Pemberley, he had done some reconnoitring and learned the astonishing news that Darcy wed an unknown woman of genteel but inconsequential birth.

He considered her dispassionately. Her figure appeared pleasing, but he could hardly imagine that dry stick Darcy noticing. While no one had word of her income, its generosity could be presumed. Which, of course, was the only likely possibility given her lack of a title, and the very fact Darcy never accompanied her on these little excursions lent credence to the theory—it was not a love match. Thus, George had no assurances that killing the female would be painful for Darcy—who might even find himself better off, her fortune in his control with no obligations.

In the case of a kidnap, Darcy would be honour-bound to launch a rescue, but there, too, the risks were greater than the potential reward. For one thing, there was no promise Darcy would put himself into George's power in exchange for her...unless she already carried the

353

Darcy heir. Judging by her slender appearance and brisk pace, George thought not. For another, the burly footman accompanying her was watchful. Granted, the only thing he watched for was the possible appearance of a wild animal, but even so.

No, George's biggest advantage was that of surprise. Darcy's sister might be a worthwhile captive, but this lady was too much of an unknown to risk it. Still, he followed her progress until he saw she and her lackey returning towards the house.

Suddenly, in the distance below, he saw his hopes fulfilled. Darcy and a female who must be Georgiana, raced across the fields towards the riding course. As swiftly as he could, he made for the end of the course. He was much closer than they were, despite being on foot, as he knew they would complete the circuitous route of jumps.

He'd had Darcy in his sights before, but conditions had never been so perfect, with George able to station himself in the exact place he wished at the exact time he wished it. He felt a surge of triumphant glee. It was time to arrange his surprise, discovering if fate would at last deliver the Darcys into his hands.

LIZZY'S ANGER KEPT HER WARM FOR SOME TIME AS SHE STORMED ACROSS the paths and lanes of Pemberley.

How dare he take Mrs Reynolds's feelings into consideration without a single thought for mine!

How dare he disregard my work without ever looking at it!

How dare he decide, without evidence, I have no talent!

Her half-boots ate up the distance as she walked off her frustration, her hurt, her outrage. Finally, though, she became aware her boots were soaked, she had neglected to wear her gloves or a muff, and she had little idea of her direction. She glanced at Andrew, the footman assigned to trail her as she thundered and blundered about the countryside. His nose was red with cold.

She sighed. "I apologise for keeping you in the chill. If you would be so kind as to point the direction, we will return to the house now."

"Right this way, madam," he said, pointing, adding politely, "And 'tis no trouble."

"Thank you." Though she kept her pace brisk, most of her anger deserted her along the way, leaving a bitter residual sadness.

What sort of marriage do I have, tramping about the hillsides instead of speaking to my husband when there are troubles?

And then, perhaps a better question occurred to her: *What sort of marriage do I wish to have?*

Why was it, exactly, Fitzwilliam understood Mrs Reynolds's sensibilities better than his wife's? Was it because the housekeeper managed to share her feelings more articulately than Lizzy? And why should Lizzy feel insulted by Fitzwilliam's criticism of art he had never seen?

I wanted to show him only perfection. Instead I showed him nothing at all.

He would not come to the studio! argued her baser self.

I did not insist. I did not tell him my feelings were bruised by his refusal. Instead, I took further insult that he did not guess at them.

Oh, shut it, Lizzy's hurt feelings muttered back. She did not wish to be reasonable while her resentment seethed. But her conscience pricked. *Fitzwilliam bought you marble, clays, tools, and supplied men to assist with the onerous tasks. He provided you a beautiful work-room. He brought the signor into your life, or you would never have known him at all. All you brought to this marriage was an alibi for his sister. With all of his generosity, mayhap you, too, can afford to be generous, now, when he requires patience and forgiveness. It is even possible you might require those things as well.*

Another thought occurred to her. A few short months ago, he hated his mother. By the time she departed, he released those resentments. He altered his opinions about Lady Anne, because it was right for him to do so. *He is capable of change. His good heart will not persist in blindness, once he understands my feelings.*

In the distant valley below, she saw two horses pounding the turf, galloping towards the northeast. Undoubtedly, he and Georgiana rode for the course; it was kept up regardless of the season, although they would not use it once the snows began.

Her first feeling was dismay that their confrontation had affected him so little, he could take pleasure now in amusements.

But I have no more idea of his feelings than he has of mine. Perhaps riding for him was like clay to her, something she could touch and mould and achieve a semblance of control. She did not know; she had never asked him, had never been to the riding course, had never taken the time to watch and compliment his skill, to express her pride in him. Because horses frightened her, she had not given his feelings about them any consideration.

Pot calls the kettle black. If the situations were not exactly similar, they were close enough to remind her she had her own imperfections.

Lizzy stopped walking. "Do you know how to reach the riding course from here?" she asked.

"Yes, of course madam," the patient Andrew replied.

"I believe my husband and sister make their way there. I would like to see it if you are not too fatigued to make the walk."

"Not at all, Mrs Darcy," he said, turning them in the proper direction.

DARCY GAVE BRIMSTONE HIS HEAD ALL THE WAY TO THE COURSE'S beginning. He heard Georgiana laughing, her gelding equally happy to be racing wild and free across the valley floor. Brimstone cleared the first jump easily, Georgiana following on her horse.

He knew he ought not to encourage her to ride like this, hell-for-leather, taking jumps many men would avoid. But his sister had an excellent seat and rode as well as any man he knew. Of course, he would not force her to a side-saddle when they were alone. Riding together was the one tie they always had, from the first time he put her on a pony. If he ever had a little girl, he would be sure she learned to ride early. He would teach her himself.

A little girl with dark eyes and Lizzy's untamed tresses.

Losing attention, however briefly, was unwise on a course of this calibre. It was all he could do to maintain his seat as Brimstone flew over the next hurdle, a potentially fatal inattention. Forcing his mind to matters at hand, he completed the course at breakneck speed. Georgiana could not keep up, being several minutes behind him by the time he rested Brimstone at the course's end.

He walked the stallion around the large clearing. Trees surrounded its edges, but there was a path leading out—rather abruptly angling steeply upwards, towards rocky ridges and some remarkable stone formations. It ended, finally, at a gritstone escarpment. One of his more blood-and-thunder ancestors named it Deap Cynll, a sheer drop of nearly two thousand feet with spectacular views of all of Pemberley.

I have never taken Lizzy here. Never shown her the sights I love. She often went walking, but he sent a footman to accompany her. Because most of this rugged land was easiest seen by horse, he had disdained her hikes and prowls. Why? Why had he dismissed opportunities to share this with her?

He watched as Georgiana took the last jump and slowed, cooling her gelding by taking a slow pass around the edge of the clearing. But he was surprised when she dismounted, tying the horse to a convenient limb and climbing a little way up the path, sitting upon a boulder.

Reluctantly he tethered Brimstone and joined her, remaining standing, looking in the direction of Pemberley, all unseeing.

"Fitzwilliam, tell me why you are distressed," she demanded.

He shrugged. "I know you have ample resources for collecting household gossip, Sister-mine. I would wager you have already heard enough."

"I heard Ruthie caught Mrs Reynolds and the signor in a passionate embrace this morning."

Fitzwilliam whirled, anger on his features. "The blackguard! How dare he—"

"Apparently, her arms were around his neck and she most certainly was not fighting him off," Georgiana interrupted wryly.

His face was a study of emotions—distress that Georgiana heard such intimate details, and dismay at the thought of Reynolds in such a situation.

Georgiana giggled. "It is an exceedingly unsettling a picture in one's mind, is it not? It was difficult enough to grow accustomed to the idea of you kissing anyone, much less Mrs Reynolds!"

His jaw firmed. "I will thank you not to picture anyone, ahem, kissing. Especially me."

She giggled again. "Believe me, 'tis not something I contemplate. Nevertheless, it is impossible to live with you and Lizzy, even in a house so large as ours, and not be confronted with a notion or two." She put her feet up on the boulder and wrapped her arms around her knees, her expression growing serious. "At least, it used to be impossible. Lately, however…there is a…a distance. I also heard the signor is to be turned out, because of Mrs Reynolds's…um…embarrassment. And I thought perhaps you ought to know all is not as, um, straightforward as it might appear. Lizzy will not be happy if you evict the signor."

"No," he said hoarsely. "She was not happy."

Georgiana sighed. "I would think, Brother, knowing you have a choice between the happiness of your wife and the happiness of your housekeeper, and understanding the situation is a complicated one, you might wish to avoid being...hasty in your judgment."

He bristled. "I must make hasty judgments every day. It is part of my life and my station. In this instance, I cannot think I have done wrong, even if what you say is true. What am I to do? Mrs Reynolds, too, shoulders much responsibility. Lizzy has shown little interest in taking it upon herself. Pemberley can live without the signor, but many more would be affected by the loss of our housekeeper."

"Are you angry at Lizzy for not...not being more involved with the household?" she asked quietly.

He shrugged again. His feelings were complicated, and not for the dissection of his young sister.

Georgiana's expression held frustration. "Because if you are, I must say, it seems unfair. You purchased me a new pianoforte, the finest I have ever seen, and hired an excellent master for me. From those clues, I surmise you wish me to practice, which I do, several hours in a day."

"'Tis not the same," he said stubbornly, and turned away again.

"No," she retorted. "Because in my case, you listen to me practice, you compliment me generously. Not so for your wife, for whom you provided the same things—tools and a master and a place to create. One cannot blame her if she is confused by your...disinterest."

Guilt lanced him, but he was affronted by Georgiana's intrusion into affairs she could know nothing about, and his instinct was to stride back to Brimstone and be rid of her opinions. Yet, he also felt compelled to explain. "I hired the wrong master. I do not like him."

"You have not tried to like him. You hardly know him. And if you have listened to Mrs Reynolds, there is every reason to believe she is, herself, um...confused."

Darcy was about to refute this statement, when, from behind him, he heard a small shriek. As he spun to face her, he heard a voice he had hoped to never hear again.

"She's quite the interfering little piece, isn't she, Darcy?"

George Wickham had Georgiana in his clutches, a pistol to her forehead, an evil, golden-toothed grin upon his scraggly-bearded face.

LIZZY FELT A TINY BIT WINDED BY THE TIME ANDREW LED HER TO THE course's end. She had expected her husband and sister might meet them on the way, but instead they found the horses tethered to tree limbs on the other side of the clearing. Georgiana's beast munched grass contentedly, but Fitzwilliam's big stallion appeared restive, giving her a rather wicked inspection. In return she gave the creature a wide berth.

"I wonder where they are?"

"There be a path from here leading to a fine prospect," the man replied. "Deap Cnyll. You can see the entire valley from there. Bit treacherous, of course."

Lizzy sighed, because they had been climbing, albeit gradually, a long while. However, this particular conversation had waited long enough.

"I will follow you, then," she said firmly.

Andrew moved in front of her; the path was rocky, but he was a neighbourhood boy and picked the best way. However, after a few minutes' climb he halted so suddenly she nearly bumped into him.

"Turn 'round, madam," he whispered so low she could barely hear him over the whistling wind. "Be quiet. Go back."

Such was the urgent tone of his whisper, she obeyed immediately. But she, like Lot's wife, twisted her head to look behind her, and felt her heart turn to salt within her chest. In the distance, a man with a pistol to Georgiana's head marched both her sister and her husband upward. Towards Deap Cnyll. *Death Knell*, Lizzy translated to herself.

She followed Andrew swiftly back into the clearing, where they would not be overheard.

"Who was it? Who was the man with the gun?" she asked quietly.

"Don't know," Andrew replied doggedly. "I must get you away, firstly."

Lizzy thought rapidly. Andrew took his duties seriously. He would never allow her near danger. Although she thought him brave enough, he was not the rash sort, accustomed to following orders rather than leading out.

"You must take one of the horses and ride back for help," Lizzy ordered.

"I cannot leave you here alone." He did not suggest she ride, her fear of the beasts well known by all.

"I am perfectly safe. I can hide in those trees," she promised, lying through her teeth. "You must hurry! You must get assistance for your master and Miss Darcy!"

He looked uncertain, but borrowing one of Fitzwilliam's masterful gestures, she flung her arm towards the horses. "Go! At once!"

To her relief, he did not waste time arguing. Quickly clambering onto Georgiana's gelding he galloped away.

He would be an hour getting help, Lizzy calculated, at very best. *I sent away my one hope!*

But in her heart of hearts, she knew there was no recourse. Andrew was unlikely to follow her orders if he felt her to be in danger. Neither, bless his soul, did he have the brains to outwit a gunman. Either she could help her husband and sister herself, or they needed an army. Andrew had gone for the army. Now it was time to see if there was any good she might do.

Carefully she picked her way up the trail, watching her step, moving quietly as possible, holding her breath around every curve of the path. Finally, finally, she saw her object, and it was all she could do to shut her mouth against a cry of distress.

DARCY KNEW HIS ONLY HOPE WAS TO KEEP GEORGE TALKING AND PRAY some opportunity for rescue presented itself. For the moment, this had not proved difficult. George was a raving madman, boasting of his prowess in the face of severe and prolonged injustices.

"Thought you outsmarted me, didn't you?" George was saying. "Leaving me with your sapscull cousin! Hah! The regiment he left me with hardly bothered to guard me! I walked away from the fools after a blasted card game!" His pistol barrel never left Georgiana's head as he dragged her along, grinning all the while. With his bushy, unkempt whiskers and filthy clothing, he looked mad indeed; nevertheless, there was a certain canniness to his expression.

Darcy dared not underestimate him, nor the strength of his hatred. *Dear Father in Heaven, protect us. Protect my sister.*

Eventually, they reached the plateau, the topmost perimeter of Deap Cynll. Large rock formations surrounded them, levelling into a wide lip of land protruding from the ring of boulders. Beyond that lip was a sheer drop of almost two thousand feet. A dusting of snow covered the ground. As soon as they emerged from the protection of the boulders, a bitingly cold wind shrieked in their ears, wrapping the skirt of Georgiana's riding habit in twisting folds about her limbs.

George yelled at Darcy to keep walking, nudging Georgiana further out, moving them ever closer to the escarpment's edge, rambling on and on about his father and some ring, how he discovered it after all of Darcy's attempts to keep it concealed. About how this ring was delivered to him by fate, a sign from heaven that Darcy was marked for death. The man was insane.

"Admit it!" George screamed. "Admit you stole it from my father! You took it, I know you did! Where did you keep it hidden? Where?"

"I hid nothing, George," Darcy replied with a calmness belied by his racing heart. "I had nothing of yours, nor of your father's."

"Liar!" George bellowed. "Your mother is a doxy and you are a liar, and yet you think you are so much better than I! Unfair!"

"No, 'tisn't fair," Darcy agreed, infusing his voice with calm command. "Let Georgiana go, George. Mete your justice upon me. I am the one you are angry with. Let her go. She will not tell anyone, will you Georgiana?"

"No," Georgiana whispered, terrified. "I will say nothing, George. I promise."

"You promise?" George bellowed. "You mean, as you promised to marry me? We all know how well you keep your promises!"

"That was my fault," Darcy called back, struggling to be heard over the screech of the wind. "I took her from you. Blame me."

"Oh, I do!" George cried. "I do indeed blame you, Fitzwilliam Darcy! 'Tis not often a man may look over the course of his entire life and find a common thread throughout all his failures and disappointments, as I can! At every single point, as soon as I neared victory, you were there to prevent it!" He jabbed the gun so hard into Georgiana's skull, she screamed.

"Let her go!" Darcy roared. "Take me instead of her! If it is all my fault, take me!" Out of the corner of his eye, he thought he saw a flash of red, but could not take his eyes off George and his sister, just a few feet away, nearly at the rim's periphery.

George laughed mockingly, launching into a long-winded ramble of lunatic proportion. He said terrible things, made awful threats, and all the while Darcy could do naught except watch Georgiana shiver while they listened to the shrieking wind and their enemy's maddened voice.

"I ought to kill her in front of you while you watch," he cried. "That would be justice for you! But I shan't do it, because I am a merciful and generous man."

"And because you know the moment you no longer hold my sister captive, I will tear you limb from limb," Darcy shouted, goaded beyond endurance.

"I have more than one pistol," George screamed, enraged. "You will never escape your fate! But as I said, I am a compassionate man. If you will jump, now, I will allow her to leave!"

"You think me a fool as well as a liar!" Darcy shouted. "We both know as soon as I am dead, any hope for Georgiana ends."

"Perhaps you would like to test your theory," George roared. "I will shoot her in the stomach while you bicker with me about whether she lives or dies!" He moved the pistol from her head to her belly, jabbing so hard she lost her balance.

At that moment, an unearthly scream startled them all. George swung around; Georgiana, already off balance, tumbled to the earth. A horse charged at them, and George instinctively dodged. Darcy, taking advantage of the distraction, shoved George with all his might.

The next two events lived on in Darcy's night terrors for years.

They happened concurrently and in mere seconds. In his dreams, they would take minutes or hours, but he forever remained a helpless witness to the dénouement.

George, with a horrified yell, lurched backwards over the edge, his arms wind-milling frantically as he abruptly disappeared from view.

The horse, Darcy suddenly recognised as Brimstone, his rider—barely seated—somehow urging him forward whilst clinging to his neck. The stallion's protest was a scream within its mighty chest, louder even than the screaming of his rider. Brimstone flung himself up, rearing powerfully, to simultaneously rid himself of the maddening aggravation upon his back and stop his forward motion.

It worked. Brimstone halted in his tracks, his rider thrown.

And Darcy watched helplessly as Lizzy flew over the cliff's edge, the red of her skirts sailing behind her in a bleeding, blooming trail.

"**N**oooo!" Darcy roared, as his life, his future, his heart and his happiness was thrown to her death.

His last view of her lovely face was her terror as she took that final plunge.

In that instant, and far too late, he suddenly saw it all: his jealousy, his small-mindedness goading him to punish Lizzy for not loving him quite enough, the petty ways he blamed the signor for his own failings.

"Lizzy!" he sobbed futilely, falling to his knees. "Lizzy!"

Georgiana, on her forearms and knees, scrabbled to the rim and peered over, something he could not yet bear to do.

But he needed to force himself up and mount a horse he could never, after this day, bear to ride again, and take him to the valley floor. He must collect the broken body of his beautiful bride, the only woman he would ever love, and carry her home to Pemberley, there to begin his lifetime of grief.

Wickham could rot where he fell, as far as Darcy was concerned.

His sister's voice penetrated his grief and pain. "Fitzwilliam! Fitzwilliam! 'Tis Lizzy!"

"Wha–what?"

"Look!"

He pushed himself to the edge, peering down.

Lizzy was not far below, folded in half over a limb growing out of the brush at the escarpment's rough edges.

"Lizzy!" he called, but there was no answer. She made no movement from her precarious perch, her hands dangling limply; there was no sign she lived.

"I must get to her," he cried. At that moment, there came the clopping of mighty hooves and the neigh of horses. Three huge Shires bearing the Adams men emerged, each picking their way surefootedly up to the escarpment's open prospect, followed by Andrew on Georgiana's gelding. Andrew had not returned all the way to Pemberley as Lizzy supposed, but instead ridden to the much nearer tenant farm for aid. Had their would-be rescuers appeared while the maddened Wickham still held a gun upon Georgiana, all might have ended dreadfully, for who knows what heinous act he might have perpetrated in his heedless, lunatic state, faced with justice? But he was gone, and the men had ropes and steadier, less fractious mounts than Brimstone.

Darcy insisted he be the one to collect his wife. He was roped to a sturdy horse, and lowered over the side. The gritstone beneath his feet, and the nearly vertical cliff face made the going difficult; every moment he both feared and hoped. If she wakened and moved even an inch, she could fall to her death. If she did not waken, she might never do so. But at last, he reached her.

"Lizzy." There was no response, nothing. Did she breathe? In the shrieking wind and dangerous setting, he could not tell. Hoping he did not injure her further, he lifted her into his arms. Nothing would make him release her, but he coiled the rope to encircle them both. There was much blood, cuts and punctures to her fair skin from the brush, and a purpling bruise upon her forehead. She had lost her hat, and her long, tangled tresses flowed over his arms.

"I have her!" he shouted.

Though the horse carefully dragged them upward, Darcy had to walk them up the cliff side, ensuring they did not grow entangled in their ropes or the scrub peppering the crevices of the gritstone. The ropes dug into his skin with nearly unbearable pressure, every muscle in his arms and thighs straining against the weight. He cared nothing for it, or for any danger. All he wanted was to see his wife's body carried safely up the hill. There was time enough to learn if she lived or died after that.

At last, he reached the rim's edge, and many hands were there to guide him and his precious burden to safety. Then, and only then did he put his hand to her delicate throat with care enough to feel the faint, fluttering pulse-beat. He put his head near her mouth, rejoicing in feeble breath upon his cheek.

"She is alive," he whispered. "Thank God in heaven, she yet lives."

Georgiana put her arms about his shoulders, a gesture of love and sisterly support. He could not bring himself to let Lizzy go, but leaned his dark head against her blonde one. There was a bruise upon her temple, her blue eyes full of tears.

"I am sorry, Georgie-my-girl," he murmured. She put her soft hand upon his face, and only then did he realise his cheeks were wet. "I am so sorry."

"Shh, Fitzwilliam," she whispered. "Take care of Lizzy."

The journey to Pemberley was a blur. He took Seth Adams's big black Shire horse, and cradled Lizzy in his arms the entire way. Though he spoke to her—words of love and devotion—she never opened her eyes.

Pemberley waited in readiness for its injured mistress, as of necessity Darcy's journey homeward was a slow one, and others arrived before him to bring word of the day's events. A doctor was fetched, who attended Lizzy and shook his head; her many wounds were anointed. The doctor warned Darcy nothing could be determined until she woke, but he was to be sent for at once if there was any sign of blood upon her lips. Lizzy was bathed and dressed in a clean nightgown; she was to be kept warm and quiet. The suggestion she would be more comfortable in her own room was summarily rejected, and she was put into the bed they had always shared. Still, she did not waken.

Mrs Reynolds stayed behind after all those assisting departed. "I would be happy to sit with the mistress if you would like to…to attend to your own needs," she said, eyes lowered as if she could not bear to meet his.

He glanced down at himself. He was filthy, bedraggled and covered in blood. He did not recall discarding his coats, but he must have done.

"Leave me a can of hot water and towels," he said curtly. "That will be all."

"Yes, sir," she said, and then paused, her hand upon the door. "If I might say, sir, how sorry I am that the mistress was hurt," she added quietly.

He nodded, and she turned to leave.

"Mrs Reynolds," he called.

"Yes, sir?"

"I expect you to resolve your troubles with the signor without my intervention. I do not wish to hear you speak of him again, unless to announce the two of you will be calling the banns. Needless to say, he will remain indefinitely. Pemberley needs you both. Learn to cope."

There was a pregnant pause. "Yes, sir," she agreed, and soundlessly departed.

A s much as he might have wished it, Darcy was not left alone for long. Perkins was first, insisting upon clean clothing. This assistance was conceded, along with tending to some bleeding scratches. Darcy refused a shave, but Perkins laid out the full costume of undress for his master—shirt, pantaloons, stockings, slippers, and brocade banyan— before finally allowing his dismissal.

Darcy donned the clean shirt and pantaloons, and had barely returned to Lizzy's motionless form when there came another tap upon the door. He did not respond to the summons until he detected the rise and fall of her chest, assuring himself she still breathed.

Then he went to the door.

Somehow, he was unsurprised to see his visitor. He was surprised, however, to see how old the man looked. Signor Benenati had aged a dozen years in a day.

The signor looked at Darcy, his eyes full of grief. "She is...she is *molto ferita*?" He looked down at his feet, scrubbing his face with his hands. "I am apologising, the English, it is–is elusive." He opened and closed his jaw, as if struggling to work it properly. "*La*–the injury?"

Darcy had made a personal vow he would welcome the signor's presence in Lizzy's life, for her sake, from this day forward, if only she was permitted to waken, to live. He expected, however, it might be difficult. But he felt only pity and shared anguish; nothing of his former malice survived seeing Lizzy nearly killed.

"She...she must waken," Darcy assured gruffly, covering his own emotions. "She will recover."

"*Sì, sì,*" the signor agreed heartily. "She must. I wished you to know...I will say the prayers and light the candles for her, *se me lo permette?*"

"We would appreciate it, Signor," Darcy replied, willing to embrace any sort of divine intervention on behalf of his beloved.

"*Bene*, good," the older man said. "She completed *la scultura*...a gift for you, only today. Her intention was to give to you immediately. I thought, perhaps, you would wish to see it. Now. And you might wish for it to be placed in here, where it would be…near."

"Yes!" Darcy said immediately. "Of course!"

The signor signalled behind him, and Darcy became aware of footmen just out of sight, carrying an obviously heavy object. Darcy stepped away from the doorway, casting his eyes around the room.

"If I might suggest," the signor said tentatively, pointing to a sturdy mahogany chest positioned along the wall opposite.

Darcy nodded his agreement, and the signor directed the footmen to place it carefully, still covered, upon the gleaming surface.

They bowed and left the room. The signor pulled an envelope out of his coat pocket. "This was to be delivered with the piece," he said quietly, handing it over.

Darcy recognised his name in Lizzy's handwriting on the front of the envelope. He took it carefully, as if it was made of the thinnest, finest china.

"Thank you, Signor," Darcy said. "Thank you for the joy you have given my…my Lizzy."

"All I have given her, she has repaid in double measure," he replied, and, bowing low, departed.

Darcy walked to his wife, so still and silent, though she yet breathed. "What have you made for me, dearest?" he asked. "What more have you done to heap coals upon my head?" He brushed aside a stray lock and pressed a kiss upon her forehead. It was cool to the touch; no fever. Why would she not wake?

Evening was falling, and he lit the tapers and stirred the fire before he returned his attention to the gift and its accompanying letter. A part of him did not want to unveil it without her knowledge…but most of him was desperate to see it. She had made this for him with her own two hands.

Carefully, he pulled back the black velvet hood, gasping at the sight of The Bride.

I did not know. I could not guess. Who could fathom the complete, utter genius and artistry one female might possess? he marvelled.

He fell to his knees, as if he worshipped. Perhaps he did. And then, of course, along with awe and pride, came a memory of a conversation he'd had with Lizzy, before they wed, when she attempted to explain what her art meant to her, and what concessions she might have to cede in exchange for the "privilege" of becoming his wife.

"What if…our situations were reversed?" she had asked. "… what if you, the master of Pemberley, had to become a sculptor so we could wed?…And what is more, you are still the master of Pemberley, 'tis still part of you and important to you, even if no one else cares, and thus you must devise a means of shoving everything being master entails into a few hours per week."

And he arrogantly thought: Not that one could compare a piece of art, even a lovely piece, to Pemberley. The two things were not at all analogous.

She had agreed to marry him, even before he promised he would not take the art away from her. Perhaps she understood what he had not: he would renege. He would not even try to appreciate what her work meant to her, beyond what little effort his money performed on his behalf. Her response was, in so many words, "Yes, I will marry you on Friday, even though you do not understand me and will not even make an attempt."

I love you, regardless, she had been saying.

And because he was too stupid to see how she spoke her love, because he was thick and could only understand something if he were beaten over the head with it, he had not heard. He had expected three little words, not one enormous sacrifice of untold generosity.

Of course, he had not demanded the sacrifice immediately. He had pretended patience. He had waited a few months for her to finish playing, expecting the novelty of the toys he had purchased to fade. But from the beginning, he had, indeed, expected her to shove every dream she possessed into a few hours per week. When she devoted more time than that, he had been hurt. And resentful. And censuring.

He looked at the brilliantly sculpted marble again. It was so beautiful. So real and true. It belonged in the gallery, just as Lizzy belonged amongst the greatest sculptors in England. Perhaps the world.

His gaze fell to the envelope in his hands. He almost did not feel worthy to read it. Carefully, he broke the seal and withdrew a single sheet of parchment.

Dearest Fitzwilliam,

I made this piece for you. It is a likeness of my sister, Jane. You dowered this girl, whom you have never met, for my sake. Because of your kindness, she married for love.

I call it "The Bride," and for me it represents your unselfish heart. Almost from the beginning, you saw me, not as others do, but with respect. Do you understand what a gift that is? So many look upon my relations with contempt, finding me unworthy of esteem or kindness. You not only overlooked it all, but you let yourself love me.

Your love is the centre of my life and the foundation of my happiness. I am dreadful at voicing the words, but pray somehow, in some way, you understand my love for you is the breath in my lungs, the sight in my eyes, and the beat of my heart.

All My Love,
Lizzy

Darcy smoothed out the letter upon his lap. His eyes filled again with tears.

He wanted to tear his hair out. He wanted to curse himself to perdition. Instead, he went to Lizzy's side.

She looked as though she slept.

"Lizzy, love," he whispered. "You mounted Brimstone on purpose to charge at Wickham, didn't you? Oh, my dearest, dearest love," he choked. He lowered his head to her chest and tried not to weep.

"I was an idiot," Lizzy said, her voice gravelly.

He startled, his head popping up, his eyes wide.

"Lizzy!" he gasped. "You are awake!"

She already struggled to sit.

"No, no," he protested. "Lie still, dearest. You have been injured."

"I have made an utter cake of myself, is what I have done," Lizzy said hoarsely, subsiding back upon the pillows, wincing a little.

He smoothed back her hair from her forehead, wanting to kiss her so much he ached with it. "Oh, Lizzy," he said thickly.

"How is Georgiana?" she asked, beginning to rise again.

"She is well," he soothed. "Please, please rest, sweetheart."

"I cannot lie here."

"You have been insensible for hours, love," he said, pressing her hand to his lips.

"Oh, dear." She struggled to sit, looking around. "Water? Throat hurts."

"Of course. Please, remain abed, my love." He poured a glass from the pitcher Mrs Reynolds left, handing it to her.

She drank thirstily, then returned the glass. As soon as he set it down upon the bedside table, she threw herself into his arms, shaking with silent sobs.

"Oh, now, my love, my sweet, sweet, love," he soothed. "All is well, I promise you." He held her as tightly as he dared, whispering nonsense, trying to calm her distress. He held her until her sobs diminished into sniffs, and finally quieted, his shirt soaked with her tears.

"And now I have completed my day's ridiculous performance," she whispered. "I apologise for behaving like the veriest goose."

"Love, you saved us. Georgiana's life and likely mine as well. You nearly lost your life in the process. I think you are entitled to feel distressed."

She shook her head slowly, as if she could not believe his description of the day's events. "A bit more water, if you would?" she asked. "I think I just leaked out all I took in."

He reached over and poured another glass, which she gratefully finished.

"My throat," she whispered, handing it back to him. "I believe I broke it with all of my screaming. And my head hurts." She snuggled back into his arms, much to his satisfaction. "Who was that man with the pistol?"

Darcy sighed. "George Wickham. A madman."

"Oh, my," Lizzy said. "Attempting to ruin Georgiana's life was not enough? He had to attempt murder?"

"Just so," Darcy agreed, relating some of Wickham's strange rantings. "Oddly enough, he was fixated upon a piece of jewellery, of all things. He rambled incessantly about his father's ring, accusing me of having stolen it from him as a young boy...but he wore it upon his finger; the whole thing was nonsense."

Lizzy sat up straight, staring at him. "His father's ring?"

"Yes."

"Is it a garnet cross with diamonds on a field of black and white enamel?"

He nodded, astonished.

"Harry Wickham gave his ring to me when I was a child! I wore it on a chain around my neck, under my dress. But the highway robbers took it from me and..."

He gathered her close again. "Hush, love. It matters not. As I said, George was completely unhinged. He must have fallen in with those thieves and...well, who can say what happened? I will see your ring is returned to you."

She shuddered a little. "Oh, Fitzwilliam...when I close my eyes, I cannot stop seeing that m–man with the pistol at Georgiana's h–head..."

He pressed a kiss to her cheek, rubbing her back soothingly as she trembled. "It all ended well, thanks to you. Can you tell me how it was you came to be there in the first place? Andrew said you came upon us on the trail up to Deap Cynll, and you promised to hide in safety, waiting for him to bring help," he chided gently.

"I could not wait, not knowing if there might be an opportunity for me to aid you in some way."

He smiled wryly. "I would have known, my love, as soon as the words 'hide in safety' came from your lips, you were gammoning me. As much as I wish you safe, always, I recognise your character is not the hiding sort." He pressed another kiss to her temple. "Andrew apologised a number of times, and I promised to kill him if he ever allows you to leave his sight again when he is to be looking after you."

"'Twas not Andrew's fault!" she protested.

"How came you to be riding Brimstone?" This was the thing he could not understand. While, as it happened, it had been the diversion giving him the opportunity to defeat George, surely there was some other means with less risk.

She gave a huge sigh. "After Andrew went for help, I ran back up the trail to you and Georgiana. I hid behind a boulder, and could not hear much over the wind, but it was plain that Wickham person threatened Georgiana in order to force you to jump. I thought perhaps I should leap out from behind the rock and scream, or make some sort of diversion...but I feared he would shoot Georgiana, or push her over the edge. They were so close. From my vantage point, I could see no one could survive such a fall."

He clutched her tightly, and she realised that she had, indeed, survived that very plunge. Shivering, she continued her tale. "I remembered seeing a saddle bag on Brimstone, and I thought you might have some sort of weapon in it. And if perhaps it was a pistol, I might be able to fire it, or at least threaten to, as a better diversion than a mere scream. If there was nothing in the saddle bag, I could try screeching at the top of my lungs. Doing nothing seemed the worst choice of all."

Emotion gripped Darcy as he relived with her those events on the cliff; everything could have ended so differently.

"I know what you are thinking," she said. "You are wondering why I did not inspect the saddle bag before following you up the trail."

Darcy managed a feeble smile. "No, dearest. I promise you, that did not occur to me."

"Oh. Well, of course you know my mortal fear of horses, so I suppose you could predict I had not wanted to go anywhere near the beast."

Before Darcy could protest, she was speaking on.

"I approached Brimstone carefully, telling him I only meant to take a quick look, but he sprung at me, trying to bite! I was already frightened and in a terrible hurry. If you remember, he was tethered to a tree with long, low branches. I thought if I climbed the tree, I might be able to snatch the bag before he could, you know, take my arm off."

"Climb the tree?" Darcy repeated weakly.

"Yes. The tree climb was the easy part, but Brimstone was already suspicious and agitated, shaking his mane and moving around. He was tethered so loosely he was almost free as it was. I hitched up my skirt so I could crawl upon the branch over his tether. I knew I only had one chance to reach the bag. I was trying to balance and reach one-handed and avoid his teeth, and most of all, to hurry...and he moved and I...I overbalanced and fell on him."

"You did what?" Darcy cried, incredulous. He scooted back to see her face.

"I know! 'Tis so ridiculous!" she replied, her ruined voice cracking on her words. "Of course, the thing he wanted most was to have me off. I grabbed onto his neck and the reins were flapping and almost instantly he was free of the tether. I held on for dear life...and of course, I lost all composure and began screaming. Even when I saw he was racing towards you, I ought to have shut my mouth to–to create some sort of proper diversion at the proper time. But I could not control myself. I could not stop screaming. And then he threw me...but I–I think I must have hit my head, because I cannot remember anything else until I wakened here with a devil of a headache."

She looked so disgusted with herself, so disapproving of her own weakness, the emotion choking Darcy loosened, and he began to laugh. Her displeasure showed clearly, and yet he could not help it, nor stop it. No mere weak chuckles, but great, whooping laughs as she continued to frown. Then, after some moments, her frown tilted upward, and finally, she began giggling, until she fell back upon the pillows, out of breath.

He leaned over her, still smiling. "You devil."

"Brimstone thinks so," she admitted, smiling back.

"I love you. Confound it, Lizzy, I love you so much. I do not deserve you, but I do love you. Tell me you know it."

Her smile widened, and she wrapped her arms around his neck, looking him in the eye. "Show me," she said.

His smile vanished. "Every day, for the rest of my life."

Darcy, holding his wife spooned against him tightly, stared across the room at the lovely marble Lizzy had carved with her own hands. She was so peaceful beside him, he thought she was sleeping. He would not mind dozing himself, but wanted to bask awhile longer in this complete and absolute contentment. For the first time, in a long, long while he felt…whole.

"I see you received my gift," Lizzy whispered.

Darcy moved so she could turn onto her back and face him. "Lizzy, I owe you so many apologies, I know not where to begin. I have never seen a creation of such beauty. Had I seen that piece in–in a home or a gallery, I would have done anything to procure it for Pemberley. I had no idea what I asked you to sacrifice. I am so sorry, my love."

"You did not ask me to sacrifice anything. You gave me the tools and the space and the instruction to improve my art."

"Compromise, then," he allowed, after a moment's thoughtfulness. "If I had bestirred myself to see what you were doing, I would have recognised your greatness at once. But the fact is, love, you have a right to your dreams no matter your ability. I did not wholly support you, as I promised I would." He stroked the wild tresses away from her soft cheeks, looking into her wide, dark eyes. "The fact of your genius only underscores my stupidity…and my–my unkindness to the wife I love. I owe you the deepest of apologies, and will do my best to make it up to you from this day forward. Tell me that, in time, you will forgive me, or you will allow me to work for your forgiveness, and I will be a happy man."

"Oh, Fitzwilliam. You should be the happiest of men immediately. I am not without fault. I should have dragged you to the studio and insisted you look. Instead, I sulked." She smiled up at him, her expression filled with dawning happiness. "On my ramble through the countryside today, it occurred to me I had done nothing to confront our difficulties. Which is why I followed, when I saw you and Georgiana on the horses. I wanted to talk to you, truly talk, and I knew you would listen, once you understood how I felt. You are the best man I know."

It struck Darcy, then, how easily she shrugged off life's blows. She looked ahead with optimism, always expecting the best from him, no matter how dismal his recent performance.

"You," he said, kissing her forehead, "awe me. Perhaps it is why you are able to create such magnificent beauty. So much is within you, I suppose some must be released through your mind and hands, before it overflows." He kissed her nose, and then her lips, reverently at first, and then with the heat that always flamed when he was close to her in this way. He managed, barely, to show some restraint. She would be sore in the coming hours, from seen and unseen injuries. Having been thrown from a horse more than once, he knew better than she how it would be tomorrow, no matter how willing she was tonight.

Lizzy reached up and brushed a lock of hair off his forehead. Her smile became a bit hesitant. "You really like it?"

"I love it," he declared firmly. "No one with any eye for beauty could find fault."

"I wanted to do a bigger piece, but my skill for the creation of a whole body is yet lacking. I have difficulties with proportion," she admitted.

He chuckled. "My love, I have no doubt you will overcome any perceived flaws, and that I would not be able to distinguish them in the first place. But if it helps, I have spoken with the signor and he will be staying at Pemberley for as long as you desire. I ought never to have threatened you with his removal. I had no right. I will never interfere again—and nor will our housekeeper."

"Thank you," she said. "I am relieved, and grateful. However, I do feel compelled to point out, you pay his wages. It gives you some rights."

"We pay his wages," he retorted. "All I have is yours."

Lizzy lifted up on one elbow, studying his expression. "I do not do well as mistress of Pemberley," she said. "I disregard much that does not interest me in favour of that which does. 'Tis not fair to you, and I understand your dismay in this regard."

He caught her hand, placing a kiss upon her knuckles, then upon her palm. "My love, a person of your gifts cannot possibly concern herself with the linen inventories. My tenants love you. You have attended well to the needs of our people. There is only so much of you to go around. Whatever time you can spare from your work and your duty, I claim in advance."

"I believe your tenants recognise I am no better than they. It is obvious I am no grand lady. And really, Georgiana does as much or more than I do," she said wryly.

He chuckled, shaking his head. "If that is the case, I am grateful. It is exactly how it should be."

"Not so," she insisted. "I am barely known to the first families here-abouts. We have paid all the requisite formal calls upon each other. But Pemberley has not entertained, nor received any of the invitations you might usually expect. I know we will be required to go to town. I fear you will be plagued by rumours of your odd wife, and you and your sister will suffer—even if the truth of my family never emerges."

He cupped her face between his hands. "Lizzy, stop. The day will come when you will be accepting the commissions of royalty. The world will someday recognise you for who you are, unlike the rest of us, for whom respect is an accident of birth. As for Georgiana, she no longer craves attention for its own sake, but has learned to develop her considerable talents with long practice and great effort. Never question that your influence upon her has been of the best possible nature. Like me, she is a better person for having known you." Bending his head, he kissed her, trying to tell her all the things mere words could not convey.

His kisses were interrupted, however, by a soft tap upon the door. Sighing, he pressed a last kiss upon her nose and arose, snatching his banyan and wrapping it around him. "Stay right there," he admonished his wife, who was already beginning to rise. He gazed at her sternly until she subsided onto her pillows.

Darcy opened the door to see an anxious Georgiana. "I am so sorry to disturb you," she said. "But I had to ask how Lizzy fares. Two of the Mrs Adamses, Mrs Smith, the Misses Peterson, and the Harrises have called, some of them twice, bearing remedies and advising poultices and tonics," she listed, naming various tenant wives and sisters. "And now Mrs Mumford of The Grange is here and will not leave without word for the neighbourhood."

"My poor girl," Darcy said. "I ought to have sent word as soon as Lizzy wakened, but I failed to think of anything except my own joy at her recovery. She is awake and not too much the worse for her fall. I believe she will be fully recovered if given several days' quiet. She now rests comfortably."

"Oh, Fitzwilliam, what wonderful news!" Georgiana cried. "I am so relieved!" She wrung his hands tightly, and then for the first time, noticed his bare feet. Her cheeks pinked.

"I have interrupted Lizzy's, um, convalescence, I think," she said, stifling a grin as she released him.

Darcy attempted his usual hauteur, but feared the reddened tips of his ears betrayed him. "You must send 'the neighbourhood' away and take time to recover yourself, as I am." He looked carefully at his sister; the bruise blooming upon her temple was evidence of what she'd endured, and yet her only concern was for Lizzy. He wrapped his arms around her in a tight hug, surprising her with his sudden display of affection. "All must remember that you, too have sustained injury. I am exceedingly proud of your bravery today, but you must not overdo. Tell Reynolds you are not at home to any more visitors, and that all is well or will be soon."

"Thank you, Brother," she said, an impish expression upon her face as she peered up at him. "I take it the signor will be staying?"

"He will," Darcy said drily, letting her go. "And now I return to my wife. You may save your 'I told you so' for later." He gentled his voice. "Please rest now, will you Georgie-my-girl?"

"Yes," she smiled. "I am able to now. As soon as I see to Mrs Mumford." She raised her voice to address her unseen sister. "Everyone wishes you well, Lizzy!" she called from the doorway, and then almost skipped down the hall.

As he closed the door, he saw Lizzy had not obeyed him, but had arisen and pulled on an undressing gown. She took a step towards him and winced. Darcy hurried to her side.

"I told you to stay in bed," he said anxiously.

Discounting this, she walked to the bust of her creation.

Darcy came from behind, circling his arms about her, satisfied when she leaned against him. The Bride stared back at them, wide-eyed, through the folds of her marble veil. "I cannot believe such a masterpiece is your first work," he murmured.

"Oh, 'tis not my first marble, although the largest I have successfully completed," she said. "I have a number of failed attempts, as well as several smaller pieces."

"It seems incredible to me," he said. "To have done so much so quickly."

"There is much I have yet to learn," she said matter-of-factly. And then, more quietly, "The signor says I...I have an unusual rapidity for— for the quality I turn out." She laughed a little. "I think it is because of all the creatures I modelled for tourists. I had to produce so many of them in order for the sales to amount to anything worthwhile, I grew adept at working quickly."

He kissed the top of her head, feeling another wave of regret. When had the master said this? Of course, she would not have felt she could repeat his compliments, any more than she could share her struggles, since he had bristled at any mention of the signor.

"I did not understand the work of modelling in clay would help so much in the practise of sculpting in marble," he commented, hoping he was encouraging her to speak of her art, to know of his interest and care.

"'Tis different, of course," she said, seeming eager to discuss it. "In clays, I mould something from nothing. In stone, I reverse the process, cutting away the excess to reveal what hides within," she explained. "If I have a real feeling for the piece, as I did with this one, the process becomes even easier."

He shook his head in amazement. "I wonder if I might visit you in your studio?" he asked. "I would love to see all you have accomplished. I am so sorry I disregarded your progress, my love...but I want you to know I am proud of you."

She turned within his arms, so she could face him. "I would love that. I have wished for your esteem nearly as much as I have wished for your...person."

"Minx," he said. "You have it, and my person."

"Does this mean, finally, you will pose for me?" she teased. "How wonderful if the gallery had a *Waking Fitzwilliam* to display beside the *Sleeping Endymion*."

He raised a brow. "It seems the height of arrogance, to memorialise myself thus."

Lizzy giggled. "Perhaps we could put it in here, for my eyes only."

"As proud as I am of you, I think not. There are far better objects for your attentions."

"I nearly died today," she murmured, her hands slipping around his neck. "You should give me what I want."

"Do not jest about today," he warned.

"I am not," she countered. "I want you. And I want you to sit for me. I want to recreate you, in clay and stone. You are perfect, every inch, and I will not rest until you let me capture you in some medium that lasts forever. I must."

If he had thought he could ever say no to her, he was proved wrong now. She shaped him with her hands upon his skin and her heart in her eyes, and his will, his happiness and his future could only follow her lead.

"You are so beautiful," he murmured, and he thought, perhaps, if her feelings were anything like his, he could understand why she wanted to preserve him in stone. Alas, he hadn't the gift to do it himself; he could but hold a vision of her within his heart, forever.

"I will take that as a 'yes,'" Lizzy said, contemplating how she would pose him, some way of capturing his nobility, his command and his...yes, his humility, as well. The perfect gentleman.

"You know I can deny you nothing," he replied. "My ruthless love."

Lizzy smiled and kissed his chin. "You will not regret a single minute of the experience," she said, "in the studio. Alone. Together."

He grinned.

"And I think," she said contemplatively, "I would like you to teach me to ride."

He burst out laughing, and she poked him in the ribs.

"I apologise, my love," he said, immediately contrite.

She huffed. "I do not aspire to your level of skill, I promise. You have disparaged yourself for discounting what is important to me, but I should at least be able to share a little more of what means most to you. And I am weary of being afraid of the beasts." She paused. "That is, if a pony could be procured who is as gentlemanly as Mr Darcy of Pemberley—with perhaps the spiritedness of, oh, say, an old cabbage leaf?"

"If you compare my animal spirits to wilting produce, we need to come to a right understanding, you and I," he said, feigning insult.

She giggled and he smiled into her eyes.

"I will teach you myself," he promised.

"Also, I believe I would like to have a baby with you, if you wish it, too."

Whenever he thought she could surprise him no more, she brought him to his knees. "I do wish it. Very much," he choked, over the lump in his throat. "And if you still feel this way in a few days, once you are recovered, and not feeling quite so vulnerable from your near brush with death, I shall be happy to apply myself most vigorously to the business of getting you with child."

"I am ready."

"Lizzy," he murmured, piercing her with his stare. "Do you know? Can you understand how much I feel? I cannot lose you, love. I nearly died with you today. If not for my sister, I might have thrown myself off that cliff after you."

She raised her hands to his face, feeling the roughness of his beard. "Shh. Do not say such things. You did not lose me. I am here, and I am yours and you are mine." The words she had always found so difficult to say came easily to her now. "I love you, my darling, with all of my heart. Nothing can change that, not even death, I am convinced."

His serious, almost grim expression softened at her pronouncement. "You love me," he said.

"Yes."

"Will you say it again?"

"For as long as we both shall live."

Several weeks later, Longbourn

Fanny spied the envelope in Thomas's hand from a dozen paces away and flew to him. She was proud of her daughters, and every one of their frequent letters sent her into raptures.

As Fanny did not write, she dictated her replies to him to write out on her behalf. When a new letter arrived, he read aloud every word. After reading dozens of these letters, he felt he knew them both, had even met the elder daughter.

But it was the younger whose letters he longed for. He awaited the post like a starving man awaiting a meal, hungering for every witty, insightful line from the daughter he had rejected and disregarded.

Fanny's pride in Lizzy was admiring, respectful and affectionate, but his was fierce and unremitting.

"A letter for you, Fanny," he said unnecessarily, his heart beating hard.

Fanny held out her hand for the envelope. "Oh, feel this, Thomas," Fanny said admiringly, smoothing her hand across it. "So thick! Do you suppose she included a drawing of her latest creation? I do hope so! But even if not, her handwriting is so lovely, it is almost artwork by itself, do not you agree?"

"Yes, yes," he said with a touch of impatience, as if she did not express his own thoughts.

Fanny discounted this, as she always did. Thomas had the strong impression she knew exactly how deep his regret and, yes, his pain. As little as he cared to think it, his wife was a fair expert on the male mind, understanding him as few could. And so they enacted this little ritual, wherein he pretended and she allowed it. He followed her into his cosy bookroom. Once, he spent many an hour alone in here, but Fanny had moved a comfortable settee in near the fireplace, and she often brought her needlework of an evening.

Perhaps his younger self might have resented this intrusion into his private domain. Now, however, he appreciated her friendly company in what could have been, what once had been a bleak and lonely life. She handed him the letter and perched expectantly upon the settee; he, remaining standing, took it from her, carefully breaking the seal.

Every word in it was both pleasure and pain. Every word was addressed to Fanny alone. It was a fine revenge, and a part of him appreciated her fashioning one so well-tailored to his sins.

Dear Mama,

Pemberley threw open its doors, inviting all the leading families in the area to a celebratory three days' worth of entertainment. Word of my ridiculous charge at the cliffs of Deap Cynll somehow spread throughout the neighbourhood.

My husband bade all the countryside to make merry with us and rejoice in our rescue. Whole families were invited, and Bishop Darcy attended to lend his consequence to the proceedings.

It was like no celebration Pemberley has ever seen, according to the redoubtable Mrs Benenati, who, of course, worked tirelessly to make it so, as the reputation of Pemberley was (naturally) at stake. Music and feasting and sleigh rides and ice-skating and wassail and plum puddings of such majesty, they will be spoken of years hence, I am assured.

"Imagine, Lizzy as hostess of all that!" Fanny exclaimed. "And the Bishop of Derby as well! Of course, he does dote upon her. Oh, my." Thomas nodded and continued reading.

Everyone was so kind and accepting, Mama. I am under no illusions London will be so easily conquered! My ostensible rescue of my very popular husband has abetted my acceptance, no doubt. Of course, I told the Bishop the whole of it when we had a private moment.

"It was an absurd accident," I insisted.

"Nonsense," he replied. "God works in mysterious ways. He chose to intervene in a rather dramatic fashion, it seems to me, and you were His weapon."

Naturally, one would assume such a sentiment from a Bishop! I am willing, I suppose, for the neighbourhood to believe me selfless and courageous, especially as these attributes reflect well upon the Darcy name. And, I am happy he now believes 'Young Fitzwilliam' knew what he was about when he asked for my hand. But I am convinced he did not think so at the time!

"As well he changed his mind. It was the most fortunate day of Fitzwilliam's life, the day he met my Lizzy, and he knows it. Didn't I say so? Absolutely nothing frightens that girl, neither bishops nor earls nor anything in between. Well, except for horses, but that's a blessing now, isn't it?"

"True, true," Thomas agreed, so he would be allowed to continue reading.

He read of Georgiana's brilliance on the pianoforte, and their pride in her performances. She also wrote of her own work, displayed for the neighbourhood at large:

'The Bride' was well received, and it seems I am to be known as an Eccentric Artist (which is, apparently, an acceptable use of Eccentrici-ty). The Bishop's open approval no doubt encouraged some in compli-ments they would not have otherwise given, but I shall nevertheless happily bask in his reflected glow.

"Balderdash," Fanny interrupted. "They all loved it for the same reason the bishop did—because it is brilliant!"

Neither Thomas nor Fanny had ever seen the piece, only drawings. Nevertheless, Thomas was inclined to believe Fanny spoke the truth. The letter finished:

You have not yet answered me as to whether you will join Aunt Bingley in her tour of the Peaks and a nice long visit at Pemberley. I do yearn to see you, Mama! Regardless, I expect to hear from you soon with all the gossip, including whatsoever you hear from Mrs Captain and her news of any anticipated special event.

With much love,
Your Daughter

SHE ALWAYS CLOSED THE SAME WAY, NEVER SIGNING HER NAME, BUT "YOUR Daughter."

Fanny was uncharacteristically silent at the completion of his recitation. After a few moments she said, "I would so like to join your sister and young Mr Bingley on their excursion to the Peak District next summer. It is awfully kind of him to offer to take me."

"And so you should," he snapped, giving expression to his jealousy. "Did I say you could not? I only think it ill-mannered our daughter invites you and so pointedly excludes your husband."

"Do you, Thomas?" Fanny said, in a voice so solemn and so unlike her usual merry tones, his eyes flew to hers. "Can it be you truly do not understand?"

In her pretty, expressive eyes, he saw compassion and pity...but also an uncompromising accord of her own: justice delivered. For all that Fanny had forgiven him, she neither expected nor required Lizzy to do the same. *This is what you lost,* her eyes said. *This is what you discarded so foolishly.* His wife might not be altogether sensible, but she understood enough, and was wiser than he in all the matters that truly counted.

"I know," he replied shortly, to words both spoken and unsaid.

In the next moment, Fanny chattered about travel plans, wardrobe necessities for said travel, the grandeur of Pemberley, and the unexampled talent of her daughter as she exclaimed over the sketches. Thomas stared into the flames, allowing the comfort of her felicity to soothe his festering conscience once more.

D arcy sighed and reread the letter from his agent, feeling the familiar sting of rage, sorrow, and satisfaction mixed with impatience. It had arrived by express a week ago; he ought to have heard more by now, and yet there was nothing!

Shortly after the notices of his marriage to Lizzy were published in the London papers, he had received a scathing letter from Lord Matlock. The letter, full of blistering recriminations announced the two families permanently severed. Worse, the earl knew all there was to know about Fanny Bennet. If Matlock chose, both Georgiana and Lizzy could be harmed. He was a powerful man, still, and despite what they knew of his predilections, they had no proof.

So Darcy set out to get it. What he discovered was worse than he imagined. The earl had nearly bankrupted himself and his estate. Darcy negotiated with holders of the earl's notes, purchasing most of them for a fraction of their cost. Some were more expensive. Nevertheless, Darcy was both determined and very, very wealthy.

He had instructed his man to hand-deliver a letter explaining the new situation to the earl. His list of demands was short, but consequential. It was a terrible game he played with a man who was dangerous, perhaps even unstable, and certainly bent on ruin. After seven days, Darcy had heard nothing as yet to indicate his demands had been or would be met.

But he thought he hid his concerns well enough.

"Tell me what is the matter," Lizzy said that evening when they were alone, and he sighed, knowing he had no defences left, for she rested inside his soul where nothing was hidden and she would have it all out of him no matter what he tried to do to protect her.

And so he told her what he had done.

"You did what? Could–could you…um, we afford to do so?"

"A goodly number of his creditors despaired of ever receiving a shilling. Many of them were purchased cheaply. But regardless of expense, I could not count the cost. I wrote him a letter explaining, in essence, I own him now, and he must do exactly as I demand."

She smiled, amazed. "Well done, sir! Why did you not wish to tell me?"

Darcy sighed again. "'Tis a delicate game. He is an earl. It is not as though I can have him tossed into debtor's prison, even owning his debts. I am counting upon the cost to his reputation and the maintenance of appearances meaning everything to him. I let it be known that anyone extending him credit in the future will have the devil to pay—I am confident no one will lend him a groat. I explicitly reminded him to whom some of those debts were owed, and for what. His private life is so reprehensible, he would be deeply humiliated were I to publish even the smallest part of it publicly. I ordered him to vacate to his country home at once, where I will keep a close eye upon him. I also demanded he retire from public life permanently, and that his son, Viscount Ravensdale, act for him in the future."

Lizzy looked up at him. There was no triumph, no rejoicing at the way he had outmanoeuvred his uncle. "Fitzwilliam, I think you act wisely. He is an evil man, possessing none of the moral compass a man in his position ought to have."

"If only I was certain I have outflanked him! What if he managed to enlist our Regent in his cause? I ought to have heard something by now from one of my agents, reporting he has departed for Matlock, and yet there is nothing. He is an abominable man. He will take out his displeasure upon his wife and his servants, to say nothing of his sons. The position I may be put into in regard to them if I am forced to act! He is a powerful and dangerous man still, and if I have read the situation wrongly…"

Lizzy kissed his cheek. "Oh, my love, I am sure you have not. At the least, he will retreat for the moment, perhaps test his new limitations. As to your cousins, they must know you will do your best to protect them from their father's sins. I have no doubt you will find a way to help them, and their mother, too. I have never heard you speak of your aunt. What is she like?"

"She is…quiet," he replied. "One forgets she is in the room, and some call her dull and timid. However, Richard and his brother respect her. I am sure they are a credit to her and not her husband."

"How awful to find oneself trapped within a marriage to such a wicked man," Lizzy said sorrowfully. "I wager she had little choice but to marry him in the first place."

Darcy looked at her soberly. "Too often, that is the case. My mother was obliged to marry my father, which begot resentment as surely as it begot her children. I browbeat you into marrying me, I know, using guilt over my sister's situation to weaken your resistance to the idea. Then I promised to see to your dreams, but because I could not imagine a better dream than the two of us together, looking after Pemberley and creating a family, I did not take your deepest interests seriously. I was so certain I knew best what would make you happy."

She snuggled in closer to him. "I wanted to be with you. You know how determined I can be when I have an idea in my head. Since I was small, I have fixed upon the notion of becoming a great artist. I could have resisted marrying you for Georgiana's sake, but I could not resist you. I was attracted by all you offered me—the studio, the signor—and I did wish to help your sister, but the promise of having you changed my idea of what I need in order to be happy."

"So, you no longer wish to become a great artist?" he asked.

"I wish to become a great artist who ardently loves her husband and dotes upon her children," she replied. "I trust you to help me with the 'looking after Pemberley and our family' parts of my new idea—I want to have it all. And even if I cannot, it will not be because we did not try."

"I have been thinking," he replied. "I believe I must change… Pemberley. Mrs Reynolds—er, Benenati manages expertly, but she has refused, in the past, to hire the assistance she requires. Hence sprung her hope for a mistress to share responsibility, I believe."

"It was not an unreasonable hope. Pemberley is a vast concern. She received the wrong mistress."

"You are the perfect mistress for me," Darcy said so fiercely, she blinked. "I am a wealthy man, but what use is my wealth if I cannot have the one I love, and if I cannot see her happy? Pemberley requires a house steward. I will offer the position to Mrs Benenati first, but only under the condition she hire an under-housekeeper, a butler, and other assistance. If I see her looking after too many details herself instead of delegating, she will lose the position."

Lizzy's brows rose. "I have never heard of a female house steward."

"I will do whatsoever is needed to ensure the comfort of my lady. If my wife can be a great artist, my housekeeper can be a house steward. I will not tolerate any disrespect towards her."

Lizzy contemplated this. "You know, I believe she will rise to the occasion." She grinned up at him. "And if the world thinks me odd, they will find you an eccentric for certain."

She lifted her mouth to his and they kissed, and he forgot about the earl and the potential for disaster, only the goodness and rightness of this.

A soft knock interrupted them.

"Enter," he called.

To his surprise, it was Mrs Benenati, who he thought long since retired for the night. But he was even more surprised at the sight of the man who pushed past her in the doorway. Richard entered, his uniform covered in road dust, his eyes red-rimmed as if he had not slept in days.

"Darcy...we are dead men," he said into the astonished silence.

DARCY STOOD ABRUPTLY. "MRS BENENATI, HAVE SOME REFRESHMENT brought in at once, if you please."

The housekeeper nodded and disappeared.

He moved to his cousin and took his arm. "Please, sit. You are exhausted."

The colonel allowed himself to be led further into the room, more or less collapsing into a proffered chair, giving a long sigh and closing his eyes.

"Perhaps I should let you and your cousin speak alone," Lizzy said, standing and moving to her husband's side.

Richard's eyes popped open and he struggled to his feet. "I apologise, Mrs Darcy—did not see you there. I am—"

Darcy pushed him back into the chair. "No matter, Richard. There is no need to talk until you have a meal and rest. Lizzy, stay if you wish. We have nothing to say that you may not hear."

Richard sighed again and gave a bitter laugh. "Have not slept in two days—or is it three? Not at my best, certainly, but I would as soon say my piece as quickly as possible."

But he did not begin speaking at once, instead, staring into the flames as if entranced. Lizzy took Darcy's hand, a gesture of support, and he brought it to his lips as she leaned into his side. Both watched the colonel with deep concern. What had happened to cause him such obvious distress?

They were all jolted from the silence by the housekeeper's knock, and with Darcy's permission, two footmen carried in trays of tea, cold meats and cheeses. Evidently Mrs Benenati had also been troubled by the colonel's haggard appearance, because there seemed enough food to feed a regiment.

When the servants had withdrawn, Lizzy occupied herself by preparing a plate for the colonel, setting it on the table by his side when he protested he could not eat, that he must speak.

"Well, out with it then," Darcy commanded, moving to seat himself beside his wife when she returned to the settee. "What is the mystery, Richard? You are not usually given to such dramatics."

This earned him the ghost of a smile, and Richard visibly made an effort to regain his composure. "Very well then. Firstly, Matlock is dead."

"Dead!" Lizzy gasped. "How?"

Darcy said nothing, but his brow rose.

Richard closed his eyes and leaned back in the chair. "Who can say? Struck by his own guilt, or by a God who suddenly chose a swifter justice than is usual? The man certainly broke every commandment on multiple occasions. Or perhaps the viscount killed him, I know not." He opened his eyes and met Darcy's. "The earl received a letter from you."

Darcy's features were as if carved in stone and Lizzy reached to clasp his hand again in hers. "Yes."

Richard closed his eyes again. "Directly after receiving it, Matlock became violent, far more than his usual bluster. My mother was injured by a brandy bottle he threw at her. Fortunately, she sent for the viscount, who was able to come at once. There was a fight, a brutal one, and Ravensdale was able to restrain him, finally. But when he insisted upon knowing what had led to such an uproar, Father refused to say and then...then, according to my brother, he went red in the face, followed by turning white as a sheet, and crumpled to the ground."

Lizzy clutched Fitzwilliam's hand more tightly.

"The doctors came. He never recovered his senses. My brother discovered your letter, and ascertained the source of his, ah, fit. It is his opinion Matlock willed himself to die out of sheer stubbornness. He would rather face the netherworld than be in your power."

"I am sorry, Richard," Darcy said solemnly. "It was certainly not the result I wished. I only needed to stop—"

"Do not apologise," Richard said vehemently. "He wronged you deeply and would have done so again. You did what you had to do. He authored his own downfall." He was quiet for a moment. "He wronged you worse than you know."

It was Lizzy who asked the question. "How so?"

"Georgiana's thwarted elopement," he said at last, "was plotted by my father. He was to receive a goodly portion of cash in exchange for delivering up the bride."

Darcy turned pale with rage, but he glanced at Lizzy and saw she had not so much as blinked at this news. "You suspected as much," he said to her.

"I thought it likely. I did not believe Lydia would do such a thing without his permission, at the least—not that she has any scruples, but because she would not dare cross him."

"You are more astute than I, Mrs Darcy," Richard said. "The idea did not occur to me until much later. But once I admitted the possibility to myself, I could not let it go. It took me a good deal of time to find Lydia Younge. I finally did, only a few days ago. She was in hiding, in fear for her life she claimed. Not from you, of course, no, but from my father, for botching the job of arranging Georgiana's elopement."

"Devil take it," Darcy muttered, no longer able to maintain his composure.

"I have sent her away, out of England, so she can do no further harm. I returned home to confront him, only to find him upon his deathbed. He passed before I could make him account for his betrayal. But you see, Darcy, my family has wronged yours in the most heinous fashion. The earl lashed out in your youth, though it was his own sister responsible for the scandal, then plotted against your young sister. You also know we haven't two shillings to rub together, and you are owed far more than my brother and I will ever have the ability to repay, even if by some miracle we are both able to marry well. Not only are we utterly in your power, but we have no right to beg for mercy." After this little speech, he stood, slowly, as if he were an old man.

"So you see why I cannot accept your hospitality."

"Do not be ridiculous," Lizzy said. "Sit. Eat."

But Richard started for the door.

Darcy shot over to him, blocking his path. Richard only stood still, swaying on his feet, slightly hunched as if expecting a blow.

"You are not responsible for your father's choices or his sins," Darcy said, gripping his cousin's shoulders. "Let those be buried with him. I am happy to offer whatever assistance I can. I will never call in those notes, Richard, and you may tell the new earl I said so. I will burn them. You are as a brother to me."

"Honour demands I refuse your generosity," Richard said stubbornly. "Burn nothing. We will pay what we can as we can."

Darcy heard a noise coming from the corner of the sofa where Lizzy sat, and he almost smiled, knowing if he looked at her, she would be rolling her eyes, and if she spoke, it would be to accuse Richard of reading too many dramatic novels. In light of his cousin's great distress, however, he kept his expression solemn.

"But Richard, I have already been repaid," he said.

Richard frowned. "Not possible."

Darcy only walked around him, holding out his hand for Lizzy. She took it and he raised her to stand beside him. "If Georgiana had not attempted to elope, I might never have come to know the one female in this world who is my happiness and my heart, and well worth any little trial we might have had to undergo in order to be together. I have been repaid a thousand times over, and would have paid a thousand times more to get her."

Lizzy looked up at her husband, her eyes shining. He smiled down at her and softly brushed her cheek.

Richard cleared his throat, his cheeks flushing slightly. "Well then," he said, looking from one to the other. "Well then."

"Sit down, Richard, please," Lizzy said. "Eat, while I see that Mrs Benenati has prepared your usual rooms—which, I have no doubt, she has already done. Talk with Fitzwilliam and be at peace. We are only family here."

"Mrs Benenati?" he asked, confused.

"Mrs Reynolds has recently wed," Darcy said, leading his befuddled cousin back to his chair. "Now do as my wife commands and eat. I will be happy to bring you up to snuff on all our doings. We have been much occupied of late, and I have been a poor correspondent."

MUCH LATER, LIZZY LAY NESTLED IN HER HUSBAND'S STRONG ARMS, listening to his heart gradually calm beneath her ear. She placed a kiss upon his chest. "What you said to Richard," she began.

"Every word the truth, my love," he averred.

"Aunt Bingley wishes to dower me, though I have told her it is unnecessary," she said. "But perhaps, in light of recent outlays, I ought to allow it."

"You ought to allow her regardless," he said. "She wants to claim her place in your life, and it is her way of doing so. And if we have ten children—"

"Ten! Saints preserve us!"

He chuckled and kissed her forehead. "Or two, it matters not to me."

After a few minutes, Lizzy asked, "The new earl...is he...?"

"Of the same stamp as his father?" Darcy finished. "No, most assuredly. He does have a reputation as a gamester, but his luck has always held. When I investigated the father, nothing in the way of indebtedness came from the son. I would guess the old earl was infrequent in payment of his allowance or used excuses of discipline to avoid doing so. The viscount...er, earl seems rather unusually self-sufficient."

"He must be feeling overwhelmed at the moment. I hope he will accept your help in management of his estate—or what is left of it."

Darcy nodded against her forehead. "But sole reliance upon agrarian pursuits, as his father and grandfather have done, will not save him. His land is overworked, and the yields are poor. I have several profitable ventures unrelated to farming, but many peers consider such things beneath notice."

"If he has a grain of intelligence, he will do whatever you suggest," Lizzy said loyally.

"Richard said he is certain the earl will lend whatever of his consequence might be useful to us. After the period of mourning is past, of course, he will throw a ball or some such in honour of our marriage." Darcy sighed heavily. "I cannot possibly mourn the old earl. And yet, it will be expected."

Lizzy shrugged against his shoulder. "At Pemberley, Matlock's treatment of the Darcys is well known. None will expect us to hang the black crape. But if we can use the excuse of his death to put off going to London for a season, I will hardly grieve. I admit I am not yet enthusiastic about spending months in town for idle pursuits. So much time would be lost from my work."

"Nor I," Darcy agreed. "I must, however, go at some point to nurture those profitable ventures. There is education for you there too, in plays, museums and galleries. Also, the polite world would think it odd if my wife never accompanied me. I would not have any believe me ashamed of you."

She touched his lips with her fingers. "I did not say I would not go with you. 'For whither thou goest, I will go.'"

He blinked in the darkness, then smiled. "Bible verse. You, my dearest love, are a female of rare capacity."

"I have always admired Ruth. She was passionately loyal." Lizzy looked down at him in the moonlight, her long hair blending with the shadows. "'Entreat me not to leave thee, or to return from following after thee: for whither thou goest, I will go; and where thou lodgest, I will lodge: thy people shall be my people, and thy God my God. Where thou diest, will I die, and there will I be buried; the Lord do so to me, and more also, if aught but death part thee and me.'" She captured his face within her hands. "It is not poetry, but it is how I feel about you."

He reached up to clasp her hands in his own. "My heart," he whispered, and drew her down to a kiss that spoke more than words could ever say.

ABOUT THE AUTHOR

Julie Cooper, a California native, lives with her Mr Darcy (without the arrogance or the Pemberley) of nearly forty years, two dogs (one intelligent, one goofball), and Kevin the Cat (smarter than all of them.) They have four children and three grandchildren, all of whom are brilliant and adorable, and she has the pictures to prove it. She works as an executive at a gift basket company and her tombstone will read, "Have your Christmas gifts delivered at least four days before the 25th." Her hobbies include reading, giving other people good advice, and wondering why no one follows it.

The Perfect Gentleman is Julie's first novel. Her second novel, *Tempt Me*, will be released in autumn 2020.

To hear more about books by Julie and other wonderful authors, please join her publisher's mailing list at www.QuillsandQuartos.com

ACKNOWLEDGMENTS

Many thanks are due to Lisa Sieck and Jan Ashton for helping bring this story to life in the first place, and to Kristi Rawley, Jan (again), and Amy D'Orazio for their superb skills in reviving it.

TEMPT ME

For Mr Darcy, a centuries-old vampyre, the Meryton assembly is his idea of purgatory. From the cloying despair of the wallflowers, the desperation of the fellows gambling in the card room, and the competition amongst the gentlemen vying for the attentions of the prettiest girls, the emotions of everyone in the room assault his refined senses in unending waves.

That is, until he meets Elizabeth Bennet. He cannot feel *her*. She is an oasis of peace in his violent world, and he would die to have her. But she might, unless he walks away.

Made in the USA
San Bernardino,
CA